MAGPIE'S RUIN

MAGPIE'S RUIN

BRIAN M. COX

To order additional copies of this book, contact:
Xlibris
AU TFN: 1 800 844 927 (Toll Free inside Australia)
AU Local: 0283 108 187 (+61 2 8310 8187 from outside Australia)
www.Xlibris.com.au
Orders@Xlibris.com.au
817830

DEDICATION

To Littessa, for your friendship and the encouragement you gave, without which this book would never have been written.

To all who read this book, may you enjoy the journey.

ACKNOWLEDGEMENTS

To Bruce Cox, Kathy Cummins, and their collaborators at Sil for their work on the Iceve language, the basis for the language that Shadow speaks.

To the editors at the Expert Editor for their work on my very rough manuscript.

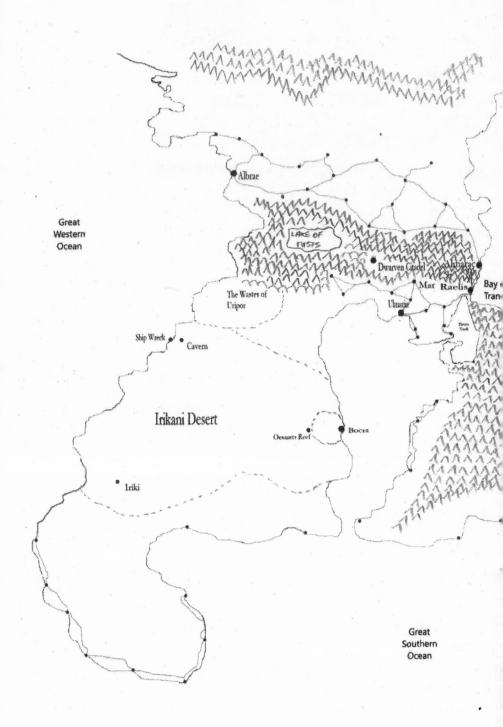

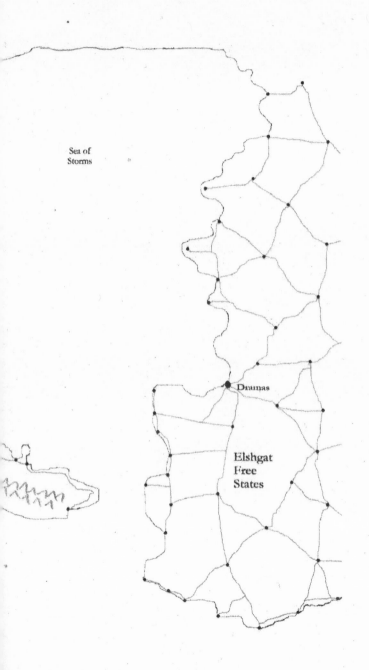

Sea of
Storms

Dramas

Elshgat
Free
States

CHAPTER 1

She was a half-breed—unnatural. She had inherited traits from a dark and secret past. Her ancestors had been a mix of the demi-human races, cross-bred with man. Not something that would be allowed, or could be admitted to, in these days of hatred and intolerance to all those with non-human blood. The Faerie had all but departed, and the dwarves had shut the doors to their deep mines and had not been seen or heard from in many generations. The Halflings, the race closest to man, had disappeared at the start of the last undead uprising. That was over four hundred years ago. The undead were no longer rife. Occasionally, reports would come forth of an uprising somewhere, and word would be sent out—a call to arms to help fight off the undead plague—but there had been no undead for 150 years. Peace more or less reigned across the nations; there was an occasional border squabble, but nothing of note. It was a time of rebuilding, of regrowth. It was a time of prosperity.

She had left her family just before her brother's marriage, twenty years ago. It was a marriage dedicated to the unification of the city states of Ulmarin and Raelis—the son of Raelis's ruling family joined to the daughter of Ulmarin's ruling family. Her brother would rule both in due course. She left to hide her family's secret, and her own. She aged slowly; she still appeared to be a lass of around eighteen years of age. She was now thirty-eight. There was something else, a secret strength, a darkness kept well hidden—a knowing, of things unknowable and untaught. It helped to keep her safe.

And now she was returning home. A vital message for her father or, if he had passed sometime in the years she had been gone, her brother. The time of peace had fled. Undead were on the move once more, and in unprecedented numbers. The vast nation of Albrae was gone. It had been overrun in a matter of weeks by the massive horde of undead. Many of the dead would join the ranks and swell the undead army to unprecedented proportions. An almost unstoppable force, one that she had been witness to. She counted herself lucky to still be alive; she was one of the very few left to spread the word. Death was on its way once more, and, what was worse, magic was failing—had failed, in fact. The one thing that could stop the undead in their tracks was no longer an option. The only thing going for mankind at this point was that they had time. It would take time for whoever was commanding the undead to regain control and gather them together again.

And so, here she was, travelling through the mountain pass from Almarac to Raelis—a matter of a few more hours and she would be home, dependent, of course, upon the poor beast pulling her cart. The horse was long overdue to be put out to pasture or sent to the knackers. A few more bends in the road and then it would be a straight run down the mountainside, through the foothills and across the grassy plain to Raelis.

There was a sudden shout, quickly followed by a short, sharp scream from up ahead. Jumping down from the cart and grabbing her bow, she ran down to the bend. Ahead of her were four men standing over another man. Bandits!

She quickly drew bead on the largest of the men and let her arrow fly. She followed with a second shot before the first had found its mark. The man dropped—one arrow in the chest and the other angling up through the throat. Two of the men spun around and then charged her. The third made a break for it. She launched one last arrow. It glanced off the buckler held by the shorter man and flew skyward.

Dropping the bow, she drew her two daggers and calmly walked towards the men. Once they came close, they separated to come at her from either side. Sensing that the shorter of the two was the lesser threat, she dived towards the taller. A quick cut as she passed him, and he was hamstrung, his sword blow passing just above her head. Rolling to her feet, she launched a second blow, and as he dropped to one knee, she cut his neck. Then he was dead.

She turned towards the other, who was upon her. A quick parry checked his clumsy blow. His buckler turned aside her other dagger. A sidestep and spin, with a cut to the back of his sword hand, and he was disarmed. It was short work after that. As he tried to pull a dagger from the sheath at his waist, she buried one of hers to the hilt in his torso, up under the ribcage and into the heart. No quarter was given. The fading sound of hoof beats told her the last man had escaped.

She made sure that the men were dead before checking on the one they had felled. He was a youth—tall, fair-haired, and strangely familiar, although she had never seen him before. Somehow, he still lived, despite his wounds. Wounds, at least, she could tend. She quickly ran back to her cart, picking her bow up on the way. Getting what she required from the cart, she hurried back. After tending his wounds, she left him where he lay, intending to investigate the bodies of her slain.

The one she had shot was a surprise. He was wearing a good-quality, fine-mesh chain mail over a gambeson. She was lucky to have dropped him with her short bow. It didn't have the power to punch through such armour; it was more for picking up the odd game animal on the trail. It was the throat shot that had done for him. A ricochet off the top of the armour had angled up into the throat. The other arrow had lodged in the chain mail but had not penetrated the gambeson beneath. His armour and cloak was not the sort to be found on common thugs, which the other men clearly were.

They were exactly what they appeared to be—common highwaymen. They could be bought and paid for by just about anyone—if one knew how to contact them and had the funds. She managed to get her unconscious patient in the cart and then loaded the other three in as well. She would burn the bodies further down the mountain.

It was well and truly dark by the time she had made it down off the mountain and built the pyre. She stripped the three bodies of their possessions before placing them upon it, and after bundling the goods into the back of the cart, she lit the fire. She could not afford to waste any more time. She needed to get the youth to some proper care. It was surprising that he was still alive, given his injuries.

So her cart rolled on. She walked beside the horse, encouraging it to continue, as she slowly made her way towards the city. As she approached the north-eastern gate, she saw that her family's sigil still flew above it—a black-and-white songbird on a field of blue. The gates had been shut for the night. She called out to the guards for assistance and asked for the portal to be opened. A young guard came out to investigate the disturbance.

'Open the gates and let me through. I have some disturbing news for King Gedry. Also, I came across this youth up on the mountain. He had been set upon by bandits. Do the Sisters of Mercy still run a hostel here? He is in need of their care. His injuries are grave. I am surprised he still lives. I am Kai, known to some as the Briar Rose, and I am a member of your royal family.'

'King Gedry died more than ten years ago, just after Prince Alaric. Regent Monfrae rules now, until Alaric's son is of age. If you are related, then you should have known. The Sisters of Mercy no longer take charity cases. The gates will remain closed until dawn. Be off with you,' said the guard.

'If you won't open the gate, at least send a message to the regent that someone claiming to be his niece is at the gate, and send this token to the Sisters of Mercy. I am sure they will send someone to assist.'

The guard moved back to the gate and called for his captain. The captain, a man who looked to be in his mid-forties, came out and, after one long look at Kai, called for the gates to be opened.

'I remember you, milady. How is it that you have not changed? You look the same as when you disappeared. You may not remember me, but I was once a member of the castle guard. I stood guard at your bedroom door many a night so you wouldn't stray. I won't keep you long. Your messages will be sent. Let's get you inside the gates and somewhere warm, whilst we wait for an answer from the palace. I doubt very much if the sisters will respond, but it will be good to have you back. See if you can talk some sense into that mad uncle of yours. But please don't tell him I said that. The demotion to captain of the gate guard is punishment enough.

'Now, let's have a look at your injured—perhaps I can assist in some way. I am well versed in the treatment of war injuries. My god, that's the crown prince you have there! What's he doing here? He's supposed to be in Almarac studying at the college. Roderick, you're on latrine duty for the next month—longer if he dies. And open that bloody gate! *Now!*' ordered the captain.

'Thank you, Captain,' replied Kai. 'I'll ensure you get a promotion for this. Let's say . . . captain of the Prince's personal guard, starting immediately. Uncle Monfrae can wait. You can guide me to the Sisters of Mercy. They will care for him. I can guarantee it. Now, let's move before he dies. I've lost a father and a brother tonight—I don't intend to lose my nephew. No wonder he looked so familiar when I first saw him. He looks like a young version of Alaric, except for that blond hair. Alaric's was as black as coal. Now, which way do I go? It has been so long since I was last here.'

'Move off down there to the right. I'll catch up in a minute. Just have to see to the men here and leave someone else in charge whilst I am gone,' suggested the captain.

Two guardsmen rode into the city with her messages as Kai moved off, the cart trundling down the laneway beside the city wall. Her nephew began to moan in the back.

'Decided to live, have you? Well, we will get you sorted out soon enough, once we can find this damn hostel.'

The gate captain caught up with her a little time later. 'Turn here, milady,' he said. 'Just a few streets further up and we'll come to a large walled-in building. That's the hostel. More like a barracks, actually. Not surprising, as they are a military order.'

As they arrived at the gate to the hostel, it opened. A small woman in a white cloak with the symbol of a blue shield twined with a black rose on the front came out. 'Ah, Captain, Sister Maria at your service. I have been ordered to attend the one who sent this token. I see that you have brought her to us. Come in, we will discuss your needs and see if we may assist,' she said.

'*May assist?* That token is a guarantee of your assistance. It was given to me by your matriarch some years back for a service I did her. It signifies a debt to be repaid.'

'Lady, I assure you the only reason you are being seen this night is because our Mother Superior does know this token. It's a reminder to our hostels of our allegiance to the Briar Rose,' explained the sister.

'*Exactly, and I am the Briar Rose.* Now, let's get my nephew under cover and see to his wounds,' commanded Kai.

Sister Maria hurried back into the compound to arrange assistance. Kai brought the cart in and parked near the main doors of the building. Sister Maria returned with two others bearing a stretcher. They proceeded to load the young prince onto the stretcher and carry him inside. Kai grabbed what she wanted out of the cart and quickly followed them, along with the captain. Once they had laid him out, the two sisters who had carried the stretcher left. He had three wounds that needed tending: one in the chest and two in the abdomen. They carefully removed the bandages from the chest wound.

'There is not as much blood as I would expect. In fact, I believe that the bleeding has stopped, although this wound still gapes,' said Maria. She cleaned away the dried blood for a closer examination. 'The flesh seems to be knitting itself back together. This may be regeneration. I have heard of it but have never seen it in action. It will prove a fascinating study,' she remarked.

Kai was incensed. 'You can study it on someone else. The prince is not a specimen for your intellectual pursuit. Regeneration is unexpected but not unheard of. It's very rare, but a few demi-humans, monsters, and undead are capable of it. Regeneration occurs every now and then in our bloodline, along with some other, hmm, benefits. We try to keep quiet about it, as some will read more into it than there is. We have demi-human blood in our family history, although none recently—at least four or five generations back. Some of us breed true, others don't. I thought I was the only one with some traits, but I see I have been mistaken. It's a good thing, though. We are going to need all the help we can get. No one must know of this. The political upheaval will not help our survival, only hasten our end.

'Captain,' Kai went on, 'you are in charge of his personal guard. You will also act as his bodyguard and manservant. That will ensure that you are the one who oversees his health and well-being, in all aspects of care. Someone you trust will be your second and aid you in your duties. If you cannot be by His Highness's side, then the other must. Find someone worthy.

'Sister Maria, I do not ask you to break any of the vows you have sworn to your sisterhood. But please remain silent as to the nature of His Highness's injuries— only say that he will survive and is recovering slowly. I also wish to keep his presence here secret until we have had a chance to locate the last man involved in the attack. I suspect he was known to the prince. Someone sought to profit from his death, and I mean to find out who. But first, I need to sleep. I was up before dawn yesterday. If Regent Monfrae requests my presence, then send a message that I am resting and will attend him at my earliest convenience. I will sleep on a pallet in this room in case the prince awakens. He and I need to talk, about a great many things.

'Captain, go back to your post at the gate. Then when your shift is over, go and find your second. Bring him here to me or find me at the palace. The prince will be safe here. For the moment, he does not exist. Everyone thinks he is still in Almarac, except for one, and that one will think he is dead.'

Kai sighed. 'This is ridiculous. I cannot just keep referring to him as "the prince". What is my nephew's name?'

'Prince Morannel, milady Kai. I will see you late today. It will take some time to find that one whom I truly trust,' said the gate captain.

Once she was alone, Kai dropped to her pallet, exhausted, and slept.

CHAPTER 2

Later that morning, not long after the sun rose, Kai was awakened by a low groan from Prince Morannel. 'Damn, I hurt. Where am I, and how did I get here? Who are you? You look familiar—a painting, I think, at home, near the one of my father. That can't be right. It's been hanging there for years. You couldn't be her. You're much too young. You are beautiful,' he said.

'Thank you for the compliment, nephew. I am your aunt Kai. I left before your parents married. You are safe and at the hostel of the Sisters of Mercy in Raelis. At this point, there are three people who know who and where you are. Now, as for what has happened, perhaps you should tell me what you remember. You were studying at the college in Almarac. What made you leave in the manner you did and without an escort?'

'My aunt? And you left before my parents married? You must be over thirty then. That can't be right. You don't look any older than I am. Truthfully now, tell me who you are,' said the prince.

'As I said, I am your aunt Kai. I am thirty-eight. I have inherited some of the benefits of our demi-human bloodline. As have you. Now, before you side-track the conversation again, tell me what you remember. This is important. I promise we can discuss other issues at length later, but tell me what I need to know,' Kai commanded.

The prince responded, more to the authority present in Kai's tone than her words, 'Let me collect my thoughts for a bit . . . I think it all started not long after we arrived in Almarac. Before we went to the college, and by *we*, I mean my sister Zephranthe and myself. We were staying at the home of some relatives of one of our local nobles. They were people we could trust, or at least my uncle thought so.'

He paused and turned his puzzled gaze to Kai. 'Are you really my aunt?' But before she could answer, the prince began to speak once more. 'Anyway, a note was delivered to me. It was a threat on my life. I still remember it, word for word. It said, "At a time and place of my choosing, you shall die. Enjoy your time at the college for it will be short." No name was given. The time set for my stay at the college was to be for five years.

'Because of the threat on my life, it was decided that I would not partake in classes or events that could put my life at risk through what could be an arranged accident. So I studied history, politics, theories on magic and theology, as well as economics. The few lessons I received in self-defence were from a friend studying the many aspects of war. I proved fairly inept. I proved to be a better strategist than a participant. I enjoyed my studies. I think they will help me rule when I ascend the throne, although I certainly am not looking forward to it. That's still a few years away yet, and a good thing too. I should like the chance to travel awhile and see some of the places I have read about . . . I digress. I received another anonymous note not long ago. It read, "Your time is due!" I did not know what to do. Who could I trust?

'I sent a note to my cousin Frederick. He graduated from the college a couple of years previously, and occasionally he would visit my sister and me. So I asked him to come and tell me what he thought, to see if he could help. He was already in Almarac. He made a suggestion to wait two weeks and then, using a disguise and telling no one of my intentions, leave for home. He gave me a pin to wear on my cloak so that the soldiers he sent to escort me home would be able to recognise me. He left that night to come home and make the proper arrangements for my safe return. I waited until the due day and then left.

'I had left a note for my sister so she would not worry and asked her to tell no one of my intentions. I met no travellers along the way until almost home. I thought this strange, as there is usually a bit of traffic heading in both directions, and it took me quite a while to walk the distance. Five days afoot. I realised that I would not make the city before nightfall and decided to find a place to camp in the foothills of the mountain.

'Then after rounding the last bend, I found myself facing four soldiers. I was relieved to see them as they had horses, and I assumed they had been sent to guide me safely the rest of the way. I approached them. Then one of them said, "He's the one. Kill the thief and take the pin."

'I recognised the voice. *My cousin!* I yelled, and they ran me through with their swords. I don't remember anything much thereafter—just a great deal of pain for a very long time, with an occasional voice filtering through. Not that I could understand anything. My cousin! Why my cousin? Why Frederick? I always looked up to him. We were friends.'

'I suspect it's because his father is your regent,' Kai responded. 'With you out of the way, and if your cousin was to marry your sister, then he would then be next in line to ascend the throne. He probably believes it should be his anyway. Then once his father passes on, he inherits. It is about politics and greed. He will have covered his tracks far too well to be caught at this. He will not expect you to survive, and as there are no witnesses who can identify him, he will believe himself to be safe. I will need to think of a way to trap him without alerting his father to what I am doing. Now, to other things—what do you know of our family and its history?'

'Just the stories of my parents. Their political marriage, my mother's death in childbirth—it was the birth of my sister—and the death of my father near the same time. A hunting accident, if I remember correctly. As to the myths read to me when I was just a boy, I don't really remember them.'

'Well, there are some truths that you need to know,' said Kai. 'We have demi-human blood in our veins. Many generations back, our family interbred with some of the other intelligent races. Most of them, in fact, if the stories I was told by my great-grandmother were true. And I think they were. It was before our family came to rule. You and I both can regenerate the wounds we receive. You heal much more slowly than I do. No magic or divine healing has kept you alive—just your body's own natural healing capacity. Your wounds are still closing. I suspect it will take close to a week before they are fully mended. Until that time, you will have to take great care to see that you do not do yourself further harm. Now, you need to fuel your body so it can heal. You need to eat. I shall go and see to it that food is sent to us. We shall dine here. I won't be gone long.'

Kai soon returned, followed shortly thereafter by one of the sisters carrying a tray laden with food. After the sister had left and they had eaten, Kai continued the conversation.

'What other abilities you have inherited, we may never find out. I hope you are not cursed, as I am, with what may be an exceptionally long life. I do not age. It is the reason I left to begin with. My growth slowed early, and then, less noticeably, I started to age slower. I have also been blessed with a remarkable agility and a muscular strength much greater than what my frame would suggest. Blade work comes naturally to me, and I can sense the presence of those around me. Now, I need to go to the palace. Rest and heal. I will be back later. The sisters may be able to provide you with a book or two to read if you become bored.'

Kai then left. Stopping a sister on her way out, she requested some books for her patient. Kai worked her way back to the guardhouse by the north-eastern gate before turning towards the centre of the city. Kai took her time, strolling along the roads and streets trying to memorise the pattern of the city. She occasionally stopped to view merchandise and talk with the populace but declined to buy anything. She slowly became aware of someone following her. Shrugging her cloak into a more comfortable position and loosening her daggers, she moved on.

She made her way to the palace—her shadow following, coming no closer but not falling behind either. She passed through the gates of the palace without stopping, as if she belonged, and the guards ignored her. That was just a bit troubling. She should have been stopped and questioned. Her shadow fell behind. She smiled to herself and then continued up the steps to the home she had left some twenty years before.

CHAPTER 3

uch a wonderful welcoming committee. No one to welcome her home, just as she wished. Now, if only she could find the chamberlain before . . . too late—here was some officious oaf come to hassle her.

'My dear fellow,' Kai said very quickly, 'perhaps you could guide me to the chamberlain. Come now, hurry up and be quick about it. Don't you know? Oh well, I shall just have to find my own way then. Be off with you now. Go on. Surely you have some worthwhile duty to attend to. No? Well, then, I'm sure you're not needed. You can leave and not come back. If I see you again, you will be food for the dogs. Good riddance, I'd say. Now where was I? That's right—the Lord Chamberlain. If I remember correctly, his office should be off in this direction.'

With that, Kai turned towards the stairs and moved off, leaving a very confused sycophant standing in the hall, wondering what had just happened. Kai quickly moved up the stairs, turned left, and moved off down the hallway. Finding a maid coming out of a room with a bundle of laundry, she stopped the lass and asked where the regent could be found at this hour.

'He is usually with the Lord Chamberlain in his private study, up on the third floor,' she said. 'There is a painting of the late king Gedry opposite the door. Shall I guide you, milady?'

'No, I don't need a guide. It has been some years since I was last here, but I still know my way around. You had best go, and be quick. You don't want to get into trouble.'

Kai moved off and found some back stairs up to the next level. She managed to avoid the few guards until she found the stairs to the third floor. There was a pair of guards at the top who looked startled to see her.

'Who are you, and where is your escort? You should not be up here, lady. If you have business with someone here at the palace, you should have arranged an appointment and received an escort to take you to them,' stated one of the guards.

'None of those in charge in this palace know that I have returned. The Lord Chamberlain is whom I have come to see. He is the only one who may remember who I am. Take me to him. *Now!* For I am Kai, aunt to your crown prince and niece of your regent. I have urgent news, and I must make myself known to them before anyone else knows that I am here. Now, if one of you cares to escort me to them, I will ensure you are properly rewarded. Oh, yes, and you had best take these,' Kai said as she offered her daggers to the guards. 'And don't lose them. I shall be wanting them back just as soon as it is proven that I am who I say I am. Now, if I am correct, we should just go up here to the third door on your right.'

Kai led the way with some protest from both guards. 'Go on, knock twice and then announce me. I shall wait,' she said.

One of the guards gave her a rueful grimace, stepped to the door, and knocked twice. When bid to enter, he opened the door and stepped through. As he tried to softly close the door behind him, Kai managed to get her foot in the doorway to hold it ajar. She pushed the door open and stepped in. The room was austere. Its furnishings limited to what was needed to fulfil the role of Lord Chamberlain. It was obvious the owner of this room did not require the trappings of power that the position usually conveyed. Lowering the hood on her cloak, she smiled at the two men in front of her.

'Surprise, gentlemen—I have returned home, and none too soon, I fear. The security of this palace is a joke. Oh, and forgive the guards. They just don't know how to do their jobs. Excuse me a moment.'

Kai turned to the guard with her daggers and said, 'I'll be having those weapons back now. Come on, hand them over. You haven't lost them already, have you?' Then she smiled. Taking back her daggers, she sheathed them and sat down in the nearest chair. 'Refreshments might be nice,' she suggested over her shoulder. Then she turned back to her uncle and the Lord Chamberlain. They looked rather astonished by her appearance.

'We thought you were dead. A search for you was instigated just after you disappeared and once again when your father died. On both occasions, no evidence of you was ever found. We must announce your return and host a banquet in your honour to welcome you home,' stated Regent Monfrae.

'The welcome party can wait, gentlemen. We have a few, more important, issues to deal with first. I must say, you are both looking well, considering your ages, and the fact that you have lost your future king. My Lord Chamberlain, what is the current penalty for regicide? Does the crown grant clemency to those of the royal family who attempt to commit murder? I myself am free of guilt, as are Their Highnesses, the prince and princess. I can't say the same for my other nephew, though. Nor can I speak on behalf of His Grace, the regent, although at this point, I have found no evidence implicating him,' she stated.

'You dare to insinuate that I or my son had the gall to commit regicide? How dare you! I loved Morannel. I have raised him as well as my own son. I rule this kingdom in his name until he comes of age. His rule begins in another six years—less if I die or deem him fit to rule. I have done my best for him and this nation!' the regent exclaimed.

'You have proof of this?' asked the Lord Chamberlain.

'Better, my lord. I have a witness. He is in safekeeping and will remain so until the right time,' Kai replied. 'My Lord Chamberlain, who may legally sit in judgement of the crime, as it stands?'

'If the regent is implicated, then it would be a panel of five lords of state. That panel would include me as the highest-ranking lord outside the royal family. Otherwise, the regent himself could be the sole judge. He should excuse himself from the role, as you imply that it is his son who must be judged. It is the right of the panel to judge if leniency may be granted. Leniency can be requested by the crown, the prosecutor, or the victim,' stated the Lord Chamberlain.

'Uncle, I assume you will allow the panel to sit in judgement?' asked Kai.

'No, I will sit in judgement, but the panel of lords shall determine innocence or guilt, and offer their verdict on punishment. I shall then issue the punishment that I deem fitting, as per the laws of the land. Lord Chamberlain, call the panel together for tomorrow afternoon. It will take place in the grand hall,' proclaimed Regent Monfrae.

'My lords, if you will have my old rooms refreshed so that I may once again use them, I would be appreciative. If the old harridan who was my nurse as a child is still around, have her present herself to me in those rooms after the evening meal. I shall return shortly with my witness,' said Kai.

'Your old rooms are currently occupied by my son. Other arrangements can be made for your stay,' stipulated the regent.

'He won't need them any longer, my lord. I shall have my old rooms back. Tonight. Your son has another place to stay tonight—a cell in the dungeon. He is guilty, my lord, and it is the only safe place to hold him. I suppose you could always have him stay in your rooms with you, my lord. Since he has gone in for regicide, killing you is his next step to the throne. Or had you not thought of that? I suppose you could just move him to another suite. Tell him that his current rooms are to be mine for the duration of my stay. Since they had been mine, they would be the most comfortable for me. Surely he could endure a few nights sleeping in another area of the palace? Besides, from what I remember, the view from that balcony is wonderful,' said Kai.

'I will see that it is done, my lady. You do realise, I trust, that you are also in line for the throne. If anything should happen to your brother's children, you would inherit,' spoke the Lord Chamberlain.

'I am aware of my precarious position, my lords. I think I would prefer to die than have to rule. There's no fun to be had, and I still have places to see and things I must do. Until later, then, my lords. Oh, by the way, there will be four of us staying in my apartments. Please ensure that the proper arrangements are made,' requested Kai.

As she left, she stopped once again to speak with the guards. 'One of you can come with me. The other can find the regent's son and escort him to the Lord Chamberlain and his father. I expect that they will want to have words with him. Come on, then. Let's go.' Kai walked down the stairs, saying, 'What's the quickest way out of here?'

'This way, Lady Kai. Follow me and I will show you the way out,' said the guard.

Once they had left the palace, Kai asked to be taken to the Sisters of Mercy hostel, and as they made their way, Kai realised that her shadow from the morning had reappeared. Kai frowned slightly. She did not like being followed by the unknown. Outside the hostel, Kai was approached by Captain Gregorson, the gate guard captain of the night before.

'I have found my second, milady. I sent him to find you. I would have thought that he would be with you by now . . . Sergeant Orset, good to see you. Still learning how to polish your boots, I see. Ah, here he is now, milady. This is Alemrae Traemellin. I would trust him with my life—already have in fact. No other would I prefer to have guarding my back. I have yet to meet the one who can best him in battle,' said Captain Gregorson. Alemrae appeared slightly stunned as he gazed upon Kai.

'Actually, Captain, you have—me! Although he might actually pose a challenge. It is a pleasure to meet you, Alemrae.' Kai smiled. 'How about we move this conversation inside, gentlemen? Fewer ears to hear, so to speak. Sergeant Orset, would you be so kind as to drive my cart back to the palace and see that all my things are taken to my suite? It should be ready by the time you return. No mauling of the luggage, mind you. I want to find all of my belongings untouched when I arrive. You are dismissed. Now, come inside, you two, and we will discuss your duties with your employer.'

Kai quickly led the men to the room in which the prince was supposed to be resting. Prince Morannel was not in the room. 'Stay here whilst I go find our missing prince,' Kai stated.

Leaving the men, she moved further into the building. Concentrating on her inner capacity for the detection of others, she managed to pick up a small group ahead and to the left of her current location. Taking the next left corridor brought her quickly to their location. She opened the door to find five sisters and the prince standing around a table. They were arguing about the use of a particular herb in the art of healing. Kai listened for a moment and then broke into the conversation.

'Sorry, ladies, but you are wrong. That particular herb has absolutely no favourable use in the treatment of the condition you are discussing. It may, in fact, do a great deal of harm. A tisane of widows' pearl used as a wash over the infected area would produce a better result. Now, I need to speak with my patient in private,' she said as she turned to address the prince. 'If you will please follow me.'

Kai then led the prince slowly back to the room. Prince Morannel paused at the doorway to his room when he saw the two armed men inside.

'Come in, nephew,' said Kai. 'These two are to be your personal bodyguards. You will not be left alone for quite some time to come. Your safety will be their sole preoccupation. They will oversee all aspects of your protection. One or the other will always be in your presence. Now, this is the former captain of the city gate guard. One of the few guards I have seen in this city who actually knows how to do his job, and one of the very few respected by your populace. His name is Geoffrey Gregorson. The other, I have only just met, his name being Alemrae Traemellin. The captain has stood surety for him. In matters relating to your personal safety, you are to obey any commands they give you. In all other matters, they will obey you. It will be up to them, not you, to determine what matters pertain to your safety, and as such, if they need to disobey a direct order from you, in order to ensure your safety, then they will do so. Have I made myself clear?'

'Yes, my lady,' responded Geoffrey and Alemrae.

'Now, we are going to transfer to the palace. I have had rooms made ready for us. We will confine ourselves to those rooms until such time as it is necessary to take our parts in the forthcoming trial of my other nephew. Once we are ensconced, I will ensure our needs are met. So, my prince, don your disguise, and we shall depart in the capable presence of your protectors,' stated Kai.

A short time later, after gathering together what few possessions were in the room, they left. Kai bid farewell to the sister guarding the front doors and asked her to pass on their thanks to the Mother Superior.

It was a long walk up to the palace. Frequent rest stops were taken to allow the prince time to recover. A short time after they left the hostel, Kai noticed her shadow of the morning had returned. Kai spoke softly with Alemrae, and he moved off into the stream of people passing by. Kai, Geoffrey, and Morannel moved on, and a short time afterwards, Alemrae returned.

'It is a young woman who follows you. She appears to belong to one of the Irikani desert tribes,' whispered Alemrae.

'Thank you. She will pose no threat. Lead us to the nearest marketplace with a well. I will await her there,' said Kai.

When they arrived at the marketplace, Kai asked the others to wait beside one of the buildings. Morannel seated himself on a wine barrel, whilst the other two stood beside him. Kai went over to the well, let down the bucket, and hauled up some water. She filled a cup, which was chained to the well head and took a drink. She then refilled the cup and placed it on the other side of the well. A hand appeared as if out of nowhere, followed by the rest of the young woman. She then drank and replaced the cup.

'Wʉyel wʉ wʉna mɛ ɛzɔl. Vakʉ ɔnʉlʉ oyen. Oku ɔvaa. Kɛlɛ ɛmɛ, mate we ɔmbɔn,' the stranger said.

'I am sorry—my Irikani is a little rusty. Do you speak my tongue?' asked Kai.

'Yes, Briar Rose, I speak your tongue. My thanks for the water. The seers have seen. Death approaches. I am to be your guide,' said the girl.

'If a guide I need, then a guide I will accept, but I must select the journey upon which you guide me,' said Kai.

'The terms are agreed, as we knew they would be. My name is Ovo-yindi, or Shadow's Hand,' said Ovo-yindi.

'Then I will call you Shadow. Go and blend, or stay with us, as your nature dictates,' responded Kai.

'I will stay with you, lady, so as to learn more of your people,' said Shadow.

'Then, come—time is short,' Kai said. Kai waved over the others and, ignoring their questions, continued on to the palace.

CHAPTER 4

After a while, they entered through the gates and went into the palace. Captain Gregorson accosted a servant and thus procured a guide to Kai's chambers. Once they had entered, Alemrae searched the apartment and, finding no one, announced the place safe. Shadow moved to the centre of the room and whispered softly in her native tongue.

'He is correct, Lady Kai. These rooms are safe. There are none in, or around, these rooms willing to do us harm. No ears to listen,' confirmed Shadow.

'Who is she?' asked Prince Morannel.

'Her name is unpronounceable in our tongue. We shall call her Shadow. She is a daughter of the desert, of the tribe Irikani. She is a shaman, a mystic of sorts and a guide. That is all I can tell you and all you need to know, except this: she means no harm to anyone,' said Kai.

'Someone approaches, Lady Kai,' said Shadow.

'I am aware of his presence, as I have been of yours every time you followed me,' said Kai. She smiled to herself again. 'Alemrae, get the door. The rest of you can move into the other rooms.'

At once, there was a knock on the door. Alemrae opened the door. A servant stood there. 'I have been sent to prepare a table for dinner,' he said.

'We shall eat in here. There will be five. I will require jugs containing water, at least three juices, including grape and lemon, and one of milk. We will also require a bottle of wine, preferably red. No ale. Ensure that one of the cups is wood, simple in design, with no carvings or other enhancements. Come to think of it, one of the wooden finger bowls would do nicely. Oh, yes, and a mixture of breads as well,' said Kai.

The servant went about his duties. He soon had a table set for five and a sideboard ready to receive the meal and drinks to be shared. He then left.

Kai went into the other room to see what the others were up to, followed by Alemrae. They were spread around the room. Shadow stood gazing out of the window, admiring the view. Prince Morannel was seated in one of the large comfortable chairs across the room and was admiring Shadow. Captain Gregorson was leaning against the wall, cleaning his fingernails with one of his daggers.

'Now, to matters of importance. First, we will be joined by an old woman after dinner. She was my old nurse. She will be responsible for the upkeep of these rooms. Anything you require, ask her, and she will see that you get it, up to a point. I do not know yet how long we will be staying here, and she will make our lives a bit more comfortable without having to depend on the less reliable staff. Second, there is a trial to be held tomorrow after the midday meal, in the Grand Hall. e will all be attending. Prince Morannel, you will remain incognito until the proper time. I will let you know when that is. You will be giving your testimony at the trial. You will wait in an adjoining chamber until called for. Captain Gregorson will be with you. I will send Alemrae in to get you both. He and Shadow will accompany me and stay by my side for the duration. Third, depending upon the outcome of the trial, we may need to stay here for some time. If so, I will ensure that we have separate rooms located near each other. Otherwise, we may be leaving within a day or two. You all may accompany me if that is your wish. I will let you know the destination once we are on our way and not before. Fourth, but certainly not the least of import, the nation of Albrae has been overrun by undead.

It has ceased to exist. Approximately five hundred thousand men, women, and children have died. This all happened within a three-week timeframe. How many undead there are is unknown. But I think that there are more now than at any other point in the history of our world. We need to find some means of stopping them once and for all. We have to forge an alliance with as many nations as we can. We will also have to find the demi-human races, for they have capabilities that we mere humans do not, and I think we will need their aid. That is all for now. Prince Morannel, if at some stage you require a champion, I will be that champion. You may discuss these things amongst yourselves, but do not let anyone overhear you. The situation at the moment is poised on a knife edge. The meal should be served shortly. Thank you.'

Kai went back into the main room. Shadow came through shortly after. 'Where am I to rest this night?' she asked.

'Where would you be most comfortable?'

'I usually sleep in the open, lady,' said Shadow.

'Call me Kai, please. If you usually sleep in the open, then there is a balcony outside my bedroom you could use. Or, if you prefer, the trellis on the balcony gives easy access to the roof. No one will disturb you in either location. You may sleep where you will.'

'Then I will sleep on the roof, Kai. There, the three moons will guide my rest. Although I may not sleep, the view is astounding—all that water. Is that the sea? I have never seen the like,' marvelled Shadow.

'Yes, that is the Bay of Tranquillity. It gives us easy access to trade, across the ocean, on the continent of Tir. If you have not seen the sea before, then how did you get here?' asked Kai.

'When I left my home at Iriki, I walked north, across the entire length of the great desert, to the wastes of Uripor. I then headed east when I reached the mountains. I know not their name. I skirted the southern edge through the foothills until I came to the village of Mar. Then I made my way to the trade road between here and Ulmarin,' she replied.

'That is a hard and dangerous journey for anyone, let alone one as young as you. That you accomplished it, alone and unharmed, is a testament to your abilities. I am pleased that you have come. Be at ease. I sense our food is about to arrive. Please wait with the others until I call for you all,' Kai said.

Shadow left. Kai walked to the door and opened it. An astonished servant had been about to knock. 'You walk loudly,' Kai said. 'Come in with the meal.'

The servants deposited the meal on the sideboard, arranging the selections in an ordered sequence and leaving the jugs and wine on the end. There was an apparent lack of bread.

'Where are the breads that I asked for?' queried Kai. 'Fetch them immediately!'

'The cook told us to serve them after the meal, my lady, as is customary,' replied the head servant.

'The cook does not determine when things are to be served. Bread will be served with our meals, not after. Once the meal is served, we are not to be disturbed. Is that understood?' Kai asked.

'Yes, Your Grace,' they responded.

'Good. Now be about your business. If this gets cold before we eat, then you will answer to me,' stipulated Kai.

The servants hurried out the door. Kai summoned the others from the next room.

'We are awaiting the breads, but we can start with what we have. Shadow, I have arranged to have some foods that may suit you. Please feel free to sample anything you desire. Let me know if there is anything else that you want. I will try to meet your needs or find something that may be suitable as a replacement. Alemrae, when the breads arrive, please take them from the servant in the hall. Do not allow them to see into the room. Please, people, start eating—I wish no formality here. Take what you wish,' ordered Kai.

Prince Morannel quickly grabbed a plate and piled it with food. He then took a chair near the end of the table. Alemrae also took a plate and, after filling it, sat at the end of the table closest to the door. Geoffrey Gregorson took the chair opposite Prince Morannel. Kai seated herself at the other end of the table from Alemrae and offered the chair between her and Captain Gregorson to Shadow. A knock on the door was answered by Alemrae, who returned with the breads. He offered Shadow her choice of the breads before putting the basket on the sideboard. He then opened the bottle of wine, poured two glasses, gave one to Kai, and took the other back to his seat and continued his meal. Shadow took the empty finger bowl from the table and went to the jugs.

After sampling each, she made a mixture of all the juices and the milk. The curdled mixture looked rather repulsive to the others, but Shadow seemed to enjoy it. After each had taken their fill, they adjourned to the next room. Kai pointed out the rooms that each of them would sleep in.

'Kai,' said Alemrae, 'you seem to have forgotten Shadow, and there are five of us with only four rooms. Where will she sleep?'

'Shadow has already told me she would prefer to sleep in the open, so she will sleep on the roof. She has access from my balcony,' replied Kai.

A loud knock sounded from the other room. 'That should be my old nurse,' said Kai. 'I shall check. Wait here.'

Kai went into the other room and answered the door. Kai's old nurse was indeed at the door. With her were two maids and three of the cook's servants who had brought the meal.

'Come in,' said Kai. The servants entered and cleaned up the remains of the meal, leaving the jug of water and some clean cups. The old nurse and the maids waited for the servants to leave before they approached Kai.

The old nurse spoke first. 'These are my granddaughters, Kira and Aleen. They will do the work, whilst I oversee them. I am not able to do as much as I used to. They will remain silent on everything they see or hear in these rooms. You have my guarantee. I have missed you, Your Grace. You were *oh, so difficult* to tend when you were young, but I am proud of you.'

'I thank you for the service you provided when I was unable to appreciate you, or the trouble I was. Please accept my apologies, however belated, for my bad behaviour,' said Kai.

'Apologies are not needed, Your Grace. Now, what are your specific orders concerning your guests?' asked the old nurse.

Kai replied, 'They are to remain nameless, and unspoken of, until I give you leave. This should be for only a short time. Either the reasons for keeping them secret will be gone, or we will be. I expect two or three days at the most. Your work is simple. Maintain these apartments with due care and attention to detail, as you used to do. Answer the door, take and send messages for us, obtain or organise for us the few essentials we will need. The young lady with me has an unusual and somewhat restricted diet. Ensure her needs are met as fully as possible. Please ignore any strange behaviour from her, as she comes from a completely different culture. Now, we will shortly retire for the night. Go about your duties as quietly and circumspectly as I require. You will be paid well for this service, and I thank you for it. Good night.'

Kai went through to the others, explained the situation to them, and then said, 'Time for bed. We have a busy day tomorrow. Good night, all.'

She then walked into her bedroom, followed by Shadow. The others organised themselves and went to their rooms. Shadow went out onto the balcony and then climbed the trellis to the roof. Kai stood on the balcony for a while, admiring the view. Then she went in, closed the balcony doors, and went to sleep.

That night, Shadow sat and watched the Bay of Tranquillity. She was mesmerised by the play of moonlight on the water, the movement of the waves rolling onto the beach, and the rising and falling of the boats at the dock. The sounds of the city and port rose up to her rooftop position, slowly dying away as the night proceeded. She felt an inner peace, a deeper understanding of her world and her place in it, and then witnessed a glorious sunrise. The sun seemed to lift itself out of the water and colour it in desert shades of orange, yellow, and gold. Somehow, it seemed a fitting end to the night.

She quietly climbed back down the trellis, feeling as rested as if she had slept the whole night. At ease with herself and her world, she slipped open the balcony doors. As she did so, a dagger slammed into the panelling of the right-hand door in front of her face.

CHAPTER 5

Shocked to stillness, Shadow waited. How could she have let her guard down so much? Who sought to harm her? As she gathered her wits and drew deeply upon her magic for protection, Kai rolled from her bed.

'Forgive me,' Kai cried. 'I reacted without thought. Who else could have been coming in that way except for you? My nerves have been wound way too tight for so long. I have hardly slept. Then, when I do finally let my guard down to sleep properly, I react when awoken, with no thought but that of survival, no care as to the damage that may occur. Please forgive me.'

'There is nothing to forgive. I did not announce my presence, just opened the doors to come in. Anyone with dire intentions could have been entering,' said Shadow. She let the forces she had gathered dissipate.

'Let us prepare. I shall summon our maids, and they will help us make ready for the day. Then we shall break our fast,' said Kai. She walked through to the main room to summon the maids, whilst Shadow waited by the doors to the balcony. She still had not moved when Kai returned.

'Do you actually need assistance to get ready for the day?' Shadow asked.

'No, but it is expected, and sometimes we must do what is expected so our enemies do not suspect us of doing something else. So a bath and change of clothes is in order and then a light meal. We have little to do until the trial, so the morning can be used to prepare and organise ourselves. Maybe do some of the planning for the journey we will be going on. Work out what we may need and how we are to transport everything, and work out how to pay for it all, if need be,' said Kai.

'What is this trial that we must attend? I am unfamiliar with the custom,' asked Shadow.

'A trial is a contest in points of law. If someone breaks our laws, then they must be tried. If found guilty of breaking the law, then they receive a punishment. The punishment depends upon the law they broke, as well as why and how severely they broke it. The trial we attend is for treason. We will be proving the guilt of the accused person. In this case, the cousin of the victim of the crime. The victim is Prince Morannel. His cousin attempted to have him murdered. He was recognised during the assault but escaped. The prince's cousin is not aware that the attack failed. So, hopefully, we can surprise him at the trial by accusing him of treason. He will be required to come to the trial but will not be informed as to why. The difficult part will be what punishment is given. The penalty for treason is usually death, but the prince admires and respects his cousin, and will probably request leniency on his behalf. It may become a very tangled business after that. The trial itself will not take that long, but determining the punishment may take quite a long time,' explained Kai.

'We have nothing like this in my country. Disagreements of this nature are unlikely to occur. We are too much involved in keeping ourselves alive to place much reliance on anyone else. Death is too easy. The breaking of our customs generally leads to banishment. Banishment in the desert by oneself usually leads to death. So most would not even consider doing something that would lead to that eventuality. If one survives their period of banishment, they may return to their tribe,' said Shadow.

'Banishment may be used as a punishment, but it is usually permanent. Banishment for a short duration would not be very conducive to stopping the infringement in the first place,' said Kai.

'I thank you for the explanation. Your ways frequently appear strange to me,' said Shadow.

'Different places have different customs, laws, and punishments,' said Kai. 'When in another land, one must learn and understand their way of doing things. You have done well so far. I have travelled widely and have been treated most harshly for little reason in some places. But I also learnt a great deal about mankind, and about myself. How we treat others is vital to how we treat ourselves. Abuse of one will eventually lead to abuse of the other. Not in the same manner, perhaps, but just as brutal in the end. You are already on a path of enlightenment. Maybe you will be nearer to its end by the time you return to your people, at least I hope it will be so. Now, is there anything else you wish to discuss? Our maids are waiting for my signal for them to begin assisting us.'

'No, nothing at the moment. I thank you for the thoughts you have shared with me. I will contemplate them when I have time. Call your maids,' said Shadow.

Kai called for the maids. When they entered, she ordered food and requested a bath be made ready and clothing set out.

She then spoke to her old nurse. 'Have my family banner raised over the palace, and have this pennant raised below it. I suspect there are very few in the city who will know it. Please send a message to the Mother Superior of the order of the Sisters of Mercy. Request that she attend the trial after the midday meal with whatever retinue she deems necessary.'

The maids hustled about, readying everything. By the time Kai and Shadow were ready, the food had arrived. The men joined them in the main room for breakfast. Whilst they adjourned to the second room, the maids cleaned up. Discussions were initiated on various topics as they began to get to know each other a little better. Time seemed to fly past, for the midday meal was suddenly upon them.

As soon as the meal was finished, Kai said, 'We must make ready for the trial. It will begin shortly. Morannel, you must remain incognito, so dress appropriately. Captain Gregorson, wear your uniform and accompany the prince to the small room outside the

Great Hall. Let no one approach the prince. Have it seem that he is your prisoner. That way, we will keep his identity a close secret until we reveal him at the trial. Shadow and Alemrae, if you have formal wear, then now is the time to use it. We shall leave in a few minutes.'

They regathered in the main room after they had made ready. 'Now let us go. Captain, wait two minutes before you follow with the prince.'

When they arrived in the Great Hall, there was a crowd gathered already. Kai made her way to the dais and stood on the lowest step. Shadow and Alemrae stood a pace behind her, one to each side, both of them looking exotic. There were six high-backed chairs, one above and behind the other five, which were set in an arc upon the dais. These would be for the judgement panel and the regent.

Frederick Monfraeson entered with a few friends. He was dressed resplendently in colours denoting the royal family. He wore a longsword on his left hip. The appearance of the scabbard suggested it had cost a small fortune.

Although, come to think of it, the pommel on the hilt of the sword looks familiar, mused Kai. It looked like that of her father's sword. *It should still be locked away in the palace armoury. It will belong to Morannel when he comes of age. The sword of the king! Has this young man had the temerity to steal it as well?*

The noise of the crowd swelled, and it drew Kai's attention to the men proceeding up the aisle. It was the judgement panel, led by the Lord Chamberlain. Regent Monfrae entered from behind the dais and made his way to the highest chair. The panel seated themselves according to rank upon the other five chairs. At that moment, the Mother Superior and her retinue entered.

She approached the dais and said, 'I was asked to present myself before the trial, and so I have come to bear witness.' She moved off to the side with her followers.

The Lord Chamberlain stood. 'We have come together this day at the behest of Princess Kai. She has recently returned to us. She has been gone from our presence these last twenty years. She wishes to present to the court formal charges of treason directed at one of our populace. Your Grace, if you would please proceed with your case.'

'Regent, my lords, my dear people of this nation, we have been betrayed by one of our own. I charge Frederick Monfraeson with the attempted murder of Prince Morannel.'

There was a huge gasp from the audience and a protest from Frederick. 'I am innocent. She has no proof. There can be no proof of something that never happened. She seeks to undermine my father's rule and take the throne for herself!' he shouted.

'I don't want the throne. I never did. That was one of the reasons I left in the first place. I have a witness to the event. But, first, let me explain the situation before I call on my witness. Three days ago, as I was coming home from my extensive travels, via Almarac, I came across an incident in the mountain pass. Just before I reached the last bend, I heard a shout and a loud scream. Someone was in trouble. I rushed forward and saw four men standing over a body on the ground. Assuming that they were bandits, I drew bead on the largest and fired off two arrows. Both struck home, and he fell. Two of the other men charged me, whilst the last ran for the horses. He mounted and, cutting the reins of the other horses, took them and fled the scene. I dispatched the two who attacked me and, after ensuring that the three of them were dead, looked to their victim. I found a youth with three dangerous wounds. I suspected that, even with my help, he might not survive. I treated his wounds as best I could and loaded him onto my cart. I then took the bodies of the men I had just slain and loaded them onto the cart as well. Once I had reached the foothills, I stripped them of their possessions and burnt the bodies. This is something that I have recently found to be necessary. I will speak to the regent and the Lord Chamberlain about why at a later time, for this is not the place. Continuing on then, I arrived at the city gate after dark. As is normal, the gates were shut. I obtained entrance and requested the aid of the Sisters of Mercy in the treatment of the victim. It was at this point that I became aware of the treasonous nature of the attack.'

The Mother Superior spoke up from where she was seated. 'I can confirm that the Lady Kai arrived at our hostel in the early hours of the morning and requested medical aid for a youth she had rescued. He had suffered terribly.'

'Lady Kai, in this we hear no evidence linking the person of Frederick Monfraeson to the supposed murder of Prince Morannel. Nor have you mentioned anything about your witness,' said the regent.

'I must allow him to explain himself, my lord,' said Kai. 'Alemrae, would you be kind enough to fetch my witness?'

'Yes, Your Grace, at once,' said Alemrae.

Alemrae went to the door leading to the small chamber, where Prince Morannel and Captain Gregorson waited. He brought them into the Great Hall.

'This young man is my witness. The other, Captain Gregorson, was once the commander of watch on the city gates and has graciously accepted the role of guarding him and ensuring his safety until his testimony is heard,' explained Kai.

'Son, if you were witness to the events just described, then tell us of your role in the incident,' said the regent.

'My lords, I was the victim of the assault. Thanks to Lady Kai and the Sisters of Mercy, I have survived the attack. The men who attacked me were led by none other than Frederick Monfraeson. I recognised his voice as soon as he spoke. He ordered his men to kill me. I was stabbed—once in the chest and twice in the abdomen. I do believe I am quite lucky to still be alive. I will show you my wounds if you wish,' said Morannel.

'That implicates Frederick in attempted murder, but I still see no link to Prince Morannel,' said the regent.

'The link is this—I am Prince Morannel,' said the prince as he removed the hood from his head.

CHAPTER 6

Chere was a gasp of recognition from the crowd as the identity of the prince was revealed.

'No! It is a lie. I did none of this!' shouted Frederick.

'How is it, my prince, that you came to be in the pass on that day?' asked the Lord Chamberlain.

'My lords, Frederick arranged it. Whilst at the college in Almarac, I received notes threatening my life. Not knowing whom I could trust, apart from my cousin, whom I have always admired and respected, I consulted with him on how to deal with the threat. He suggested that I make my way back home, alone and in disguise. I was to wear a pin he had given me so that the guards he would send to escort me home would be able to identify me. I did not immediately know the four men who attacked. Two had the look of common thugs. One other wore chain mail from the palace guard. And then there was my cousin. I knew him when he spoke. He called me a thief and told the others to get the pin. This pin.' The prince held up a silver pin in the shape of a charging boar.

'Frederick Monfraeson, I find you guilty of the charge of treason!' yelled Regent Monfrae in anger. 'What have you to say in your defence? What have you in mitigation of this foul attack on our realm?'

'I did this only for you, Father. You are the true ruler of this land, not this cowardly youth. If he had shown any fighting spirit, some gumption, during his stay at the college, I would not have been forced into this. But, no, he chose what he should study based solely on his personal safety. No risk to himself. No attempt to learn to wield a weapon of any sort. Just ridiculous things like ancient history. Even when his friends tried to get him to learn to wield a weapon, he refused, claiming to be inept. He was not inept—he was afraid! No king can afford to show fear. Thus, he is no king. He has no right to the throne. An accident of birth does not make you a king. It takes leadership, drive, and passion—the traits that you possess, Father. You should be, and are, king!' exclaimed Frederick.

'I am *not* the king. Nor will I ever be,' thundered Regent Monfrae. 'I am regent for Prince Morannel until he comes of age. Here, now, in this place and at this time, I renounce all ties to the royal family on my behalf and that of all my kin. I believe you have done this for yourself, my son, so that, in the course of time, you could be king instead. Look at you. Your clothing betrays you—they are in the colours of the royal house, not those of my house. Your true colours are those of the charging boar—brown on a black field. That silver pin is the emblem of our house. I gave it to you when you came of age, and you have treasured it ever since, and that sword. That sword you're carrying—it was not of our making. Where did you get it? The palace armoury, perhaps? The sword of my late brother, Gedry. The sword "Soulburner". The sword of the king! What has it done to you, my son, that you should seek to rise above your station, to strive for the very throne itself? Its name is apt, for it burns the soul of the one who wields it. It is a most perilous weapon to wield, for it attacks the user as much as it inflicts damage upon its victims. Lord Chamberlain, could you and the other lords adjourn to the small chamber to discuss the punishment to be meted out to my son? I shall await your decision.'

'Wait, my lords. As the prosecutor and initiator of these proceedings, I would like to countenance mercy. If the prince agrees, then Frederick Monfraeson can challenge me for freedom and the right to bear the sword—a trial of combat in the style of the Elshgat Free States. If he defeats me, then he keeps the sword and goes free.

If he fails to defeat me, then he suffers the fate of those who lose, the same fate as that in Elshgat,' requested Kai.

'My lady, we know not the rules, nor the results of such a trial, should he lose. So, as such, we cannot grant the permission for that to go ahead. We cannot, I am sorry, take your word on it,' said the Lord Chamberlain.

'My lords, will you accept mine?' asked Alemrae. 'It is well known that I have spent time in Elshgat. I have seen several such trials and know how they should be conducted. The trial is conducted as such. Within a circle of fire, not less than twenty feet wide, and not exceeding fifty, the two combatants fight until one of the two admits defeat, is slain, or the bandage of the champion is removed. It goes thus. Both enter the circle bearing their weapons of choice. The circle is lit, and the fight commences. No onlooker may influence the fight in any way, either through voice or action. Silence must rule until the fight is complete. In the case of a trial, as we have here, the champion's bandage covers all sight. They must fight blind. Only thus can the will of the gods be truly understood. Should the champion fall, then the other is set free, to once more take his place as if the acts had never been committed. If the champion wins, then the loser becomes the bound slave for a period of one year to the champion. If at the end of that time, the slave still has not redeemed themselves sufficiently for the act that initiated the trial, then they are banished for the term of their life. They are also tattooed with the mark of their crime, so that all may know. In this case, it would be a blooded crown and dagger on the forehead. If, at any time during the year of enslavement, the champion believes the slave has redeemed themselves, they can be set free immediately. It is left to the champion and the slave to work it out between them.'

'I accept the challenge,' shouted Frederick, 'if the lords will allow it. I shall obtain my freedom once more.'

'Have you seen the pennant flying this day above the palace, Frederick? Do you know its significance? For I very much doubt that you will leave the circle alive,' said Alemrae.

'Aunt Kai,' said Morannel, 'I would not have you risk yourself on my behalf or that of my cousin. But if you truly wish to do this thing, then you have my blessing. I only hope you may spare the life of my wayward cousin. Yes, cousin, I mean you no ill will. Nor have I ever. If you should survive this contest, win or lose, I would still request your presence at my council when I am king. For you did but seek what you thought was best for this nation of mine. Such loyalty to my people should be availed upon, not thrown on the trash. But know this: any hint of betrayal a second time will not be greeted with so lenient an answer. It will cost you your head. Lady Kai, when should such a contest be run?'

'At dawn, in three days. Time for preparation is required. Here in this hall, where the number of viewers is limited. Access shall be by lot, drawn from amongst all the populace of the city. For this is how it should be done. Equal numbers in proportion to the numbers in the city, my prince. The regent, three lords, the Mother Superior and three of her sisters, the Lady Shadow, Alemrae, yourself, my liege, your bodyguard, Captain Gregorson, and enough of the household guard to provide adequate safety for all. Until this is settled, Frederick should be allowed to go free if he agrees to remain in the custody of his father. If he doesn't, he should be locked in the palace dungeon,' said Kai.

'I shall remain in my father's custody,' said Frederick.

'Then, since our future king wishes this contest to go ahead, we, the lords of the inner council and panel of judgement, will allow its result to stand, and may the gods have mercy on you all,' said the Lord Chamberlain.

CHAPTER 7

A s the crowd dispersed, Kai approached the panel.

'My lords, Regent Monfrae, may I have a moment of your time? In private. There is another issue we need to discuss,' requested Kai.

The regent and the lords of the inner council left with Kai. Shadow, Alemrae, Prince Morannel, and Captain Gregorson went back to Kai's suite. Frederick Monfraeson was escorted by the guards to his father's chambers.

When Kai and the lords met in a secure chamber with Regent Monfrae, the Lord Chamberlain asked, 'Are you sure that this bout is necessary, milady?'

'Yes, my lord, I am. It is the only means I have to save his life, and we need all the men we can get. And this brings me to the reason I asked to speak with you and the reason for burning the bodies on the mountain. For the last five years, I have been living and training in the capital of Albrae. In that time, I attained a title, The Briar Rose. It is only given to a warrior who manages to defeat the top-five elite guards of the king of Albrae. This is a single, prolonged battle, where the warrior must fight each man in turn, from weakest to strongest. There is no gap between the duels. The warrior must defeat one after the other, tiring as he goes on, to then fight a better opponent than the one he has just fought. The title has been won only three times in the entire history of Albrae—all 1,500 years. I tell you this not to boast of my accomplishment but to give you fair warning. The army of Albrae was made up of the best warriors that I have ever seen. They had many mages and clerics in support. The army was around fifty thousand strong—a vast and formidable force.

'This is supposed to frighten you, my lords. Albrae is no more. It has been overrun by undead. It took the horde of undead a little over three weeks to destroy the nation of Albrae. I was there at the first major battle. We thought that we had eradicated the undead with a magnificent victory. Then overnight they arose from where they had fallen and fell upon us. That is why I burnt the bodies on the mountain—to stop them from rising as undead. I was one of a very few who managed to make it out alive. It has taken me over two months to get here even travelling as swiftly as I could. I do not know how long it will take the undead to move on, but move on they will. I am seeking assistance from whomever I can so as to mount a defensive action—a containment, if you will, of the undead. I have had assurances from those I have spoken to along the way. They will be sending representatives here. I wish to create a council of nations to bring about the defence of our continent. We have access here, through our trading empire, to most of the nations. Word can go forth by ship far more quickly than I can carry it myself. I also seek the lost races: the Elves, Dwarves, and Halflings. I have researched their locations over the many years I have been gone. I believe that I may be able to find them, and it has always been my intention to do so. I recently found the location of one dwarven mine on an ancient map. I have not yet been able to seek entrance. I also recently found traces of where the elves may be, although I have not yet been able to afford the time to search them out. I am hoping that they may know where the Halflings are, for I have found no trace of them.

'Undead were first created by man. It is up to us to see them defeated. But for this, we are going to need assistance. The demi-humans' capabilities may well be the difference in the end. I intend to take a select group in search of allies. I shall leave the gathering of the human nations to your capable hands. We, here, have the most extensive trading empire. We also control the greatest amount of fluid wealth. It will be up to us to finance this undertaking. We might bankrupt the nations to see this out, but failure is not an option. If we fail, the world dies. The Sisters of Mercy have many hostels across the nations. Their order was founded on the destruction of the undead menace. They must form the backbone of whatever standing force we can muster. Call on the Mother Superior and advise her of the undertaking. Call Princess Zephranthe home. It may pay to send her to live with her grandparents for the time being. They will ensure her safety, and it may help clear the way for the political upheaval we are about to unleash. Now, I have to go. I need to speak to my small group and prepare for my duel.'

'Lady Kai, I have witnessed Frederick Monfraeson in the combat ring. He is certainly no slouch with a sword, and no doubt he will request the use of Soulburner in the bout. You are aware I trust of the abilities of the sword. It is a fearsome weapon on its own. In the hands of a skilled warrior, it will be even more deadly. Are you sure you can survive this bout? He will use all his skill to try to kill you. His victory won't be complete until you are dead. He will not take a lesser option,' said one of the lords.

'The weapon will be needed when we face the undead. Its flaming blade will offer more defence than an ordinary blade. I intend for Frederick to be the one who wields that blade against the undead. For that, I must see him brought down alive in the ring. The sword has already bonded to Frederick. No one else will be able to summon forth the flame for another generation, and that will be too late. I have fought in the rings of fire many times in the Elshgat Free States. I have been successful before. Even blindfolded, I believe I am a match for Frederick, and as my slave for a year, I can tutor him in those fighting techniques I have mastered. By the time I finish, he will be worthy of the blade and be its master, as he will be the master of himself. He and the blade will be one.

'Before the bout is undertaken, I shall complete a written record of my findings, fighting techniques, and training programmes for your use. We shall need silver weapons for those who achieve a certain level of skill. Silver is anathema to most undead. If our better warriors are using silver weapons, it will make the fight go easier.

Summon all the mages and clerics you can. Magic will also be of great importance. There is one downfall. The more undead there are gathered in an area, the less magic works. Permanent effects, like the sword Soulburner and my dagger, are unaffected, but the gathering of magical energies around large numbers of undead is almost impossible. I learnt that the hard way! The pass between here and Almarac is one of the most defensible positions we have. Guard it well. Now, I must be off before you can think up any more distractions. You have your orders, gentlemen.' Kai smiled. 'Now, be good little boys and obey.' She smiled, again. 'Only kidding,' she said and then left.

The raised voices of the inner circle followed her out the door as they began their discussions in earnest.

When she reached her apartments, the others surrounded her.

'Alemrae has been telling us about this form of combat. How is it that you know of it? Fighting Frederick would be risky enough, but to do so blindfolded—that is insanity. You could burn yourself in the flame or depart the circle, and that would give the combat to Frederick,' said Prince Morannel.

'I have fought this way before. I am accustomed to fighting without sight. I have trained for it. The lack of vision will not be a problem. The only problem will be if there is any sound. I must be able to hear his movements. I will fight barefoot. No doubt, he will be wearing boots with metal studs for grip. The noise they create on the floor will guide me to him. With that, and knowing the weapon he uses, I can predict, to some extent, the moves he will make. It is not precise, but my many years of training and combat experience should give me a great enough edge to bring him down. If nothing else works, I have one other desperate move I can try—very risky, it could cost me my life. I will say no more on it. But if I have to use it and it works, I might be out of action for a while. If so, you will need to begin a journey. The one I am about to tell you of. When Princess Zephranthe comes home, we will escort her to her grandparents' home. She will live with them until other matters are dealt with. This should help reduce the political tensions that have been building between the two nations. Added to that is the second reason for our journey. Albrae has been overrun by undead.'

There was a murmur of dismay amongst the group at this news.

'Wait, hear me out,' continued Kai. 'I won't go into details, but believe me when I tell you that the entire country has been overrun. We go to find allies for a defensive action. The command centre for whatever forces that can be raised will be here. Word is being sent out by ship. Once we have informed the ruling council of Ulmarin, we shall leave. Our goal is to locate the missing demi-human races and enlist their aid. Our first target is the dwarves. I know the location of one of their mines. We will start there. Hopefully, we can gain entrance and persuade them to assist us. Their metal smiths are the best in the world and can turn out armour and weapons much faster than anyone else. They will also have some fierce fighters amongst them—at least the histories all agree on that. Their numbers may not be that great, but we need all the help we can get.

'The big problem, then, will be to locate the elves. I have a vague notion of where to search, but we can't afford to lose too much time in the looking. Of the Halflings, I have no idea where to begin. I am hoping that if we find the dwarves and elves, they might be able to give us some indication as to their whereabouts. Then, if we succeed, I intend to take a small mobile strike force and go where no sane person would go—into the black hole that is the northlands—to find and destroy whatever it was that created this plague. May the gods grant us some measure of success!

'Shadow, when I travelled in your lands, there was a tribe in possession of a powder that turned a normal flame into a cold white flame. Do you know of this powder? If so, do you have any, or can you make it?'

'Yes, Kai, I do know the powder. I have a small amount with me. It is not something that I know how to make,' said Shadow.

'Do you have enough to turn the circle of flame white? I need to change the nature of the circle so that I can tell the difference between it and the blade that Frederick will be using. Frederick's blade will flame for him if he wills it. I am sure that he will make the blade flame for the duration of our fight,' said Kai.

'It will use all the powder I have, for the circle is large, but if it will give you an edge, then you can have it,' promised Shadow.

'When Alemrae sets up the circle, use the powder. He will be the adjudicator for the match. No one else knows the rules,' said Kai.

'Huh! What rules? Two enter and fight until one is defeated. The means of defeat is not an issue. Only one will leave the circle by their own means. Always the other requires assistance,' countered Alemrae.

'Prince Morannel, if I am unable to lead the journey in search of the lost races, then you must. You are young, I know, but in you runs the blood of a line of kings. You will do well. If Frederick somehow defeats me—and he might—then take him on the journey with you, for you will have need of him. Amongst my possessions are a number of manuals. These are to be given to the Lord Chamberlain. He will know what to do with them. One other thing—you must conquer your fear. If you don't, you will die,' said Kai.

'It was not fear I felt. It was a glory, a lust for the fight. I could not stand it. My opponent in my first combat was a friend, and I wanted to see him dead! So I dropped the sword, and every time, no matter who it was, if I started to use a weapon or was near a fight, I felt like killing whoever was in front of me. So I feigned ineptness. That way I could avoid the combat drills, and I would not have to feel the insanity within, for it was insanity to feel what I did,' insisted the prince.

'What you felt was no more than the darkest nature of our heredity. It is a part of you. You must learn to control it, or it will always control you. There will come a time when you have no choice. You must enter a fight or join men bearing weaponry. If you are overcome by your bestial nature, you will destroy the ones you seek to help. Both Alemrae and Captain Gregorson can help you with this. They can train and spar with you. They are both skilled enough to withstand your worst, and knowledgeable enough to help you. I will do as much as I can to assist you as well. Even Shadow may have some insights into how to control such emotion. If you had consulted with the war masters of the college, they may also have been able to help. Much time has been wasted by you in this. I admire your dedication to peace and the gathering of knowledge to help you rule, but, first, we must ensure that there will be a nation left to be ruled. I kid you not—this is the most important undertaking in the history of mankind. We all must play our part. I hope I have not scared you all too much. We embark on the most dangerous of undertakings. I hope we can find some enjoyment on the way. Now, I need some time alone for contemplation. Please leave me be,' requested Kai.

CHAPTER 8

K ai stood and walked through her room and out onto the balcony. There she sat in a chair and watched the ocean. She felt drained. So much energy, thought, and willpower had been used during the afternoon; she was exhausted. She sat and watched, allowing the back and forth flowing of the water in the bay to wash away the angst inside her. Quite some time later, Alemrae came out and joined her on the balcony.

'The evening meal has been served. You should come in and eat. Then sleep this night. I must talk with you tomorrow. I have something important that we need to discuss, but it can wait,' said Alemrae.

Kai acknowledged his exit but continued to sit and watch the waters. Long after the sun had set and the others had retired for the night, she came in, ate a little of the food that had been left for her, and then went to bed.

Some hours after the sun rose the next morning, Kai awoke. She was alone. The others had all gone, exploring the markets and enjoying the day, looking for those items that would be of use to them on their journey.

In one of the many marketplaces, the group was strolling amongst the stalls. Attracted by the sparkle emanating from a particular shop, Shadow left the others and approached the merchant. 'May I view your merchandise?' she asked.

'Customers are always appreciated. I do not recognise your accent or your state of dress. Where have you come from, lady?'

'I am a daughter of the desert, known as Irikani to your people. What are these things you sell?' asked Shadow.

'This is jewellery, lady. Items to be worn on one's body to enhance one's look. They are beautiful, are they not?' he replied.

Prince Morannel came over. 'Is there anything you like, Shadow?' he asked.

'They are all beautiful, Morannel. But I don't know what they are for,' said Shadow, sounding a bit perplexed.

'There are rings for one's fingers, necklaces, and bangles, even a pin and a brooch to hold one's cloak on. Have you any special items, merchant?' asked Morannel.

'I do have one item. I don't show it to many, and even fewer could afford it. A golden egg—about five centis across and nine long,' the merchant replied.

'May we see it?' asked Shadow, suddenly even more interested.

'Certainly, my lord, milady. Please come through. Sarah, man the front, would you? I must show these two my other collection,' said the merchant.

His daughter came to the front of the awning and stood behind the bench. The merchant gestured for them to come around the counter and into his home. Inside, the merchant hurried to his chest, unlocked it, and drew out the precious egg.

'You see, my lord? This is my most treasured piece. I don't know where it comes from, but it has a nice patina of red blended in the gold.'

Seeing Shadow's adoring look, the prince asked for the price. The merchant gave it, saying, 'I cannot part with it for less than 1,000 dracma, my lord. It is an extremely rare piece. I have never seen one like it before.'

'May I hold it for a moment?' asked Shadow.

Looking carefully at Prince Morannel, the merchant nodded. Shadow held it in her hands and then raised it to her cheek. She whispered a few words in her native tongue. It grew warm in her hands.

'It's alive,' she whispered. 'Prince Morannel, can you afford this? Would you buy it for me?' requested Shadow.

'This means something to you, doesn't it?' asked Morannel. 'You know what it is. Is it truly worth what he asks for it?'

'It is beyond price. These golden eggs are fabled, even in our desert, which is where it comes from. I really must have it,' pleaded Shadow.

'Then have it you shall. Merchant, I do not carry that sort of money around with me, but if you come to the palace with us, bringing your egg, I will see that you are given a warranty from the state treasury upon which you may draw up to the value of 1,500 dracma. My lady requires that egg, and I intend that she shall have it. Do you agree to it?'

'Yes, my lord. I shall come at once. Sarah, close the shop. We are done with business for the day. I am to attend the palace to close a deal. Now, what shall we carry the egg in?' asked the merchant.

'I have something, if you don't mind,' said Shadow. 'Wrap it in this cloth, and I will carry it in my pouch, where it will be warmed by my body.'

They left the shop together and made their way back to the palace, where the prince completed his end of the bargain. The merchant left feeling very happy for himself—he had just made the best sale of his life.

When they had made it back to the rooms, the prince asked Shadow just what it was they had bought.

'An egg!' she answered with a laugh. 'This is no piece of jewellery—it is a living egg. It will hatch. Then I will have a desert companion. I must keep it warm. The heat of my body will not be enough. The egg must stay near one of your fires until it hatches. I hope it will hatch soon. I cannot afford to leave it to hatch alone, and it had almost died from the cold.'

'Yes, but what is it?' asked Morannel.

'It is a creature of the desert, a flying lizard. It will, when grown, be able to breathe fire. It will be about the size of my hand at full growth. The adults are extremely rare, and to find an egg, here of all places, is truly remarkable. This is the most wondrous gift you have given me. How will I ever be able to repay you?' asked Shadow.

'I am sure you will think of something,' said Morannel.

'We will be travelling together for quite some time. Who knows what that will bring?'

Meanwhile, Kai, after breaking her fast, decided to spend some time outside the city. So, gathering what she wished to take with her, she left. Not wanting any company, she used the servants' passageways to get down to the ground floor. She left via the kitchen and, after having words with the chief cook, passed through the gardens and out the back gate. The guards said nothing as they let her out. She made her way quickly down to the city gate leading to Ulmarin and, after passing through, headed uphill away from the trade road.

She wandered with no real destination in mind, passing through copses of trees and crossing meadows. She took her time with her meandering. With the sun overhead, she stopped to quench her thirst by a small stream and, seeing a small meadow on the other side, leapt across. She moved around the clearing and, seeing no paths entering, decided that she would be unlikely to be disturbed. She left her possessions on a rocky outcrop and stripped off her excess clothing. She even removed her boots. Then she walked to the centre of the clearing. She began to dance. Or at least that is what it would look like to anyone watching her. She was practising her fighting moves, slowly stretching her muscles and loosening her tendons. She slowly increased her speed, flowing from stance to stance.

By the time she had been through all her moves, she was at full speed. She was a blur of motion. Then she drew her daggers and repeated her manoeuvres. She stopped suddenly, as still as a statue, her daggers flying across the clearing and burying their blades into a tree.

'You can come out now,' she said.

Alemrae stepped out from behind the tree. He removed the daggers and tossed them back to Kai. 'If you would prefer to spar with a moving target, you have one. You move smoothly, even at speed. But you have a hole in your defence,' he said.

'I know,' said Kai. 'It is something that comes of having no fear of being wounded. I heal.'

'You are an enigma, Kai. You look young, yet you have a nephew who appears older than you. And you demonstrate fighting skills that few could master, even after decades of intense training. You collect knowledge. Showing a great mind at work, yet you pretend to innocence, allowing others to make up their own minds and come to their own conclusions. Thus allowing the beginnings of wisdom to flower within them. You look to protect everyone who comes in contact with you, yet you kill freely and easily. You are compassionate and deadly at the same time. I would know more of you, if you would tell me.'

'We are to be travelling together. It is only right that you should know more of me. You shall have to trust my judgement, and I, yours. My story is a long one—make yourself comfortable.'

Kai made a pillow of her cloak, placed it on a flat rock outcrop, and sat upon it. Alemrae sat at her feet on the grass.

'Begin,' he said.

CHAPTER 9

'I had a sheltered upbringing. I showed extraordinary intelligence when I was very young. So my father had me taught early. Whatever my tutor could cram into my brain. I learnt, reading, writing, and numbers. My tutor really taught me one most important thing—to have a love of knowledge; a love of the history of man, and especially of my family. He explained about the missing demi-human races. The undead wars and the political ramifications of various decisions that my father was making. The possibility of an arranged marriage. It was when I started to collect the stories of our family that something struck me—we were different. There was always some strangeness about us. Something we could do that other men couldn't. Sometimes a madness within. I began to wonder why.

'So I talked to my great-great-grandmother. I asked her to tell me all the stories she could remember of our family. I wrote them down as she spoke, without really taking them all in. Then I asked all the other elders I could find about anything they could remember about my family, anything at all. Again, I wrote it all down. Once I had finished, I reread the lot. I collated all the stories and rewrote them into a single volume, working out what they all meant and where they fit within the family history. I discovered something then that few know. We are other—no longer human. No more will I say on that.

'When I left twenty years ago, I went seeking the Elves, Dwarves, and Halflings. Trying to find them has been a passion of mine. I took ship and crossed to the far continent. I went alone, telling no one of my plans or where I was heading. Because I am a royal personage, I thought I would be assisted on my journey and did not think about my personal safety. I was naive. Three days outside the port city of Dramas, I was abducted—captured really—by a band of bravos. They were thugs, with little intelligence to be had amongst them. They thought to use me for their pleasure. I had other intentions, so I tried to fight them. I was untrained and my hands were bound, but I was quick and small. I had downed three of them when their leader stepped up and knocked me out from behind. When I awoke, I was in his tent, and I hurt all over. They had abused me whilst I was unconscious. Then they had bound my arms and my legs whilst I was still out. "You are a hell cat," he had said. "So I am going to take you to hell." The band took me across the sea of grass to Elshgat. There, they sold me to a slaver. He would sell me at auction.

'When the day of the auction came, I resisted. The guards beat me, and I was whipped. I told the man with the whip, "If you use that again, I'll stuff it down your throat." They laughed at me. The guards then dragged me to the auction. I was a mess, but I was up on the platform. Then the idiot with the whip tried to use it again. I saw his movement and turned, catching the whip between my bound hands. I pulled sharply, and the guard lost it. I quickly pulled the whip to me. The guard rushed at me to get it back. I kicked him in the groin as hard as I could. He buckled and fell at my feet. I proceeded to do as I had threatened. The other guards jumped me and pulled me off. The auctioneer was furious and ordered me beaten again. One of the buyers stopped them. "I'll pay fifty drac for her, twenty if you beat her." That was not much for a slave, especially a young woman like me. The pleasure houses would pay over 1,000 drac for the right slave, but none would risk the violence I had just shown. I was told that if I behaved, I would be treated well. If not, he would have me bound, stripped, and chained to a wall in the slaves' quarters. The other slaves could do what they liked to me.

'The man who bought me owned a fighting school. He bought slaves and had them trained to fight. The fights were in rings of fire, either to first blood or to the death. He made money on the betting. It was there that I first learnt to fight. There were three fighting schools in the city. All had slaves trained for the fighting pits, the rings of fire. The schools trained in different methods. The students of the first school specialised in a single weapon, used to the exclusion of all others. The second school taught the use of all weapons, specialising in none. The third school trained the body and the mind, the thought being that if you trained your body and mind, then anything coming to hand could be a weapon, and if there were no weapons, you could fight with your body. I had been sold to the owner of the first school—the specialists. Because of my small stature, they gave me a dagger to use. I took to the training with a passion. No one would treat me again the way I had been treated. I would have my revenge.

'Within one year, I was almost at the top of our ranks. I was having a practice bout with another fighter when the owner and head trainer of the third school came to arrange a match between the schools. The trainer watched me fight. He had words with his owner. The upshot of that was that I was bought by the third school. They paid 2,500 drac for me. I was given specialised individual training to boost my speed and my stamina. And then they tried to strengthen me. That turned out surprisingly. For all of us. They loaded up some weights for me to lift, and I lifted them, over and over again. They increased the weight beyond what I should have been able to lift, and still I managed to lift them. They toned my body, made my muscles rock hard. Then in a fit of inspiration, the trainer sent me to a dance school—a school for slaves being taught the many different dances, so as to please their masters. I learnt them all. In the end, my body was supple, quick, and strong. I had also increased my stamina. I was able to work harder and longer than my fighting comrades. My trainer said I would be the best. I had already made it to the elite. I was called on to fight in the rings of fire many times. My master made an obscene amount of money on me, much more than he had paid for me and the expense of keeping me. People kept expecting me to lose, and I never did.

'Then, one day, my master was insulted by a visiting schoolmaster. A death challenge was issued, and I was selected as the champion for my school. I was thrown into the ring of fire with this hulking brute, the visitors' champion. He laughed at me and said it was an insult for him to have to fight me. I said I agreed. I bandaged my eyes and said, "Now it is even." I told him he could not win. If he killed me, it would be because he was so much bigger than me and I was blindfolded. If I defeated him, he would be laughed at for the same reason. He was finished as a fighter. He would only be remembered as an incompetent fool.

'He growled and sprang forward. My daggers took out his throat before he had taken three steps. I whipped off the bandage and then leapt over the flames. I saw the visitor standing near my master. "Instead of sending an oaf, why don't you fight yourself?" I asked. "Because I don't have to," he replied. "Well, fight this," I said and threw my dagger. It pierced his left eye and entered his brain.

'My master gave me my freedom that day. It was my last fight in the ring. I was free. It was unheard of—no slave was freed from the rings of fire. I tried to convince my master to free the other fighters. "You make the money on the wagers," I said. "Why waste money buying slaves only to see them killed? People will pay you to teach them to fight." I changed the system. Fewer men died. Not many slaves were freed, though.'

'You, you are Crimson. I heard about you when I visited friends in the Elshgat Free States' interrupted Alemrae in a shocked whisper.

'That is a name I have not heard in many years. I never divulged my true name in case someone tried to make a profit from it. And at the time, I was ashamed of what I had become. They called me Crimson because when they first bought me, I was covered in blood,' responded Kai. 'I stayed in Elshgat for a while, learning all I could about their neighbouring lands and doing what I could to improve the lot of the slaves. I was about twenty-one or twenty-two when I left, as skilled a fighter as any. I was confident. Too confident. I accepted challenges, even those that required me to fight multiple opponents. None could touch me. Then, one night, after having a little too much to drink, I accepted my last challenge. The fight took place in a clearing. No one to witness. As I fought the challenger, another man crept up on us. He had lost a lot of money wagering on an opponent of mine. He took his chance to get even. He sank three arrows into me. His friend stripped me of my daggers and other items and then they left me there, naked, to die.

'Somehow, I lived through the night. I awoke in agony the next morning. I felt around to my back and touched the first of the arrows. Pain shot through me. My training allowed me to concentrate despite the pain. I managed to pull the arrow out. Its head was not barbed. The pain was excruciating. But I did not black out again. The pain began to recede. When I felt my back, I could not feel where the arrow had been. I started to feel a little better, a little stronger. I reached around to the second arrow and pulled it out as well. Once again, I was almost overcome by the pain, but I gritted my teeth and waited. Again, the pain receded, this time quicker than before. Once again, I could not feel where the arrow had been. The last arrow was harder. It was more difficult to reach. I could barely grasp it. So I had to pull it out slowly. It actually seemed to feel better the more I pulled. I rested a moment and, once again, pulled on the arrow gently, slowly removing it. Again, it started to feel better. So I pulled more slowly. There was less pain.

'When I finally removed the arrow, I actually felt fine. I stood up and, clutching the arrows, began to walk back to the inn where I had been staying. I looked the arrows over. Two were covered in blood. The third was clean. It was as if my body had healed the wound as I slowly pulled the arrow out. I realised then what it meant. My body would regenerate the wounds I received. So as long as I was not actually killed in a fight, any wounds I suffered would heal. I also realised that if the two men who had sought to kill me saw me, they would set the mob on me. I snuck inside the back of the inn and made my way to my room. I found one of the men in there. He died, fast and quietly. I got what was left of my money and possessions and then slipped out of the inn without being seen.

'I decided to go in search of the lost races once more. So I travelled the continent. I accepted no more challenges. I looked for clues but did not find any. These lands had been settled for so long by man that the other races must have disappeared long before. I almost gave up. I had wasted six years on this continent, only to realise that nowhere in the history of these nations were the demi-human races even mentioned. I was on the wrong continent! I made up my mind to go back to my homelands. We, at least, had much history with the lost. I thought to search the other lands around my home.

'It took me another year to travel back to the port where I had first arrived. I managed to buy some daggers. It took almost all the money that I had left. Then I started asking questions around the docks and the stockyards, searching for information—this time about bands of bandits in the lands around the township. I found what I was after. The men who had taken me were still in business. I found out which area they frequented. I walked out trying to find them. They found me instead.

'I allowed them to take me back to their camp. My hands were bound, but they had left my feet free. Their leader came out to see the catch. He did not recognise me. So I said to him, "I am your hell cat. I have come back from hell to get my revenge." Then I snapped the bonds on my hands and went into action. He died first, with a broken neck. My next target was the one who had my new daggers. He went down, hard. Once I retrieved my new daggers from him, the others were already backing off. "Come and die," I said. "Surely one of you pathetic slugs can kill me?" They turned and ran instead. I let them go. I searched the tents for anything of value. There was enough money for passage on a ship and a few other things I thought might come in handy.

'The first ship leaving the port was going to Albrae. I purchased a working passage. It should have taken about eight months to sail there. Stopping and trading at places along the way. Giving me plenty of time to rest and make plans. Learning the ways on a ship. And asking more questions to learn more of the continent and its peoples. We did not make it to Albrae. The ship went down during a massive storm off the coast of the Irikani desert, still a month's travel from Albrae. Five of us made it to the shore. The rocky cliffs were being pounded by the storm, but we couldn't stay where we were. We found a place to make the climb. By helping each other, all five of us made it up. We rested on the cliff top. Feeling miserable and tired, the storm still raging, we suffered through the night. The storm abated near dawn. The next few days were bad. We knew nothing of the desert or which way was safety. We headed east. In the end, I was the only one left alive. My body was slowly repairing the damage that the exposure to the elements was causing. I had started travelling at night and tried to find somewhere to hole up during the day.

'Then one evening, not long after I had set out, I realised that I was being followed. I looked around but could not see anyone. I continued on a short way. Again, I could sense something behind me. So I waited, not looking in that direction. It slowly came closer. I could sense it about twenty feet away. So I turned around. I could see nothing there. I closed my eyes, and then I could feel the presence— waiting, just ahead of me. With my eyes closed, I walked forward, slowly, feeling the way with my feet until it was there, at arm's reach. I took another step forward and raised my hand. I reached out and touched whatever it was. It felt like a body, a person. When I opened my eyes, nothing was in front of me, but my hand was still touching something, or someone. "Show yourself," I said. There was no answer. I felt a hand touch mine, guide it to a shoulder, press down, and then let go. I gripped whoever it was.

'They led me to a cavern. I had passed it sometime the previous night. There were people in it. Suddenly, my mysterious helper became visible. She motioned towards the fire, so I went. They fed me and looked after me. They slowly taught me their language. Haltingly at first and then more quickly. They taught me much about the desert, their history, and the power of their mages and holy men. I spent two years with them, learning all I could. When I decided to go, they guided me to the badlands, the wastes of Uripor, at the northern most point of the desert. From there, if I travelled along the coast and into the Northlands, I could find my way to Albrae. This I did. I used Albrae as a base and continued to search out information on the whereabouts of those lost races, on magic and what it could do—anything that might give me a hint as to where to look next. I would hear a rumour, and off I would go.

'I was returning from another fruitless chase when I came across an ambush. A large group of women was being overrun by goblins. I joined in the fight. I was surprised to find that they did not really need any help. They fought well, aggressively and as a unit. It was just the even larger number of foes, almost twice as many, that had them in trouble. My own style favoured a lone assault. So I ploughed into the rear of the mass, causing havoc. I kept moving from here to there. Not staying anywhere long enough for the goblins to realise, I was alone. I managed to break them up a bit. It seemed to do the trick.

'As the pressure on the front eased, the women pressed forward. The goblins fractured even more. A few started running. I took advantage of that, and then the rout started in earnest. They left more dead on the field than were able to run away. One of the women greeted me, thanked me for the help, and asked if I needed any help with my wounds. "I don't have any," I said. "None of them were able to breach my defence." She was amazed. "We are on our way back to our motherhouse, outside Albrae. Would you like to journey with us?" I agreed, for I had never heard of a group of women fighters. They were part of the Sisters of Mercy. Their chapter house near Albrae was the first to be founded. They had been escorting their Mother Superior back to Albrae when the goblins had struck. They had split into two groups; one rushed the Mother Superior to safety, and the other stayed to combat the threat.

'We discussed many things on the way back, enough to get me interested. I stayed with them as a guest, learning from them and teaching what I could. They were very impressed with my fighting techniques and asked me to instruct them. I had already decided to move on at that point but thought that if I wrote it all down, it might be of some use. It took many weeks to work it out and get it all down in writing, both the movements and the philosophies. Once I was finished, they had many copies made.

'During my time with them, I had been introduced to some of the guards in Albrae. They thought it might be fun to play a bit of a joke on one of their captains. He was an excellent swordsman but also a bit of a braggart. I went with them to the tavern where the captain liked to take his ease and asked if he liked to dance. He admitted that he did not dance—he was a swordsman, not a dancer. "Pity," I said. "I am not a swordsman, but I do dance. I wonder who is better with a blade—a swordsman like you or a dancer like me." "The swordsman, of course," he said. "I disagree," I replied. "Would you like to test your theory? Say, tomorrow—in your training area at the barracks?" He could hardly refuse since his men were around him, and they would have been at him for it.

'So the next morning when I turned up, the training area was full. Word had been passed that the captain was to get his comeuppance. I decided to put on a show. I pretended that he was a dancing partner, and, weapon to weapon, I parried his blows in a way that it made it look like we were dancing, turning him around and around. I stepped away from him and stopped. "You dance well," I said. "Now, can you really fight?" With a whoop from the crowd, I came at him, both daggers—a blur. It took all his skill to keep me at arm's reach. He was wholly on the defensive. Then I sped up. I aimed for his weapon, not wanting to actually hurt him. Just when he realised he was overmatched, I tripped him and then leant down and gave him a kiss. The crowd hooted. Then I backed off and walked out. They parted to let me through.

'He came and found me later and apologised for his boorish behaviour the evening before. I told him he had been set up, and I thanked him for putting on a good show. He told me I was the best he had ever seen and asked if I would train with him and his men—set a new level for them all to strive for. I agreed, since I had nothing else planned at the time. My training manual was adopted. They incorporated it into their existing training. It slowly filtered throughout their entire army.

'After a few years, I began to get bored. Once again, I sought to find the lost races. I was allowed to read volumes that normally I would not have had access to. It led me to the location of a dwarven mine on an old map—in the mountains near my home town of Raelis, almost due north of Ulmarin. I had finally found a solid clue to what I was after. I would be off just as soon as I could. Then the morning before I was due to leave, my friends told me of a tournament that had just been announced—the tournament for the title of Briar Rose. It was named after the first winner. A woman. It was said about her that you had to get through the thorns in order to reach the rose within. The tournament was held once every five years. It would be a challenge, they said. Only two others had ever won it. In four hundred years, two people had earned the title of Briar Rose. Any and all who wished could enter. Over the period of a month, the contestants would fight to first blood. The eventual winner would go up against the five best warriors in the king's personal guard. His champions. The winner had to fight all of them, one after the other. No break for rest. The winner tires, whilst his next opponent is fresh. If the contestant manages to defeat all five warriors, then they receive the title of Briar Rose and military command, in times of war, of the Sisters of Mercy. The first winner had founded the order as a response to an undead uprising and women not being allowed to fight in the war.

'I decided to take the challenge. Surely someone in the contest would manage to defeat me. I liked the sound of the title but didn't want the command. So we fought. The preliminary rounds were easy. Few had my skill. No one had abilities like mine. By the time I came to the final bout to decide who would challenge the champions, I was a favourite, but so was my opponent. It was going to be close. We both used two weapons—me two daggers, him short sword and dagger. The stadium where we were to fight was packed. Standing room only. The king and his five champions watched on with the rest.

'At the ring of the bell, it started. We danced and we danced and we danced. The crowd was going wild. Then they stood mute. Awed. And we continued to dance to the ringing of steel. They had never seen anything like this. We did not slow down. We even sped up. Everything was a blur. Then we stopped—face to face, hands outstretched to the sides, chests touching. We were both breathing hard. He looked down at me, and I looked up at him. We both smiled. He was beautiful. So I kissed him. I had forgotten the tournament. He took a stumbling step back, shocked, and I accidentally nicked him on the hand with my dagger, drawing blood. I hadn't meant it, but it was over and I had won. I would face the five champions. Not a very good way to win, I suppose. He was angry and came back at me. I dropped my daggers, and when he came close, I threw myself on him. Then I kissed him again. I kept kissing him until he calmed down. The crowd had, once again, gone wild. "We are not through," he said. "Never," I replied. "Together always," I said. His name was Brelldan, he said. So I kissed him again. "I am Kai," I said. Then he kissed me. We laughed and kissed again. We left the stadium together.

'We stayed together the whole of the next week, enjoying the pleasure of our dancing together, and we talked as well, a great deal, amongst other things. He was still by my side when the final of the tournament was to begin. He had known all five of the champions for years. He knew their strengths and their weaknesses. He told me everything he could remember about them. He had planned this for a long time—to become the champion of champions, to be the Briar Rose. And then I had come and destroyed his dream at the very moment that he had expected victory. I had also stolen his heart. But he had mine. So in that, too, we were even. We were one—two sides of the same coin.

'The time had come. There we were, the six of us, standing in the centre of the stadium, untold thousands watching in the stands. I was concentrating on my opponents. This would be harder than I had thought. It was not going to be to first blood. I had to make them yield, to truly defeat them.

'My opponents were thus: Riddik the Giant. He stood well over seven feet tall. His weapon was a huge axe. He was first. The weapon looked ponderous, but I had been told he could wield it like it was a feather. One hit from that, and I would be done for. The second was Hergath, a swordsman. He favoured his left side and used a shield to cover his weakness. The third, Laksha the Small, was my size—very quick, like a serpent. According to Brelldan, my best bet would be to wear him down, tire him out so he made mistakes. He also preferred using two daggers. Grellor would be my fourth. He was not very intelligent, according to my Brell. "Get him into a pattern and then change it before he realises." But he was strong and had a lot of stamina. The fifth, Druban. He was the complete swordsman, according to Brell. He used two swords of unequal length, was quick, and had good stamina. He knew every dirty trick in the book. He had a temper, which was his only weakness.

'I awaited the bell. I stood calmly, hands by my side, daggers in their sheaths. Why waste the energy of holding them until I needed to? The bell rang, and I walked forward. Riddik came at the trot. He took a couple of practice swings to loosen up on the way. When I neared him, I pretended to stumble. The axe quickly came down in an arc, but I was gone, up and over the weapon and then back to the ground. Before he had finished the swing, I reached down to make a grab for his leg. Using all my strength, I heaved, managing to unbalance him. He toppled over, the weight of the axe helping in pulling him down. My dagger came out and was at his throat before he could blink. The crowd roared.

'One down, four to go. No time wasted. Now where was Hergath? There he was, already on his way in. I went to meet him. I turned to his right, his stronger side. I circled him slowly, always going in the same direction, making him turn. I turned him right around, twice, watching for his reactions. When I had him positioned where I wanted him, I made my move. A highline attack to the sword arm. He squinted as the sun hit his eyes, even whilst he made the parry. Then I spun as fast as I could to his left, managing to get behind the shield. Out of his line of sight, I ducked low and rolled back the other way, as he quickly turned around, trying to cover the blow to his weak side. My dagger came up under his sword arm and raked across his side and around to his back. He dropped and signalled his defeat. That was number two. Three to go!

'I turned towards Laksha, took three paces towards him, and then stopped. I would let him come to me. I could catch my breath whilst he crossed the distance. I watched him closely, seeing how he moved. He walked calmly, taking his time. He showed no emotion. Was he stressed? Was he feeling some pain and trying not to show it? Surely his face should show something. I watched more carefully. Was that a limp he was trying to hide? Maybe. I needed to get him to move quickly so I could see if he was faking or trying to cover something up. I sprang at him as quickly as I could. As I approached, I spun to the side and then cartwheeled behind him. I watched him spin. He grimaced as his left foot hit the ground trying to halt his spin. Success. An injury, perhaps. Could I make use of it, or was it a lure?

'He stepped forward, trying to lessen the distance between us. I moved sideways and away, keeping him turning and away from me. He kept approaching. I kept moving, first in one direction and then another. I kept him on the move. It was frustrating him, I could see it, and he wanted this game of cat and mouse over. I decided to oblige. Instead of leaping back, I came forward. I was within striking distance. Our arms moved. Fast. Attack and parry—a ringing of steel on steel. His hands were blisteringly quick. But so were mine. He balanced himself, with one foot slightly forward of the other but at an awkward angle. His balance was off. My chance came. I changed my centre of balance and then leapt straight up. His eyes widened in surprise as my foot connected with his chin. He went straight back, flat on his back. He did not move.

'Now for number four. Grellor. I had to get to him quickly. I ran at him, and he readied himself. I decided for speed, to overwhelm his slower reflexes. Blow after blow, I rained on him. He parried them all. He was sweating, using all his skill to keep me at bay. Then I stopped suddenly, and he attempted to parry a blow that I didn't send. It left him wide open. I tapped him on the centre of his chest with the tip of my dagger. I smiled at him. He knelt in front of me. I turned from him and walked a few steps away.

'I was up to the final champion. The time it took to dispatch the first four had not been great. But I was beginning to tire. I had expended a great deal of energy, both physical and mental, in such a short space of time. And this was Druban—the supreme champion of the king's personal guard. He wore chain mail, head to foot with plate greaves, pauldrons and arm guards over top. It would take a heavy blow for one of my daggers to have any effect. Plus, he was good with his weapons. As good as Brelldan. We stood there, facing each other, neither making a move. Each waiting for the other to strike. I sheathed my daggers and spoke instead. "You don't deserve to dance with me. You're not as good as my Brell." His face turned red. When he leapt forward, I parried his sword with my hand, flipping it to the side and interrupting the thrust from his other weapon. Then I slapped him in the face, hard. He roared, dropped his swords, and swung a punch at me. I turned inside it, reached up, grabbed his hand, and pulled him towards me as I turned my back. Then I flipped him over me, onto his back. I knelt with my knee on his chest, pulled my dagger from its sheath, and held it to his throat. The crowd went berserk. It was deafening. I had won.

'I stood up, sheathed my dagger, and walked towards the king. I knelt at his feet. "I am Kai, princess of Raelis. My honour to serve Your Majesty." "Rise, Kai. The title of Briar Rose is yours. You are the third to win the title. Never before have I seen such skill combined with such an understanding of the nature of combat. With each of your opponents, you determined his weakness and then exploited it," said the king. "I accept the title, Highness," I replied. "But please relieve from me the necessity of command of the Sisters of Mercy. Don't misunderstand me—they are a fine order—but I have no experience with command, or with the way both they and your armies fight. All my knowledge and technique is based around individual combat. I could not serve you well in that regard. My opponent Brelldan has the knowledge and the capability to serve in that capacity. Name him as your commander. He will serve you well. I will be staying by his side." "It shall be done as you ask," said the king. "If there is anything else that I can do for you, then let me know." "I will,' I replied. "Now I must go. Brelldan is waiting. He will wish to celebrate."

'The capital celebrated my win for a week. Wherever Brell and I went, we were cheered, invited to parties, or asked to give a display of our skill. I decided to make a break for it. Taking Brell with me, I set out to find a way through the mountains on a direct route to the dwarven mine. We did not make it. The mountains proved impassable. Still, we had been gone from the capital for weeks, and by the time we returned, things had settled down. What followed were two years of bliss. Then came our last year together.

'I had been learning all Brell could teach me of command. We often went out with various groups—Sisters of Mercy or units from the army—patrolling the northern borders. It was a wild land up there. We started getting large groups of humanoids coming south. These weren't just raiding parties, the likes of which we had seen before. These were entire communities of goblins, orcs, and their ilk. They numbered in the hundreds, each band moving fast, moving south, and we were in the way. Many pitched battles were fought. We could not understand it, this sudden drive south. The goblins and other monsters had lived in the Northlands for centuries, with only a little trouble for those in the south.

'Then the first encounter with undead was made. It was just a few. The soldiers who fought them shrugged it off as nothing to worry about. The number of undead had not been great for centuries. Two weeks later, a unit of fifty men was wiped out. They had failed to return from a short and routine patrol. Brell rode out with a handful of soldiers in support. He was the only one to make it back. He raised the alarm, rallied the troops, and sent word to the king. The king passed the word to all the towns and cities. "Call in the troops. We are in for a fight. There are extremely large numbers of undead out there." It was why the goblins had tried to come south. They were fleeing the undead. We should have learnt their lesson and followed suit. Small contingents of the army were left scattered around the nation to serve as protection from the bands of goblins. The rest coalesced into an army, the likes of which I had never seen—fifty thousand strong, plus the odd mage and cleric.

'We formed up on the grassy plains south and east of Albrae. Then we rode forth. We would push the undead back in one fell swoop. We found the undead quickly. They had left the forested hills and wandered out onto the plain. We formed up the ranks and charged into them. It was a massacre. We killed them all, and quickly. Scouts were sent out. They returned, having found nothing. Whilst we celebrated that night, the undead rose again, or came in from elsewhere.

'Just before dawn, they attacked our camps, en masse. They outnumbered us, and we were surprised. We responded well, though, I thought initially. Soldiers died, as did undead. Accidents happened. Men fled in terror, whilst others stood and fought. Fires spread. Sparks from the cook fires caused some tents to burst into flame, lighting the scene. The undead veered away from the flames. "Spread the fire!" I yelled. Some heard and did as I commanded. We managed to form a complete ring of fire around us. The flow of undead eased, and we downed the rest inside the ring. "Burn the bodies, all of the fallen, including our own!" I cried. I tried to find Brell. We had become separated during the battle.

'Then I saw him. His back to the fire, he was fighting for his life. Almost surrounded. He was stunning in his ferocity. This was his true battle self, not the shadow he showed whilst he and I fought. He was magnificent, untouchable, but he was also tiring. Someone started shooting arrows at the undead near him. Others threw some firebrands to give him room. The undead backed off. He turned and leapt, trying to clear the flames. A spear, thrown from somewhere out amidst the undead, took him in the back. He crashed into the fire and screamed in pain. I froze.

'When the screaming stopped, he was dead. Gone. The love of my life. I could not look away from his corpse. I watched it burn. I collapsed, bereft. I just sat on the ground and did nothing. A young soldier rallied the troops who were there. He kept the fires going until well past dawn, kept the fires burning until they ran out of fuel. It was closer to midday. It did not matter—the undead had gone. He had the men gather up all the useable equipment and round up the few horses that were still near. He found me still sitting there, staring at the spot where Brelldan had died. He brought a horse and had me tied to it. He went to where I had been staring and, seeing a flash from some metal, scattered the ashes away. He found a dagger, made of gold, silver, and some other strange grey metal. It was glowing, a light blue light. It faded as we watched. He picked it up, surprised that it was cool to the touch, and put it in his pouch.

'He gathered the men and led us back to the capital. We picked up the occasional soldier on the way. By the time we reached Albrae, there were maybe two thousand of us. That was all that was left of that vast army. I was roused from my stupor by the king. He asked what we needed to do. "Flee," I said. "There are too many undead. Take all your people and flee." He did not take my advice. He summoned all the mages he could, and all the clerics. He rallied the people for a massive strike, backed with magical powers. Those not going with the king fled. I was one of them.

'Before I left, the young soldier came to me. He gave me the dagger he had found in the ashes. "It was Brelldan's," he said. "Take it. Use it. Find some way to defeat the undead. End this plague for all time, if you can." Then he left. He went with his king. He was perhaps the bravest man I had ever met. I never knew his name, and I never will.

'When I left, I went alone with horse and cart carrying my few treasured possessions. I went south and made for the mountains. Once there, I turned east. I moved as far and as fast as I could. I spread the word as I went, but it was too late. The undead were everywhere. I kept moving, fighting when forced to it, but fleeing most often. I took many wounds before I left them behind. My body slowly healed each one. The farther away from the undead I got, the faster I healed. I heard later the result of the king's stand. The magic had failed, that of both mages and clerics alike. Nothing worked. The undead sapped the magical energies from whatever was around them. That was something that had never been written about in the histories. Maybe they did not know, or maybe something had changed. Anyway, now I knew it. Something else to explain. Another aspect of our defence, one string in the tangle unwound.

'I finally managed to get to a town and exchange my horse and buy provisions. They had not heard the news. I talked the mayor into leaving and spreading the news. Then I left. I moved on. I headed for home. I had nowhere else to go. The rest you know.'

CHAPTER 10

K ai fell silent for a moment and took a deep breath. 'Now, tell me why? Why the interest? Why me? How did you find me? *And who are you?*'

'I . . . I am Alemrae, the last living member of my family. Many years ago, when I first left my family's homestead, I went in search of the answer to that question. *Why me?* We were different from all the others around our village. We lived out in the forest, quite a distance from the village. It was my grandmother's house. Her husband had built it. It was a strange house. It blended into the forest. It was peaceful there. It contained a peace that I have not felt since. My friends were beginning to age—I was not. This, I must say, was a long time ago.

'I talked with my grandmother. Her husband had left with his family, and she had stayed to take care of her father, who was ailing. Not long after her husband had left, she found out that she was pregnant. She gave birth to my father. The family stayed aloof, out in the woods, away from everyone else. Then when my father was old enough, he ventured from the forest and met my mother. They married, and soon after, I was born. My mother died giving birth to me. My father could not cope with his grief. He walked away into the forest and never returned. My grandmother raised me. I roamed the forest. I learnt all I could of forest lore. How to hunt and dress game. How to move through the forest without trace. My grandmother knew a lot. Mostly about the plants: how and where they grew, and how they could be used, both as food and for healing. I thought it strange that she knew how to heal. We never got sick.

'Just before she died, my grandmother told me that I was the last of my line. But there was a family tie, she said. Her great-great-grandmother had had a sister. This sister had disappeared. They had been travelling to a wedding when they were attacked by a tribe of trolls. By the time the fight was over, the sister was gone. No evidence could be found. Sometime later, there was a rumour of a maiden giving birth at a monastery. A human compound. The woman had died giving birth. But the child, a boy, had lived.

'When my grandmother died, I went in search of that child and, as time passed, looked for clues as to the whereabouts of that child and any family he may have created. That was two hundred years ago. You may have guessed by now that I am part elven. I do not know where the elves have disappeared to. I also would like to find them so that I can learn more of my heritage. I have not returned home, for we lived in the far north—farther north than the mountains north of Albrae, a land where winter can last for more than five months and nights can be long. I came south looking for family. I have wandered the continents, never staying anywhere for long, moving on so that none would suspect my heritage. Always moving, always seeking. Until I met Geoffrey and saved his life. He invited me to visit the city where he lived. The city of Raelis. I have been in and around the city for about five years. And now I have met you. I believe that your family is the one I have been searching for. You look like my grandmother in appearance. So similar it is eerie, you could be her sister, almost a twin. Now you know why I wanted to talk with you.'

'We had best be getting back—it has grown late. Come, cousin, I will escort you to the palace.' Gathering her things, Kai got up and left, accompanied by Alemrae.

They managed to return to the city just before the gates were closed for the night. The city grew quiet as dusk settled, and they made their way up almost empty streets to the palace. The lamplighters were at work, igniting the torches and lanterns at the crossroads of streets—a measure to make the streets a bit safer. It was the dark alleyways between that provided the dangers now.

They made it safely to the palace and entered through the kitchens, where Kai requested that the dinner for her group be set on tables out in the terraced garden, with plenty of braziers, as it would start to get cool. Kai and Alemrae then returned to their rooms.

Shadow was hovering over her egg by the fireplace, with Prince Morannel reading in a chair nearby. Geoffrey sat attaching yet another patch on his already much patched cloak. Kai called the maids to have a bath readied and retired to her room. Alemrae also retired to get ready for the evening meal. He preferred to wash with a damp cloth and cold water. When he returned to the main room, he found Shadow there alone. The other two had gone to their rooms to get ready as well. He approached quietly across the carpeted floor— no sound to give away his presence.

Yet before he could speak, Shadow said, 'I sense that you have some questions for me, Alemrae.'

'Yes, I do,' he replied. 'But they can wait until another time.'

'You seek to possess the life within the egg. Remember this always: it is its own being. It may decide to accompany you, or it may not. It is not your choice.'

'As it is with all things. All I seek is its survival, nothing else. They are extremely rare, even in my own land. I will be saddened if it chooses to leave me, but I could never force it to stay. I am unsure if it will survive. It was almost dead of cold when I first laid my hands upon it. I used my magic to see if it was what I thought it was. I felt it grow warmer as I held it. Now I keep it near this hearth to ensure its warmth.'

'You would do better to enshroud it with magic to wrap a layer of warmth around it,' suggested Alemrae.

'I know not how to do this thing,' replied Shadow.

'Here, let me show you. Embrace your magic and follow what I do.'

Shadow's eyes widened as Alemrae spoke fluently but softly in her tongue. 'Do you see?' he asked as he wove magic. 'The pattern of warm air flows constantly around the egg, encasing it in a cocoon. If done in such a fashion, the egg may be taken away from the fire and it will stay warm.'

'Can such an approach be done with other things?' asked Shadow.

'Yes, although the area to be encased must always remain small, maybe one foot square, no larger or the spell won't take. You can also reduce the temperature in the same way. I will go now. I shall meet you all in the gardens when you are ready,' said Alemrae.

With that, he left. Shadow returned her focus to the egg. She felt the egg and realised it was definitely warmer. She then studied it with her magic and was surprised to learn that the egg was absorbing her magic along with the warmth. She decided to try something. She cast another spell she knew, a spell of growth. She had learnt it whilst trying to make plants grow in her desert home. Once again, the egg absorbed the magic, although nothing else appeared to have happened. She decided that she would try a few other spells in the coming days just to see what would happen. Geoffrey, Kai, and Morannel entered the room.

'What have you there?' asked Kai.

'Oh! It's my egg,' replied Shadow excitedly. 'Morannel bought it for me today, down in the market. Isn't it exquisite? It was very expensive! I could never have afforded it, even over a lifetime.' Her eyes were aglow with appreciation as they turned upon Morannel.

Kai looked at Morannel and raised an eyebrow. He blushed.

'Oh, I see,' said Kai, turning back. 'Yes, Shadow, it is very nice. Let's go. It is time for our evening meal.' And she led them down to the gardens.

Shadow wrapped the egg in cloth and took it with her. The dinner in the garden was a fine affair. Alemrae joined them, as he said he would. The good food and pleasant conversation with trusted friends made a nice evening. The braziers warmed the air enough so that they were not cold, but did not overheat them either. They could see the bay to the east and the mountains to the north and west, the tips of which slowly changed colour as the sun's light receded. When the first moon rose above the bay, the snow and ice on the tip of the closest mountain gleamed silver. Far off to the west, a flash of blue light from the mountains appeared. It passed unremarked, for none had seen it.

'We should have an early night this night,' said Kai. 'It will be a long day tomorrow, with little time for sleep tomorrow night. We will have to prepare for the trial in the ring of fire the next day and be up early for it.' She rose from where she was seated and went up to the rooms.

'Shadow, please wait a moment?' asked Prince Morannel. Shadow stopped, whilst the others went upstairs. 'There is something I must tell you,' said the prince. 'I have realised that I have acted in a rather foolish way. By obtaining the egg for you, I had hoped to win your affection. But my life is not my own to live as I would choose. It belongs to this country and its people. I would not have you think that I trifle with your affections. I must marry for the benefit of my country when they require it, even if I would prefer it to be otherwise. We have a journey ahead of us. We will be travelling together, and I would not have any awkwardness between us.'

'Prince Morannel, your heart is your own. You may give it where you choose. I am a daughter of the desert, and I shall return there when my time here is done. If I return alone or with another, matters not. I count you a friend, and you will always have a place within my heart. I must go up. I have a need to speak with Alemrae before he sleeps.'

'Then go, Shadow. I shall remain here in this garden for a while.'

Shadow left, feeling that something important had been said but could not figure out what. When she got to the rooms, she quietly knocked on Alemrae's door. Alemrae opened the door and stepped out, shutting it behind him.

'Alemrae, can you tell me more of the egg and the magic you use?' asked Shadow.

Alemrae answered. 'The Elgrae Amaf, or lizards of light in the common tongue, are creatures of magic. They absorb it, change it, grow it, and then they return it to the world as life. Magic is life, life is magic. The more magic they absorb, the more powerful they become. The more powerful they are, the more life they can sustain. Check your egg. The reddish tinge grows and changes shape as the life within quickens. When the markings make the hatchling, then it will unfurl. The magic I use is not mine. It belongs to no one. Magic is only limited by the scope of the one who seeks to manipulate it. How you see the world determines how you see magic. It is for you to discover your limits, for magic has none! Now, you must sleep well this night, for you will be needed in the morning.'

Alemrae left the room, firmly shutting the door behind him. Shadow did not think that she could sleep that night. So much had happened that day. Needed in the morning? How could he know what was yet to come? This would need some thought—a lot of thought. She settled down in a large comfortable chair, intending to work out the things that were rattling around in her mind. She fell asleep instead.

CHAPTER 11

She was awakened the next morning by the sound of someone vomiting noisily. The sound was coming from Kai's room. She quickly got up and rushed in. Kai was lying upside down on the bed and being sick into the chamber pot.

'Gods, I feel awful. What's the matter with me? I've never been sick in my life,' groaned Kai. Then she threw up again.

'Here, let me help you,' said Shadow, and reaching over with a damp cloth, she began to clean her face. 'Just lie back and stay calm. You will be fine. Let me get you some water to rinse your mouth . . . There, that's better now, isn't it? Just sip the water. You will feel a little better shortly.'

'I can't just lie here. I have things I must see to today,' responded Kai.

'Just rest, Kai. We can organise all that needs to be done. You must keep your strength for tomorrow. Try to get some more rest. I will look in on you again shortly. You are in no condition to do anything just yet,' replied Shadow.

With that, Shadow rose and walked out, shutting the door behind her. Alemrae was waiting, sitting on a chair in the main room.

'How could you know!' exclaimed Shadow softly.

'She doesn't even know herself,' Alemrae replied. 'My magic allows me to read the aura of anyone near me. It clearly showed me Kai's condition. You did not tell her, I trust. She must find out for herself. She can have no worries until after the fight tomorrow. It must consume her—mind, body, and soul. If she has doubts or worries other than the end result she has set herself, then she shall fail. If that happens, we are all in a great deal of trouble.'

As the day passed, Kai issued orders from her bed, and they were carried out. She managed to take some water and then solid food. It stayed down. She wanted to get up, but the others would not let her. 'Save your strength,' they said. 'You will need it for the fight tomorrow.' She acquiesced.

So they talked and joked throughout the day. They came and went, going to do the tasks they had been set, whilst the others continued to talk. They each told parts of their life story; it was a short time of bonding and tranquillity. It was a preparation of sorts for the long journey ahead. Shadow continued to use her magic on the egg, and everyone was interested in the colour changes induced. The pattern was becoming more distinct. There were the vague hints of legs and wings, a long neck, and an even longer tail began to show. It was beginning to resemble a lizard. The egg no longer looked gold; it was more of a dirty bronze colour.

'Soon, so very soon,' said Alemrae. 'A few more days, at this rate, I think.'

Night fell, and they all sought some rest.

Sometime before dawn, they were awoken by Alemrae. 'It is time,' he said. 'We must prepare for the trials of the day. We have about two hours to be ready. The Great Hall is already beginning to fill.' Everyone began to prepare themselves. Kai did not suffer the sickness of the day before; her body had already adjusted to the changes occurring within.

When they arrived, the Great Hall was packed. Everyone who had been successful in the lottery for admittance had come early. There was a crowd outside the doors, trying to get in. The guards had barred the doors. 'No more to be admitted,' they cried. 'Wait peacefully or you will be dispersed. The result will be announced soon enough. Your neighbours who won admittance will tell you about it. Please be patient.'

The crowd grumbled but quietened. None wished to be forced to leave. Inside the hall, all was ready. Kai waited patiently beside Shadow and Alemrae. Prince Morannel was seated on the throne. Beside him were the inner council and Regent Monfrae. They were surrounded at the foot of the dais by a ring of guards. The Mother Superior of the Sisters of Mercy and her chosen retinue were seated in a boxed stand near the throne. Opposite them were the other lords and upper class who had gained entry. The rest of the hall was filled by the commoners.

The guards bringing in Frederick Monfraeson halted in front of the dais. Prince Morannel stood. 'Frederick Monfraeson, you were charged and found guilty. This trial at arms is for the benefit of your life. If you win, you will have your life and freedom. If you lose and you survive, you will be bound to Kai, the Briar Rose, as her slave for the period of one year. She may, at her discretion, release you at any time if she believes your actions warrant it. If, at the end of that year, she is still of the opinion that you have not redeemed yourself, then you will be banished from Raelis and its lands upon pain of death. You have agreed to these terms.'

'Yes, Your Grace, I have,' said Frederick.

'Alemrae Traemellin, you have agreed to oversee this trial. It is time to do your duty,' said the prince.

Alemrae moved to the circle of oil-soaked wood and began to outline how events would proceed. 'The trial will soon commence. The following is to be obeyed by those who watch. Those who do not obey will be forcibly expelled. From here until the end, no sound shall be made. This fight will be conducted in silence. The two contestants shall enter the ring and stand opposite one another. The entrance to the ring shall be closed, and the ring shall be lit. The victor is the last one to be able to stand without contest. The one who loses will either have admitted defeat, be unconscious, or be dead. Kai and Frederick, please take your place inside the ring. Once the ring is lit and Kai has donned her blindfold, the match may begin. Once the ring is lit, anything that happens inside the ring stays in the ring.'

Kai followed Frederick into the ring. She stood near the opening and watched Frederick walk to the other side and turn around. She took note of his weapon, as well as the armour he wore. Frederick was wearing a chain mail hauberk and carried a buckler. The sword was, as she had thought it would be, Soulburner. He wore leather leggings and iron-studded boots. They made a grating sound on the floor as he walked.

Kai, on the other hand, was bereft of armour. She wore a tight-fitting cloth bodysuit of dark colours and carried two daggers, one of which was Brelldan's. She carried it in her left hand. A guard came forward and pushed a wood pile over to close the opening and then stepped back into place. Kai took out the blindfold and knotted it into place, covering her sight totally.

At this point, Shadow stepped forward. She whispered something in her own language and drew on her magical powers. Fire spilled from her hands onto the wood, igniting it in a blaze of cold white flame. The crowd slowly became silent. The trial had begun.

CHAPTER 12

K ai concentrated on her hearing as she turned her head slightly from side to side and listened to the sounds around her. She closed her eyes to help her concentrate. There was a whoosh from in front of her; Frederick must have called on his sword to emit flame, she thought. She took two steps forward, silently, and began a weaving motion with her daggers. She sensed the placement of Frederick, and then to her astonishment, she could see him, a vague and faint outline of red, blue, and green heat patterns.

The sword was almost white; the ring of fire, black. It gave her a basis for her defence. She relaxed a fraction and turned slightly off-centre so that she was not truly facing Frederick but to the right of him. She was happy to let him think that she did not know where he was. She advanced in the direction she was facing. Frederick also advanced slowly and then swung a solid blow towards Kai's side. Her left hand darted out and engaged the sword, and there was a ringing tone of metal on metal, the white of the sword dropping to a deep red. The dagger in her left hand noticeably cooled, as if in response to the flame on the sword blade.

Then they began to fence. Sword and shield versus two daggers. They tested each other for weaknesses, and despite the blindfold, Kai knew she held the upper hand. Kai began the sequence she had practised in the meadow. Frederick matched her, time and again, parrying and attacking, as the opportunities came and went. Until the fateful moment.

Frederick saw the hole in Kai's defence but delayed too long to take advantage. Kai repeated the sequence, and this time, Frederick attacked. A hard straight thrust, it slid between the daggers and into her left side, angling up from just below the ribcage and exiting just below the scapula on her right, narrowly missing her backbone. Kai screamed in agony and vomited blood. But she did not fall. She lashed out with the hilts of both daggers towards the face of Frederick. She struck hard, felt bone crack, and Frederick fell back, losing his grip on the sword. The flames on the sword died out immediately.

Dropping her daggers, Kai grasped the hilt of the sword and pulled it clear and then threw it behind her. Kai knelt, still fighting the pain in her side and back. She felt around her for her daggers. She located one. It felt cool. *Brelldan's*, she thought. She transferred it to her right hand and then stood up. She heard Frederick rising to his feet, gasping, so she moved towards him. The pain began to lessen, and she stood straighter.

'You cannot win,' she said, spitting out some blood. 'Your one chance has fled. I shall give you no other.'

With that, she made a cut at him. He blocked it with his shield and was astonished to see the dagger cut straight through, slicing off about a third of the buckler. Even as he recovered from his astonishment, Kai made another blow. This one created a large slice in his chain mail but failed to find the skin beneath. The chain parted as if it were silk. Then Frederick knew he was in trouble. There was no way he could win this fight. In his moment of victory, he had lost. Kai was a far superior fighter than he had thought possible. How she could stand, let alone fight, with that wound? It was unbelievable, and her dagger made his armour useless. All it did was slow him down, and he was unarmed. It was inevitable. He was going to lose or die. He did not wish to die. *If I must lose, then it will be in my way*, he thought.

He knelt and looked up at Kai. 'I surrender myself to your command, mistress,' he said as he bowed his head. 'Please be merciful.'

Kai stood where she was, looking down upon him. Then she removed her blindfold. It was over. 'I accept your admission of defeat. Come, kinsman,' she said. 'We have much to do.'

Then she collapsed to the floor, holding her side. 'Damn, that hurts. First, you had best get me a stretcher and carry me to my room,' she managed to say before she fainted.

CHAPTER 13

Shadow was the first to Kai's side, having leapt over the flames. Once more, she drew on her magic and cast a minor healing spell—something to stop the bleeding—unaware that it had already slowed considerably. It was the best that she could do.

Alemrae walked through the fire, untouched by the flame. 'A stretcher is on its way,' he said. 'We shall take her to her rooms and care for her there.'

The stretcher was brought in, and Kai was laid upon it. She was hoisted aloft by Frederick and Alemrae, and then they slowly and carefully carried her out of the room. Shadow followed. A buzz of sound grew in the Great Hall as everybody began talking about the duel and the probability that Kai would not survive, for it was a hideous wounding. It would be talked about for a very long time.

The doors were opened, and the crowd in the hall began to disperse to their homes. Prince Morannel retrieved Kai's daggers and the sword Soulburner from the now burnt-out ring. He passed them to a guard and told him to ensure that they were returned to the Lady Kai.

Then he turned to his uncle. 'She will survive this wounding. I received wounds almost as severe, and it has taken me only four days to heal. Kai heals faster than I do, she has admitted as much to me. She will be up and about in no time. We need her. I need her. The country, even the world, needs her to do what she does best—to fight for all our lives. She fights for us, for she has no reason to live for herself.

'My lords, we need to begin stockpiling weapons and armour. Oil as well. Prepare as if for the longest siege imaginable. Then double the amount required. Then we might come close to having enough. Send out requests to every ruling body we know. Ask for men and supplies. Take all those who are willing to respond! We will train as many as we can. Those unfit for fighting can do the myriad of chores required to sustain the fighting force that we are going to need. Send a request to the fighting schools of the Elshgat Free States. Tell them we need as many skirmishers as they can raise. However many come, send them to assist in Almarac—they are the best suited to delay the assault on Almarac by the undead. Give the citizens of Almarac time to get out. Send a message to Almarac that they should evacuate their region. Get everybody to come here. We will send those not involved in the defence on to Ulmarin. We will need as many armourers and weapon smiths as we can get. We need mages and clerics as well, though these will need to stay clear of the actual fighting. In the meantime, double the guard on the palace and the walls. I want twenty guards sent to get my sister from Almarac. Captain Gregorson can lead them. They can take two extra mounts apiece, and make the trip as fast as they can without killing the horses. Hopefully, Zeph will already be on her way home. I shall now go and check on how Kai is faring.'

Once outside the Great Hall, Frederick and Alemrae halted. They had no choice. The hallways were packed with servants and others awaiting news of the trial. Alemrae yelled for room to be made and, when no apparent movement was made to clear a path, called for guards.

The guards who came through the door after them formed a shield wall and started pushing the crowd out of the way. The guards yelled for the crowd to make way, and slowly they edged forward. It took time to manoeuvre the stretcher through the crowd and up to the second floor. Once there, they were clear of the crowd and they made better time.

They arrived at Kai's room and very carefully moved her onto her bed. Shadow called for the old nurse. When Kira, one of her granddaughters, came through, she was sent to get her grandmother and was told to run, as Kai was seriously wounded. They waited anxiously for the old nurse. When a knock sounded on the main door, they were puzzled, as they knew the nurse would not bother with such formalities. Alemrae went to the door and opened it.

One of the Sisters of Mercy was standing in the hall. 'I am Sister Seraphine. I have come to offer my services,' she said. 'I am the best healer of our order in the city.'

Alemrae replied, 'You are welcome—your expertise is needed. The wound is grievous. Quickly, come in. She is on her bed in the other room.'

The sister went straight through to the bedroom. 'Please open the window and the balcony doors,' she said. 'I shall need more light.'

Then Seraphine began to examine the wounds. 'We need to keep these wounds free of infection. I shall make a wash to rinse the wounds before we bandage them. The bandages we use should be first boiled in water for a while. This will help prevent the wounds turning septic. We shall also need to sew the wounds closed. We will soak the needle and threads to be used in a solution I shall make. Then we will rinse our hands with that solution to purify them before we attempt the surgery.'

Seraphine turned to Shadow. 'Excuse me. Shadow, isn't it?'

'Yes, that is the name I am using here.'

'Your garments have some very fine stitching. Did you make them yourself?' asked the sister.

'Yes, I did. What interest have you in my clothes? You should be concentrating on Kai!' stated Shadow, annoyed by the question.

The sister replied, 'My skill with the needle is not as good as yours. It would be good if you did the stitching of Kai's wounds. I will oversee your work, but many small, neat stiches will be required.'

'I would be honoured to work with you in treating her wounds,' Shadow replied.

It took some time to boil the bandages and create the antiseptic solution, but once that was done, it did not take them long to sew the wounds closed and bandage them.

When they left Kai's room, they found the old nurse treating the injuries of Frederick. Frederick shook off the attentions of the nurse and approached the sister and Shadow. 'How is she?' he asked.

'She is still unconscious. Until she awakens, she is in a grave condition. We can only wait and see what happens. We have done all we can for her,' responded the sister.

'May I wait with her?' asked Frederick.

'No,' said the sister. 'Shadow will be the one to keep an eye on Kai. I will come back and relieve her when needed.' With that, Sister Seraphine left.

Shadow went and gathered her egg before going back into Kai's room and shutting the door firmly behind her. Frederick went back to his seat and sat down, willing to wait as long as necessary to ensure Kai recovered. He could not think what would happen if she died now.

Alemrae came over to Frederick and said, 'I may be able to help you, if you will trust me to.'

'Whether or not I trust you is unimportant. Kai trusts you. Do what you will.' Alemrae spoke in a low voice, in a language unknown to Frederick.

Frederick felt his face bathed in warmth, and then there was an intense pain in his jaw. He felt it straighten, realign, and then click into place. 'Try not to talk much until you give it a chance to heal. It is now set correctly and should heal over a period of a few weeks. That's better than the four or five months and a crooked jaw you were going to have, is it not?' said Alemrae. Alemrae walked away before Frederick could answer and went into his room.

Prince Morannel came into the main room, glanced over at his cousin, and then quietly knocked on Kai's door. Shadow answered.

'Kai is not to be disturbed, Highness,' she said.

'Just tell me how she is doing and I shall go,' he replied.

'She is doing as well as can be expected after having three feet of steel run through her chest. She needs rest, care, and no disturbances.'

'Thank you, Shadow. I know you care for her. We all do. She will be fine. She will heal as I did,' said Morannel. 'It is you I am worried about.'

With that, he moved away from the door and sat in a chair to wait. Shadow returned to her seat beside the bed and continued her contemplation of her egg whilst she waited for some response from Kai. Occasionally, Shadow would bring forth her magic and wrap her egg in it, watching as the egg absorbed the magic. The patterned lines deepened, indicating the form of a lizard of light. Oh, how she wished it would hurry up and hatch. It did seem to be a little bit bigger and heavier to her than when she had first gotten it. So maybe it was growing a touch.

Late that afternoon, the sister came back. 'I will take the watch until the second moon rises,' she said. 'I have made arrangements for another sister to then come and take the watch until dawn. If Kai lives until tomorrow, then we can hope that she will survive. Now, go and get some rest. I will call if there is any change.'

CHAPTER 14

The next morning, they all gathered in the main room hoping for some good news. The Sister of Mercy came out and said, 'There has been no change. Kai still lies unconscious. We will change the bandages this morning and again in the afternoon. Shadow will assist us. Go about your duties. There is nothing else to be done here.'

Shadow went with the sister back into Kai's room. Morannel, Alemrae, and Frederick went to the training grounds to work out.

'Frederick, you were wrong about me,' said Morannel. 'I am not afraid of the battle. I am afraid of my emotions when I wield a weapon. You must assist Alemrae in teaching me what I must master.'

Alemrae took two wooden practice swords and gave them to Morannel and Frederick. 'Face each other. Morannel, I want you to defend yourself, but do not attack. When you feel the need to attack, lower your weapon and step back. Frederick, attack Morannel—use attack patterns of the first level. If Morannel lowers his sword, then step back and lower yours. Allow him to regain control. Then we will start again.'

They practised, stopping frequently at first and then less often. Occasionally, Alemrae would show Morannel some footwork and defensive manoeuvres to incorporate in his defence. He improved steadily. They stopped for the midday meal and went back up to their rooms. Kai had still not shown any sign of waking up. They ate in the room with the sisters and Shadow.

Alemrae slipped into Kai's room and, using his magic, viewed Kai's aura. She was healing slowly. He came back into the main room and said, 'Kai is healing slowly. She may not awaken until she is fully recovered. The wounds are closed and the stitches may be removed. Until she awakens, there is nothing more we need do for her. Kai will be very hungry when she awakens. We must have some food ready for her at all times.'

With that, Alemrae left. Shadow collected her egg and went out onto the balcony. Morannel followed soon after. Shadow continued to cast her magic about the egg. Its colour had changed even further. It was now a deep bronze, as if highly polished. It had blue edges on what appeared to be scales.

'Shadow,' queried Morannel, 'the other day when you first joined us, we could not see you. Was that a spell of yours that caused it?'

'Yes, it was,' she replied.

'Have you tried casting it upon the egg?' he asked.

'No, because it would turn the egg invisible, and I need to be able to see it,' she answered.

'Why don't you try it? You can lower the spell if it turns invisible, can't you?' said Morannel.

'It does not work that way. I could lower it if I cast it upon myself, but not if I cast it upon an object,' she replied. 'It is a powerful spell, though. I have not cast anything that powerful on the egg yet. It would prove interesting to see what would happen.'

So, gathering her magic, she wound the egg in the illusion of invisibility, letting the spell seep into the egg as she watched. The egg unfurled. There was no other way to describe the process. It did not hatch, as there was no shell left behind. The entirety of the egg was consumed in the formation of the lizard of light. It was twelve inches long. The body was about three inches, with the neck also about three inches. The tail was five inches long. The head was an inch long. The wings, when it finally opened them, were leathery and shaped like a bat's. They were a resplendent blue in colour, matching the edges of the scales. It hissed, and a small spurt of flame escaped its mouth.

Shadow gasped. 'It's almost full grown,' she cried. 'It's no wonder the young are never seen.' The lizard turned to face her, its eyes glowing a bright red. 'He's hungry! I know he's hungry. Quickly, we must feed him.'

Shadow slowly reached out and let the lizard walk onto her hand rather than trying to grab him. 'He trusts me,' she whispered wonderingly before slowly standing up and walking inside, with Morannel following. 'Is there any meat here?' she asked.

'I'll order some raw meat for you. You might try some of that cooked chicken in the meantime,' suggested Morannel.

Morannel went to the door and asked the guard there to send to the kitchen for a small plate of raw meat, a couple of varieties if possible. Shadow picked up a few small pieces of chicken and fed the lizard. It seemed quite happy to take the food from her hand.

When the chicken was gone, Shadow poured some water into her finger bowl and placed it on the table. The lizard of light flew from her hand and landed on the table beside the bowl. It took a sniff and sneezed. Then it inserted its mouth into the water and drank. Once it had had its fill, the lizard began to explore the other objects on the table. It walked around, its wings furled tightly to its body. The legs were long enough so that the rounded belly of the lizard was held well clear of the table. It appeared almost catlike in its grace. It sat on its haunches and used its nimble forepaws to handle the objects that it was interested in. Despite its small size, the lizard seemed capable of lifting some quite heavy things—at least enough to handle them or topple them over, as happened to a vase of flowers on the table. The water went everywhere. The vase righted itself with no apparent help, whilst the flowers bound themselves together in a tight and colourful knot. The water stayed where it was. The lizard was distracted by a knock at the door. It flew straight to Shadow's shoulder, where it nuzzled at her neck. She reached up to stroke it gently.

'That was amazing,' said Morannel. 'What shall you call him?'

'I have no idea. Would you get the door? I don't want anyone to see him yet,' said Shadow as she walked into the other room.

Morannel answered the door and received the small platter of mixed meats from the servant, thanking him for his prompt attention to the odd request. Shadow had taken a seat by the time Morannel came through with the meat tray. Morannel passed Shadow the tray and took a seat nearby. The lizard, smelling the meat, crawled down the front of Shadow's chest and on to her lap. It stood up on its haunches and tried to reach the platter. Shadow brought the platter down and rested it on her thighs, where the lizard could help himself. He proceeded to do just that, daintily picking up each piece and giving it a good sniff before eating it. When he'd had enough, he curled into a ball on Shadow's lap and promptly went to sleep.

'What do you call an inquisitive ball of mischief?' Shadow queried softly.

Morannel chuckled softly. 'No idea,' he said. 'But he is wonderful, I'll give you that. Worth every drac I spent too.' He smiled at Shadow.

'I think I shall call him Rad—short for radiance,' said Shadow. 'For that is how I feel when I look upon him, as if my whole being is full of light.'

'That is how your presence makes me feel,' said Morannel. With that, he got up and walked out the door.

'You are very strange, Morannel,' said Shadow unto herself. She put the platter of meat on the floor and, after carefully lifting Rad so as not to wake him, curled herself into a more comfortable position, put Rad back on her lap, and went to sleep.

She was awoken by the unpleasant feeling of something long and wet lashing her nose. She opened her eyes to see Rad perched on her face, licking her. She reached up and gently removed him. 'I am going to call you Rad,' she said. It bobbed its head as if it understood and then rubbed its head against her hand.

'Come on. It is time for you to meet the others,' she said.

Alemrae, Morannel, and Frederick were seated around the table when Shadow walked in. 'Woken from your nap, I see,' said Alemrae, smiling.

Shadow moved to the table and sat down. 'This is Rad,' she said, placing the lizard on the table for all to see. Rad sat up and cocked his head at a raffish angle and peered back at the others around him.

Alemrae laughed. 'Quite the little charmer, isn't he?' he said.

Rad galloped up the table for a closer inspection of Alemrae. 'This is one of those mythical lizards, I take it?' said Frederick.

'No myth, obviously,' said Alemrae. He placed his hand on the table, and Rad walked up to it and gave it a sniff.

'No biting,' said Shadow. 'You don't need to taste him—he's not for eating.' Rad looked over his shoulder at her with a doleful expression. 'He thinks you smell good, Alemrae,' said Shadow.

'How is it that you know what he thinks?' asked Morannel.

'I don't know, but I do,' said Shadow.

'It may be that he has become your familiar,' said Alemrae.

'I have heard of similar things happening to a few great seers, but not with anything as intelligent as a lizard of light.'

'I think you may be in for a very informative time,' said Alemrae. 'These lizards are of an extremely magical nature and thought to be highly intelligent, and he is obviously very inquisitive.'

Rad stretched his wings and bounced up and down as if agreeing. Then he took flight around the room. Gliding more than flapping, he circled the room a couple of times and then made for Shadow. He landed softly on her shoulder, chirped in her ear, and then looked at the others.

'Yes, definitely intelligent,' said Alemrae. 'Perhaps you should look through Kai's books and see what she has in relation to magic and familiars. You should also check out the palace library as well.'

'Interesting colouration—bronze above and blue beneath the wings,' said Morannel. 'Is that the normal colour for them?'

'The bronzing, yes. The blue, no. They are usually a light reddish colour beneath,' said Shadow. 'At least that is what I have been told.' She blushed and looked at Rad. 'It's for attracting a harem apparently.' Then she laughed, a delighted, silvery laugh. 'No, there are no females for you around here, Rad. We shall see . . . at some point, I expect.'

'Interesting, only hearing one side of the conversation, don't you think, Morannel? You had better be careful about that, Shadow—people will say you've gone mad talking to yourself like that,' said Alemrae, who then laughed.

Shadow gave him a surprised look. 'I was not aware that I was talking out loud,' she said.

'What is all the noise about?' queried Kai. The others jumped up, startled. Then they all tried to speak at once. Rad screeched. Kai appeared surprised by the noise and then had a closer look at Shadow. 'You have your miniature dragon, have you?' she asked with a smile. She held out her hand. 'Feel free to bite, if you wish,' she said. Rad flew to Kai and landed on her hand. He sniffed and then bit softly just enough to break the skin of a finger and taste her blood. 'Taste good, don't I?' she said to Rad.

Rad looked up at her and nodded, eyes wide, as if astonished. Then he flew back to Shadow. 'He is . . . confused,' Shadow said wonderingly. 'Why are you confused, Rad? No wings? Of course, she doesn't have wings. She isn't supposed to have wings . . . Oh, I see you think it would be better if she did have wings. How can you do that? Give her wings, I mean . . . Magic? I should have known. It's always magic with you, isn't it?' she said, giving Rad a light stroke on the side of his long neck.

'I don't need wings, Rad. Now, is there anything at all to eat around here?' asked Kai.

'Actually, it is past time for the evening meal. I wonder what the hold-up is,' said Frederick.

'I shall go and find out,' said Morannel. 'In the meantime, there is a little food left on the sideboard, Kai.'

Morannel then left, accompanied by Alemrae. Kai moved to the sideboard and heaped a plate full of greens and bread, there being no meat left. Then she sat at the table and began to devour it.

'Mistress, forgive me, but what will my duties be?' asked Frederick.

Kai paused in her eating. 'Call me Kai. Your duties are simple. Do what is needed of you. Obey your instructions. Otherwise, be yourself. Your slavery is not meant to be demeaning of your spirit—it is just for the assurance of your behaviour,' said Kai.

'Thank you. I shall strive to meet your needs to the best of my abilities,' said Frederick.

'Then you shall do well, from all that I have heard about you,' replied Kai. 'Now, let me eat.'

Prince Morannel and Alemrae went in search of a servant or the guards. None of whom were to be found on the top two floors of the palace. Something was obviously very wrong. They made their way down to the first floor before finding anyone. Morannel called to the servant, who was hurrying towards the far end of the corridor. The servant stopped, turned, and yelled, 'Sorry, Highness—emergency—must run.' And that is what he proceeded to do, going through the door at the end of the corridor.

Alemrae said, 'That was very strange. Let's go find out what this emergency is.' They strode off the other way, towards the stairs leading to the ground floor. There was a mass of people at the foot of the stairs, some talking, some yelling; people were coming and going in a rush.

'What has happened?' yelled Prince Morannel. 'Quiet! Let me know, now! Whatever has happened, it is mine to deal with.'

One of the servants came running up the stairs.

'Highness, Almarac is under attack.'

CHAPTER 15

'What are you saying? What is happening?' demanded Prince Morannel.

'The people are fleeing, trying to come here,' the servant answered breathlessly. 'Regent Monfrae and the inner council are dealing with the populace. We are all under orders to assist.'

'Here are my orders. Go to the kitchens and get food enough for six and take it up to Aunt Kai's rooms. When you get there, pass on the news and tell them we will be with them shortly. Now, where are my uncle and the inner council?' said Prince Morannel.

'They are at the palace gates, my lord,' said the servant.

'Thank you. Go and do what I have asked. Then be about your duties,' said the prince. 'Alemrae, come!'

The prince, followed by Alemrae, left the palace and headed for the front gate.

'My lords, what news?' shouted Prince Morannel when they had arrived at the gate.

'A messenger just in. The undead have attacked Almarac—no large numbers yet. The populace are en route here. No news about your sister yet, but she should have already left. The soldiers and guards are mounting a rear defence to hold back the undead,' said one of the lords.

'Begin the defence of the pass,' said the prince. 'Move our soldiers and guards to the rim. Start sending up barrels of oil and spare armour and weapons. Stockpile all we have. Create a base camp at the foot of the mountain pass. We can transfer men and supplies from there. Begin immediately. I suggest we also send our light cavalry and the horse archers by boat to somewhere north of Almarac. They can join up with whatever horse units Almarac has left. Order them to do a roaming defence. Have them lead the undead away from Almarac if they can—they can live off the land. Only engage the undead when absolutely necessary. It will be a delaying tactic. The more they can spread the undead out over the great plain between Almarac and the ruins of Albrae, the better. We need them to give us as much time as they can. Have them split into small groups once they have succeeded in luring the undead away from Almarac—ten or fifteen men per group. We can't use them at the pass. This way, they can assist us and be of use. I don't intend for it to be a death sentence. They are not to risk themselves and are to fight only when necessary or if it is reasonably safe to do so. I will go to inform the Lady Kai. She may have further instructions.'

Prince Morannel and Alemrae headed back into the palace at a run. By the time they had reached the third floor, Morannel was out of breath. Alemrae, on the other hand, was barely breathing any harder than before. They entered the room to find the food Morannel had asked for already in place. The others were seated around the table and already eating.

'Bad news, I'm afraid. The undead have attacked Almarac. Their populace is already on their way here. The troops in Almarac are going to try a retreating defence for the length of the pass. We are sending men to assist in both the evacuation and the defence. No word yet of my sister,' summarised Prince Morannel.

'The regent and the inner council can handle the defence. We shall leave tomorrow or the day after at the latest. We ride for Ulmarin,' stated Kai.

Alemrae went to the sideboard and took some food and sat down to eat, and Morannel followed suit.

They slept that night, but it was an uneasy rest for all of them. Thoughts of the coming troubles and their journey to who knows where ahead of them. The problems of searching for the lost races kept Kai awake for a long time. When she finally did sleep, her dreams were troubled, of vague disturbances, and an amorphous shadow covering the unknown. Then her nightmare: she relived the horrid moment of Brelldan's death and her inability to act, of being surrounded by undead and slowly torn apart, again and again and again.

She woke up and sat bolt upright, shaking with intense fear. Suddenly, Alemrae was there, holding her, whispering all would be well. She collapsed back into a deep sleep and did not dream for the rest of the night.

When she awoke the next morning, she was troubled. She barely remembered her dreams. Only the nightmare stood out and her reaction to it. *How did Alemrae come to be there? And where is he now?* She decided to get up and check on the rest of her group, but, first, she went out and sat on the balcony overlooking the bay. Shadow was there, sitting on one of the chairs, Rad on her shoulder. They were watching the bay and conversing silently with each other apparently, as they would turn their heads and look at each other occasionally. Rad would sometimes rub his head against Shadow's cheek and neck affectionately.

Rad turned and looked at Kai and then squawked softly. 'Good morning, Kai,' said Shadow, not looking in her direction. 'I hope you slept better than me. I kept having these horrendous nightmares involving the death of my Rad here. I finally decided to stay awake the rest of the night and just watch the bay. Your own sleep was troubled, I gather?'

'Yes, I suspect we all had a rough night. Wake the others, Shadow. We must talk. I believe we should leave as soon as possible,' commanded Kai.

Shadow went inside and began moving through the rooms and waking the others. They all met in the main room. Kai ordered some food readied and then spoke to them. 'I believe our restless night was given to us by our enemy, whoever that is. We are planning to do something that they do not want us doing, and they are trying to impede our progress, even if it is only by causing sleep deprivation. We are on the right track. We will go to Ulmarin first and then head due north to that dwarven mine in the mountains I found reference to. What we find there will determine our next move. We shall break our fast and get ready to leave at once. We can delay no longer.'

They all went to their rooms to get ready whilst they waited for their food to arrive. Kai sent messages to Regent Monfrae and the Lord Chamberlain. Once they had eaten, they headed down to the front of the palace to find that Kai's requests had been fulfilled. Horses and supplies were waiting for them in the courtyard.

'Morannel, Shadow will have had no experience in riding. Stay by her side and instruct her as we go. Frederick, stay near them and provide assistance should they need it. We will not be travelling at speed yet.'

As they prepared to mount, a disturbance at the gate drew their attention. A cavalcade rode through. It was Captain Gregorson and his men. With them was Morannel's sister, Zephranthe.

'Captain Gregorson, sorry about this, but you shall all be coming with us. We are leaving as soon as you can swap horses and get more supplies. We are heading for Ulmarin. Lady Zephranthe, pleased to meet you. I am your aunt Kai. We are going to take you to Ulmarin for your safety. You will stay with your mother's family until the present troubles are over. If we don't succeed in our task, then you will be the last of the ruling family. I know you are young for it, but you have your training at the college to help you. It will be your duty to ensure the safety of as many as you can. Rule well.'

It took time for the change of horses and gathering of supplies for Captain Gregorson and his men. It was closer to midday than Kai liked before they managed to leave. Morannel spent the extra time instructing Shadow how to ride. At last, it was time for them to leave the city.

CHAPTER 16

They left at a walk, and when it was time to eat, they continued on, consuming their meal whilst riding. There was a lot of traffic on the road. It slowed them down somewhat, and Kai was getting impatient. She decided to pick up the pace. Using the techniques she had learnt from Brelldan in Albrae—trotting, walking, and leading the horses, as well as swapping mounts from time to time—they were able to increase their pace. They continued moving until well after sunset and were off again before dawn. The people on the road gave way to the heavily armed group passing them.

They made it to Ulmarin without incident in just under four days. They were stopped at the gates to the city by the guards. Kai proclaimed the presence of Prince Morannel and Princess Zephranthe. Messages were sent ahead to the palace whilst the group was escorted by guards. It took quite a long time to get to the palace from the gate. The local populace came out to watch the procession. Such a diverse group under guard had not been seen in the city for a very long time, and rumour had it that the prince and princess, whom they had never seen, were part of it. Extra guards sent by the palace to ensure their rapid passage through the city caught up to them. They opened up the crowd and let them increase their pace.

Ulmarin was a beautiful city and well planned out. The rulers had spent much of their income on rebuilding works, cisterns, and the removal of refuse from the city streets. The streets were well paved and kept in good repair, allowing for good traffic flow through the city. The docks and associated shipyards were also well funded. The citizens, however, were a bit more slovenly than was expected. The cost of food was much higher than in Raelis, and there was a much greater divide between the rich and the poor. Taxes were higher and wages were, in general, lower. The greed of the wealthy was on show. The merchant class was akin to nobility here. In all, it was a good place to live if you had wealth. If you didn't, it wasn't. Kai noticed the injustice of it all, and even though it was not her place, she was determined to make a difference.

They arrived at the palace to a fanfare of trumpets. The guards, resplendent in their regalia, and the lords and ladies of the realm dressed in their finery made a spectacular sight. But the display of wealth on show after the state of the commons made it seem overtly extreme. At the front of the group stood the city state's rulers, Prince Morannel's grandparents: King Darian and Queen Elspeth. Prince Morannel rode to the fore.

'I am Prince Morannel!' he exclaimed. 'Those with me are as follows: Lady Kai, the Briar Rose of Albrae and my aunt; Princess Zephranthe, my sister; the Lady Shadow, a daughter of the desert; Alemrae Traemellin, my protector; and Capt. Geoffrey Gregorson, also my bodyguard. The other guards are my personal retinue and that of my sister. We require your assistance, both in matters of state and personal care. Have rooms prepared for us, for we have journeyed from Raelis in four days. Our nations face an emergency the likes of which we have never seen. Aunt Kai and I shall explain as soon as we have been able to refresh ourselves.'

He then dismounted, as did the others of the group. Handing his reins over to a waiting servant, he stepped forward to greet his grandparents for the first time. 'I am sorry that we have not yet been able to make your acquaintance. The political differences you share with my uncle, the regent of Raelis, must be put aside. I may not be here for long, but whilst I am, I intend for us to get to know one another and become a true and loving family,' said Morannel.

'We welcome you to our home, Prince and Princess,' said King Darian. 'You may stay for as long as you wish—your aunt and friends as well. We shall have a celebration to mark your arrival tomorrow night. There will be many wanting to meet you in the coming weeks. A series of small dinners and balls will be used to allow them the opportunity. Come, let us see you settled. We shall meet you all after breakfast tomorrow. We have much to organise before then.'

They were escorted deep within the labyrinth that was the Palace of Ulmarin. It was certain that they would require servants to escort them from place to place during their stay, for the size of the palace was daunting. It was easily five times the size of the palace in Raelis and with more levels, both above and below ground. The palace occupied the summit of a large hill and had grown down the sides and into the core of the hill over the centuries of its existence. Some parts were almost in ruin. Builders, along with the architects and engineers, were working on reclaiming the currently unusable sections.

After they had been shown their rooms, the group assembled in a small dining hall for the midday meal. The hall would comfortably hold fifty guests. The food on offer was plentiful, if not the best available. Shadow found it difficult to follow her strict regime. Almost every dish had something that she was forbidden by her oaths to consume. Morannel came to her aid by requesting a greater selection of breads and juices than what was currently on offer.

When the meal was almost over, Morannel suggested to the servants that they take the food when they were done and have their own meal using the leftovers. There would certainly be enough to go around. The servants were almost overwhelmed by his generosity.

Back in their room, discussion raged over how they could take their leave without further damaging the poor relationship between Raelis and Ulmarin. They came to no conclusion. They needed to talk with King Darian and Queen Elspeth first. More discussions after the evening meal also led nowhere. Frustration was mounting amongst them, and so they retired early.

The next morning, when the time came for the formal introduction of Prince Morannel and the others, they were escorted in a more deferential manner than they had been on the way in. It seemed that the servants had a bone to pick with their masters and did so in ways that were not obvious. The hall they were led to had obviously been ornate once but now was looking decidedly the worse for wear. King Darian and Queen Elspeth were sitting on a couple of antique lounging beds, enjoying the exotic fruits in the bowls beside them. Nothing of the like had been offered to their guests.

'My king and queen, may I please introduce to you my companions?' asked Prince Morannel. 'Shadow, a daughter of the Irikani desert; Alemrae and Capt. Geoffrey Gregorson, my bodyguards; my cousin Frederick; my sister, the princess Zephranthe; and this young beauty beside me is actually my aunt Kai. She happens to be eighteen years my senior. It is she who carried the dire news that has alarmed the nations of the known world.'

'That is quite enough, Prince Morannel,' said Kai. 'King Darian, the news I bring is catastrophic. Albrae has been overrun by undead. The nation has ceased to exist.'

'My lady, the loss of Albrae means nothing to us. Little of our trade comes from there. I doubt very much if a few undead in that heathen land will worry us here at all. As long as the trade from the south and east remains, we shall continue to prosper and enhance the beauty of our city,' said the king.

'King Darian, you are gravely mistaken. The loss of Albrae will very much impact upon you. Albrae was attacked a little over two months ago. Since then, we have begun to form a defensive coalition based in Raelis. Five days ago, the undead struck at Almarac. We had not heard the outcome of that sortie when we left Raelis to come here. Princess Zephranthe will stay here with you for her own safety. The rest of our group will undertake to find support in other areas. We cannot afford to lengthen our stay. We must continue in our search for assistance, wherever that takes us. Raelis has undertaken to create a defensive line, holding the entire length of the pass to Almarac. When we left Raelis, citizens of Almarac had already begun to come through the pass. Any and all assistance that you can muster should be sent to Raelis.'

'And just why should we send any assistance to Raelis!' shouted King Darian. 'They have done nothing but seek to harm the alliance I formed with King Gedry.'

'Your alliance still stands, in the form of Prince Morannel and Princess Zephranthe. Your political differences need to be put aside for the greater good,' said Kai forcefully. 'The stake of the known world depends upon it. I don't think you understand the significance of what I have told you. Albrae, all its citizens—five hundred thousand men women and children—are dead. Their army rode out to confront the undead and were slaughtered. I happened to be in Albrae at the time. I am one of the few who managed to escape. The undead host is large enough to swallow every nation of man if we don't work together. If they get through the pass from Almarac, then Raelis and Ulmarin are doomed, as will be every other living thing on this continent. The continent of Tir is no safe haven either. There is a land bridge in the far north, across which the undead will pass once they have finished with this side. The mountains to our north are deemed unpassable, yet there are enough undead to find a passage through. If they come, how will you stand? Your defences are slight. I suggest that you commit all your resources to helping Raelis with whatever they need, primarily food, weapons, armour, and as many men as you have.'

'We shall discuss these matters at council next week. Until then, you will join us at the forthcoming events in the honour of our prince and princess, who have finally returned home. I bid you good day,' said King Darian coldly.

At that, Kai left, followed by Prince Morannel and the others. Once they were back in their room, she let out her anger and frustration in a torrid burst of vituperation. They had been escorted by guards who remained posted by the door to their rooms. They were in effect hostage to the king's wishes.

'It will not be the king you must convince but the Privy Council and the Council of Merchants,' suggested Alemrae. 'They are the ones who truly manage this city and its coffers. Get them onside, and the king will fold. To do that, you will need to play host to all of them at these functions the king has orchestrated. I know we cannot really afford the time from our search, but this must be done, and with the guards on our door, I don't see another alternative. If we fail to get Ulmarin to assist Raelis, there will be no point in doing anything else, for the continents will fall.'

CHAPTER 17

When the others left, Princess Zephranthe decided to stay with the king and queen. At first, she spoke to them in a conciliatory tone and tried to gently impress upon them the seriousness of the situation.

'Aunt Kai is correct. I was in Almarac when the undead struck. They came out of nowhere. It took the combined might of all the forces there to defend the city for one day. The populace fled to the pass, looking for safety. I went with them, along with the few guards that we brought with us. The numbers of undead I saw were overwhelming, and according to Kai, what I saw was only a small fraction of the entire horde. I can assist you with determining what can be done. Organisational ability is my strength. I beg you to allow me to assist.'

'I am sure that the congress of merchants shall know what must be done,' said the queen.

'The congress of merchants will look to profit from the turmoil, nothing else,' said Princess Zephranthe. 'It is up to the two of you, as well as my brother and me, to lead the way. You have lost your nation's respect. Now you must do what is needed to regain it. I may be young, but I have been taught well the needs of a country and how to rule it properly. You have made a fine mess of things with your inattention and by allowing the Council of Merchants and the Privy Council to rule in your place.'

'She is right, my dear,' said the king. 'We must seek to survive this mess before it overwhelms us all. I will begin to change things at the next meeting of the Privy Council.'

'Why wait? Release a proclamation! Your word is law. You need not wait upon others to make your decisions for you. Tell them what to do! If they refuse, remove them from office, confiscate all of their assets and holdings, and use what you get to finance the aid that Raelis requires,' pleaded Zephranthe. 'Whilst you're at it, divest the Council of Merchants from all monetary control in the city. The funds are yours to use, not theirs. Have a respected moneylender go over the books to ensure that they are correct. If they are not, then I suggest that you have the funds of the entire Council of Merchants taken and put into the treasury. I hope you realise that most of the wealth in this city belongs to the members of the Council of Merchants, and that includes what is in your royal treasury.'

Meanwhile, Kai had gathered the others together. 'When we leave here, we shall head north. There is a dwarven mine almost due north of here, just slightly to the west, in the mountains. I am hoping to find it and evidence that will lead us to where the dwarves have gone. It has become much more urgent that we find them. We need supplies and perhaps a guide who knows the area of the mountains that we need. Alemrae, go into the city and find the guide we require, and also some supplies. You have travelled much and are the most likely to be able to obtain all that we may need. Take Frederick with you. Captain Gregorson, see to the men. Ensure that some stay as bodyguards to Princess Zephranthe. The rest can go back to Raelis. I will leave it up to you as to how many will stay. I intend on making our stay here as brief as possible. I want to be ready to leave as soon as we can.'

Captain Gregorson, Alemrae, and Frederick left, servants showing them the way and guards tailing them. Shadow took Rad into her room and tried to teach him a complex game with sticks and pebbles. She did not have much success. Rad kept trying to use magic to cheat. 'Magic is not allowed,' she told him. Rad tossed his head and turned his back. Games weren't fun if he could not use magic.

Shadow laughed and then reached out and took Rad in her hands and kissed his neck. 'Oh, you are a funny little lizard,' she said, and when Rad rubbed his head against her cheek, she relented. 'OK, you win. You can use magic.'

Rad jumped back onto the bed and started the sticks and pebbles twirling with magic. They came together in the image of a man, who proceeded to walk around the bed. He walked to the edge of the bed and appeared to look over the edge. He then turned back to face Rad and shook his head. Rad nodded in return. The stickman shook his head again. Rad croaked, and the stickman flew backwards off the bed and crashed onto the floor, separating into many pieces.

'I think you broke it, Rad,' said Shadow, glancing over the edge at the mess on the floor. Rad gambolled over to the edge and peered over and then looked up at Shadow and nodded. Then Rad walked over to Shadow and climbed up onto her lap. Shadow lay back on the bed and caressed Rad until they both fell asleep.

Kai and Morannel were alone in the main room of their complex. Morannel was telling Kai of his practice sessions with Frederick and Alemrae. He had been annoyed that all they worked on was defence.

'Defence is everything,' said Kai. 'If your defence is strong, then their attack will become weak. It is at this point that you can determine when and where you should strike. If you attack without learning to defend, then you leave yourself open to their response. If you defend well, you can open a hole in their attack through which you may strike. The purpose of the training is to accustom the body to moving without thought. If you have to think about what to do, then you are slowed down. By training your muscles to remember what to do, you can react without thought.'

'So it is a matter of training one's mind not to think so your body may react to what you can see?' Morannel asked.

'To a point. It is sometimes necessary to react to things you cannot see, only feel or hear. Too much reliance on sight can also leave you susceptible to attack. Learn to feel what is around you. Trust all of your senses and use them all. Once you can learn to do that, even a little, then we can start to teach you to attack. You have a lot to learn in little time. Perhaps to begin with, you should learn to shoot a bow. That may prove much more beneficial in the long run—you can also hunt with it. Alemrae can teach you,' said Kai. 'Since we are going to be here awhile, we may as well put the time to good use.'

As dusk approached, Captain Gregorson returned. 'Eight men will stay and guard Princess Zephranthe. The rest will return to Raelis,' he said. 'I have heard some rumours. There has been some unusual activity in the mountains to the north. The one who told me could not tell me anymore, but a strange light has occasionally flashed from the top of the highest peak.'

'That could be something or it could be nothing. We shall just have to be aware of what is happening around us when we travel into the mountains. You have done well, Captain. Thank you,' said Kai.

Not long after, Alemrae and Frederick returned, followed by a number of servants lugging the extra supplies that Alemrae thought that they would need.

'I have found us a guide,' said Alemrae. 'When we decide to go, he will join us outside the main gate. There have been some unusual sightings, by hunters and the like, in the mountains to the north. Bands of humanoids, mostly man-sized with some larger than man-sized, in small numbers, are roaming the region. Also, strange flashes of light have been seen coming from the area of the highest peak. Possibly some form of magic. It's hard to tell. The descriptions have all been vague. One of the mountains farther back in the range appears to be smoking. It may be a volcano, either active or dormant. It may even be close to erupting. It could become quite dangerous for us all up there, and that's aside from the scattering of monsters that usually roam the hills hereabouts. We shall have to be careful in our travels.'

'Captain Gregorson also gave us warning of strange happenings in the hills to the north. We shall be doubly on our guard when we leave. Now we must make ready for this ridiculous ball that we have to attend,' remarked Kai.

The ball that night was a magnificent fiasco. All those invited, of course, turned up dressed in their best. Except for the guests of honour. They were dressed in their everyday travelling clothes. They stood out in the throng. The food provided was sumptuous but cold. The musicians played very well, but the conversation was rather lacking in anything that even remotely sounded like polite banter. They were all harangued at tedious length by whoever could grab their attention. Everyone was at pains, it seemed, to point out that they were the only ones who would be able to help with the current crises, and how much they would like to do so, if only they could; alas, with such and such doing this or that, it would only be after whenever this other thing happened that they would be able to do anything. In all, no one would actually agree to do anything.

Shadow had acquired quite a large group of admirers, or rather Rad had, and Rad stayed with Shadow. Shadow was bombarded with questions about Rad—so many and so quickly that she couldn't answer one before the next was asked. Tiring of the noise, Shadow made her way to the buffet. Prince Morannel joined her there. Shadow let Rad climb down onto the table, where he made straight for the meat trays. He sat there munching his way through the various selections, occasionally burping.

'Enjoying yourself, aren't you, Rad?' said Shadow, picking up a plate and beginning to load it with food. Rad climbed back up Shadow to sit on her shoulder, and he warbled softly into her ear. Morannel, who had already filled a plate, guided Shadow to the seats at the edge of the room. There, they sat and ate, watching the crowd swirl around as if trying to tie itself in a knot.

Alemrae moved through the crowd as if it did not exist. He passed by people, who would barely realise he was there before he had moved on. Frederick proved to be in his element. This was the sort of thing he was used to, and enjoyed. The political manoeuvrings of the upper classes were his bread and butter. He probably gained as much information from each of the various members of the Council of Merchants and Privy Council as they gained from him.

Kai, on the other hand, hated these sorts of gatherings. She dealt with them all in the straight-faced way she had of dealing with anyone. She told the truth and cared not for the opinions of the rich and spoiled rabble. When asked to dance by one young buffoon, she replied, 'I only dance to the ring of steel, and I see none here who could accompany me, nor keep up, for that matter.' She walked away, with her hands resting on the hilts of her daggers, leaving him alone and confused.

She found Shadow and Prince Morannel at the side of the room. 'Come, it is time to take our leave. Let's get the others and get out of here.'

CHAPTER 18

It took four weeks of political wrangling, debate, and intimidation before the Privy Council and the Council of Merchants buckled to the throne. Frederick and Princess Zephranthe made a formidable team. Between them, they discovered and eliminated each and every threat, turning those responsible into firm believers in the action of the throne or into paupers. The city slowly responded to the firm rule they were being shown. Raelis would receive the full support of the city and whatever aid they needed. The guards were finally removed from their rooms.

News from Raelis and Almarac had come through during their stay. The first attack on Almarac had been repulsed, and no further attacks had eventuated. Almarac had been evacuated except for military personnel. The mounted troops sent from Raelis had used Almarac as a base for three weeks before the second wave of undead approached. Then they had ridden out, scattering across the land, trying to entice the undead to move away from Almarac. To a large extent, they were successful. Few undead came upon the city, and for quite a while, the soldiers left in Almarac were able to destroy them with relative ease.

The pass between Almarac and Raelis was still in the process of being fortified when the largest body of undead to be seen in the local area encompassed Almarac. The few soldiers left in the city had managed to escape and flee up the pass, giving those on guard there plenty of warning. The first of seventeen gated walls across the pass had been completed. The others were still under construction, but it was reported that they should be completed by the time it came necessary to defend them. It would cost the undead plenty to bring down each barrier across the pass. No further word from the cavalry had been received.

Their final day in Ulmarin went by fast. By late afternoon, with their goodbyes all said, they retired to their chambers. 'Let us take our evening meal and have an early night. We are to be ready to leave the palace and be at the city gate at dawn,' Kai said.

The servants brought food for them, food of better quality than what they had eaten earlier in their stay. They also brought enough breads and juices to satisfy Shadow's requirements. Once again, Prince Morannel told the servants to finish off what they themselves could not eat. The servants thanked Morannel for his generosity.

'Please organise a breakfast for us two hours before dawn,' said Prince Morannel. 'And send someone ahead to ensure we are awakened in time. You can also share whatever is left after our breakfast.'

The following morning, they were awoken and served their breakfast well before dawn. They were mounted and riding towards the city gate by the time the sun rose. The gates opened just as they arrived, and they rode through. They stopped on the side of the road to await their guide. The guide rode towards them from the line of trees to the north.

Alemrae went to meet him and brought him to the group. 'This is our guide, Lakira Terino, and he is the only hunter to regularly go deep into the mountains—most will only skirt the edges.'

Kai spoke. 'I am Kai, and I lead this group, and before you say anything, I am older than I look. The others are Shadow, Prince Morannel, Capt. Geoffrey Gregorson, Frederick, and you already know Alemrae. When we are away from the road, I will tell you what I need you to do for us.'

'Follow me, then, Kai. I shall find you a secluded spot so that you can tell me what I need to know. Then I will tell you how much it will cost.' Lakira rode off through the trees, followed by the others.

They rode quietly for about an hour before they came to a small clearing. 'Few people come this far into the forest. We should not be disturbed by anyone. The bears may be another matter, but I do not expect them to come by. They should be finding places to hole up in, as winter is closing in.'

'This will do,' Kai replied. 'We are in search of the lost races: the Elves, Dwarves, and Halflings. I found reference to a dwarven mine in the mountains, almost due north of Ulmarin. Do you know of it, and can you guide us to it?'

'Aye, lady, I have seen the entrance. It will take us four days to travel to the mountains from here and at least three, possibly four, to get to the mountain you require—longer if we have to side-track. There are many small bands of orcs and ogres in that area. The numbers have been increasing for some time now. It may be difficult to find a way through without a fight. The last valley before we get to the mountain will certainly be occupied.'

'We can deal with a fight or two. We have four experienced fighters and two with us capable of some magic. That does not include you. I would expect that you are quite handy if it comes to that,' said Kai.

'Right you are, Kai. You need not worry about me. My price is thus: ten drac a day, twice that in the mountains, and I get to loot the bodies of anything we kill,' said Lakira.

'I will see that you receive twice that, and any loot shall be split evenly between us all,' said Kai. 'Oh, and we shall need to burn the bodies if at all possible.'

'That may prove a hindrance. Others in the area will certainly come looking for the cause of the smoke,' said Lakira.

'I may be able to do something about that,' said Shadow. 'Let me think on it.'

'You will have plenty of time. It is going to be a few days before we get to that,' said Lakira. 'Shall we get going, then? There is a remote cabin that we may be able to use for the night. It is a long way from here, but if we get a move on, we should make it by nightfall.'

Lakira mounted his steed and led the way, going in a slightly west of north direction. The tracks and trails he followed meandered through the forest, going northwards and westwards. At times, the forest was so thick that there was barely any trail to follow; at others, they could ride four abreast.

They stopped at midday to eat and let the horses graze in a small meadow. Some discussion arose as to how the horses would do in the mountains. 'There is a small outpost for trappers and furriers in the foothills. We can leave the mounts there and proceed on foot,' said Lakira. 'If we have to go around some areas, it may be easier to do so by climbing.'

At the smell of food, Rad made an appearance. He had been sleeping in one of the saddlebags on Shadow's mount. He flew across the clearing to Shadow, much to the surprise of Lakira. 'Now there's something that you don't see every day—a lizard flying. Best be careful that the birds don't see it, or they'll try to eat it,' he said.

Shadow retrieved some meat for Rad and let him feed himself. When they mounted up again, Rad flew to Shadow's shoulder and stayed there. The sun was just setting when they made it to the cabin. It was little more than four log walls and a thatched roof, but it would be more comfortable than out in the open in the days ahead.

'We shall mount guards tonight and each night forthwith,' said Kai. 'Two at a time. Prince Morannel and Shadow, if you could take the first shift. Alemrae and Lakira, the second. Frederick and I will take the third. Captain Gregorson, you will rest tonight. You will have the first and last watch tomorrow night. We will cycle through this order each night—one of us will have a night of complete rest, followed by two shifts the next night—unless something unforeseeable happens. Shadow, if you will help me to prepare tonight's meal, the others can see to the horses and do a quick sweep around the area. By the time they are done, the meal should be ready. Once we have eaten, we shall get some rest, whilst those on guard duty protect us. Wake the next pair after two hours have passed.'

The night was quiet. Everyone slept well, and there were no disturbances to alert the guards. Kai was difficult to awaken when it was time for her watch; she was soundly asleep, dreaming. Alemrae finally managed to wake her with some effort.

'You have been hard to wake,' Alemrae said.

'That is unusual. I normally wake easily,' she replied, yawning hugely.

'Perhaps it was the dream you had,' suggested Alemrae.

'Perhaps. It was a strange but fascinating dream, both poignant and disturbing,' said Kai. 'I was in a forest, at night. The forest was ancient, primordial. The trees were immense, and there was a feeling of peace about it, a peace that I have never known. There was a flash of colour between the trees, and as I approached, I saw a clearing. There was a girl there. She had what I thought was the most extraordinarily red cloak about her. Then the cloak unfolded into a pair of magnificent wings—she was naked. She leapt up and flew into the sky. I went with her. She flew above the trees, high into the sky. The forest stretched out far below. To the far north, I thought I saw a hint of the ocean. To the east, the sun was beginning to rise. Light blossomed around us. It fell upon the girl and lit her up in a majestic beauty, and she was dazzlingly beautiful. She hung there in the sky, enjoying the moment, but I sensed something about her, a feeling of profound sorrow, as if something was missing and had been missing for a long time. She slowly spiralled her way back down into the clearing. Someone was waiting there for her. She looked up, and I saw her face for the first time. Her eyes . . . her eyes were an emerald green. They were a colour I have only ever seen once before. In Brelldan. She had Brelldan's eyes. How could this be? He is dead. He had no children.'

'The mind can play many tricks on you, but perhaps you saw what you needed to see. A vast and peaceful forest with an ocean to the north. I have heard rumours of a land far to the south, across the southern ocean. A land covered by forest, with few safe places to land a ship. A steep and rugged coastline. The rumours have always been vague. As if the instigator did not believe what had been told them. Few ships built these days could sail to where this land is supposed to be, so far to the south. It could be that refuge of the elves that you have been seeking. The child you saw with Brelldan's eyes—it could be your psyche responding to your need for something of him. You have not yet had the time to mourn him properly, and you may be regretting not having had his child. Her wings may be a symbol of freedom, the possibility of escaping all that has troubled you. Try not to dwell on it. It's your watch. Keep your mind on the job at hand, although it has been a peaceful night. I'll see you in the morning,' said Alemrae, who then retired to his bedding.

Kai went outside to where Frederick was on guard. 'I'll cover the other side. Slowly circle your way around, move anticlockwise, and I'll do the same. We wake the others at the first hint of dawn. I want us to be on the move by the time the sun is fully up,' she said.

Dawn crept up on them, but they were on the move quickly. They travelled for an hour before stopping to break their fast. 'Any thoughts about your dream?' queried Alemrae softly.

'No, nothing. It was just unusual, that's all,' said Kai. 'You may be right, though. I have not had time to mourn, and someone may be guiding my dreams to show me where to go. I followed a dream once. It led me to Tir, all those years ago. So why not follow one to this forest? But after we have found the dwarves—they still must come first.'

'Agreed to that, since we are already on our way,' said Alemrae.

They moved on shortly after. It would be another three days of travel before they made it to the outpost in the foothills. They arrived late in the afternoon. By the time they had done all the business they needed to do, it was too late to continue on.

'We shall stay here this night and leave in the morning. I want the sun well up before we leave. We should be relatively safe here. One guard only on watch tonight. Change at the normal interval. I want as many rested up as possible. It will be much more dangerous from here on in,' said Kai.

'I will take the first watch tonight,' said Alemrae. 'I will wake Frederick when it is his turn to watch.'

Everyone was relaxed, and they had a pleasant evening. They talked about the coming difficulties that the mountains might provide and how they would surmount them. Slowly, they sought their beds, until only Shadow and Alemrae were still awake.

'Kai is still unaware of her condition, isn't she?' Shadow asked Alemrae.

'Yes,' he replied. 'But not for much longer, I think. She has been putting on some extra weight—her clothes are becoming tighter. Her balance is also changing as her centre of gravity is lowering. She will notice that first, I think. Especially if she has to fight.'

'Keep an eye on her, then. Protect her when she needs it,' said Shadow. 'I will rest now.'

Alemrae kept watch. He did not sleep that night. He woke the others just after dawn. Kai was furious that he had stayed awake. 'I need little sleep, and you wanted as many to be as well rested as possible. Besides, it gave me time to think,' he said.

Before they left, Shadow cut down a small tree and cut off its branches to make a walking staff. Rad decided to help her. As she trimmed the branches and bark off the trunk, it became drier and harder. By the time she had finished, she had a stout staff that could be easily turned into a weapon if need be.

'Thank you, Rad. That was my intention all along. How kind of you to speed up the process,' she said.

They walked off, Lakira taking the lead, moving directly towards the mountains, with the smoking peak ahead of them. Clouds gathered about the peaks, thick and dark.

'That looks ominous,' said Lakira. 'Storm or snow is my bet—could be both. Should not affect us down here, though. Would hate to be up there right now.'

They spent the day wriggling their way up through the valleys, coming ever closer to the storm raging about the peaks. 'We need to start to look for shelter,' Lakira reasoned. 'That may be upon us shortly.'

A small cave at the bottom of a cliff gave them just enough room to get out of the weather. 'Hope this blows over soon,' said Frederick. 'I don't fancy spending the night in this cramped little cave.'

'That's okay. It will be less cramped in here for us when you are standing guard out there in the rain,' Kai said with a smile.

'Rad says that there is magic in this,' Shadow stated. 'Lots of magic.'

The storm blew out within the hour, and they made their way out into a much changed landscape. The land was drenched. Rivulets raced down the hillsides, and some snow covered the higher regions. Little moved.

'We will be easily seen. Nothing is moving around out here, except for us. We shall need to take extra care not to be surprised with a visit tonight,' said Lakira. 'Bands of orcs were seen not far from here. Keep close.'

They made camp before dark. It was a cold camp. They could not afford the risk a fire would present. They were barely settled in when there was an almighty bang with an accompanying flash of light. The ground trembled. Lightning struck the top of the smoking peak, again and again and again.

'Magic, more magic,' stated Shadow. 'That is one powerful mage up there!'

'We won't be able to sleep for a while. Let's move on,' suggested Kai. 'Lakira, scout ahead. Leave a trail for Alemrae to follow. We will move out in a few minutes, to give you time.'

Lakira moved off, and they followed a while later. Alemrae followed signs the others could not see. They moved slowly in the darkness, trying to make little noise. Alemrae halted them and signalled to take cover, not that there was much cover to be had. Lakira appeared in a hurry. 'There is a large group of orcs heading this way. It looks like they have already tangled with something tonight. Most have injuries. Do we take them or hide?'

'Hide,' stated Kai. 'At the top of the ridge. If they come for us, we hit them with everything. Arrows first.'

They arranged themselves at the ridgetop, those with bows, arrows knocked, aiming over their comrades. Then the orcs appeared.

CHAPTER 19

Fifteen orcs rounded the rocky outcrop lower down. The first glanced towards the ridge and, seeing the group, yelled. Then they charged up the slope. Arrows flew. The four leading orcs all dropped, but the others came on.

Another round of arrows and two more orcs fell, and then they were too close for bows. Frederick leapt forward, shield forward, and rammed into the leading orc, his sword finding flesh in the second. Shadow swung her staff to the head of the orc Frederick had knocked over, ending its existence. Her staff swung up in time to block a blow delivered by another. Morannel ploughed into it, his sword making short work of the job. He spun and found another, sword ringing as metal struck metal. Alemrae, Kai, and Lakira passed them and engaged the orcs behind. Geoffrey Gregorson moved up and signalled for Shadow to drop back. Her staff would prove more of a hindrance than a help in the close fighting that was about to take place. He moved past her and finished off the orc Morannel was fighting, taking it down from behind. He signalled to Morannel to do the same. Working as a team, they quickly sent the last of the orcs to oblivion.

'Search the bodies quickly,' commanded Kai. 'We need to be gone as soon as we can. Is anyone injured?'

No one had taken a wound. It had been a lucky encounter. The orcs had behaved in a strange manner, with no thought involved. It was as if they had been forced into it.

'Time to go!' yelled Kai, and she led the way back up and over the ridge.

After a short time, she paused. 'We need rest. Are there any caves nearby?'

'One,' replied Lakira. 'This way. Follow me and be quick. The fight will have attracted others.'

They moved off at a trot. In ten minutes, they were safely ensconced in a double curved cave system, and they lit a small fire up against an inside wall, where the light couldn't reflect back to the cave's entrance. Geoffrey took up guard at the entrance without being asked. After the long, hard, cold day and the interrupted evening, the added warmth of the fire to the cave induced them to seek rest quickly. After sorting out who would take watch and when, they slept.

It was an uneasy sleep that night. Most of them woke at some point, awakened by some unknown disturbance. They were almost as tired by the time dawn came around. 'It may be wise to stay in here for the day and rest,' said Lakira. 'We can move out at dusk and travel through the night. It will be slower going, but it just might prove to be safer.'

'I don't think it will be safe at any time,' replied Kai. 'But we do need some decent rest. We can rest until midday, and then you and Alemrae can do some scouting. I want to get to the valley of the mine before dawn and find somewhere to hole up in. Check out the possibilities, would you? It will be a hard trek.'

'In that case, we had better start immediately. It's quite a way to go. I'll send Alemrae back for you when it is time for you to move out.'

Lakira and Alemrae left silently. Shadow and Rad followed them to the entrance and took guard, replacing Frederick.

'Eat, everyone. Then try and get some more rest,' said Kai.

Alemrae returned about four hours later and reported to Kai. 'We will not make it through tonight. There are way too many bands of orcs between us and the valley we want. Lakira is trying to find us a way through. There may be a lot of climbing involved. I shall rest until he returns.'

It was almost dusk when Lakira returned. 'The orcs are beginning to flee. From what, I don't know, but there is definitely something in that valley that is trouncing them. That mage is still at work, hammering away at the mountaintop with lightning. I think he means to ignite the volcano. This is going to be a most dangerous area in the next day or two if he succeeds.'

'Alemrae! Gather everyone together. We leave now!' exclaimed Kai. 'Lakira, we have a new target. We must stop that mage. Take us to him.'

Lakira walked out, muttering hysterically to himself. 'Magic, more bloody magic. Next time, take a holiday to the sea instead.'

Under cover of darkness, the group made their way towards the high peak. They moved as quickly and as quietly as they could on a path leading directly towards the peak and all that lightning. Dawn came and went whilst they were still on the move, and they ate as they marched. They had managed to avoid the few bands of orcs they came across. The orcs were much more concerned with what was behind them than looking for someone ahead. They had moved at pace, leaving their wounded behind to catch up later, if they caught up at all. It took much longer than Kai had thought it would for them to get to the mountain, which was under attack by the lightning. The sun was beginning to set.

'We must rest,' she said. 'It will be a long climb up to where the mage is. It would be better to take him on once we are refreshed a bit. Take what rest you can. Share the guard duty between you.'

Kai unrolled her bedding. She felt exhausted. She had expended a great deal of energy and felt much more tired than she had expected to feel. She wondered how the others were coping. She slept despite the rumble and clash of the lightning.

She was awoken some six hours later. Alemrae offered her some hot food. 'We are about to get under way again,' he said. 'We have all managed to get some rest—you, the most, as you seemed to need it. Rad thinks that the mage is not that far away. He also thinks that there is more than one involved.'

Kai got herself organised and ate her meal. The others were all ready to go. When they left, Rad led the way. Somehow, he could detect where the magic was coming from. The others had to move quickly to keep up. It was much easier to fly over the obstacles than wend their way through. Shadow quickly admonished Rad to have some care not get too far ahead and to wait for the rest of them. He alighted on a boulder and began cleaning himself until the others caught up. He kept them waiting until he finished.

Oh, you're here. I thought you would take longer, he thought to Shadow. Shadow grumbled at him and then softly laughed at his response. Rad took to the air again—flying more slowly this time—and led them around the side of the mountain.

They were about halfway up the mountain when Rad stopped on another boulder. *Just ahead, up over that black-and-red striped ledge,* he thought. Shadow passed on the message to the others. Alemrae and Lakira crept closer for a look.

'Ogre mages—three of them,' they reported when they came back.

'No wonder that lightning has not stopped. We get as close to them as we can and hit them with all we have,' said Kai. 'Don't let them get any magic off. If they do, we are done for. Their expertise is in battle magic.'

'I have some magic that may assist us,' said Shadow. 'We had better move back a bit, though. They just might sense it when I cast.'

They backed up until Shadow stopped them. 'This should do. I intend to camouflage us a bit. I don't know how much it will help, but it should allow us to get much closer without being seen. It won't last long.'

The others gathered close, and she began to cast the spell. Rad added something to it, somehow magnifying her ability and the strength of the spell. Once the spell settled upon them, they found it difficult to see one another, and they knew where everyone was standing. It would be almost impossible for the ogre mages to see them initially. They carefully moved back towards the mages until they were in position.

'Now!' shouted Kai.

The ogre mages turned rapidly, casting magic in the direction of her shout. Kai flattened herself to the ground. The lightning bolts flew over her head, striking the boulders behind her in a blinding flash of light and a deafening peal of thunder. Rad cast a spell, and small patches of darkness appeared around the heads of the mages, temporarily blocking out their sight. The group piled in to them, weapons flashing, but their blows apparently doing no harm. Frederick called on his sword to flame, and, suddenly, the ogre he faced yelled in pain, the sword cutting into its side and giving it a tremendous wound. Kai's dagger pierced the thigh of the mage she faced, dropping it to one knee. It appeared that the defensive magic that the mages had raised was failing. Rad's spell lifted, giving the mages back their sight. The two injured ogres were quickly despatched. The last was too busy trying to hold off Alemrae and Geoffrey to realise it was the last. It did not take long for the two competent swordsmen to finish it off.

The lightning on the peak dissipated. There was silence, a vast and profound silence, as if everything was holding its breath for the lightning to begin again. They searched the ogres, finding a substantial amount of wealth upon them. Rad kept tugging at a small, almost insignificant bronze ring in the ear of the largest of the mages. Shadow went to help him. It had a cunningly hidden clasp, quite difficult to unlatch. Shadow queried Rad as to its importance. It looked worthless, which explained why no one else had bothered to try to take it.

Rad hissed at it, and it glowed a soft green light. 'Magical,' Shadow said. Rad nodded. 'What's it do?' Shadow asked. Rad did not know.

'Burn the bodies,' ordered Kai. 'I seem to have lost my balance a bit. I am not as agile as I once was.'

They piled the bodies in a heap and covered them with the small amount of brush they could find. Rad breathed fire on them to light them up. A pillar of thick black smoke rose from the burning bodies. 'That is definitely an indication that something is up here,' said Shadow. 'I wonder if anything would be brave enough to come looking, though.'

They left the ledge and headed in the general direction of the dwarven mine. They walked slowly down the mountain, looking for any trouble heading their way. They came across none. Near the base of the mountain, they came across another cave, well hidden behind a few larger boulders. It seemed to be quite deep. It would take too long to explore, but it would be a fairly safe place to camp whilst they recovered. They had not escaped the fight without injury; cuts, bruises, and strains abounded amongst them. It would only take them a short time to recover, though; there were no serious injuries. Once again, luck had been on their side. Kai wondered how long that would last. She feared for the safety of the others. Surely they could not keep this up, this occasional fighting with no major injuries. It was inherent with risk.

They rested comfortably within their shelter for the rest of the night and well into the morning. When Kai awoke, Alemrae was just returning from exploring deeper into the cave. 'Come, you must see this,' he said.

Taking some extra torches, the group followed him deep into the cave. 'This has been worked,' he said, pointing to a section of wall and floor. 'It is not natural—it is too smooth.'

Shadow quietly discussed something with Rad and, upon finishing their conversation, cast a spell at the wall. It revealed a faint outline of a doorway. 'You are quite correct, it seems,' said Shadow. 'Now, how do we open it?'

They all searched for some means to open the now visible door. Morannel found a small depression in the wall just above waist height, about where a handle should be. 'What if I press here?' he said. There was a soft click, and the door moved inwards a fraction and then slid sideways into the wall, leaving an opening big enough to walk through easily.

'Go back and collect all our things,' said Kai. 'We shall see where this takes us.'

Once they were ready to enter, Rad gave a chirp. 'Save your torches,' said Shadow. 'I shall provide us with light.' Then she cast a spell—a ball of soft white light arose from the palm of her hand to hang just above her head. It lit the way for a short distance but was better than the torches.

'We had better map this as we go,' Alemrae said. 'We don't want to end up lost down here.'

Frederick pulled out some parchment with a quill and some ink. 'Give me the dimensions as we go, but take it slowly,' he said.

They moved off, Frederick marking off the passages on the parchment as they went.

'Ignore the side passages,' said Kai. 'Let's just go straight on for now, deeper into the mountain.'

The air smelled fine, if a bit dusty—not stale, so it had to be circulating somehow. There were faint sounds coming from ahead, too soft to make out what they were. The group continued on. The noises could be heard intermittently as they progressed.

'My magic is about to fade,' said Shadow. 'Someone, light a torch.'

Geoffrey quickly did so and took the lead, Alemrae joining him. 'Stay just behind me,' Alemrae said. 'I can see further if the light of the torch is not in my eyes.' He drew his weapons and moved forward silently. 'Wait here a moment,' he said and quickly moved off up the passage into the darkness. They waited for a while and then longer.

Alemrae suddenly returned. 'Come quickly. Forget the map. We are going to have some trouble.' Then he turned back the way he had just come and proceeded at pace down the passageway.

CHAPTER 20

T he others rushed to catch up, making quite a deal of noise as they went. It took some time to reach him, and when they did, they realised what he had meant.

They had stopped at the opening to an immense cavern. There was a large crevasse running across it, over which a rope suspension bridge had been raised. There was a small group of humanoids battling a much larger group of orcs, goblins, and ogres at the far end. Those not involved in the actual fighting were carrying torches. They had found the dwarves at last!

'Spread out to either side,' ordered Alemrae. 'Unlimber your bows and get ready. Shadow, go forward and tell them to retreat across the bridge. We will cover them with supporting fire.'

Those with missile weapons did as ordered, whilst Shadow carefully moved out upon the bridge. She crossed slowly and, when she got close enough, yelled out to the dwarves. 'We will give you covering fire—retreat across the bridge!'

She turned and hurried back without looking to see if they had begun to retreat. One of the dwarves looked back and, seeing the group readying support, ordered a fighting withdrawal. Step by step, they backed across the bridge, Kai's group giving fire to those not in combat, dropping a few. Once back on firm ground, the dwarves formed a shield wall and retreated no further, holding their place so that the archers could do their murderous work. The goblinoids pushed forward, trying to use brute force to shove the dwarves out of the way and break the line. The goblinoids numbers fell away under the onslaught. The dwarves fought fiercely.

In the end, all their opponents had fallen; none ran or surrendered. Once again, the single-mindedness of the group astounded Kai. Something definitely had control over the goblinoids in the area.

There were many wounds to be attended to and introductions to be made.

'Many thanks to you and your group,' said the leader of the dwarves. 'Much as I hate to admit it, I don't think we could have defeated them all without your assistance. How did you come to be here?'

'We came looking for support for our own problems,' Kai replied. 'It was sheer chance we found our way to you at this time. We had taken shelter in a cave after a vicious fight, and one of our number found the location of a hidden door. Thinking it may provide us with some idea where your race was located, we came through in search.'

'Perhaps we can assist each other,' replied the dwarf. 'Our citadel has been under assault for quite some time now. We have had things under control, but lately they have been throwing a lot of magic against us. We have some natural resistance to such, but it has been almost overwhelming. I was ordered to find some way of stopping it. I took my men—this small group is the last of us—out through some secret passages. We managed to surprise the mages who were launching the assault. We slew some of them, but an extremely large force of goblinoids attacked us. We were forced into a retreat. Once free of them, we fled. We have been trying to fight our way clear for some days now. I think that group was the last of those who were following us, but I can't be sure. We need to get to a safe haven. I was leading my men to one not far from here when that bunch overtook us.'

'If you lead the way, we will escort you,' said Kai. 'We need to work together, first to save your citadel and then to see if you are able to support our needs.'

'As soon as we have seen to my men, we will go,' the dwarf said.

Not long after, they were on their way, the dwarves forming a clump at the head of the group. It did not take long until they stopped in the middle of a passage. 'There is a door in that wall,' said the chief dwarf. 'Once through, we shall be safe.'

It took some time for the dwarves to find the opening mechanism. It had not been used for quite some time, and its location had been forgotten. Once opened, they piled through into a series of large and comfortable rooms. These rooms had obviously been set up as a refuge, one that could be used in just the kind of circumstances they now found themselves.

'We are safe here. Few could find the door, let alone open it,' said the dwarf. 'Now, let's get these introductions out of the way, shall we? I am Bradur Ironfist.' He then proceeded to name all of his men, and Kai did the same.

'We had hoped to find you for aid with our own problems,' Kai began. 'The undead have arisen once more. The nations of man are gathering to try and stem the invasion, but I am afraid we will not succeed by ourselves. That is why I decided to come looking for the vanished races: you, the Elves, and the Halflings. I thought a small group of well-armed men may have an easier time of finding them than trying to do so with an army. I sought out the dwarves first, as I had located a reference to one of your mines. I was going there when we stumbled upon you. I believe that there are more undead now than ever before. Once, all races fought together in what we thought was the war that destroyed them all. I believe we need to do so again. Whilst our armies hold the undead in place, I intend to find and destroy their source. Once that is done, we can force those that are left to disperse until they have all been disposed of.'

'A worthy cause and a worthy fight,' said the dwarf. 'We shall see what aid is forthcoming. I will assist you in this when we have delivered my citadel from its enemies. And no matter the result of that exchange, I will join you in your task myself, if you will have me.'

'You would be welcome, Bradur,' said Kai. 'Now, how are we to save the rest of your people?'

'There are two main problems that I am aware of,' Bradur replied. 'The host attacking the citadel and another, smaller, are those causing havoc within our territories. There is a group of ogre mages trying to reignite the volcano within which we reside. If they are successful, then we are all doomed. What gets me is that they have to know that they will die if they do it.'

'They have already failed,' stated Kai. 'We killed them late last night, as well as a band of orcs that was fleeing from a lower valley. There is something strange going on though,—the orcs, ogre mages, and those we fought today seem to have no regard for their lives. I think something or someone has managed to gain some sort of hold over them all. They are not thinking properly, just reacting hostilely to whatever is in front of them. If we can eliminate whatever is controlling them, we might get a pleasant result. The goblinoids should flee, if they don't actually turn on one another.'

'Well, that's more good news. You are definitely earning your aid. We had some beasties keeping guard on the valley entrance to our lands—seems like they might just be doing their job. Didn't expect that they could take on an army, however, so maybe they are just attacking those that come too close to their nesting sites. That mine you were going to is not a mine. It is a passage through to the interior ring of these mountains. We have all we need within these mountains, so we had no reason to go looking for others, and we needed to replenish our numbers. We lost a large proportion of our population in that last undead war. The gates in the tunnel were destroyed just over three months ago. We have been fighting ever since. Not undead, though—just all these darn goblinoids.'

'It seems we fight the same war. The undead first attacked Albrae just over three months ago. The two battles must be linked somehow,' said Kai.

'That means it will be in the magic. Whoever controls the undead has taken control of the goblinoids. They are forcing them to attack us so that we cannot come to your aid. If we destroy the mages at the main battle, I think we might find that link you are after.'

'Either them or someone else controlling them,' suggested Kai.

'I am beginning to suspect the latter.'

'Time to get some rest, I think. I seem to tire more easily than I used to,' said Kai.

She moved off to where the others had set up some bedding for her. The two groups settled down for some well-earned rest. Kai slept much longer than she thought she would. When she awoke, the others had already eaten and were doing domestic-style chores, cleaning rust off weapons and armour, mending clothing and the like, as well as sorting through all the gear they were carrying, trying to figure out what they would need from here on. They were going to have to travel light.

'We'll be guiding you through the mountain to one of the lower portals. It comes out on a ledge that looks out over the citadel and the army camped outside it. I would like to get someone back into the citadel and tell them that help is at hand,' said Bradur. 'Without alerting our enemy, if at all possible.'

'I may be able to help with that. I would need to see the distances involved first,' offered Shadow.

Once Kai had eaten and they had all packed up, they set off. The walking pace of the dwarves was fine for the humans, if just a bit too brisk to keep up for a long time. It was a long and twisted path, with many turns from one passageway into another before they reached their destination.

'We can stop and eat here whilst we see what we can, and make a few decisions too,' said Bradur. 'If we keep the noise down, no one should know we are here.'

Shadow went out for a good look, being careful not to get close to the edge or risk being seen from below. They were almost directly above the citadel. It backed up against the cliff face upon which the ledge she was standing on extended. They were so far above that she did not think anyone looking in her direction would even see her. The army below looked like it was made up of ants; they were that small. There appeared to be little movement in the citadel.

Shadow went back inside. 'I have an idea,' she told Bradur. 'Write your message and I will deliver it.'

'I would like to see you try,' he said. 'It is too far to throw it and be assured of its delivery.'

Shadow went and got some cloth from her backpack. Putting the message and a small rock she had found in the cloth, she tied it in a knot. *Not too heavy*, she thought. 'Come, Rad,' she called, walking back out to the ledge. Rad poked his head out of a sack he had been hiding in, much to the astonishment of the dwarves. They had been unaware of his presence. He flew after Shadow and landed on her shoulder. 'I need you to take this down to that building and drop it near one of the dwarves,' she said. 'No, not on him, near him. Just be sure he gets it.'

Rad took hold of the small bundle with both forefeet, tested its weight and, without warning, dived from Shadows shoulder over the edge. Shadow watched, but he was soon out of sight. She waited on the ledge for quite a long time before she noticed Rad winging his way back up towards her.

When he arrived, Shadow walked with him back into the tunnel. 'Your message has been delivered,' she told Bradur. Then she laughed. 'As well as a sore foot, apparently.'

'What?' queried Bradur.

'Rad dropped your note on the foot of one of your kin. He hopped around, whilst one of the others picked up the package and unwrapped it. Your kin was given the rock, and the note was taken inside,' she replied.

Bradur laughed. 'Serves them right for not looking up,' he said. 'Rad is one of those lizards of light, isn't he?'

'Yes,' Shadow replied. 'He only unfurled about six weeks ago, but he seems to be much older than that.'

'I know some things about them,' he replied. 'They start learning from when the egg is laid, not from when it unfurls. It can take them many centuries to absorb enough magical energy to hatch. He appears to be an almost fully grown male. He must be very old to have grown so much before unfurling.'

'He was almost dead before I got him,' said Shadow. 'A merchant was keeping him in a chest until Morannel bought him for me. I started casting magic at him from when I first got him. It seemed to help.'

'Aye, it would have. They can absorb any magical energies that they come into contact with. How long did you have him before he unfurled?' asked Bradur.

'Only a few days. I used all the magic I could raise in those days, though.'

'He must have been near to unfurling before the merchant got hold of him,' suggested Bradur. 'Only the fact that he had been starved of magical energies delayed the act, most likely. Has he bathed in fire yet?'

Rad perked up at that, suddenly interested in where the conversation was going.

'Not that I have seen. Wouldn't the fire burn him?' Shadow asked, and Rad's eyes rolled.

'He unfurled from a metal egg, did he not? Metal doesn't burn, so then, how the hell could he?' replied Bradur. 'A cousin of mine once bragged of having one of these fellows play in his forge. It could be true—his forge turned out some amazingly good pieces for a good long while after it happened. My cousin was not noted for the quality of his work, usually, so this made somewhat of an impact. Enough to be remembered anyway. I know of a few dwarves who might be interested in having this fellow come and visit their forge.'

'We could do quite well out of it. Make them pay for what this one would love to do anyway,' Shadow laughed. 'I thought you might bring some way of making a bit of gold into this. I just didn't know how.'

'Our reputation has preceded us again, has it?' Bradur laughed.

'I don't mind. I just thought it might make an interesting diversion,' Shadow replied. 'We might do it. Do you think we could convince these fellows to do a commission based on Rad, here, swimming in their forge?'

'Probably,' he said. 'We will need to get rid of that army out there first, though.'

'Well, I'll let you handle that. I've done my part in delivering your note,' said Shadow with a laugh.

'Thanks a lot!' said Bradur with a grin. 'You're all heart.'

'That's why Rad stays with me,' replied Shadow, also with a grin. Their friendly banter went a long way to easing some of the tensions that had developed since the two groups had merged. Together, maybe they could just pull this situation out of the fire it was in.

CHAPTER 21

Kai called everyone together and explained the situation to all.
'Any suggestions as to how we go about it?' she asked.

'Camouflage worked up on the hillside,' commented Frederick.

'Too large a group this time,' stated Shadow.

'We need a distraction,' said one of the dwarves. 'But what could
distract an army?'

'Burning their food supplies,' stated Alemrae. 'Everyone needs
to eat.'

'That still incorporates getting in there in the first place,'
stated Kai.

'But not everyone needs go. I was thinking perhaps two—Rad
and I,' Alemrae offered. 'I can sneak better than the rest of you, and
if I can get Rad into the right place . . . well, you saw what he can
do when he burnt the ogre mages up on the mountain. He would at
least stay safe. He can fly out of there. I would be the one in trouble,
and if their supplies go up, it should not cause me too much difficulty
to get out again.'

'Fair enough,' said Kai. 'But that still leaves the rest of us.'

'They don't really look to their rear all that much,' said one of
the dwarves. 'Go in just after dawn when their sight is at its weakest.
Time our arrival with the supplies going up, and we could be well in
towards the command centre before we run into trouble.'

'Let me lead,' said Geoffrey Gregorson. 'I can speak the orcs' tongue, and I might be able to fool them long enough to get us by.'

'I knew there was a good reason to bring you along,' replied Kai.

'You're all mad,' stated Lakira. 'There is no chance of you all getting in and back out again.'

'You may be right,' said Kai, 'but some of us don't have a choice. I think we should put a guard on the tunnel where we expect to return to. If you, Lakira, and Shadow would be willing to stay behind, I would be that much more comfortable.'

'I'll wait with them,' stated Morannel. 'Three left to guard, whilst the rest do the job.'

'Settled,' said Kai. 'I shall, along with Captain Gregorson, Frederick, and all the dwarves, attempt to eliminate the command centre. Alemrae and Rad will provide the diversion. Lakira, Shadow, and Morannel will guard the escape route. Bradur, guide us to where we need to be to start this fracas.'

'On your feet, men!' commanded Bradur. 'We've a job to do.'

He led them out the way they had come and then down, changing corridors and tunnels, seemingly at whim. Until at last, he stopped. 'This is as close as we dare go. We stay here until dawn. I suggest we give Alemrae an hour to get the diversion in place before we start out. May fortune favour us all. We are going to need it.'

He sent one of his men to the entrance to keep watch and ordered him to let them know when it was time to go.

Alemrae left early with Rad. It would take time, he said, to get everything in place.

'This is the part I hate most,' Kai said to Bradur. 'I always hate the waiting.'

'You wait for enough fights. You get used to it,' replied Bradur.

'I am used to it, but I still hate it,' replied Kai with a smile.

'Aye, it is always more fun to be in there swinging than awaiting your turn,' said Bradur.

The dwarf near the entrance signalled. 'Time to go,' ordered Bradur.

Geoffrey led off. 'Look downright evil and nasty, would you? It will help when I have to talk sense into them,' he said.

They made it to the rear lines without being confronted and had started on their way through before one orc stood in their path. Geoffrey confronted him, speaking orcish. The orcs behind took note of what was said. Geoffrey said something again. The orc in front replied, also in the harsh and guttural dialect. Geoffrey looked at the other orcs behind and ordered them on. The one in front of him spoke again.

'Because you're already dead!' Geoffrey yelled and then stabbed the orc through the chest with his sword. The dwarves, along with Kai and Frederick, drew their weapons. The orcs in front ran towards the front lines.

'What did you tell them?' asked Kai.

'Ordered them to start the attack on the city walls. This one refused, effectively challenging me, so I did what any self-respecting orc would do—killed him, thus asserting my dominance and right to order them about.'

'Don't do that again,' Kai said. 'We can't fight our way in from here.'

'We won't need to. The others were watching—word will spread, and they will stay out of my way. It should be a clear path.'

Just then, there was a loud bang and a great whoosh as a pillar of fire shot up high into the air. 'Defend the supplies. Attack the walls!' yelled Geoffrey in orcish.

The orcs started running around in all directions. 'To the command centre. Now!' ordered Geoffrey. 'This won't last long.'

CHAPTER 22

They started running towards the command centre, Geoffrey shouting out conflicting orders in orcish as they went. An occasional enraged orc would plough into them, only to be cut down by the dwarves. Then off they would race again. They made it to the command centre and barrelled straight into the guards without stopping. It was a short and ugly melee.

At the end of it, one dwarf was dead and two others were seriously wounded. Fifteen orcs were dead. Leaving the wounded where they were to play dead, they went inside. There were two orc guards at the inner portal. These charged forward at the sight of the dwarves. Captain Gregorson engaged one; Bradur, the other. Kai bypassed the fray and moved into the next room. She was followed by Frederick and the rest of the dwarves. There were three ogres and a human mage in the room. The human appeared to be in charge. He looked withered, as if he was exceptionally old, older than he had any right to be and still be living.

Kai did not hesitate. Ignoring the ogres, she rushed the mage, Frederick on her heels. Frederick parried a blow from an ogre aiming for Kai and then engaged it in earnest. The dwarves piled on to the other two ogres.

Just as Kai reached the mage, he let off a magical blast aimed at her. She had no chance to dodge. It hit her straight in the chest, lifting her from her feet. Her momentum carried her forward, and she crashed into the mage, knocking them both down. They were both stunned for a second—Kai from the blast, the mage from the failure of his attack. Kai reacted first, Brelldan's dagger finding its way into the side of the mage, interrupting his casting of another spell. A flaming sword blade suddenly appeared in front of Kai and passed clean through the mage's neck, removing the head from the body. It did not bleed.

Kai was helped to her feet by Frederick. The ogre he had been fighting was lying in a pool of its own blood. The dwarves, having finished off the other two ogres, were searching the room. One of the dwarves outside gave a yell, bringing assistance from those inside. Looking out through the doorway, they saw pandemonium—ogres, orcs, and goblins were running everywhere, fighting with each other and looking for some means of escape.

The gates to the citadel opened with a loud clang, and out flowed the dwarves into the frenzy. Their solid wall of defence crushed the demoralised horde. Even outnumbered three to one, it didn't matter. The dwarven force arrowed through the fray, heading for the command centre.

'Help is coming!' yelled Kai. 'Let's get your fellows in here and out of sight.'

At that point, Alemrae closed in from around the side. 'Get undercover now!' he yelled as he dived through the doorway.

A small force of goblins charged around the corner, straight into the group. The dwarves held firm, knocking the leading goblins from their feet and attacking the second row. Kai, Geoffrey, Bradur, and Frederick joined the fight. The goblins went down fast. They dragged their wounded into the structure and guarded the entrance. Alemrae used what little magic he could raise to help the most seriously injured. All would recover, if they were given the time to do so.

'What happened here?' asked Alemrae. 'All was fairly normal out there until suddenly all hell broke loose. Every group of goblinoids started hacking away at each other, as if they had suddenly gone mad.'

'We killed the mage controlling them, I think,' said Kai. 'He's in the other room.'

Alemrae went through to take a look and search the place for information. By the time he returned, there were more dwarves at the entrance.

Bradur stepped forward. 'We have killed the mage running the show here,' he said. 'But the job is not finished yet. Clear the area of all the goblinoids. They should be starting to flee—let them go if they are, and kill the ones looking to stay. The injured here need a guard until more help from the citadel can arrive.'

Kai went to Alemrae. 'Where is Rad?' she asked.

'I don't know. He disappeared directly after he blew up the stores. I haven't seen him since. I hope he is back in the tunnel with Shadow or safe high above this mess.'

'The tunnels are not safe. This horde has run in every direction. Those tunnels will be almost as dangerous as out there. I hope Lakira, Shadow, and Morannel are safe,' Kai whispered.

'Are you all right?' asked Alemrae. 'You look rather faint to me.'

'I got hit in the chest with a magical blast from that mage just as I leapt upon him. We both caught the blast. I recovered and stabbed him as he tried to cast another. Frederick cut his head off whilst I was lying on top of him. Damn, I hurt.'

'The adrenalin from the fight is wearing off. Your body is reacting to all you have been through,' Alemrae said. 'Lie down before you fall down. We will take care of things.'

Kai collapsed to the floor, almost unconscious with fatigue and injury.

'Bradur, we need a force to go and collect Shadow, Lakira, and Morannel,' said Alemrae. 'Also, get someone to bring a few stretchers. We are going to have to carry our comrades out of here.'

'Already on it, Alemrae. A troupe of thirty dwarves is en route to the tunnels now. I have already sent to the citadel for more troops, medical supplies, and a healer. You lot are going to be heroes because of this,' replied Bradur.

'I don't need to be a hero. I need Kai to survive. She's pregnant, Bradur, and the child is special. We all need her to survive!' yelled Alemrae.

'Are you mad, letting a woman fight in that condition!' exclaimed Bradur.

'It's not as if we could stop her. She is a force all by herself,' said Alemrae softly. 'But she does need our aid. Oh, and one other thing—she does not know that she is pregnant.'

'And how is that possible?' asked Bradur.

'Ask her to tell you the story of her life, and you just might figure it out for yourself,' Alemrae answered.

'What are you two yelling for?' asked Kai sleepily.

'Go back to sleep, Kai,' Alemrae answered. 'No need for you to wake up just yet.'

The noise outside began to fade, as the dwarven army began to gain control over the immediate area. 'Tell the troops to start creating a funeral pyre. We need to burn the dead before they start waking up,' Captain Gregorson told Bradur.

'They're dead. They can't wake up,' replied Bradur.

'Yes, but we're dealing with undead and necromancers. We can't take the chance. Do you really want to have to kill them all again?' said the captain.

'I take your point,' said Bradur. He signalled to one of the younger dwarves nearby. 'Further orders—you are to begin burning the dead.'

'Yes, sir,' the young soldier replied.

'Just what rank do you carry in the citadel?' asked Captain Gregorson.

'Oh, just supreme commander of the field troops. My brother doesn't like it when I stay too long in the citadel. He keeps finding me odd jobs to do, like dispersing this rabble.'

'And who is your brother?' asked Frederick.

'King Gralden Ironfist III,' he replied. 'I try not to make an issue of it.' Then he laughed. 'Come on—let's get all the wounded back to my brother's palace. I am sure he will want to talk at you.'

'Don't you mean *with* us?' asked Frederick.

'No, definitely *at* you. He loves the sound of his own voice, does my brother,' replied Bradur.

They slowly moved out of the command centre and towards the citadel. No word of Shadow and the others had reached them by the time they were safely ensconced in private rooms at the palace. More dwarves were sent out to search for them.

CHAPTER 23

Lakira, Shadow, and Morannel had stayed inside the tunnel
mouth, watching the horde as the sun rose. They saw the
explosion as the supplies were set alight and the start of the enraged
melee. It was as the first goblinoids started to flee that they realised
they were in trouble. The sheer magnitude of the numbers trying
to flee meant that every escape route would have hundreds of the
enemy running down them. They could not fight—they needed to
find a hiding spot. Inside the tunnels was a death trap. They needed
to get outside and somewhere up the slope before those first fleeing
goblins arrived.

They rushed outside, looking for any easier way up the steep
slope. Lakira motioned them further along the cliff face. 'Up there,'
he said. 'A small ledge. From there, we can climb to that small
opening a little higher to the right. If it is large enough, we stay and
defend it. If not, we go higher until we find a likely spot to rest. Follow
me. I'll show you the way up.'

After hiding their belongings, they climbed to the ledge and then
up to the opening. It was barely big enough for one, let alone three.

'Up and to the left—another ledge, wider than that one lower
down. We can rest on that,' stated Lakira.

They climbed up again, having a few anxious moments as they
crawled onto the ledge. They could stay here awhile and get their
breath. They were high enough up not to be in immediate danger

from the goblinoids below, but they would need somewhere safer to spend the night. Going back down was not an option.

Lakira looked around the ledge for somewhere else to go. A dark hole in the cliff wall high above looked to be the only promising target. He did not think that they could make it, until he spied the chimney. It was just a crack in the rock face, really, but it would provide the easiest and safest means of ascent that he could see.

'I have found us somewhere to go, but you're not going to like how we get there. We will wait here for a bit longer to regain our strength, and then I will lead the way,' stipulated Lakira. 'Shadow, you follow me. Morannel, bring up the rear. Put your hands and feet where I do. Move one limb at a time and have the other three anchored at all times. Right hand, right foot, left hand, left foot—that is the order for movement. We are going straight up a crevice in the rock to what appears to be a deep cave. We don't stop until we get there. No one can help you. You have to do it all yourself. We have no other options. The sooner we do it, the better. We don't want to run out of light, and this is going to take some time. Now, follow me and I will show you how to go.'

He moved to where the crevice started and, showing the others how to place their hands and feet, slowly began to climb the wall. Shadow followed suit, finding it a lot harder than she had imagined it would be. Morannel began to climb behind her. Lakira moved up steadily and quickly outpaced the other two. Shadow climbed steadily but slowly, feeling as if her arms would pull loose from her shoulders with the weight of her body. Morannel stayed close behind Shadow, having to wait for her to move on before he could move again. He felt as if his strength was being slowly leached out of his arms and legs.

'Try to move a little faster, can't you?' he whispered to Shadow. Shadow failed to reply. Either she had not heard him or she was using all her energy in the climb. Hand by hand, foot by foot, they made their way up the crevice. Lakira was waiting at the top, with his body braced in the widening section of the crack.

'You have done well,' he said to Shadow. 'Now is the hardest part of all. You have to use me as a ladder up to the lip of the cave. Then haul yourself over the edge. Once you're in, move towards the back and make room for Morannel. He will be following you.'

Shadow slowly moved higher. She found it harder and harder to maintain her grip. She stretched up a little too much to make a grab for Lakira. She slipped. If Morannel, who had climbed directly after her, had not been solidly anchored, they both would have fallen. As it was, Shadow gave herself an almighty fright. She froze, clinging to the rock face, supported slightly by Morannel.

'Come on, my love. You can do it,' he whispered.

Shadow took heart from his words and proceeded to move up again. This time, she did not stretch out for Lakira but sought a handhold lower in the crevice. She slowly worked her way up, climbing over Lakira and towards the ledge. She slid the fingers of one hand up to the lip and held on. Releasing the other hand, she slid that one up the rock face until it, too, was holding on to the ledge. Then she heaved with all the strength left in her arms and legs and catapulted herself up. She managed to get her forearms over the ledge and, finding toeholds for her feet, managed to wriggle her way on to the ledge and roll into the cave.

She crawled towards the back and collapsed, exhausted. She was asleep before Morannel made it into the cave. He crawled over to her and cradled her in his arms, leaning against the wall before he, too, slept.

Lakira was in trouble. He had wedged himself tightly into the crevice, and when the others had climbed over him, they had forced him physically farther into the gap. He could rest without fear of falling, but he could also die of starvation before he could escape. Knowing it was his only chance, he risked everything. If he fell— well, it would be a quick death, and he had never feared death.

He reached above for two handholds, and pulling hard with both arms and pushing with the one free foot, he launched himself up as hard as he could. His other foot came free. He lost a fair amount of skin as his boot came off. He would have trouble walking if he managed to survive the rest of the climb.

Up he went, managing to reach the lip of the cave. Grasping the lip, he called for some help, but there was no answer. He struggled to reach higher and finally managed to get one arm over the lip and then the other. After that, it became easier. Inch by inch, he crawled his way into the cave, collapsing on the edge. His body was safely supported, but both legs were dangling over at the knee.

Morannel was the first to awaken. It was dark, and he had a hard time working out just where he was. Then it all came flooding back— that harrowing climb. He was still holding Shadow, but where was Lakira? He looked about the cave, and there, over by the very edge, a large lump was sprawled on the ground. He gently laid Shadow down on the rock floor of the cave and crawled over to Lakira. He found a pulse and, so, slowly pulled him further into the cave beside Shadow. Then, energy gone, he slept once more.

Sunlight woke them the next morning. The floor of the valley was still in darkness. The sun shone straight into the cave, lighting up the back. There was a passage back there. A way out perhaps? Together, Shadow and Morannel helped Lakira to his feet. He could not walk, but by using them as support, he could hobble along. A short way in and the light from the cave mouth all but disappeared.

Shadow cast her spell of light. 'We will have light for an hour,' she said. 'We must move on continuously until the light fades. Then I will try to cast it again. If I can't, we will stay where we are until I can gather enough magical force to cast it again.'

They moved off, slowly going further into the mountain. The tunnel floor was slanting up, so they were also climbing higher up. The tunnel did not deviate much. It was almost a continuously straight passage, leading to the upper levels of the mountain. They came to a junction just as the light died.

'Let me rest a bit before you try the spell again,' said Lakira.

'We could all use some rest,' stated Shadow.

After a while, Shadow tried her spell again. It worked. 'Which way do we go?' she asked.

'Upwards. Always move upwards,' said Lakira. 'There will be less chance of running into any goblins the higher we go. Unfortunately, it also means moving further away from any rescue.'

They continued on, coming across more and more junctions as they went. Each time, they selected the one they thought would take them up. They seemed to be slowly travelling in a circle but climbing higher on each circuit. They noticed a light ahead—another tunnel opening, letting fresh air and more light into the caves.

'Let's stop here and rest,' said Lakira. 'We can see what approaches even when the light goes out.'

Morannel moved to the mouth of the cave and looked out. The mountainside was covered with snow. There were no tracks to be seen. The view was marvellous but unappealing to someone as tired and hungry as he. He stumbled back to the others. 'We need to find another way to go,' he said. 'It is all snow and rock out there. We are almost at the summit.' He collapsed on the ground beside them and fell asleep. The others did the same.

Rad found Shadow whilst they slept. He curled up on her chest to wait for her to awaken. They slept for a long time. A lack of food and the cold conditions were sending them to the brink of survival.

It was almost dusk when Shadow finally roused. She was not only surprised to find Rad there but also extremely happy. She woke Morannel and Lakira. 'Time to move on,' she said. 'We have to get warm, or at least find somewhere a bit more protected than here to wait.'

'I still have some parchment and ink,' said Morannel. 'Send a note with Rad. Tell him to find Kai. She can send help if she knows where we are.'

He gave Shadow the ink and parchment and then tore a piece of cloth from his shirt to use to attach the note to Rad.

'Go find Kai and the others,' Shadow ordered. 'Tell them where we are. They need to get here in the next day or so, or we're going to die.' Rad squawked at her. 'Go now, Rad. Fly as fast as you can. Go to the citadel. They are our only hope.'

Rad left, flying out the cave entrance and out of sight. 'Nought to do now but rest and conserve our strength,' Shadow said. She pulled Lakira up against Morannel and then clung to Morannel's other side. It did not take long for them all to fall asleep again.

CHAPTER 24

Kai was anxious. Another day had passed, and there was still no word about Morannel, Shadow, or Lakira. She had been forced to stay in bed. She had a remarkable lack of strength as a result of the blast of magic from the mage. Alemrae and the others visited from time to time, but they were all worried and started to get on one another's nerves. A major search was under way, but there were so many passages to check and not many guards available to do the checking.

It was late in the afternoon when Alemrae came in. 'I have both good and bad news. The bad news is that there is still no sign of the others. The good news is that I think Rad has been sighted. At least a small creature has been seen flying above the citadel.'

'That does it. Help me up. I need to get outside. Rad is looking for me. Shadow will have sent me a message.'

Alemrae assisted Kai in rising and helped her walk out on to the balcony outside her room. 'Rad!' Kai yelled as loudly as she could. Then she yelled again. A blur of screeching bronze and blue came streaking over the rooftops and thudded into Kai.

'Look, he has a streamer. I bet there is a message,' said Kai. 'Get it now, whilst I hold him.'

Alemrae quickly freed the streamer from around Rad's leg. 'The message is short,' he said. 'Near summit, opposite citadel, injuries, near death, exposure, come soonest.'

'I'll get this to Bradur immediately,' Alemrae said, racing out the door and yelling for help. Alemrae found Bradur racing to find him, having heard the commotion.

'We have a note. They're in serious trouble. Get your men. Here, read this,' Alemrae said, shoving the note towards Bradur.

They raced down to the gates of the citadel. Bradur called orders as he ran. It took but minutes for a large rescue team to begin the march across the valley to the tunnels opposite. The dwarves who were still searching the mountain had occasionally run across bands of goblins in the tunnels, so care would have to be taken. Bradur, being the one who knew the tunnel system the best, decided the path to follow.

They raced along, not slowing even for the steepest paths. They halted at one junction. 'We need to make a choice,' said Bradur. 'The tunnel to our right is the shortest route, but there is a very large band of goblinoids residing in one of the largest chambers. The left-hand tunnel will take about an hour longer but bypasses the chamber where the goblinoids are.'

'No choice at all,' said Alemrae. 'We go right, barrel straight through without stopping. We can't afford to waste any time by going around.'

'Right, then, we charge in. Arrow formation as soon as we have the room. Fight towards the tunnel to the left of the one straight ahead.'

They moved off at the trot, and within minutes, they found their way into the large chamber. There were a huge number of goblins and orcs in the room. The dwarves charged off towards the exit they required, the goblins and orcs running to meet them. Alemrae moved to the point of the arrow formation and drew his twin swords. He did not bother with his usually elegant form but went in brutally, hard and swift, not stopping to fully engage before moving on to the next enemy.

He cut his way deeply into the mob before the press of bodies slowed him down, but he did not stop moving forward. The dwarves behind, attacking ferociously, also kept moving. Within minutes, they had fought their way clear and were racing up the tunnel. Some dwarves slowed to provide a fighting withdrawal and discourage pursuit. They had received many minor wounds during the brief encounter, but they ignored them in favour of getting to Lakira, Shadow, and Morannel.

Within three hours of Kai receiving the note, they had found the lost, who were huddled together, trying to stay warm, and barely responsive to the arrival of their rescuers. Lakira, Shadow, and Morannel were bundled in blankets and strapped to stretchers. Alemrae used what little magic he could raise in an attempt to revive them.

The descent back through the mountain to the citadel began. They bypassed the chamber with the goblinoids, not willing to risk fighting their way through again. By the time they reached the exit to the tunnel system at the base of the mountain, Shadow and Morannel were responsive. But Lakira had passed on. The blood loss from the injuries to his foot, on top of the long exposure to the elements, had taken its toll on the rugged hunter. A larger group of dwarves met them as they crossed the valley. Bradur sent them to eradicate all the goblins left in the mountain, blaming the creatures for the death of Lakira.

They arrived at the citadel to much cheering; until news of the death of one of the heroes passed amongst the populace. Shadow and Morannel were rushed up to the rooms near Kai, and she came and spoke with them. The injuries to Alemrae and the dwarves of the rescue team were treated, and everyone was allowed to rest. Rad went mad with joy upon seeing Shadow again, for Kai had kept him with her. He flew back and forth across the room, doing acrobatic feats in the air that amazed all those who saw him. He landed on her bed and danced up her body until he was near her face and then proceeded to give her face a bath with his tongue.

'Rad, stop that,' said Shadow. 'I will be all right. Calm down.' Rad settled down, curling up beside her neck and rubbing his head against her cheek. 'I love you too, Rad,' whispered Shadow. 'Now let me rest.' She shut her eyes and slept, with a very happy Rad crooning softly in her ear.

CHAPTER 25

It took time for everyone to recover. They all attended the funeral for Lakira the morning after their return. He was honoured by all for his heroism. The climb up the cliff would become a legend amongst the dwarves, and a challenge for the young to exceed the expectations of their fellows in feats of bravery and loyalty.

Messages were sent out to other dwarven compounds in the mountains. A call to war. The undead had arisen again, and they were needed. The weather turned for the worse. Winter storms unleashed their burden of snow, making travel all but impossible. The toughest scouts carried messages back and forth between the clans. The dwarves readied for war. As soon as the weather broke, they would march for Raelis to join in the defence of the world. King Gralden Ironfist III would lead the dwarven forces. Bradur would join with Kai and her group to find the Elves and Halflings.

Whilst they recovered in the citadel, waiting for the weather to break, they learnt what they could from the dwarves. Keeping his word, Bradur introduced Shadow and Rad to Kralmar Hammerhand, the best of the metal workers in the citadel and chief forger of weapons. He was delighted to experiment at his forge whilst Rad played within, and was aware of the magical nature of the famed lizards of light. He promised to do the work that Shadow had asked of him—to turn the magical earring Rad had identified into a cloak pin shaped in the design of a briar rose. He could not say what the result would be in terms of the magic. 'That is up to Rad to deal with,' he said.

On the day they chose to begin the work, the worst storm of the season erupted around the citadel, as if the weather itself was trying to halt their progress. Shadow, Rad, and Bradur went to the forge. Kralmar was already there, and he had already prepared all that he needed to do the work. Shadow let Rad go, and he flew straight into the flame of the forge, chuckling with joy at the warmth he felt. Rad began to glow as he absorbed the warmth. Kralmar took the ring and placed it in a crucible to melt. Then he moved the crucible into the depths of the forge. As the ring heated, the flames around it changed colour. Magic began to flow from the ring, and Rad started to absorb the magic, changing its nature and returning it to the molten metal in another form. The metal changed. It was no longer bronze but something else. It was a black so deep that it caught all light and gave no reflection, but it did shine with a dark blue glow.

Kralmar removed the molten metal and poured it from the crucible into the mould of the pin he had already prepared. Still glowing, Rad flew from the forge and breathed on the mould. He chirped once and then flew back into the forge. He began to play amongst the flames, manipulating magical forces as he did so. The forge itself began to glow with a bright white light. Then the forge went cold. All the heat was gone. The fires were out, but the centre of the forge still glowed as if it was still alight.

Rad walked out. His scales gleamed as if highly polished. He looked like a newly completed work of art, perfect in its entirety. His eyes glowed, his pleasure apparent to the three looking on.

'What has he done?' queried Kralmar.

'I don't know,' said Shadow. 'But I don't think you are going to have to heat your forge again. Look at it—it shines as if still alight and ready to be used. Don't be surprised if the items you make with this forge do some strange things. Rad sometimes has a warped sense of humour.'

'Now you tell me,' Kralmar said with a laugh.

Rad, still glowing, flew to Shadow and landed on her shoulder. He rubbed his head against her cheek. 'Oh, you are toasty warm, Rad,' said Shadow. He happily clicked an agreement.

Kralmar opened the mould to see the pin. It was flawless. It was a black briar rose with just the faintest sheen of blue amongst the petals. It shone as if highly polished. No more work was needed; the pin was finished. Kralmar removed it carefully from the mould and gave it to Shadow.

'What magic does it hold?' asked Bradur.

'If I understand Rad properly, it will provide some protection to the wearer from both magical attack and flame,' Shadow replied. 'I intend for it to be a gift to Kai.'

Bradur and Shadow, with Rad still perched on her shoulder, left the forge. Kralmar stayed, determined to experiment with this newly magical forge. In the days that followed, he grew more and more in awe of the nature of the magic that Rad had instilled into the forge. He vowed to repay them before they left—making the trinket was not enough. He made two matching items, both in silver. One was a circlet for Shadow to wear, which featured two winged lizards playing amidst waves of fire. A large blue sapphire centred the piece. The other item was a small chain necklace and pendant just large enough to fit over Rad's head. It was made in a pattern of snowflakes and had the appearance and delicacy of lace. Both were master works that few other smiths could have made. The intricacy of the detail was phenomenal, down to, and including, the scales of the lizards. They almost looked alive.

They were confined to the citadel for a month. When the storms finally stopped, the dwarves began the march to Raelis. Kai and her group went with them. They needed to take ship, and the largest ships available were in Raelis.

On the night before their departure, Kralmar presented the gifts to Shadow and Rad. Everyone was astonished at the quality of the work. Shadow placed the circlet upon her head. It expanded to fit perfectly. It suited her as no other jewellery ever would. Rad was unsure about his gift— he could sense an amazing level of magic within—but he allowed Shadow to place it over his head and down to the base of his neck, where it fitted neatly. Then an amazing change occurred. Rad seemed to absorb the necklace, leaving a white pattern of snowflakes around his neck and down onto his chest. He changed colour to a brilliant silver. The blue highlights of his scales remained, as did the colour on the underside of his wings. His eyes turned blue. He was astonished. Then he began to grow. He doubled in size. He was the largest lizard of light to ever have existed, and the only silver one. He was unique.

Kai had trouble with her clothes. Nothing seemed to fit. Her pregnancy was finally beginning to show. She could not understand, and then it dawned upon her. All the little clues had been there all along—the way the others treated her, the nausea on the day before her duel with Frederick, why she was eating so much, and why she felt much more tired than usual. This was something that she had never thought about. She and Brelldan had never discussed having children; she had just assumed that she was barren. Her periods had always been few and far between. She never knew when they would occur and so never gave them a thought. She did not miss them, which was usually the first indication a woman had that she may be pregnant. She was embarking on the next leg of a dangerous journey. How would this impact upon it? She had no idea. She did not even know when the child would be due, but it had to be in six months' time, at the most. Where she would be then, she had no idea. She called for Shadow and Alemrae to attend her.

'You knew and did not tell me!' she yelled at them as soon as they were alone with her.

'Knew what?' asked Alemrae.

'That I am pregnant!' shouted Kai.

'We all knew,' said Shadow. 'Calm down. You had to find out for yourself. You would have denied it if we told you, even though it would have been the truth.'

'What does this mean for our journey? How are we to deal with a newborn child when we go into such danger as we must face?' asked Kai.

'We have time to sort through the issues. Are you not pleased to carry Brelldan's daughter?' asked Alemrae.

'How do you know it is his daughter?' Kai asked.

'You told me yourself. Your dream—do you remember?' answered Alemrae.

'But that was just a dream,' whispered Kai.

'Sometimes, during periods of great stress, we can have visions of the future. We were all under a lot of stress when you had that dream. Don't forget Rad said "she should have wings". He was talking about your daughter, and he has given her them.'

'How do you know this?' asked Kai.

'Every night when you sleep, I use my magic to check on your health, and that of your daughter. You are both important to us,' said Alemrae. 'I know not why.'

'I have something for you, Kai,' said Shadow. 'I did not know when I would give it to you, but this is the moment. Here, take this.' Shadow gave the briar rose pin to Kai. 'This was the first item to be produced in Kralmar's new magical forge. Rad took the magic from the earring and transformed it. Kralmar used the metal and made this pin. Together, they completed the design I asked for, and it shall offer some protection from both magical attack and fire to whoever wears it.'

'I thank you for your gift, but why are you giving it to me?' asked Kai.

'For all that you have given and will give in the future,' said Shadow. 'About your clothes—we had new ones made. They have already been packed. There is one change left for you in that cupboard.'

Alemrae walked out so that Kai could change. Shadow helped Kai with the garments and insisted that she wear the fur-lined cloak and matching boots. Kai did as asked, not wanting to appear ungrateful after all the help she had been given. She used the briar rose pin to fasten the cloak closed. She was as ready as she would ever be.

'Let's get a move on, or the king may decide to leave us behind,' Kai said.

'Not likely. He would start a revolt if he did that, and his brother would take the throne,' chuckled Shadow.

They walked out to where Alemrae waited, and with him, they went to where the rest of the group waited. They walked out of the citadel and went west towards the main entrance tunnel leading to the outside world. They passed many reminders of the recent goblinoid incursion—derelict homesteads and workshops left behind by the evacuated dwarves. Some were only just being revisited. Smoke rose occasionally from a fireplace, an indication that the stubborn dwarves would soon put things back to rights. Fields with crops abounded, not so the livestock. The goblins and orcs would have taken them for their food supply. It was going to be a tough winter for the dwarves, but at least the citadel had plenty of supplies to ration out. The other holdings in the area away from the citadel had been left alone, and so they were well stocked. There would be food for all as long as the winter was not too bitter.

The dwarves marched on, knowing that their relatives would fare better with fewer mouths to feed. They were to be on the trail for a week, so the usual travel rations would be their sole sustenance. It would be unlikely that they could hunt anything along the way. The wildlife would scatter from the presence of such numbers as the dwarven army possessed.

They made it to the trade road between Ulmarin and Raelis in four days. It would be a further three before they had arrived at their destination, Raelis. A few horses had been procured, and Kai was given one to ride, the state of her pregnancy giving her precedence. As Kai's companion, Shadow also had a mount, although she let Morannel ride most often. Shadow still preferred to walk rather than ride.

Rad enjoyed the travel. He flitted from here to there, exploring everything and spending time with each member of the group. Despite his greater size, he remained an inquisitive ball of mischief, albeit a much more powerful one. He still needed to physically connect with Shadow throughout each day.

Shadow studied her circlet when time permitted and was much impressed by what she learnt. It was a magnifier. Any spell she cast would work better and last longer. It also gave off a blue light at any time that she found it too dark to see, without her having to do anything. It was not a strong light, but it was steady, and it allowed her to move around at night comfortably. It was much better than a torch.

CHAPTER 26

Their arrival at Raelis was welcomed with a great show of appreciation. The various leaders were introduced, and a meeting of the War Council was planned for the following day. A banquet was held on the first evening, and it was a great success—tales were told, histories were exchanged, and Kai's small group was rewarded for their achievements. When Kai made it known that they would need a large deep-water vessel to take them on a long journey far into the great southern ocean, a number of merchants offered the use of the pride of their fleet.

Between them, they determined the best ship and crew for the group to take—*Storm Dancer*, the biggest and fastest of the deep-water ships in port. It could be sailed for three months without the need to return to land for supplies, such was the size of her hold. Her crew of thirty-eight had sailed some of the most dangerous waters in the north and were keen to face the challenges of the southern ocean. They could take ten passengers aboard comfortably, fourteen if they didn't mind being cramped and sharing bunks. Kai spoke with the captain of *Storm Dancer* and engaged his services. It would take a week to prepare the ship and stock it with supplies. No room would be left in the hold for cargo. They would purchase supplies as they travelled south, stopping at various ports, searching out rumours of the southern land.

With a week to wait, Kai and her group moved into the palace, back to the rooms they had vacated seven weeks before. Bradur was assigned a room befitting his rank nearby.

One morning, Kai, Morannel, and Capt. Geoffrey Gregorson met with Regent Monfrae and the Lord Chamberlain to discuss how the defence was going.

'It is hard to say, really. The undead have not come in any great numbers yet. We are holding the first defensive wall easily. The other walls are still under construction. We are hoping that the dwarves you have brought us will be willing to assist in the construction,' said Regent Monfrae.

'That is unlikely. The dwarves who came with me are all warriors, and the construction crews are not due to leave the citadel for a week or two. They have their own repairs to see to before coming here,' Kai replied. 'It might speed things up if you arranged some transport, as well as horse relays for messages and the like between Raelis, Ulmarin, and the dwarven citadel of Rockholme. Send a message to Rockholme asking if a specialist engineer could come and oversee the construction of the walls. You may get a positive response from that. I think we may leave Capt. Geoffrey Gregorson with you for the time being. His many years of experience may come in handy during the defence. Have him take over the defensive line on the walls. He would also be the best one to liaise with the dwarven soldiery.'

'My Lady Kai, I object. My place is with you and by the side of my prince,' argued Captain Gregorson.

'The prince is no longer in need of a bodyguard, and dragging you across the southern ocean would be a waste of your talents,' replied Kai. 'No, you are needed here much more than on a ship at sea. I will promise you this: before I set out to the north in search of that bottomless hole these undead have come from, I will come back here so you can join us again. There is no other that I would have defending my back on that trek.'

'For that, I thank you. I will accept the role you have given me, albeit unhappily,' said Geoffrey.

'May I suggest,' broke in Prince Morannel, 'that the captain be given a new title and promotion for services to the nation, above and beyond the call of duty—field commander of the city guard.'

'It shall be done as you wish,' said Regent Monfrae.

Leaving the newly promoted field commander with the regent and Lord Chamberlain, Kai and Morannel left the palace and headed for the Sisters of Mercy chapter house. The streets were a throng of people, and it took much longer than Kai had expected to make their way there. The gates were open, much to their surprise, and there was a crowd of women in the courtyard.

Prince Morannel and Kai managed to push their way through to the front door of the chapter house, Kai's obvious pregnancy giving them the excuse of seeking a healer. One of the sisters who was guarding the door recognised Kai and Morannel from their earlier visit. She allowed them entry, much to the anger of some of the waiting women.

'Compassion first, ladies!' the guard shouted above the noise of the crowd. 'Be at ease. You shall all be seen in turn.'

The noise quietened somewhat and then even further as the door closed behind them. 'Allow me to escort you to our healers,' said one sister.

'No need,' replied Kai. 'We have come to speak with your Mother Superior. Tell her that Prince Morannel and the Briar Rose are here to see her.'

'You are the Briar Rose! I shall escort you to her at once. Follow me,' the sister said.

They followed the sister to the receiving hall of the sisterhood. There, the Mother Superior was questioning a young lady over her reasons for admittance to the order.

'You must remember that the oath is for life. Once you become one of us, there is no going back. You will be put to whatever tasks are suited to your abilities. You very well may end up doing exactly the same job as you already have and are trying to escape, with no recourse to avoid it. You may, of course, undergo the trials, but once the oath is given, you are to obey. You may leave now. Return in two days if you wish to partake in the trials. I have other urgent business to attend.'

A sister guided the young woman out.

'Lady Kai, Prince Morannel, I am pleased that you have come to see us. Welcome,' said the Mother Superior.

'I have come to renounce my role as the commander of your forces,' replied Kai. 'I will not be around to do the job, so someone else should oversee the role. You will no doubt be involved in the defence effort. Your order has the finest fighting force left to us, excluding the demi-humans, and so far we only have the dwarves on our side. They are great warriors but few in number. Whomever you choose, have them consult with Field Commander Geoffrey Gregorson. He has just received the tactical command for the defence.'

'And what role will you play in this conflict, Kai?' asked the mother. 'Your pregnancy must surely limit your search. You will require assistance when you are due.'

'My role stays the same. We travel by ship, so I will be able to take my ease. When the time comes, I will no doubt have able assistants for the birth. Both Shadow and Alemrae will see to that,' said Kai.

'They're not the only ones, Kai,' said Prince Morannel. 'I was going to ask you, Mother, if you would spare one of your healers to join with us in our search—first and foremost to oversee the care that Kai will need.'

'I protest, my prince. I am not an invalid,' announced Kai.

'You can barely see your feet as it is, and you are going to get much larger. You will require the expert attention of a trained healer, and I, for one, shall see that you get it. Consider it a royal command from your future king,' said Prince Morannel.

'So be it, Majesty,' spat Kai furiously.

'Mother Superior, if you would please send your representative to the palace at the earliest convenience,' requested Morannel. 'We are due to board ship in six days, and it would be good to have the entire party together for a day or two before we go. There will be some discussions to be had over the roles we all will play.'

'I will ensure that she arrives at the palace this evening,' replied the Mother Superior.

They returned to the palace as slowly as they had left. They arrived after the midday meal, just in time for the meeting of the Council of War. Morannel showed Kai to a seat at the table and took the seat next to her. Then he summoned a servant and requested food for the two of them. Kai indicated that she was not hungry.

'You can eat anyway,' Morannel replied. 'You need to eat regularly for the health of your child.'

The rest of the council came to the room in ones and twos, dribbling in over the space of a quarter hour. Bradur and his brother, King Gralden, were the last to arrive. Regent Monfrae called the meeting to order and explained the recent promotion of Capt. Geoffrey Gregorson to the post of field commander of the forces.

Field Commander Gregorson then stood to speak.

'The most recent news from the front line is that there has been a build-up of undead in the lower reaches of the valley before the entry to the pass proper. We expect to see battle engaged within the next day or so. King Gralden, if you would please send some of your troops to support the front line, we would be immensely grateful, and if any of your troops has experience with construction, could they please aid the builders constructing the other protective walls? We have already sent a message requesting aid from your specialists back in Rockholme. Mother Superior, your sisters are the most skilled of our fighters. I wish to use them as shock troops to push the undead back when we have to retreat. Until we require them, could you have them begin training the unskilled warriors we have gathered? A rotation of troops has begun to be sent to the lines. In case of emergency, all troops at the camp at the top of the pass will respond. Hopefully, they can give the rest of us enough time to respond. At all times, one-third of our force shall be within the pass. The other two-thirds shall be training, resting, or recuperating.'

A commotion outside forced the silence of Geoffrey Gregorson, and then the doors suddenly crashed open. A young soldier in the guards' colours rushed through.

'Message just in, my lords. The defensive wall has fallen. We are in retreat. The undead are storming into the pass!' he yelled.

CHAPTER 27

There was an audible gasp from those gathered, as the young solider continued to relay his message.

'The force at the top encampment has marched into the pass. Aid has been requested urgently. A sorcerer riding an enormous flying black steed and two giants led the attack on the wall. Magic broke the wall, and the giants cleared a path for the undead to use. The soldiers manning the oil barrels above the pass were attacked with magical energies and forced to flee.'

'King Gralden, Mother Superior, can you please send, as quickly as possible, all the troops you can muster to turn back the undead horde?' commanded Geoffrey Gregorson.

The king left at a run, and the Mother Superior sent for a messenger. Two messages were sent: the first to the Sisters of Mercy, giving them orders to defend the pass and hold at all cost; the second to the commander of the forces in camp at the base of the mountain to move all his troops to the holding area at the start of the pass.

When King Gralden got to his men, he ordered them to march. 'Forced march, at the run. The pass is endangered. Form a shield wall and stop the advance of the undead. Then clear the pass if we can. Move out!' he yelled.

The entire dwarven host was on the road and running to the mountains within five minutes. It usually took three hours to ride to the base of the pass; the dwarves ran it in two. They slowed to a walk until they reached the top and then began running into the pass. The human forces moved aside to let them through. They continued to run through the night, passing soldiers coming back from the front line. All the time, the messages were repeated: 'Being forced back. The numbers overwhelming.' The advance of the undead was slowing, not because of the resistance but because of the small number of undead that could advance past the unfinished walls at once.

The dwarves continued to run. On the evening of the third day, they arrived at the front. They crashed through the weakening defensive line and onto the undead horde. There, they formed their shield wall. The undead were stopped in their tracks. As they slowly tired, the dwarves at the front stepped back, allowing fresher arms to continue to rain blows down upon the enemy. The undead piled up beneath them. Then the dwarves began to advance, their sheer savagery in battle unmatched by the undead.

The fight continued, pressing back down the pass to the remains of the first defensive wall. The press of undead eased, and the dwarves surged forward. There was no sign of the sorcerer or either of the giants. The dwarves managed to clear the pass and then the valley leading down to Almarac.

King Gralden called a withdrawal. They regrouped at the remains of the defensive wall. Roving patrols were instigated, and they turned up few undead. The disappearance of the sorcerer and the giants led to an increased sense of trepidation. They could return, at any time, and with more undead. The human forces also reassembled. Messages were sent. The story of the dwarves' destruction of the undead awed the populace. Then the story of Kai and her search became known, and it was enthusiastically embraced. The journey by ship to search the southern ocean for a lost continent and the other lost races became the talk of the city.

Storm Dancer moved out of port to the cheers of the populace. The search for the elves had met with public approval after the dwarves had shown their capabilities in battle. Their emergency holding defence and advance after the undead had destroyed the first defensive wall had been nothing short of miraculous. Kai's group stood at the rail as they moved out, the hope of the nations going with them. They were heading for Tir. From all indications, the continent that they searched for would lie somewhere to the south of that landmass.

They sailed south, down the west coast and along the southern coastline, searching for rumours at each port along the way. Shadow spent part of each day in the crow's nest with Rad, marvelling at the magnitude of the ocean and experimenting with magic, trying different ways to manipulate it and determining what she could do.

CHAPTER 28

They had been sailing south for more than a month. Their last stop, at a small village of fishermen, had given them the hint they required. An old sail hand had remembered a storm-tossed voyage far into the southern ocean from his youth. They had not found land, he said, but they had seen seabirds, which were always within a short distance of land. He believed it was just over the horizon. It had taken them six weeks to sail back to known waters. They had made it to an island with fresh water and food sources. From there, they had sailed back to civilisation.

Storm Dancer had left the small village three weeks ago, and the captain thought that they were as far south as any recent voyage had gone. If he was right, then it would still be another two weeks before they neared the unknown land in the south.

Shadow resumed her usual spot in the crow's nest of the foremast with Rad. They both enjoyed the wide open view of the sea. Rad often took short flights, delighting in the freedom of the air and the chance to try and catch some fish. After his first taste, fish had become his favourite meal, and catching them had become a hobby of sorts. It certainly reduced the time Shadow had to spend feeding him.

It had been a fine morning, and they were both looking forward to a pleasant afternoon. The sun shone bright, and the sky was free from cloud. The wind was blowing steadily from the north-west, and the ship was racing ahead of it. Rad came to rest on the rail and chittered his pleasure of the day. Shadows return smile was brilliant. Rad turned and looked north and then croaked. *Magic, lots and lots of magic, bad magic* was the thought Shadow received.

The sky to the north turned green—a sickly, putrid, dark and bilious green. Rad clicked a *'Hurry'* to Shadow as she began to climb down the mast. He took the easy route and flew down, clicking and squawking his displeasure at her slowness. They rushed to where the captain stood on the rear deck near the helm.

'Look behind us, to the north,' said Shadow. 'Have you ever seen a sky like that before?' she asked.

'No,' he replied.

'This will be bad,' said Shadow. 'I can't tell you how I know. I just do.'

'Anything unusual at sea is bad,' replied the captain. 'All hands on deck!' he yelled. The wind dropped to nothing, and the ship slowed. 'Check the hold, fasten down all cargo and loose items. Close and batten the hatches. Reef all sails but leave the fore. Prepare for a storm the likes of which we have never seen. Move, now, fast! And light the storm lanterns. It's going to be dark in a few minutes.'

Shadow raced to the room she shared with Kai, grabbed her circlet, and put it on. Then she went looking for the storm lanterns. She found one sailor struggling to light them. 'Here, allow me,' she said. Using her magic and concentrating on the circlet to empower her spell, she cast a spell of light on each of the lanterns. 'I don't know how long they will last, but they should get us through the night. They won't go out if they get inundated with water,' she said.

The sky to the north darkened considerably. Clouds rolled in from nowhere, thick and black, with a purplish hue. Impossibly fast. In no time at all, rain began to lash down in torrents. Then the wind started. It howled through the rigging. The foresail billowed to its full extent and pulled the ship forward through the tossing sea. The sail hands were still lashing safety lines about the deck when the storm's fury hit. The crew worked in pairs for safety. They worked hard and furiously; they worked to save their lives.

The ship lived up to its name. It danced with the wind amongst the waves, flying before the storm. The storm drove them south, far faster than they could possibly have travelled under normal conditions. Kai's group tried to keep to their rooms and out of the way, allowing the crew to go about their work.

It was two days of running before the storm, with little food available for anyone. Dry rations and a little water were all that the cook could do. The sea was just too rough to risk anyone in the hold. The rear mast came crashing down, followed by the main. The only good thing about it was that they acted like storm anchors, helping to steady the ship. The foremast was beginning to creak alarmingly when the captain ordered the foresail cut loose. The ship no longer danced, she stumbled. The competence of the captain and crew was the only thing that lessened the fear in the hearts of the passengers. They were unaware of just how much danger they were all in.

At dusk on the second day, the storm blew itself away. *Storm Dancer* limped along, still heading south. The captain ordered the day crew to stand down. The night shift would try to repair some of the damage. The cook, finally able to prepare a meal, set about his duties. A light soup was all he managed that first night, but it was enough. It gave them the fluids they needed and the sustenance their bodies craved.

By the next morning, the captain had a better idea of how badly the ship had been damaged. He came and spoke to Kai. 'We need to find somewhere that we can stop and do repairs. We need land. I cannot guarantee that the ship will survive a strong blow, let alone another storm like that last one.'

'I doubt that we will have another storm,' replied Kai. 'Shadow said it was induced by magic. If so, I doubt that whoever was responsible could raise another for quite some time. Do you know how far we travelled?' she asked.

'At a rough guess, I would say that we are at least a week's travel farther south than where that old sailor thought they had reached. I am hoping that land is relatively near.'

Both Shadow and Alemrae climbed the mast. It creaked alarmingly as they looked for any sign of land. None could be seen. Rad joined them, chirruping happily now that the immediate danger had passed.

'We could try magic to locate the nearest land,' said Shadow, 'except that I have no idea how to proceed.' Rad clicked and clacked at her. 'Oh,' said Shadow, understanding his meaning. 'Join your magic to mine, and I will then join both of ours to Rad. Together, the three of us should be able to locate the nearest land,' she told Alemrae.

Alemrae sought his magic and sent a coil spinning to Shadow. She also brought forth her magic and, wrapping it together with Alemrae's, passed it on to Rad. Rad sat on the rail, rearranged the strands, and added his own form of magic to the mix. He formed a lattice work that whorled and twisted into a globe that encompassed the ship. Rad then released the magic. The ship reacted, turning slowly. It was no longer pointing south but to the east.

'Keep this heading!' Shadow shouted down from the mast. They climbed down, their job done.

Shadow went to the first mate who had command of the ship. 'The closest land is straight ahead,' she said. 'I don't know what we will find when we get there.'

By mid-afternoon, land had been sighted, but it did not look promising. There were high cliffs for as far as the eye could see in either direction. Above the cliffs was a forest, tall and thick. A jungle of immense proportions, the smaller trees were twice the height of the tallest trees they had in the north—between 90 and 120 feet high. The tallest towered above them, going up over three hundred feet in height, and this was just at the edge. How tall the trees grew nearer the centre of the forest was beyond anyone's reckoning.

'Which way do you wish us to travel?' asked the captain.

'North. Follow along the coast until we find an inlet or river that we can safely navigate. Then we follow it until we find a safe place to stop and repair,' Kai replied.

They stopped as the sun began to set. The captain was not willing to risk further damage to his ship by sailing through unfamiliar waters at night. Dawn came, and they set under way again, rounding a headland and running east. Near mid-morning, they came across a deep water lagoon surrounded by reefs. The tidal flow showed a usable entrance between two higher sections. *Storm Dancer* limped through into the calmer waters beyond, scraping her keel in a couple of spots.

Once through, they saw a marvel ahead. There, running out from the sanded beach, was a stone dock. How and when it had been built was a mystery, but it was ancient. Some sections near the end had eroded and fallen into the sea. Closer to the beach, it was still sound. They pulled up alongside and tied off to the pillars and then ran out a boarding plank. Everyone left the ship. They carefully walked up the stone pier to the beach and collapsed with relief upon the sand, enjoying the feel of solid ground beneath them once again.

Once they had rested for a while, the captain ordered his crew to search the surrounding area carefully, but without straying too far into the forest, and to begin setting up the necessary encampment. The ship was to be under guard continuously. The remains of stone buildings back in the forest were discovered, as was a faint trail leading deeper into the jungle. The buildings proved to be unusable. Some of the blocks were taken to use as a base for their fire and supports for stakes to hold up tents and sailcloth for shade. Food was not going to be a problem. There were plenty of fruit-bearing trees along the coastline, as well as further into the jungle. There was also the lagoon full of fish—all they had to do was catch them.

It took three days to set the camp up as they required and to find a source of fresh water nearby. Once the immediate needs were met, Kai consulted with the captain about the repairs for the ship.

'It is likely to take us ten to twelve weeks to replace the masts. All the other repairs needed should be completed well before then,' he said.

'I think we shall leave you to your work,' said Kai. 'We may as well follow that faint trail and see where it goes. It gives us a starting point in our search for the elves. We shall get an early night tonight and start after we break our fast in the morning. We shall search for eight to ten weeks and then seek to return, letting you know what has been found. If we have not returned by the end of fourteen weeks, then consider us dead. Do not come looking for us. We are an able group and should be able to overcome any difficulties we encounter. That gives you an extra two weeks to get the ship ready to sail. When the time comes, leave, without us if you must.'

A feast was held that night in honour of the brave adventurers who would be departing in the morning to face the unknown. In the morning, their last goodbyes said, Kai's group walked into the jungle, following the faint trail that led away from the ruined buildings.

CHAPTER 29

After they had travelled for a short distance, Bradur knelt upon the trail and searched through the leaf litter. He found paving stones. 'I knew it!' he exclaimed. 'There had to be some reason for this trail to still be visible, considering the state of disrepair of the buildings. This was once a major road to somewhere, well paved and maintained.'

Alemrae took the lead, his skills in the forest the best of the party. He was easily able to follow the trail, and the others followed him. Morannel took the second position, followed by Shadow, Kai, and Maria from the Sisters of Mercy, who was the healer for the party. Bradur and Frederick brought up the rear. Rad flitted from the front to the back of the party and occasionally off into the trees, but usually spent the time resting upon Shadow's shoulder, occasionally commenting to Shadow about the forest.

They followed the trail for two days before it began to deviate in its course. It had been heading in a straight line in a south-easterly direction, but now it veered to the south. A high ridge appeared before them, a break in the tree line showing nothing ahead but a sharp drop down the other side. When they reached the top of the ridge, they saw an awe-inspiring sight. Far in the distance was a line of mountains, so high that clouds covered the top two-thirds of them. In front of the mountains was more forest, tall and dense. A series of large clearings or grassy plains were visible, some along the line of their march. A large, wide river flowed from the mountains to the north-east, cutting through the forest.

'That will prove difficult to cross,' said Alemrae.

'We can always hope that we won't need to, or we could go around. How about we camp here for the night and continue on again in the morning?' Kai said, feeling a bit more tired than usual.

'We could all use the break an early stop would give us,' replied Alemrae.

They camped that night just below the top of the ridge, off the trail and on the other side from the mountains. Their smokeless fire gave them warmth and kept the local wildlife at bay. They had kept a watch every night up to this point—not knowing what to expect—but there had been no encounters of any sort. Despite the ease of the trail, no animals appeared to use it, leading Alemrae to assume that there was something out there, in the forest, which would occasionally hunt along the trail.

Once Kai was asleep, Alemrae spoke with the others. 'She nears her time. She will give birth within the month. If we don't find the elves soon, then we should turn back. She would be more comfortable on the ship when she gives birth, and it will be safer for all of us.'

'You know something,' said Bradur. 'Spit it out. Let us know the worst.'

'I don't know anything, but I suspect that there is something that hunts along this trail. That is why we have seen no other animals using it. When it comes for us, and I suspect it soon will, we must protect Kai. She is in no condition to protect herself. I have removed her daggers from her possession. She must learn to rely on us for her defence. Morannel, would you please take her daggers and carry them for her?'

'Certainly. I shall remain by her side and be her defence,' he replied.

'I shall assist,' said Shadow and the Sister of Mercy simultaneously. They smiled at each other. Shadow had spent much time with the sister, trying to learn what she could of healing and childbirth so that she would be of assistance when the time came for Kai to give birth.

They had become close friends through being of a similar age, the sharing of knowledge and the time spent together.

They arose at first light the next morning and set off before Kai could realise her daggers were missing. She was the only one in the group not weighed down by the equipment they carried. She was carrying enough extra weight as it was. They travelled for an hour before stopping for their morning meal, a small stream running beside the trail giving them access to fresh water. The noises of the forest died away.

Alemrae was instantly on the alert. 'Caution, all,' he whispered. 'Something comes. Hide.'

CHAPTER 30

They all tried to find a place to conceal themselves. Some were more successful than others. Bradur stayed where he was, out in the open, delivering himself up as prey for the hunter and trusting in his armour and the others to come to his aid, hopefully surprising the beast.

The attack, when it came, was swift. Three large bipedal lizards raced from the forest edge and hit the sturdy dwarf front on, knocking him from his feet. The largest lizard attempted to bite through his armour and found the task most difficult. An arrow whizzed through the air, striking one of the smaller lizards. A second followed.

Frederick rushed out, flaming sword swinging at the other smaller lizard—a partial hit, enough to cause a wound but not severe enough to kill the beast. It roared in pain and then leapt at its attacker. Bradur, still on the ground, tried to swing his axe at the large lizard above him. He succeeded in hitting one of its legs but did little actual damage to it.

Alemrae let loose another arrow into the first beast he had shot. This one found its true mark and pierced the heart. Frederick had his hands full trying to keep the other smaller lizard off him. The flame of the sword seemed to worry it more than anything else, so he tried to lash it across the face with the flame. It seemed to work, and the lizard backed off. Another strike at its face sent it fleeing back into the forest.

The larger lizard, now alone, realised it could do little to hurt its victim, so it, too, fled into the forest, screaming its frustration. Before long, the sounds of their flight disappeared, and the normal sounds of the forest resumed. The group gathered together and checked one another for injuries.

The only one with an injury was Bradur, who had a large bruise on his chest from where the lizard had tried to bite him. 'Nothing more than a love bite,' he muttered. 'Used to get worse from the wife when she was feeling frisky.'

'Let's move on,' said Alemrae. 'We don't want to waste the daylight.'

Once again, they set off. By mid-morning, they had crossed through the first of the many open grassy areas.

'Things don't feel right,' said Shadow. Rad clicked his agreement.

'What do you mean?' asked Morannel.

'I don't know. It just doesn't feel the same as it did before we came into these grasslands. It feels sort of wrong, as if things are not quite as they should be,' she replied, shuddering.

'She is right,' said Alemrae. 'Now that I am aware of it, I can feel the difference as well. It is as if things have been twisted or bent out of shape.'

'Keep alert and stay close together,' commanded Kai. 'That may be the only warning we have in this place.'

They moved on, the feeling of wrongness growing, until everyone could feel it. Rad kept up a constant string of whistles clicks and clacks at Shadow, complaining of the wrongness. 'There is nothing I can do about it,' she told him. 'Until we leave this region, I think just about anything may have the capacity to do us harm.'

'Stay on the trail. It feels like the one safe spot,' said Alemrae.

Sister Maria laughed at him. 'You think that grass and flowers may attack?'

'I don't trust anything here,' he replied. 'Any field of this size should have grazers of some sort, yet we see nothing, just the plant life. That suggests to me that there is something terribly wrong out there.'

The group began to prepare a quick meal. Maria walked away from the path towards the red and white roses in the field. No one noticed her leave the path. It was tough going—the long waist-high grass was tangled and difficult to walk through. She leant over one of the roses to smell the flower when she noticed something white on the ground by her feet. She bent down even further to pick it up. *How strange. A small cat skull. It died here.*

As she began to stand, she felt something prick through her clothing and wrap tightly around her legs. Looking back down, she saw the rose wrapping itself about her, its thorns piercing her leg. Something else was entangling her arms—the long grass. She became alarmed. Before she could do anything else, the white rose struck at her inner thigh. It began to turn red. It was feeding on her. Another rose twined around her left arm and began to feed as well. She was shocked by the suddenness of it all and felt herself growing weak and dizzy. She tried to call out but was overcome. She collapsed, the long grass wrapping itself tightly around her, hiding her from view.

CHAPTER 31

Kai was the first to notice that someone was missing and called the alarm. They looked around but could not see any trace of the sister. She had vanished.

'Move out,' ordered Alemrae. 'Something is very wrong here. We need to remove ourselves from this area as soon as we can. It feels like something worse is on its way.'

The ground out in the field buckled, and soil flung up into the air. The group ran, not waiting to see what had caused the eruption of the ground. They passed back under the canopy of the trees, still with the feeling of strangeness about them. The trail widened a fraction. More of the paved surface had become visible, and the trees overhead closed in, forming a tightly closed archway through which the path continued. A series of low-slung lianas crossed the path.

Alemrae pushed through. Morannel and Shadow were in their midst, with Kai just about to enter the tangle, when Morannel cried out, 'Ow, beware the thorns.' He began to pull one of the lianas from him, bleeding as he did so. The lianas seemed to come alive, writhing around Morannel and Shadow. They were both bound tightly and hauled upwards.

Looking up, Kai saw four large eyes and two gaping mouths full of large teeth—they appeared to be all head. 'Monsters!' she yelled, reaching for her daggers on her belt. Her daggers were gone. *Where are they?* She had them earlier, she was sure. She backed off, feeling helpless, but knowing that there was nothing she could do. Even with her daggers, she realised, there was no way that she would have been able to assist. She would just cause more problems for everyone— another who would need to be rescued.

Frederick rushed forward, his sword enveloping itself with flame as he did. Alemrae turned around and brought his bow to bear. He quickly loosed an arrow into the large lumpy head of the thing holding Shadow. It appeared to do no harm whatsoever. Bradur came forward and jumped, catching onto Shadow's legs. Their combined weight was too much for the beast to lift. It came to them instead, lowering itself upon them from the trees. Frederick swung at the limbs holding Morannel, striking and severing one and burning it as well. It did not appear to bleed; a thick and sticky substance oozed from the wound. It looked more like sap than anything else.

Bradur cleared himself from the beast holding Shadow and pulled his axe from his belt. Two large, long tentacles came over the thing towards him. He stepped forward and, with a mighty effort, slammed his axe into the beast. It was like chopping wood. The creature screamed and dropped Shadow, sending eight of its tentacles towards the dwarf. Alemrae brought his twin swords into the action, assisting Frederick with hacking the limbs holding Morannel.

Rad, in a fit of fury over the attack on Shadow, breathed fire upon the creature suspended above her. Flame encircled the beast. Thick, oily smoke rose from its body and flames shot up along the tentacles, as it writhed in agony, burning to death. Bradur dropped his axe and grabbed hold of Shadow, pulling her out from underneath the burning hulk. She was a little bit singed and unconscious but still alive.

The other beast started to pull itself, along with Morannel, higher into the trees. Rad took to the air and sent flames flowing through the foliage about it. The creature dropped Morannel in its haste to escape the flame. He fell to the ground with a thud, groaning. Slowly, peace returned once more.

Kai raced to where Shadow lay. She inspected her injuries and decided on the best course of treatment. 'We shall have to carry her until she regains consciousness,' she said. 'Build a stretcher, but stay close in case there are more of those things out there. We dare not stay here long.'

Kai then checked on Morannel. He was bleeding from the many small wounds inflicted by the thorns on the tentacles, and he had a large bruise on his shoulder from when he had fallen, but was otherwise okay. He slowly got to his feet. 'What were they?' he asked.

'Some sort of twisted, intelligent plant,' responded Alemrae. 'A monstrosity created by mages trying to meld plant and animal life together. I've read about them, never thought to see one. Don't ever wish to see another.'

Rad flew back down to Shadow and gently nudged her cheek. He whistled sadly when he received no response.

'Let's get this stretcher built,' suggested Morannel.

Kai oversaw the project. They gently laid Shadow upon it, and Bradur and Morannel lifted it. 'Now let's get out of here,' Morannel said.

Once again, Alemrae took the lead. The rest followed closely behind, surrounding the stretcher. Rad rode upon the stretcher and rested his head upon Shadow's cheek. They crossed through the forest and another grassy plain before stopping to rest. The feeling of wrongness was still as strong as ever.

'I would hazard a guess that some great mage tried to do some evil works and they backfired upon him,' said Alemrae. 'That might account for this feeling and those monsters we came upon.'

They moved out again, with Morannel and Bradur carrying the stretcher as quickly as they could. They passed back into the forest and slowed a little, not wanting to attract any more unwanted attention. They stumbled forward, exhausted after the day's events, not wishing to stop but having little energy to continue on. They came to a river. The path stopped at the edge, and there was a stone bridge leading across to the other side. Like the dock they had come across, this was ancient. Parts had crumbled into the river below, but it looked sturdy enough to hold them, if they were careful about it. They moved across the bridge and on into the forest on the other side.

'The feeling of wrongness is gone,' said Alemrae wonderingly.

'We should be safe here. We'll stop for the night,' commanded Kai.

They organised their camp, set guards, and checked on their wounded. Shadow was still unresponsive.

'I am worried about her,' said Kai. 'She should have awakened by now. What does your magic tell you, Alemrae?'

'There is something in her system, maybe a poison of some sort. There is little we can do for her but keep her warm and hope she recovers,' he said.

They kept watch all through the night, but there was little change in Shadow's condition. They left as the sun rose, the path slowly rising before them. They were climbing the foothills of the great mountain range they had seen. Somehow, in that strange land, all distance had been skewed as well. The thick jungle thinned as they climbed. Looking back, they could see the path that they had followed clearly. It meandered all over the landscape. How was it possible? They all remembered following a straight path, always heading in the one direction. Had time altered along with everything else down in that horrid valley? They could not tell.

They stopped again at midday, and, once again, Alemrae checked upon Shadow with his magic. 'I fear we are slowly losing her,' he said. 'Unless we get some help soon, she will die.'

'Then we continue on,' said Kai. 'We eat on the move. Somewhere ahead is the place we seek. I can feel it.'

'What you feel . . .' said Alemrae. Then he stopped. 'Peace,' he whispered in wonderment. 'I have not felt this since . . .' Again, he paused. 'You are correct, Kai. Help is near at hand if only we can attract its attention.'

'You already have,' said a voice from above.

CHAPTER 32

The group jumped, surprised. Looking up into the trees about them, they saw people. They were different—slim, lithe, and graceful. They walked upon the branches through the trees as if on the ground. They were all well-armed.

'You have entered our lands. Whether or not you leave them again has yet to be determined.'

'We have one here who is sorely in need of aid,' said Kai. 'Is there nought that you can do to assist us? We have already lost one of our number, and we do not wish to lose another!'

'We may provide assistance, but that in itself may prove costly,' the elf replied.

'We shall pay the price—whatever is asked,' replied Kai.

'We shall hold you to that agreement,' said the elf. 'Come, follow.' He motioned to two of his fellows to take over the carrying of the stretcher. Then they began to run. It took all the effort that the group could muster just to keep up. It appeared that the elves were running slowly so that they would not fall behind, so gracefully did they move.

Just as they thought that they could go no further, the elves stopped. They walked through into a clearing. Within that clearing stood the largest trees they had ever seen, and within those trees dwelt a city—not upon the ground but hundreds of feet in the air.

'Rest here. One comes who may provide the assistance that you seek.'

The group sank to the ground, half stunned, not just by what they saw in front of them but also by their exhaustion. An aged elf slowly glided to where they were. She spoke to the other elves, and they left. Then she turned to Kai. 'You trespass upon lands you have no right to enter, but we shall assist you at a cost—the cost to be paid at a later date. Now, I shall see to your companion, Kai.'

She turned from Kai to Shadow and knelt beside her. Seeing Rad beside Shadow, the elf looked up surprised. 'How is it that one of the dragons of old has survived and come to be here?' she asked. 'No matter. I shall hear the tale later.'

She turned to Rad and spoke a strange language. Rad replied, also speaking that language. 'She has been poisoned by the death balls from the Valley of Scraethius. This may take some time, and she has little of it left.'

The elf bowed low over Shadow's head and began whispering. Goosebumps appeared upon Shadow's flesh as the elf worked her magic. Rad sat up and worked some magic of his own, linking the magic of the elf to Shadow's circlet and, thus, more directly into Shadow. The goosebumps faded, Shadow's colour resumed a healthier tone, and her breathing deepened, as if she were merely sleeping and not near the point of death. Her eyes opened.

'I know you, but I don't,' she whispered curiously upon seeing the elf. Then she turned her eyes upon Morannel, who hovered close by. 'I have missed you,' she said.

Morannel leant forward and took her hand in his. 'As I have missed you,' he replied.

The elf turned to Rad. 'I am amazed at your capabilities. How is it that you are what you are and that you may do what you have done?'

Rad squawked an apology, for he was unsure as to the nature of the question.

Shadow moved as if to get up, but Morannel held her down. 'You are still weak. Let me carry you,' he said, and then he picked her up in his arms and held her close. She rested her head against his shoulder, content. 'Where are we to go?' Morannel asked the elven woman.

'Rooms have long been prepared. Shall I guide you?' she asked.

Kai replied, 'If you would be so kind, or if there are no others who may show us the way.'

'There are many who know where you shall reside but few who may willingly guide you,' she said.

'And why is that?' Kai asked.

'Come, follow me, and whilst I lead you to your dwelling, I will answer your questions. It is because of the prophecies,' the elf replied, leading off.

'Which prophecies am I supposed to fulfil?' Kai asked.

'All of them and none,' she replied.

'That is a ridiculous answer,' Kai stated.

'As with any prophecy, the interpretation is open to misjudgement. If you were to literally fulfil some, then doing so would preclude you from fulfilling others,' the elf replied calmly. 'Thus the contradiction within the answer. The prophecies themselves are so archaic that the means to understanding them has been lost. Some are simple—the means of your arrival by following the Path of Icarian through the Valley of Scraethius and the timing of your arrival to coincide with the Pillar of Demitrial. Others not so—the deliverance from safety to the world of peace at war; the destruction of our death only to lead us to death. So, you see, the confusion is there within. How is it possible to destroy death and then lead us to death? Many have read the prophecies in their original form and fail to find anything to give us hope. I prefer to rely on hope and watch how you fulfil them. Now, here we are. Your accommodation awaits. I hope it meets with your approval. There are those within who will guide you whilst you stay. I shall return at the close of the day.'

With that, she left them standing near the base of one of the trees. 'Do any of you see a dwelling?' asked Frederick.

Rad clicked at him. '*Up*, he said,' Shadow replied.

They all looked skyward, and high up, in the topmost branches, were pathways and buildings.

'How are we supposed to get up there?' asked Kai. 'We certainly can't climb that tree!'

'You walk up the pathways, or if a mage obliges—teleport,' said an elf, walking around from the other side of the tree.

'We have three capable of magic with us, but none can teleport,' Kai replied.

'Then walk it is. This way,' replied the elf as he turned and walked back the way he had come.

Kai's group followed. On the other side of the massive tree was the beginning of a ramp leading up, spiralling around the tree towards the pathways above. 'If you are fearful of heights, then please stay close to the trunk,' recommended the elf.

The ramp was wide enough to walk two abreast. 'Surely there must be a faster way to arrive at the top than this slow walk up,' said Kai.

'We do have baskets and the like for raising goods and food. They cannot bear a great deal of weight. As with all things, assistance must be asked for before it can be given.'

'Well, then, considering the state of my health at the moment, can we receive aid in getting up to our dwelling?' asked Shadow.

'Certainly,' replied the elf. He pulled out a horn and blew a series of notes upon it. A few seconds later, everything blurred and shifted. Instead of standing on the lower part of the ramp, they were on a platform at the top.

Another young elf greeted them. She was wearing little in the way of clothing, just a filmy light covering of some unknown cloth. 'I am here to assist, if assistance you require,' she said.

Kai replied, 'Your assistance is required and also appreciated. Guide us to our rooms and have brought to us all that we require, preferably before we need to ask for it.'

The young elf smiled. 'Gladly,' she replied. 'Please follow me. Your rooms are through here.'

She led them to a series of buildings that appeared to have grown out of the tree rather than be built upon it. 'These were grown for your use, centuries ago. Please, enjoy your stay.' She opened the door and let them enter.

CHAPTER 33

The rooms were fine, if lacking in comfort. Everything was made from wood and finished with a high polish. There were carvings everywhere. Some were extremely intricate; others were very simple, but no less impressive—they showed the nature of the forest in all its entirety. They moved through the rooms, exploring the building and deciding on who would stay where. Each room seemed, by some marvellous method, to have been created for one particular individual, fitting their taste.

They all settled in. Rad went out to explore the tree city. Shadow had been the first to select a room. The large window with a view over the grassy plain surrounding the tree city with the forest in the background gave her a sense of openness—a feeling that she had missed during their travels through the jungle. The window also allowed Rad to fly in and out whenever he wanted to stretch his wings or explore.

She was standing there at the window, gazing out to the horizon, when she felt arms close around her and pull her from behind. 'I was afraid that I had lost you,' whispered Morannel in her ear.

She turned in his arms and embraced him. 'You will never lose me. I will always be in your heart, for you are in mine,' she replied. Then she looked up at him.

They kissed, gently at first and then more passionately. Together they moved slowly to the bed and tumbled down upon it. 'Ow, that hurt,' said Shadow, breaking the mood that had arisen. The bed, also made of wood, was, of course, hard and unyielding. They laughed at themselves.

'We are definitely going to need some padding on this,' said Shadow.

'I like that *we*,' said Morannel.

Shadow smiled at him, a broad and beautiful smile. Morannel could not resist and reached out to take her in his arms once again and kiss her. Shadow did not resist but embraced him eagerly in return.

'When you are ready—nephew, Shadow—could you join us in the front room?' said Kai, interrupting them. Shadow and Morannel both jumped and blushed when they looked at Kai, embarrassed to have been found in such a compromising position.

Kai laughed at them. 'There is nothing to be embarrassed about, you two. We have expected this for months. What took you so long?' she asked. 'Come on—the others are waiting.' With that, she left.

Shadow and Morannel looked guiltily at each other, blushing even more. Then they arose and, with arms around each other, left the room.

They took a late midday meal together. Shadow realised that someone was missing. 'Where is Sister Maria?' she asked.

It was Alemrae who responded. 'She disappeared along the trail amidst one of the grassy areas, don't you remember? We could not see her anywhere, and it was too dangerous to go looking. She was warned not to leave the trail, but she must have and paid the price for it.'

Shadow looked distraught, and Morannel held her in an attempt to provide comfort. 'We all share your grief,' he whispered to her. Shadow's tears flowed, and she sought to bury her face in Morannel's shoulder.

Not long after, a small group of elves joined them. 'We are the elders. It is we who must impose upon you the obligations due for the healing and safe conduct into our realm. We are here to tell you your price.'

'Before you do, could you explain a few other things to us?' asked Kai.

'If we have the knowledge, then, yes,' replied the eldest.

'We were told earlier that we would fulfil some prophecies. Could you elaborate upon them a bit more?' said Kai.

'It is you alone, Kai, who will fulfil the prophecies, not the others with you,' said another of the elders. 'The assistance of others is not mentioned, nor is it necessary. The prophecies all relate to an individual. *The daughter of the world*. That is you, Kai. For within your family background, you have a relationship with all.'

'That is not quite accurate, but I certainly am related to many races, as is Morannel,' replied Kai.

'Morannel is a son, not a daughter, and the prophecies relate to a woman, not a man,' explained a third elder.

'It was your decision to follow the Path of Icarian, which led you, in turn, to the Valley of Scraethius. That is where you lost your "protector of health", as she was called in the prophecy. You have arrived before the Pillar of Demitrial is at its conjunction, thus fulfilling a few of the prophecies already,' said the fourth elder.

'Who were Icarian and Scraethius, and what is this pillar you keep mentioning?' queried Kai.

'Icarian, the Mad Seer, was one of us. He lived over five thousand years ago. It was he who looked into the future and spoke the prophecies. It was also he who designed and built the stone dock your ship used and the pathway you followed. No others have ever used them. Scraethius was an evil arch-mage of immense powers. He sought to destroy us, but instead his creations destroyed him—not before his evil will had tainted and twisted everything in his valley, however. His magic still holds sway there. Powerful as we are in things magical, we cannot extend our control over his domain. Everything that has been tried has been twisted awry. Unless his power is destroyed, he will eventually destroy us. The evil slowly spreads. Thus, the next step along the prophecy—you will destroy our death and lead us to death. The Pillar of Demitrial we can show you tonight. It is an alignment of both stars and planets in our sky.

It has happened only three times in our history, all thirty thousand years of it. Each event heralds a massive change in the world as a whole. Each time, a son or daughter of the world has come forth at the culmination of the pillar to lead the world into its next stage.'

'Excuse me,' interrupted Shadow, 'but may Alemrae, Rad, and I spend some time with your mages, learning something about how you manipulate magic?'

'It was expected that you would ask. It has been allowed for,' replied the first elder. 'They await you even now, amidst their grove. Just ask any one of the young to guide you.'

Shadow and Alemrae rose to their feet and walked out. 'You others may wish to avail yourselves of our training grounds,' said the second, a polite dismissal of them.

'Come,' said Morannel. 'They obviously have things to discuss with Kai in private.' Frederick and Bradur stood and followed Morannel out.

'An easy way of ensuring our solitude,' said Kai. 'What is the meaning of separating us like this?'

'You must return, alone, to the Valley of Scraethius. There you will find a tunnel in the field where your comrade fell. Enter the tunnel. It will take you to that which must be destroyed.'

'I am unable to do so at this time. Until my child is born and I have recovered from the birth, I must stay here,' replied Kai. 'Also, I seem to have lost my weapons somewhere along the trail. Could they be replaced?'

'Your companions took your weapons to protect you from yourself. Were they wrong to do so? I think not, for they ensured your safety. No doubt they will return them once you are delivered of your child. Speaking of which, prepare yourself, for your time is due. You could have had the child at any time in the last three weeks. I suspect it will come within a day or two. Aid will be provided.'

'I would ask that you care for my daughter as if she were one of you for as long as she is in the care of your people,' said Kai.

'That is the second part of your penalty—that when you leave us, your daughter remains, as you knew she would.'

'Then it was you who gave me the dream of my daughter flying over the forest,' remarked Kai.

'We did not know the substance of the dream, just the time frame of the future for which you had to see,' replied the eldest elf.

'Give me one boon. Please ensure that she can cope with the differences of her heritage and all that it brings her, for she shall have a troubled life,' asked Kai.

'It shall be done. Come. It nears time for the evening meal. We shall all join together on the forest floor for a feast. Once the time is right, we shall show you the Pillar of Demitrial,' said one of the elders.

The four elders and Kai left as a group, and they walked out to the edge of the platform. 'Do you truly trust us?' asked the first elder.

'I trust everyone until they do me wrong,' replied Kai.

'Then allow us the privilege.' She reached out and took one of Kai's hands; the second eldest took hold of the other. The other two elders joined in, forming a circle, and speaking softly, they proceeded to walk off the edge and out onto the air. Taking Kai with them, they gently fell towards the ground. Going slowly the whole way down, they landed softly.

Kai grinned with delight. 'That is a much easier way to travel,' she said.

'Only if you're going down. It won't take you up,' replied one of the elves with a laugh.

They continued along a forest path, many other elves joining with them. They arrived at a huge clearing. A bonfire was burning in the centre, and trestles laden with food were scattered around the field. 'Go and mingle. The others will find you,' said the eldest.

CHAPTER 34

Kai left the elves and wandered across to one of the tables. She picked up a wooden platter, polished to a high sheen, the grain of the wood showing the hints of a face—decoration enough. She walked the length of the table, taking selections from a wide variety of dishes, unsure what any of it was. Once her plate was full, she moved towards the bonfire, seeking a place where she could seat herself comfortably. She found a large log on which to sit, far enough away from the fire that she was not too hot, but close enough that as the evening cooled, she would stay warm. She ate her meal amidst a small group of young elves who were all chatting away about the visitors, oblivious to her presence.

Alemrae was the first to join her. He brought a waterbag and a couple of cups, as well as his own meal. Setting his plate on the log, he poured a cup of water for Kai before getting his own. Then sitting beside her, he consumed his meal in silence.

'Did you learn much in the short space of time you were able to spend with the mages?' Kai asked.

'A different way of thinking mainly, I suppose,' answered Alemrae. 'They work with the things around them, not against their natures, as most others do. It makes it easier to do some things, but others are almost impossible. There are benefits to both. To blend the two together will take much work. Shadow has proved adept. It is amazing just how much she is capable of doing, even without her circlet. I think it is because of the way she thinks. She tends to experiment a lot, just shifting magical energies around to see what happens. If she finds something unusual, she tries the same thing on something else and compares the results. I think she actually understands the nature of magic better than just about anyone else that I have ever met, even though she knows very few actual spells. Once she begins collecting an assortment of spells, she will become exceptionally dangerous. Her defensive magic is astounding. I would be hard-pressed to better her defences, and I have spent over ten times the length of time she has actually working magic!'

'And what of Rad?' queried Kai.

'Rad is a freak.' Then he laughed. 'He can manipulate magical forces in just about any way imaginable. He just takes the raw force or what someone else is doing, and adds to it, or changes it slightly, to make it behave how he wishes. He does not have rote spells like the rest of us. I think that is why he took to Shadow. Her abilities lie closest to what he does. Their minds are linked. They boost each other's abilities—Rad's manipulations added to Shadow's creativity. Why do you ask, Kai?'

'There is something in our future. A bare hint is all I feel. The three of you are going to be very important to us. Do me a favour—when the time comes, accept my decision and back me up. I am sure you will know when.'

'I shall do so, even at the cost of my life,' he replied.

'It shall not cost you your life—it will save it,' said Kai. 'There may come a time when I might have to do the unthinkable, to risk it all. If it comes to that, I want everyone out.'

'I've already promised to do as you ask. Just don't expect us to be happy about it.'

'If you all live, then I can die happy, for I will go to join my Brelldan. But we have a war to win first,' replied Kai.

Bradur, Morannel, and Frederick came over. 'I have been searching for Shadow. Have you seen her?' asked Morannel.

'She said that she needed some time alone but would join us after the feast,' said Alemrae.

Morannel frowned. 'I hope my actions have not caused her to rethink,' he said, worried.

Rad glided down from somewhere above, his silver scales reflecting the firelight in a myriad of patterns. He landed lightly on Kai's leg and walked up to her lap. He gently rested his head on her stomach, listening to the sounds within.

'Do you mind?' said Kai. Rad looked up at Kai and chirruped happily. Then he looked back over his shoulder.

Shadow appeared from the crowd and hurried to them. She stood beside Morannel and put her arm around his waist, pulling him closer to her and laying her head upon his shoulder. Morannel's arm went around her waist.

'Apparently no harm done,' said Alemrae, smiling.

'What?' asked Shadow.

'Nothing—just passing a comment,' said Alemrae.

'I feel better now that we are together again,' said Kai. 'Does anyone know anything about this Pillar of Demitrial?'

'Demitrial was a sage,' replied an elder, just walking up to them. 'Many thousands of years ago, he was the first to record the position of the stars that heralded the cataclysmic event that originally saw the end of the second age and ushered in a short ice age. Few of any race survived. Those that did prospered in the ages to come. The elven race is one of the last with a knowledge of that first event. It is time to see the pillar for yourselves. Come along.'

They all trooped after the elder to a small secluded clearing. Many other elves were already there. A clear crystalline dome was hovering in the air above the grass. The grass was short, thick, and soft.

'Please lie down. There is space enough for all,' said one of the elders. 'Make yourselves comfortable. The Pillar of Demitrial will culminate at midnight, so we have an hour to wait. The dome above you will magnify the view of the stars, making it easier to see the pillar as it forms. If you wish, the dome can be removed.'

'The dome is fine where it is,' answered Kai in a strained tone.

'I see that it has already begun,' said an elder.

'What has begun?' asked Frederick, looking up.

'The birth of the new world,' answered the elder.

They lay down on the soft grass and looked up at the dome. There, enlarged by the magic within the dome, they saw two columns of stars, almost perfectly aligned, with four more forming a triangle across the top. The point of the triangle was missing.

Kai was moaning softly to herself occasionally, trying to ignore the pain as her contractions intensified.

But she knew that her labour had begun.

CHAPTER 35

The feeling of magic surrounded them, intensifying as the night went on. Kai's birthing moved along smoothly, assisted by the magic. Her pain was minimised and went largely unnoticed by the others. It was Alemrae who alerted the rest to Kai's imminent delivery. It was just minutes to midnight. All of a sudden, they were not interested in the stars but in the progress of the birth. Kai moved into a squatting position. Her clothing had already been stealthily removed to allow for the birth.

Bradur knelt behind her. 'Lean back upon me—it will be easier,' he said.

With his solid support, Kai did indeed find holding the birthing position much easier. Rad and Shadow began using their magic to assist Kai, whilst Alemrae moved in to catch the child as she was born. Morannel and Frederick stood well clear, not wishing to intrude too much, and decided to look back up at the stars.

As they watched, there was a burst of red light at the point where the missing star should have been just as the pillar was fully aligned. The light struck the dome and passed through, narrowing, and focusing to a small circle. The circle anointed the newborn head of Kai's daughter just as she howled protest at her birth. Cloth was presented to Alemrae to clean off the child. She was inspected with magic to ensure her health. All was okay. She was a healthy young babe with all the right number of fingers and toes, with only one difference—an extra pair of limbs.

Rad flew down to where Alemrae knelt and inspected the child for himself. Happy with what he found, he carolled his delight. *She has wings.* He flew back to Shadow and landed on her shoulder, still making a joyful noise. Shadow tried to quieten him but with little success. Kai lay back in the grass, allowing the elves to clean her properly. Her daughter, wrapped in a soft, clean cloth, was placed in her arms.

Kai looked at her. 'Your name will be Bell,' she said, 'for you have rung in the dawn of a new age. May you find the peace that few of us have ever had!'

Kai then turned to one of the elders. 'I have seen my daughter and held her. Take her to that place where she will be cared for. If possible, I will see her again before I leave.'

'As our agreement stands, it shall be done,' he replied. Taking Bell, he handed her off to one of the elves waiting nearby.

'What is this? What did you agree to? How could this be?' asked Shadow angrily.

'Peace, Shadow. It is for the best. Bell will grow and learn here in peace. There are tasks that we must yet do, and the trail is no place for an infant. We would all be distracted by her, and trouble would come of it. I am hoping that there will come a time when we can come back for her. All of us. But if not, then at least I know that she will grow up. Here, she will learn to be at peace with herself and her surroundings. That is all I can ask. At least, here, she has a chance at life. Besides, we have just seen another part of the prophecy fulfilled. I have delivered Bell from a place of safety into a land of peace, which is at war.'

They waited in the glade for Kai to regather her strength. When she was ready, they made their way back to their dwelling. Once again, mages provided assistance by teleporting them up to the platform from below.

'I think I'm getting the hang of that,' said Shadow. 'I shall have to work on it.'

'I would suggest attempting to teleport small inanimate objects a short distance first,' said one of the elders, 'before attempting it on yourself.'

'Noted,' said Shadow with a grin. 'Now, if our beds have some decent padding on them by now, then I shall seek my bed. Coming, Morannel?' she asked, smiling shyly at him.

'As you wish, my love,' Morannel replied.

They entered their dwelling and moved to Shadow's room. The others all went to their rooms and prepared for sleep. Morannel and Shadow embraced and kissed.

'We need to discuss our future together,' said Morannel. 'I would not have you at risk in childbirth until after our journey is complete.'

'I shall not conceive this night, or in any time in the near future. Besides my magic, there are herbs that I can take to prevent conception,' Shadow replied. 'We have other issues more important in front of us than bringing children into the world. I must return to the desert. How long I will need to be there is unclear.'

'That is not at issue. You shall do what you must. I will stay at your side for as long as may be,' stated Morannel.

'But you have responsibilities, a nation to rule, laws to govern, decisions to make,' said Shadow. 'I would not have you ignore those responsibilities because of me.'

'I have come to realise that there are some things that are more important to me than ruling. You are one of them—the most important in fact,' stated Morannel. 'There will come a time when I must make some important decisions, but that time is not now. For now, we two can be as one, and I fully intend to make the most of it.'

With that, Morannel picked up Shadow, carried her to the bed, and lay her down upon it. Shadow was a bit shocked by the intensity of Morannel's statement, and it took her a while to respond. When she did, she did so with full and enthusiastic participation.

CHAPTER 36

Shadow and Morannel enjoyed each other until the sun rose. Then they slept. They arose after the midday meal, but even so, they beat Kai up by a couple of hours. They left their room in search of food. No one was in the main room when they entered. Some food was left in the centre of the table—some fruits and leafy vegetables. There was no meat, although an empty platter was near the other bowls.

'Looks like Rad has been here and gobbled all the meat,' said Morannel.

'Quite likely,' replied Shadow. 'You were much more interested in eating something else earlier. Don't blame him if you let him get to it before you,' she said, laughing.

'Hmm, perhaps I should start on that again,' Morannel murmured, nuzzling at Shadow's neck.

'Stop that. We came out here to get sustenance. We can play again tonight.'

'Well, that's only a few hours off. I suppose I can wait,' remarked Morannel.

They helped themselves to some of the food and adjourned to the platform outside. Rad, who had been sitting by the edge of the roof and looking over them whilst they ate, wafted down from above and landed on Shadow's shoulder. He rubbed his head against her neck and cheek, looking for affection. She returned the gesture, gently caressing his head and neck, resuming their bonding ritual.

'I wonder what the others have been up to today,' said Morannel.

'Something more important than sleeping all day, I expect,' replied Shadow.

'We didn't sleep all day,' said Morannel.

'No, just most of it,' said Shadow with a grin. 'I wonder if we could go and see Bell.' Rad clicked an agreement; he also wanted to see her again. 'You just want to see her wings again,' said Shadow. Rad carolled his answer, happy for Bell to have her wings.

'Let us go and find out,' said Morannel.

They got up and, after returning their plates to the table, went looking for a guide to show them where Bell had been taken.

CHAPTER 37

K ai awoke shortly after they had left. She took her time in arising, first doing a slow stretch, tensing and loosening her muscles. She felt much more relaxed. The extra weight from her middle was gone. She no longer felt any soreness or pain from the birth. Her body had already repaired the small amount of damage that had occurred. She climbed out of the bed and stood in the middle of the room. She slowly began her exercise regime that ensured her suppleness and kept her strong. In short, she danced, slowly at first until she had completed all the moves and then again slightly faster. By the time she had completed a third repetition, she was almost back up to her full speed. She had already worked up a sweat and decided that it was enough for the day. She would do more on the morrow.

She searched her room for some means to clean herself and, finding nothing of use, decided to dress and find out where to go to bathe. She obtained a guide to a grassy grove beside a small stream. She was left there alone when she admitted a wish for privacy. She cleaned herself in the stream, the cool water refreshing her. Once she had finished, she returned to the dwelling. Walking up the spiral ramp left her feeling rather tired and very hungry. Calling out for assistance, she walked back into the dwelling and waited.

A young elf came in. 'You asked for some assistance?' he said.

'Yes. Can you have the evening meal brought up here now? I don't know how many will be eating here tonight.'

'Yes, Kai, food shall be brought,' he answered. Then he left.

Kai went back into her room and lay back down on the bed, waiting for the food to be brought and someone to talk to. She fell asleep again. Noise from the other room woke her up. It sounded as if the rest of the group had returned. She arose once more, only to find a group of elven children surrounding Shadow and Rad. They were all chatting away. Rad was in his element; he did so love to be admired. He was stretching out his wings and returning them to their folded position and cleaning himself for his admirers.

'Has our meal arrived yet?' Kai asked Shadow.

Shadow arose to her feet, glad of the distraction. 'Not yet. The others are all on their way up. The food should get here by the time they do,' she replied.

The children left quietly, knowing without being told that it was time to leave. Rad flew out the door behind them.

'How are you feeling today?' asked Shadow.

'Lighter, definitely lighter,' Kai laughed. 'I seem to have recovered somewhat from Bell's delivery. Tomorrow, I think I shall attend to the problem of the Valley of Scraethius. Something definitely needs to be done about it. The elves will not be free to assist us with our undead problem until the valley is dealt with, so down the tunnel I go.'

'Could it not be the same problem? Everywhere we have gone so far, there has been a sorcerer or necromancer to be dealt with. Could one have taken over the valley? They seem to be adept at controlling things,' said Shadow.

'I don't know. You may be right. I shall find out in the next few days, I imagine.'

'You're not planning on going alone, I hope,' said Shadow.

'I was told I must,' replied Kai.

'Since when has that stopped you from doing what you believe is the right thing to do? We shall all be needed.'

'Why do you think that all of us are needed?'

'You mentioned a tunnel,' replied Shadow. 'You are going to need light to find your way, and I have the best and steadiest source you could possibly want. If I come, then Morannel will. He will seek to protect me. Besides, he is an able hand at mapping the tunnels and will help to ensure we don't get lost. Bradur is a must. His nature is such that he will provide insight into how the tunnels are built, or if they are natural. He is also a sturdy and ferocious fighter. Frederick has a magical blade. It can harm most things we might come across. Its flame would also provide a little bit more light. Last is Alemrae. He always has insights into what is around us. He has lived longer than the rest of us. He is also a formidable fighter and mage.'

'Don't count on any magic. The valley twists all magic cast in its vicinity to its own purpose,' said Kai.

'And that is why we need Rad. His innate understanding of the nature of magic just may help us in overcoming whatever is causing the valley to do what it does. Besides which, even if you went alone, the rest of us would follow you.'

'All right, you have convinced me. But how do you intend on convincing the elders?' asked Kai.

'I don't. That's your problem,' said Shadow with a laugh. 'And if we may, I would like to see if we can find Maria and give her a decent funeral.'

'We will certainly try. It did not sit right with me that we just left her there,' replied Kai.

Just then, the others walked in. The food followed on their heels. Once the meal was served, the elves departed. Kai served herself first, too hungry to wait any longer. The rest all took plates and helped themselves. Once they had finished, Kai stood to speak.

'Tomorrow, we will go back to the Valley of Scraethius. There we will look to accomplish two things: find Maria, so that we can give her a decent funeral, and try to determine what is causing the valley to be the way it is and fix it if possible. Shadow has convinced me that we all will be needed. Magic gets twisted there, so we will probably have to rely on brute force. So I will need my daggers back!'

'I would suggest that we wait one more day,' said Alemrae. 'Tomorrow, you and I can spar, barehanded. If you last the distance or defeat me, then you can have your daggers back. If you don't, then we wait one more day for your recovery to be complete.'

'And who gave you that authority?' said Kai.

'You did, when you became pregnant and could no longer protect yourself,' said Alemrae. 'Someone had to oversee your health. You were oblivious to your condition. That someone was me. Since then, any and all decisions regarding your safety have been mine.'

'Ha! So be it. Since you are all in collusion, I doubt that trying to go anyway would work—it is just as likely to lead to a rebellion,' said Kai.

'Only for your health,' replied Shadow gleefully. It was rare that they could convince Kai to do anything against her wishes, and now they had done it twice in one day.

'Well, I am in for an early night,' said Kai. 'You had all better do the same, because as soon as I am done with Alemrae tomorrow, we will be leaving.' With that, she walked back into her room.

'A bit conceited, isn't she?' stated Bradur.

'Not particularly. She is just very sure of her capabilities,' replied Alemrae. 'I suspect that we will be leaving no matter the outcome of tomorrow. Shadow, do you have anything that will heal bruises quickly? I think I am going to need it. I have just given Kai an excuse to hit me, and she has wanted to do just that for quite a while now.'

'I have seen you in action. Are you sure that she can defeat you?' asked Bradur.

'Easily. If I can drag it out a bit, then maybe I might have a chance. It will all depend on how much her stamina has improved. If she is anywhere near her best, then I am going to be thrashed, probably deservedly,' replied Alemrae, laughing. 'I had better get some rest as well,' he concluded and then also left.

'How is it, that Kai has such martial skills?' asked Bradur.

Morannel replied, 'It is all in her history. She left her home, when about my age, in search of the lost races. Not long after she started out, she was captured by brigands and sold into slavery. The one who purchased her ran a school dedicated to fighting. His slaves fought in individual combat, either to first blood or to death. Another school bought her from the first one and improved upon her techniques. She eventually fought her way to freedom. Her owner granted her freedom after a death bout that she won when blindfolded. Her opponent's vision was unimpaired. She spent many years travelling and ended up in Albrae. Whilst there, she won the title of Briar Rose in a competition to find the best fighter of the populace. According to custom, the winner then has to fight the king's five champions—one after the other, no chance to rest, weakest to strongest. Kai defeated them all, thus earning herself the title. On top of that, our family history is rife with interbreeding with the demi-human races. She has abilities that few others have. You will see just how good she is tomorrow. None of us have seen her fight to the best of her abilities. I am sure that tomorrow we will see something special. Mind you, Alemrae can certainly fight much better than he is letting on.'

Morannel moved to where Shadow sat, took her by the hand, and assisted her to her feet. He then guided her to their room, his arm around her waist and whispering in her ear.

'And then there were two,' said Bradur.

'Make that one,' said Frederick, leaving as well.

Rad flew in through a window and landed on the table.

'Well, you're it,' said Bradur getting up. 'I'm off to bed as well.'

Rad looked around the room and croaked. The door and windows were shut. The torches went out. Rad stealthily made his way to Shadow's room, where he hid. A light appeared, a nice bright, flickering orange flame. Then another, but this one was green; five more dancing lights came up, dispersed evenly around the room, each one of a different colour. They began to swirl around the room, making the shadows jump around crazily. Then a wave of darkness rolled up from the bed and swamped them all. Rad crawled up the side of the bed and curled up on a pillow beside Shadow, miffed. Shadow was too preoccupied to notice.

CHAPTER 38

They arose with the sun. It was going to be a hectic day. They dressed and gathered in the main room to break their fast. Kai had already left by the time Shadow arrived. When she finally did appear, the others burst out laughing. Shadow could not understand why, but then she could not see herself. Her face looked like it had been painted with many coloured dots.

'Why do you laugh at me?' asked Shadow.

'Have you looked in a mirror lately?' asked Frederick. 'You seem to be a bit spotty this morning.'

'What do you mean "spotty"?' said Shadow.

'Your face is covered with spots, many of them, in a nice rainbow of colours,' replied Frederick.

'I suspect Rad may have had something to do with it,' said Morannel.

'Why blame him?' asked Shadow.

'You did cover his lights last night with darkness and ignored him,' replied Morannel.

'But I did nothing,' replied Shadow. 'I used no magic.'

'Then I have no idea what happened,' said Morannel.

'You go and watch the bout. I am going to stay in my room until Rad turns up and we discuss what he did to me and why,' Shadow stated, walking back to her room.

The others left for the training grounds after breaking their fast.

After spending some time gazing out the window of her room, Shadow went and broke her fast. She was annoyed with Rad. Why would he do such a thing and not even communicate his displeasure to her? She went back into her room and lay down on the bed, intending to wait for Rad to return. She fell asleep waiting.

The others had made their way to the training grounds. Some young elves were learning how to use different weapons. The bow was favoured, as it could be used to provide sustenance as well as in warlike activities. Various types of swords and other melee weaponry were also on offer for use. Various-sized rings had been carved into the sod. These were the combat rings.

Kai was standing in the middle of one of the smaller rings, a faint sheen of sweat already upon her brow. She had completed her warm-up and was ready for Alemrae.

Alemrae stripped off his excess clothing and began stretching. When he was ready, he stepped into the ring. 'Whenever you are ready,' he said, moving into a crouched position.

Kai leapt forward. Alemrae dodged to the side, and, spinning, he sent a kick flying towards the back of Kai's unprotected legs. She back flipped over his kick and sent one of her own towards his chest. Alemrae leant back and let it pass. Then they began to spar in earnest. Blows flicked back and forth between them, punches and kicks, even an occasional throw attempt. Kai sped up. She wanted this farce over and done with. She needed to be on the move, not delayed by some silly upmanship.

Alemrae began to become more and more defensive, using all his skill to keep Kai away. Even so, the odd blow found its mark. She was just too quick. Alemrae managed to grasp Kai's left arm and throw her over his back towards the ground. Kai spun in the air and landed on her feet; she sent a terrific kick at Alemrae's stomach. It landed, partially winding him. He backed off, hoping to gain some time to recover. Kai pressed the attack, sensing her advantage, landing many more blows to the torso and head.

Alemrae stepped forward to stop the assault, giving Kai no room to throw any more blows. He grasped both of her arms with his and pulled her closer. Kai kicked, not to the legs or body but at the head. Without any room to manoeuvre, she somehow landed the telling blow. Her foot connected with the point of his chin. He flew backwards, unconscious before he hit the ground. Kai sat down beside him.

'I am exhausted. You may have been right to want to delay another day, but I had my reasons. You win. Now we have to wait until you awaken and recover.'

CHAPTER 39

They left the elven city at dawn the following day, heading back down the trail the way they had come. The forest seemed to become darker as they proceeded through. A feeling of foreboding surrounded them. Perhaps it was aware of their intentions to end the evil in the Valley of Scraethius. They all kept alert, not wanting to have some unforeseen accident upon the trail. Thus, with tensions raised, they came at last to the field where Maria, the Sister of Mercy, was lost.

The field was vacant. There was nothing to see, except for the long grass and the occasional red or white rose. Somewhere out there was the reason they were here. No one wished to be the first to walk out into the field. After a long pause, Frederick ventured out, sword drawn and flaming.

'Let's have a better look, shall we?' He thrust his flaming weapon into a thick clump of grass. A tremor ran through the field as the grass took flame. Astonishingly, a ring of bare earth opened up around the burning patch of grass, as if the grass had moved itself away from the flames.

'Light torches. Burn a wide swath through this field until we can find this tunnel we are supposed to take,' ordered Kai.

Frederick continued to advance slowly, swinging his flaming sword at every clump of grass he could reach. The others, torches lit, moved out to flank him. The grass seemed resistant to the flame, taking a much longer time to catch alight than normal.

They advanced through the field, the grass and roses giving way to the flame. Looking back across the area they had already cleared, they saw the grass returning, slowly moving back to encircle them. There were many bones where they had burnt the grass, some recently stripped of flesh, others obviously old—a part of the strangeness of the Valley of Scraethius, where the plants could move about and feed upon the animal life.

They came to the area where the ground had heaved up the last time they were there. A freshly formed tunnel sloped steeply down under the field. It was lined with some sort of sticky slime or ooze, remnants of whatever had formed the tunnel—some magically developed beast or giant worm maybe. The tunnel was close to eight feet across—just wide enough to walk together in pairs, but not wide enough to fight together. If it came to battle, one person would have to take the lead.

Shadow donned her circlet. Giving them good light, it lit up an area for about thirty feet around them. Frederick's sword, still flaming, added to the light, but not by much. Bradur knelt in the tunnel to examine the floor and walls. 'Some sort of giant worm made this. It has not been carved out by tools or limbs,' he said.

'The sand worms of the Irikani Desert leave similar tunnels but nowhere near as large. They are only about a foot across, and they do not last for long—a day at the most, less if it happens to storm,' said Shadow.

'The nature of the ground would lead to their collapse. If they tunnelled through solid earth as is here, then the tunnels would remain for much longer,' replied Bradur. 'The walls are solid. There is little risk of collapse. We can proceed.'

Bradur put words into action and slowly moved off, drawing his axe from his belt as he did so. He was followed by Kai, Frederick, and Morannel. Shadow, with Rad again on her shoulder, and Alemrae brought up the rear. It was tricky going until the tunnel levelled off. The ooze coating the walls of the tunnel was making it slippery.

The tunnel meandered in a somewhat southerly direction, heading further into the Valley of Scraethius.

After travelling for about an hour, they came across another tunnel. This one appeared to be much older but well used if the build-up of slime was any indication. This second tunnel crossed the first at an angle, heading towards both the south-east and western parts of the valley.

'Keep heading south,' ordered Kai. 'I sense that that is where we need to go. The centre of the valley should still lie ahead of us somewhere.'

Once again, they moved off down the tunnel. A while later, Bradur called a halt. 'Wait here a moment.'

He moved off into the darkness alone. Fifteen minutes passed whilst they awaited his return.

'He is taking too long,' muttered Frederick quietly.

'We wait,' said Kai. 'Bradur can sense things about this environment that we have no idea about. We dare not proceed without him.'

It was another ten minutes before Bradur returned. 'There is a wide section of the tunnel up ahead. It appears to be a natural cavern with many entrances into it. There is a large bulbous mass of what may well be eggs off to one side. We need to be very careful as we pass through. Follow me.'

CHAPTER 40

It did not take them long to reach the cavern. The light they had did not reach to the far sides or the roof. The floor of the cavern was some fifteen feet below the exit of the tunnel. 'Move down to the floor, slowly and as quietly as you can. I sense a great deal of danger around us,' whispered Kai.

Bradur began the descent. Once he was on the floor of the cavern, Frederick followed. Each of them made their way slowly down. 'There is something moving over there,' whispered Frederick, pointing towards the western side of the cavern. A long white worm, about eight feet long and a foot across, was wriggling its way towards them, attracted by the light and heat.

'It must have just hatched. It will be hungry,' said Bradur. 'Do we run or kill it?'

'Kill it,' commanded Kai. 'We don't want it following us all the way.'

They spread out but stayed within the circle of light provided by Shadow. The worm, confused by the splitting up of the party, halted briefly and then came on, heading directly towards Shadow. The party encircled the worm and attacked it from all sides. It let out a piercing shriek as it died. Looking around them, they saw more movement heading in their direction—three more of the small worms.

'Frederick, use your sword to burn the egg pile before the rest of them hatch.'

The party raced towards the young worms whilst Frederick bypassed them, heading towards the egg pile. Rad flittered after him. It took no time at all before the three worms were dead, each one giving off a shrill sound as it died. Frederick thrust his flaming sword into the pile of eggs, causing a column of greasy oily smoke to arise, but they did not catch flame.

A loud shrill scream sounded from the other side of the pile. Looking up over the top, Frederick saw a giant worm rear up, ready to protect its young. It was close to eight feet across and forty feet long. Frederick glanced back towards the others and realised that they were in a great deal of trouble. Two other giant worms had moved up behind them, summoned by the death cries of the young.

He rushed back to assist. Rad breathed flame upon the eggs. His breath, far hotter than Frederick's sword, caused them to erupt into a mass of flame, lighting up the cavern. Two more giant worms were heading towards them from the north-east.

'There are too many. Run. There is a passage too small for them to fit through towards the south-east!' shouted Bradur.

They rushed away, the worms following hard at their heels. It was a strange chase—the party dodging around stalagmites, the worms crashing into them, breaking many, the ooze from their skin eating away at the limestone. One chunk of falling stalactite crashed into Morannel and knocked him from his feet. He rolled to the side just as one of the worms struck at him, a glancing blow but one that nearly shattered his arm. Pain flared up, his skin blistering from the acidic ooze. He stumbled back to his feet and into another stalagmite, its support helping him to steady himself. The worm reared back to strike again. Morannel prepared to dodge. The worm let out a sudden shriek and turned from him. Morannel took the opportunity provided to stumble towards the exit, where the others were waiting. He looked back.

There was Frederick battling the giant worm with his flaming sword, cutting large holes in its body. The other worms were closing in. Realising his peril, Frederick swung one last mighty blow, nearly severing the head of the worm, before fleeing towards the dubious safety of the small tunnel. The worm burnt, causing the others to move away. The party would be safe for the moment.

Kai quickly inspected Morannel's injuries. 'This is going to take a while to heal. We must bandage it, and you shall have to carry your arm in a sling. Stay in the middle of the group. Take no action. Just stay alert and warn the rest of us if you notice any danger. Frederick, your deed has earned you your freedom. From here on, you are no longer bound, for without your help, Morannel would have been killed. You risked your own life to save the life of your king. That is all I needed to see. Now, let's move out slowly and stealthily. Bradur, take the lead.'

'This passage is not natural, nor has it been carved out by hand,' said Bradur. 'I think we may be close to Scraethius's centre of power. I believe this has been made with magical power.'

Bradur led off, followed by Alemrae. Frederick brought up the rear, being the only one with a weapon suitable for defending against the worms should they manage to tunnel through. Kai and Shadow assisted Morannel. Rad was chirruping encouragement until Shadow admonished him into silence.

They walked on, the tunnel becoming more and more regular as they went, until it had the appearance of a building. Corridors crossed the way forward and delayed their progress. They took time to ensure the safety of the party before proceeding. The occasional empty room, with nothing but dust or a broken crate or two, broke the monotony. There were no doors. Kai moved to the front, sensing trouble ahead. When it came, it came fast—and on six legs.

CHAPTER 41

A large black cat with two long tentacles attached to its shoulders suddenly appeared. It barrelled straight into Alemrae, knocking him from his feet.

Bradur's first stroke with his axe sheared through where it was but missed completely. 'Shadow cat!' he yelled.

Kai moved in, eyes closed, focusing on her inner talent, sensing the true location of the beast. She struck hard, one dagger entering the left side behind the foreleg; the other piercing the back, cutting into the muscles of one of the tentacles.

With the beast distracted by Kai, Alemrae was able to rise to his feet. Drawing his twin swords, he struck out, not to where he saw the beast but to the side where Kai was focused. One blade struck home; the other missed and narrowly missed Kai as well.

'Douse the light!' shouted Alemrae as he backed off. 'Kai will fare better alone and without sight.'

Shadow stopped her circlet from emitting light, and darkness reigned. Alemrae continued to weave a defensive pattern of blade work in front of him, hoping to dissuade the beast from further attack. Kai stepped up her assault, striking faster and hitting more often than she missed. Bradur stepped forward, unimpeded by the darkness, and swung a hefty blow towards the front of the beast. The strike connected, and the beast collapsed to the ground. Kai called for the light again.

'What did you call this thing?' Kai asked.

'Shadow cat, also known as a displacer beast,' explained Bradur. 'They are known to haunt ruins and the like. They are solitary in nature. The skin of the beast alters the light patterns around it, making it appear somewhere other than its true location. The skins are valuable. If you don't mind, I would like to skin it and keep the hide.'

'You are welcome to it,' replied Kai. 'We need to take a short break to recover anyway.'

Shadow and Alemrae assisted Bradur with the skinning of the beast, the three of them making short work of the gruesome task, although working by touch made the job just a little more difficult. Morannel kept an eye on the corridor, ensuring there were no more unpleasant surprises whilst the others were occupied.

'Since that beast was lurking in these corridors, surely an exit to the surface must be nearby,' mentioned Kai. 'I would suspect an arch-mage to have a tower, not reside underground, especially since he seemed to work at combining plants and animals together. Surely he would require some form of garden to work in.'

'He could just as easily transport them from above ground to a much safer abode under the surface and then release them when he was done, if they lived,' replied Alemrae. 'I will concede, though, that finding his laboratory will probably necessitate a search of the grounds above us.'

Rad chittered at Shadow. 'There is a great deal of magical energy in use a little to the west of us,' Shadow informed them. 'Rad is sensing its use.'

'Time to go, then,' said Kai. 'We continue heading in a generally southern direction but bearing to the west whenever possible. Shadow, use Rad to guide us. Frederick, move back to the front. I will guard the rear, whilst our two wounded stay towards the middle. Bradur, stay by me.'

Shadow moved to the front, with Rad upon her shoulder, and took the lead. She walked at a slow, comfortable pace, which the others had no trouble with. She had no hesitation in turning off the corridor at the first westerly joining intersection. A faint whiff of fresher air encouraged their movement, and they proceeded at a faster pace. She stopped at a stairwell. It spiralled up towards the surface and down into the depths of the earth. The corridor also continued on beyond the point where her light reached.

'Rad says that magical forces are being wielded below. Down the stairs. But I think we should first determine what, if anything, is above us. It may be our escape path,' stated Shadow.

'Good idea—up it is,' replied Kai.

They climbed the spiral stairs. Eventually, a small window in the side wall showed a view of lands to the north of their position. They were about three storeys above ground, yet there had been no exits.

'Keep going until we reach the top,' said Kai quietly. 'I want to know what it is we are dealing with here.'

They continued up, arriving at the top a short time later. The tower they were in was about seven-storeys tall and had no other exits. They had come out into a single room at the top of the tower. It encompassed the whole floor—just one large single room with open windows on all sides. A large summoning circle was in the centre of the chamber, with torch brackets upon the walls at each compass point. The circle and glyphs were exceptional, made out of precious metals and gemstones—a permanent structure for the summoning of extremely dangerous entities. It could also be used as a portal, a place to transit to and from another place. It absolutely reeked of magic!

'There is nothing else up here that we need to see,' stated Kai. 'We need to go below and see what is stirring up the valley.'

Once again, they set off back down the spiralling staircase and into the depths of the earth. They paused for a rest at the junction where they had first found the staircase. Morannel removed his arm from the sling. It was beginning to feel much better, and he could actually move it without any pain, but it still lacked the strength that he would need to fight. He took up his share of their possessions and then added Kai's to his load, freeing her from any burden.

'Time to readjust our order again,' decided Kai. 'Bradur, take the lead with me. Alemrae, come after us. Morannel and Shadow, with Rad, to the middle. Frederick, bring up the rear. Try and keep our light low. We don't want to inform whatever is down here with our light.'

Shadow removed her circlet, and darkness reigned, until Frederick drew Soulburner and brought forth its flame. The small amount of light it produced would be enough for them to find their way without being bright enough to alert anyone of their approach.

'Shadow, signal when we are on the same level as the magic. Now, move out.'

Kai and Bradur moved off down the staircase, side by side. They stopped at each level, waiting for Shadow to tell them which way to go. The answer was always the same: 'Deeper. We must go deeper.'

They were at least seven levels beyond the ground surface when they reached the bottom of the staircase. Unlike the rest of the levels, this one was well lit. Globes of light hung on the walls at even spacing. One small corridor led directly away from the stairway and ended at a closed door. Two other corridors of the normal size led off to the east and west.

'We go straight ahead,' said Kai, walking forward. 'A door in a place without doors is a dead giveaway.'

When they reached the door, Bradur reached out and turned the handle slowly so as to make as little noise as possible. He pulled the door open a fraction and risked a peak through. Seeing nothing of note, he opened the portal fully and stepped through. Kai followed on his heels. This was an entrance chamber to a series of rooms, each room dedicated to a different branch of magical study, the subject indicated by glyphs etched on the doors. Shadow indicated a room to the left was where the magic emanated from. They moved across to the door and pushed through. This was a large circular room with an altar in the middle, and upon the altar was a body.

Maria.

CHAPTER 42

Standing on the other side of the altar was a desiccated mage—another necromancer.

'Ah, you have made it at last. I was beginning to wonder if you would. You are just in time to see the final act in the transfiguration of your colleague.'

He cast a spell upon Maria's body, and she began to move. 'Please welcome the new addition to my forces. I hope you enjoy her company. I see you have brought me another plaything. How kind of you.'

As the undead thing, which had been Maria, arose from the altar, the necromancer began to cast more magic. The group spread out, hoping to reduce the number impacted by whatever spell he cast.

The undead thing attacked. It was not slow and ponderous like the zombies that had attacked Albrae but quick and surprisingly strong. Alemrae and Frederick converged on it, allowing the others to concentrate on the necromancer. They had just begun to move forward when a black, oily beam, which was giving off a noxious grey smoke, shot forth from the necromancer's hand and struck Rad, enveloping him. Shadow shrieked and collapsed, having been clipped by the edge of the beam. Some of the foul smoke stayed attached to Shadow and slowly covered her form.

Kai moved towards the altar, only to be intercepted by the undead. Morannel rushed to Shadow to see if he could aid her, but there was nothing he could do. Bradur, guarding the doorway, called for aid. A host of zombies sought to gain entrance, and he was hard-pressed to hold the door by himself. He was being overpowered by the sheer number and strength of those trying to enter the room.

'Alemrae, help Bradur. Kai, take down that necromancer. I'll deal with this one!' shouted Frederick.

Kai backed off to allow Frederick more room and then raced around the other side of the altar. Alemrae went to help stop the flood of zombies from entering the room. Frederick attacked with all his might, his flaming weapon slicing and burning the undead before him. He was struck in return. For every wound he inflicted, he received another himself. It was a war of attrition. Who would outlast whom?

Kai slammed a blow into the necromancer, knocking him away from the altar. 'Your puny attempts can do me no harm,' he said. He struck back with a taloned hand, clawing a vicious wound down Kai's arm and forcing her to drop one of her daggers. 'You are overmatched.'

Kai struck again, this time with Brelldan's dagger. This one penetrated the side of the necromancer and cut a large slice across the torso. To Kai's horror, the wound immediately began to heal, closing up as fast as the injury had been caused.

'Now you see the futility of your predicament,' cried the necromancer. The black, oily, smoking ball that engulfed Rad began to show signs of a bright white light piercing through the darkness. Then the ball exploded into incandescence, and a white beam shot out, striking the necromancer in the dead centre of his chest. The necromancer rapidly changed. He was no longer desiccated but had the appearance of a healthy, normal individual of about middle age.

Kai struck again whilst the necromancer was stunned. This time, the dagger pierced the chest, and blood flowed. It did not heal. The necromancer screamed. Kai, pressing her attack, brought him down.

Rad swooped upon the undead that Frederick was attacking, his silver claws ripping through the neck of the monster, dropping it to the ground. Frederick stabbed it through the heart and kept his sword there until the body was engulfed in flame.

By this time, Bradur and Alemrae had downed five of the zombies seeking to gain entrance. The dead were piling up in the doorway and impeding those still trying to enter. Yet still they came. Frederick joined the fight at the door, allowing Alemrae to back off.

'See to Shadow,' called Frederick as he chopped at another zombie. 'We'll keep the doorway guarded.'

Between them, Frederick and Bradur managed to kill off the rest of the zombies, burning them in the process. Alemrae, using his magic to assess Shadow's health, was disturbed. 'Something is seriously wrong here. Whatever that beam was, it has done a tremendous amount of harm. The smoke is continuing to do damage. She is barely alive.' Rad landed on the ground beside Shadow and crooned to her. 'She needs help, but we dare not move her,' said Alemrae.

'Rad and I will guard her until you can bring us assistance,' said Morannel. 'The rest of you can seek to end the menace of this valley and then bring in the elves to help Shadow.'

'We will search these rooms first. There may be something here that will help her, or end the work of Scraethius,' said Alemrae.

'But not before we have dealt with everyone's injuries,' said Kai. 'The battle has taken quite a toll on us.'

After seeing to the wounded, Kai, Bradur, Alemrae, and Frederick began to search the other rooms. Kai called out to Rad, requiring his presence. He reluctantly left Shadow's side and flew to her. 'I need you to determine what is magical and what is not. Can you do that for me?' she asked.

Rad nodded. He began to manipulate the energies around him. When he was done, many items in the rooms around them began to glow.

'These all have magical properties, do they?' asked Kai. Again, Rad nodded.

Then he flew back into the room where Shadow was lying on the floor. The group gathered up the glowing items, unsure of their use, and brought them back into the altar room. The wall behind the altar began to glow as well.

'Could that be a doorway?' inquired Alemrae.

Bradur moved over and examined the wall closely. Brushing his hand across the face of the wall, he was surprised that he felt nothing. He pressed his hand forward, and it went straight through the wall. 'There is nothing here,' he cried. 'It is an illusion.'

He stepped forward and disappeared through the wall.

CHAPTER 43

K ai and Alemrae leapt after Bradur. They emerged in a short corridor, which led to another small room. There, upon a large, throne-like chair, rested the remains of Scraethius the Arch-Mage. Before him, in the centre of the room, was a pedestal. On the top of the pedestal rested a glowing green gem the size of a clenched fist. It radiated menace.

'That is the source of corruption,' stated Alemrae. 'We need to destroy it.'

Without warning, Bradur swung his axe with all his might and struck the jewel with the flat of the blade. He was sent crashing back against the wall of the room, where he crumpled in a heap.

'That was an idiotic thing for you to do,' stated Alemrae to the unconscious dwarf. 'We need to disrupt the arcane protections before we can physically destroy it.'

'And how do you propose we do that?' asked Kai.

'No idea,' replied Alemrae. 'Rad may be the answer.'

Kai moved back to where Rad and Shadow were. 'I need you again, Rad,' said Kai. 'For something special. If you can help, we can get aid for Shadow much faster.' Rad flew up and perched on Kai's arm. 'I take it that's a *yes*—you will help,' said Kai, walking back towards the illusion.

As they passed through, the illusion collapsed. 'We need to destroy this gem. It has arcane protections. Can you do anything about it?' asked Kai when they had reached the pedestal.

Rad inspected the gem. Alemrae had been searching the room and had found a small golden hammer upon the remains of Scraethius. It was about the size you would use to crack open a nut.

'Would this help?' asked Alemrae, holding up the tiny hammer. Rad looked at it and then nodded.

An image came to Kai then of the gem resting on the altar and being struck by the hammer. 'Can you take the gem and place it on the altar in the other room, Rad?' she asked.

Rad gently picked up the gem and flew into the other room. Kai and Alemrae followed. Rad placed the gem in the centre of the altar and then flew back to land beside Shadow. Taking the small hammer from Alemrae, Kai strode to the altar.

'Brace yourselves. I have no idea what is about to happen,' she said. Then she knapped the gem with the hammer. It exploded in a burst of green energy, throwing Kai and the others back towards the walls.

A dazzling green plume of smoke arose above the altar and coalesced in the air. The ball that formed hovered there briefly before moving over Shadow and settling upon her. The mist spread out, engulfing her and the grey smoke. Light flickered over her body as if the two smoke plumes were doing battle. There was a groan from the other room, followed by a few curses. A battered and bruised dwarf accompanied the sounds coming into the room.

'What the heck happened?' he asked.

'You did something idiotic, and then we destroyed the gem,' replied Alemrae, laughing at the disgruntled appearance of the dwarf.

'We have done what we came to do. This valley will return to its natural state. The monsters abroad should eventually succumb unto death. It is time to return,' said Kai.

'I may be able to assist with that,' said Alemrae. 'If you all wait here, I will attempt to summon some assistance in that tower room above.'

'Do not go alone. Take one of the others with you,' stated Kai.

'If I must. Bradur, come along. We have some stairs to climb.' Alemrae left, followed by the surly dwarf.

'Let us see if we can make Shadow a bit more comfortable,' said Kai.

Shadow's circlet rolled free from her head, untouched by any hand, and remained lying on the ground by her head. The green mist dissipated; the grey smoke had vanished.

'Search the rooms. Let's see if we can find something to put Shadow on.'

They left quickly and quietly.

CHAPTER 44

All was darkness. Shadow was lying in a silver boat; a roiling black cloud of oil and grey smoke surrounded her, trying to smother her, but it could not pass into the boat. She lay there forever, unable to move, only seeing the cloud above her. A bright green mist began to descend through the black cloud. A vast rumbling sound came to her ears, as if both clouds were trying to stop the other from reaching her. A green island formed by the boat, and a man appeared upon it.

'Only together can we stop this destruction,' he said. 'Join me on my island, and I can aid you.'

'Who are you?' Shadow replied.

'I am Scraethius, Arch-Mage of Ildrakol and healer extraordinaire. I am your last hope of survival, as you are of mine.'

'You are dead. You have been dead for centuries. How is it that your spirit lives on?'

'I never died. My spirit was instilled in my final magical triumph by an enemy I never met. In the last moments of its completion, I was attacked—my spirit stripped from my body and locked within the construct I had made. My physical body perished, yes, but my spirit remains. With the destruction of my masterpiece, I have been released. I immediately sought a body to finish my work. Yours was the only one available.'

'You cannot have it. It is mine.'

'You are dying, almost dead already. If you die, then everything is for nothing. If you allow me to coexist within, then I can heal you and destroy this attack. Only within a physical form can I do this. In return, I ask that you help me end the presence of the undead in our world. I can give you knowledge and power. Once the undead are dealt with, I will be free of the obligations set upon me, for I was their creator. Yes! Me! I am to blame for all the centuries of chaos that has ensued. In my haste to learn all that I could of healing the body and spirit, I created the first undead. I also created a tool to further my research into them. That tool was taken from me when I was entombed.'

'If you created the undead and this tool, then surely you know how to destroy them.'

'The undead fall readily enough to magic, the blade, or fire. I know of no means with which to destroy the tool I created. You must choose, now! You have little time left, if I am to keep us alive. Join me here, for I cannot step within your protections.'

Shadow made her decision. She rose to her feet and stepped from the silver boat onto the island of green mist.

'Now you are mine,' said Scraethius.

Green mist surrounded her, bathed her in its soft and gentle touch, and seeped gradually within. Then the pain began, as the oily black smoke, which had been attacking her, resumed its assault. She could feel the turmoil within as the two opposing forces collided—one full of destruction, hate, and death; the other a renewal of body, of peace of mind, healing, and comfort.

She gathered what forces of her own she could and hurled them into the fray, siding with what she felt was right and good, siding with life. She felt her body begin to heal, the pain receding. The dark, oily cloud was shunted apart from her, and it slowly dissipated. It faded into visions of the past, of another life led, of lessons learnt and power gained. The life of Scraethius. They were one.

Shadow began thrashing on the floor. Her eyes opened and glowed an emerald green. Rad began screaming in agitation. Smoke rose from her body—a ghastly oily black smoke, reminiscent of the black beam that had struck her. She contorted in pain as the opposing forces battled for supremacy within her. A green mist enveloped her head and slowly spread down her body. As it progressed, her thrashing decreased, until she was immersed fully within the fog of green.

The black smoke rose and dispersed. The green fog also slowly dissipated. Shadow was calm, at peace—healed. Her eyes remained emerald green in colour, a bit disturbing in their brightness, although they no longer actually glowed.

CHAPTER 45

Frederick had been searching through the other rooms looking for something to use as bedding. He was unsuccessful, but he did find something else of importance. With the destruction of the gem, other magical protections had also failed. An extra doorway was now visible off the front room.

He called for Kai and Morannel to assist with this new discovery. This final room was of the greatest importance. Scraethius's magical tomes and spell books were lined up on the bookshelves, along with many potions and other items, including a crystal sphere, a staff, and a dagger. The whole room screamed of power. This was the true refuge of Scraethius, where he had finalised his research and collated his knowledge. His most prized possessions were here, and theirs for the taking.

Faint sounds gained their attention. Shadow had regained consciousness.

'Help me up,' she whispered. Morannel and Kai aided her as she rose to her feet. 'I've just had the most horrendous nightmare. Where are we?'

'We are in the tunnels under the valley of Scraethius the Arch-Mage,' replied Morannel.

'I remember. I remember that black beam. It was then that the nightmare started.'

'You don't have to tell us,' said Morannel. 'Just let it go. You have been healed, and by Scraethius the Arch-Mage, no less.'

'I dreamt of him, or maybe it was not a dream. I was battling a sea of undeath. He pulled me up out of the morass to safety and passed to me his lore. I know what drove him insane and why he did what he did. He sought a cure and, in his thirst for knowledge, unleashed a horror—the first plague of undead. His creation was stolen from him. It is that which is the source of our current issue with undead. Have you found his workroom yet, his lair?'

'We did,' replied Kai. 'Just before you awoke.'

'Then take me there,' she said.

With Morannel offering his arm as support, they made their way back into the first room and, from there, into Scraethius's private study. Rad flew after them, still unsure about the nature of the change in Shadow.

'Just as he left it,' Shadow muttered softly. She gathered up the crystal sphere and placed it on the table. 'Watch this,' she whispered. Then she cast a spell softly and in her native tongue, as was her fashion.

The globe began to shine with a faint white light. Within that light, a myriad of colours formed and coalesced into an image. Alemrae and Bradur were entering the top of the tower. The image faded from sight until the crystal globe was as it had been.

'How did you do that?' queried Kai.

'As I said before, Scraethius gave me his lore. I know everything about magic that he knew. I just don't have his power yet.' Shadow sat on the edge of the table. 'I am still weak. Pass me his staff and dagger. I shall take them, for I alone know their use. When Alemrae and Bradur return from the tower, we shall leave.'

'They were going to try and summon some help with the use of the ring,' said Frederick.

'I know they won't be successful. Alemrae does not have the power to work the ring. We shall leave by another route, after I dismantle these ruins,' said Shadow. 'Come, Rad—let me hold you.'

Rad landed on the table near Shadow, still wary of the change. Shadow offered him her hand. 'Go on. Bite me.'

Rad stepped forward, still unsure but did as requested. He bit hard, savouring the essence that was the newly improved Shadow. He let go and warbled a strange but happy sort of tune. Shadow lifted up her hand, looked at it, and then muttered a few words. The bleeding stopped as the wound healed. 'Happy now?' she asked him. He flew up to her shoulder in response and nuzzled her neck. She stroked him in return.

'I thought you didn't know much about healing magic,' said Kai.

'I didn't, but Scraethius was, first and foremost, a healer. All his work was done in relation to healing. The fact that he created as many problems as he fixed somehow escaped his notice. His cross-breeds were more in the nature of a hobby as a plant enthusiast. He tried to improve upon their perfection, giving them the ability to move about and seek better living areas. The fact that they became carnivorous and semi-intelligent was a side effect that he ignored.'

'If he was by nature a healer, then why did he create such an evil piece of self-sustaining magic?'

'He didn't—not intentionally. Just as he finished the last of his incantations to form the jewel to preserve his work, he was assaulted by a necromancer. The blending of the two magics led to the disaster you rectified. The necromancer managed to kill Scraethius before trying to escape. The monsters, which Scraethius had set free, finished him off. The elves confused that necromancer with Scraethius, as they had been unaware of his presence.'

'That means there have been four necromancers killed, with at least one, probably more, still at large. This is one large cult we are dealing with, not a plague at all. Things are beginning to make more sense,' said Kai.

'And they control, or have unleashed, whatever horror it was that Scraethius created,' said Shadow softly.

CHAPTER 46

Alemrae and Bradur returned a while later. 'I was not able to raise the circle to power. It is beyond my means,' said Alemrae sadly.

'It no longer matters,' replied Kai. 'Look who is back with us.'

Shadow walked in from another room.

'You look a little better than when we last saw you,' stated Alemrae.

Shadow grinned. 'That's an understatement if ever I heard one,' she laughed. 'Kai, these rooms are safe. How about we rest and recuperate before we leave?'

'That is a fine suggestion. We've been on the move for more than a day now, and we still have a few injuries to attend to.'

They made a cold camp in the front room of the complex, closing the door to give a little warning if something should try to come upon them. Shadow used her newfound knowledge to assist the recovery of the injured. Food and a good rest restored their vitality. By the time they were prepared to leave, it was the afternoon of the following day.

Shadow took the lead, with Rad on her shoulder and Morannel by her side. Frederick, Alemrae, Bradur, and Kai followed after. She led them back up the stairwell to the corridor they had first been in and, turning the way they had not yet explored, moved on. Shadow ignored many other passageways until they finally came to another, much smaller, sloping passageway—the one that would lead them to the surface.

But Shadow wished to try something before they left. Sending the rest of the party further up the passage, she prepared to cast a spell that she never would have even thought of, let alone attempted, before her recent experience. She gathered all the magical force that she could muster and, channelling it through her circlet, cast the spell.

At first, nothing seemed to happen. Then, slowly, the passageway in front of her began to shrink. The entire edifice shrunk to a diminutive size. The eighteen-storey complex now looked to be a model about four inches tall. It sat on the ground of the passage, just in front of her. She picked it up and put it in her backpack. Where the building had been was now a vast hole in the ground. She could see the sky—on the far edge, she could even see the cave of the white worms. She suspected that this would eventually become a lake, if there was ever enough rain to fill it up. She turned around and saw the others watching her, astounded by what they had just seen.

'Shall we go?' she asked, walking past them and heading up the passage towards the exit.

Once she reached the floor of the valley, she turned north, heading back up the grassy plain towards the Path of Icarian the Mad Seer. There were no interruptions to their journey. The grab grass and vampire roses had moved on, searching for some place safer in which to grow. The party found the path just as the sun began to set and made camp. Shadow had been ignoring the rest of the party all day, but now that they had made camp, she could no longer do so. She would have to answer some of their questions. As they settled down after the meal, she made up her mind.

'What do you want to know?' she asked them.

'What happened to you, and how did you gain such power?' asked Alemrae. 'One minute you are almost dead, and the next time I see you, you seem to be an arch-mage's equal in power.'

'I survived the assault meant to turn Rad into an undead. It almost succeeded in doing the same to me. When Kai destroyed Scraethius's magical gem, all his power stored in it had to go somewhere. His spirit had been infused in the gem and contained within it all of his knowledge and power. It needed a vessel capable of using the power it contained. I was the only one available. My own magical defences flared up, along with the power of the circlet, and saved me from total possession. We reached an agreement, his spirit and mine. I would allow his partial possession until the end of the undead menace— it was what he was aiming for anyway—and he would share his knowledge and powers with me. Once the undead are gone, he shall move on. His existence will be ended for ever, and I shall be left with whatever power I have developed and all the knowledge that I can remember.'

'What do you intend on doing with the tower complex?' asked Frederick.

'Ildrakol. Its name is Ildrakol. I will provide a bastion for my people. I want to set it up somewhere near the sea and allow my people to live within its walls. It is a more substantial home than the caves they currently reside in.'

'And the library of magical research—what do you intend on doing with it?' asked Kai.

'Study it, of course, and use it to bolster my attempt at world domination.' She laughed at the startled look upon their faces. 'No. I will try and help my people. I wish to try and change some of the desert wastelands into an arable area. If we can grow more food, then my people will prosper. Scraethius's work with plants should come in useful. I have no plans to try and change their nature, though. I may destroy some of his works so that others do not do the same as he did. I must admit I was fascinated with his ideas of experimentation, but I have also suffered from the results of those experiments. I think I shall be a little bit more circumspect in how I go about my own experiments from now on. I never really gave it much thought before, just tried different things to see what would happen. I have become much more aware of my responsibilities as a mage now. If we are done, I would like to get some rest.'

Shadow turned away from the group and went to her bedroll. She was asleep before Morannel lay down beside her. With both

Morannel and Shadow asleep, the others were free to discuss the situation.

'This bears watching,' said Alemrae. 'Any sort of possession can be extremely dangerous. In this case, both to Shadow and to us.'

'Keep an eye on her,' said Kai. 'If you notice anything out of the ordinary with Shadow, then inform me. I don't know if there will be anything that we can do about it, though.'

In the morning, they arose with the dawn. After breaking their fast, they continued on, back to the elven city. Once again, they arrived late in the afternoon. At least this time they were not in a hurry because of injury. They headed straight back to the lodgings they had used before. Once at the base of the tree, Shadow used her newfound knowledge to teleport everyone up to the platform. They startled a number of elves with their sudden arrival.

'Not bad for a first attempt, even if I do say so myself,' said Shadow gleefully. Rad chirruped an agreement and then clicked off another message. He took to the air, winging his way through the treetops. 'He's off to see Bell again. He's spending more time with her than me! I am beginning to think he is infatuated with her,' she laughed.

They spent the evening resting and seeing to their belongings and making repairs where needed. After breakfast the next morning, they gathered together with a few of the elders of the elven nation.

'It is time for us to return to Raelis. We have found what we have been searching for—one of the keys to solving the problem of the undead. If you could provide us some assistance, either in returning us to our home or in the battles that lie ahead against the undead, we would be grateful.'

'We cannot assist your return, but once you are there, have your mages create a portal using this gemstone as a focus. We can then transport those who are willing to assist through to you. Magical aid or fresh food could be as readily passed through. Your wounded could then also make the crossing and come to us for their healing. Your ship is repaired and awaiting your return. The sooner you return, the quicker it will be for us to assist.'

They left the meeting and gathered together their belongings. Leaving the elven people behind, they retraced their path to the bay where their ship awaited.

It was a fast-paced journey, with little to trouble them on the way. They used the magic learnt from the elves to help hasten their march and to increase their stamina and tolerance for hardship. They covered the distance quickly and easily, reaching the ship on the evening of the fifth day.

A small celebration was held that night for the success of their mission. Now they had to return home across the sea. They caught the dawn tide and sailed north. With magic to guide them, landfall on the southern coast of Tir, the eastern continent, was easily achieved. They then turned west, following the coast until they could once again head north towards Raelis.

CHAPTER 47

After six weeks of further sea travel, they arrived back at Raelis; good winds and magical guidance the reason for their speedy arrival. Their appearance was unexpected. They had been gone so long that the populace had almost given up all hope of their return.

, The city had changed in the time they were gone. Once a thriving mercantile port, it was now more in the nature of a giant militarised camp. An orderly progression of drays and carts flowed from the docks into the heart of the city and out to the armed camp. Others returned, carrying empty crates and barrels to be returned across the sea for replenishment. Space at the docks was limited.

The ship hove to. A lighter was sent in to arrange for a berth for the ship and to send messages on to the palace. Kai went with it, leaving the others to make their way when the ship docked. Once ashore, Kai seconded a horse and rode to the palace. The main thoroughfares were choked with the drays and carts, so she took to the back streets and meandered her way through the city. Entering the palace through the rear gate, she left the horse with the guards and continued afoot. Once again, she managed to surprise Regent Monfrae and the Lord Chamberlain with her return.

'We have much to discuss, both in terms of the ongoing war here and our successes and losses far away from here. Be at peace, Regent Monfrae. Frederick is well and has earned his freedom. He is with the others, awaiting passage from the ship. If you could please arrange transit for them to the palace and ensure rooms for all of us are made ready. But, first, I must take some sad news to the Mother Superior of the Sisters of Mercy. I will return shortly and give you the rest of the news.'

'The Mother Superior is currently in residence here at the palace, recovering from some injuries. The cause—a stupid accident. She's in your great-grandmother's rooms, I believe. Ask one of the maids for guidance to her.'

Kai left in search of a maid. Finding where the Mother Superior was ensconced was easily done. Down on the ground floor near the entrance to the kitchens, two of the Sisters of Mercy stood guard at a doorway. Upon seeing Kai approaching, one immediately ducked her head through the doorway and spoke to those within. She re-emerged and waved Kai straight through. The Mother Superior was lying prone, heavily wrapped in bandages. One of the sisters was slowly spooning a light broth into her mouth. She stopped and made to leave.

'Please continue your duties. I have returned with both good news and bad. Alas, Sister Maria has fallen. I shall spare you the details until later. The good news is that we managed to find the elves. We have assisted them with their own problems, and in return, they have agreed to aid us. We shall set up a portal to allow travel between the elven city and Raelis. They shall send through what aid they can. Any who require healing and can be transferred through will receive medical aid there. We can also summon one of their healers if there is great need. As soon as the portal has been set up, I shall ask for a healer to come through to aid you. In the meantime, I shall see if Shadow can assist in any way. She has become far more powerful than you would believe possible in such a short time. I shall tarry no longer, for I must let Regent Monfrae and the Lord Chamberlain know the whole of it.'

Kai departed and returned to the regent and Lord Chamberlain. Their meeting lasted for hours. Many messages were dispatched and decisions made. Other leaders came and went as their duties dictated. When the group arrived, Kai sent them up to her suite. Shadow was asked to look in on the Mother Superior to see if she could be of assistance. Alemrae volunteered to attend her as well. Bradur headed off to find his brother and let him know the tale of their success.

It was late evening by the time Kai was able to return to her suite of rooms. The others had already gathered there. Food had been left on the sideboard for her, and she immediately went to fill a plate. Whilst she ate, she filled in the details of what was to occur. There would be a short respite from their journeying, at least until the elves had arrived and things had settled down. Time to relax and refresh, tell tales, and attend state functions, as well as an opportunity to attempt to bolster the morale of the populace.

Two days after they had returned, Geoffrey Gregorson made an appearance. He had finally made it back from the encampment at the top of the range. He had arranged for others to take over his duties. An informal party was thrown now that they were all back together. There had been two more major attacks by the undead on the defences at the end of the pass in the time they had been gone. They had been repulsed, although not easily. Since the last major attack, there had been little in the way of assault. It appeared as though the undead had dispersed a bit.

CHAPTER 48

They had been back in Raelis for a month when Kai called the group back together.

'Everything seems to be under control and going according to plan. The Mother Superior is rapidly regaining her health and will shortly be able to return to her duties. The elves are assisting where they can. All is quiet on the war front, and there are plans under way to retake Almarac from the undead. As they are beginning their push to do so, I believe we should be on our way also. We head for the far north to try and find the bolthole of this necromancer cabal, but, first, I need to return to the desert and talk with Shadow's people. Prepare yourselves. We ride for Ulmarin at dawn in two days.'

Once again, they were on the trail. They left Raelis through the western gate and headed towards Ulmarin.

'We have a choice to make,' stated Kai. 'We can take ship from Ulmarin to Bocra and then proceed from there across the desert to Shadow's home, or we follow the mountains west and then turn south, crossing through the desert until we come across her people. Any suggestions?'

'Go via Bocra. We can gather the requisite supplies for a desert crossing there. It will also be the shorter journey,' replied Geoffrey.

'That will also require crossing the Plains of the Lost, which we would bypass if we came in from the north,' stated Shadow.

'What are the Plains of the Lost?' asked Morannel.

'A vast, flat, sandy patch of desert—no water, no shelter, constantly shifting winds. It takes five days of travel without respite to cross it, if we are lucky. If we aren't . . . well . . . they are called the Plains of the Lost for good reason,' replied Shadow.

'Alemrae, I would have your opinion,' stated Kai.

'The choice is between three weeks of dangerous and uncomfortable travel as opposed to eight to ten weeks of slightly less uncomfortable travel. As time is of the essence, I think it may be wiser to take the more dangerous but shorter journey. I have travelled the Plains of the Lost before. The dangers are well known by both Shadow and I. They can be minimised with a little planning. We are all accustomed to the rigours of travel, and those not experienced with the desert can learn from those of us who are. The longer and safer journey could bring up the more unexpected danger; something we could not anticipate that would cost us even more time. We go via Bocra,' stated Alemrae.

'Decision made. Thank you, Alemrae. We go to Bocra. Shadow, you and Alemrae must gather what we need for the crossing. Start when we get to Ulmarin. It will take a day or two to arrange passage on a ship bound for Bocra. Let's move on.'

They pushed hard, forcing themselves and their horses to press beyond their limits. They made it to Ulmarin in just three days. The horses would be useless for anything after such a taxing journey. They headed straight for the docks. Taking a room at a wharf-side inn, they made their plans. Kai would go and find them a ship. Alemrae and Shadow would search the nearby shops for what they would need in Bocra and the desert. Morannel and Frederick would sell the horses for whatever they could get and then go to the palace to inform the king of the current state of affairs. Captain Gregorson and Bradur the dwarf would wait at the inn and pass on any messages as the others came and went.

By evening of the third day, passage had been arranged. Little in the way of supplies had been bought. The specialised equipment needed would be more easily obtained in Bocra and for far less cost. The ship would sail with the dawn tide, so little sleep was had on the last night. Final arrangements and packing kept everyone busy until it was time to go.

On ship, they kept to themselves. There were no other passengers, and the ship's crew were a surly lot and not to be trusted. They had the look of pirates rather than honest traders, but no other ship in port was bound for Bocra. Besides, they were a well-armed and capable group, and it showed. It was a fast trip. They arrived a day earlier than they had expected, making up a little of the time lost in trying to get passage.

Bocra—the tent city of the desert tribes, one of the few permanent towns anywhere in the desert region, trading outpost and port, a place of thievery and lawlessness, where anything was possible if you had the right amount of money, or could get away with it without being caught. One's safety was one's own concern. Sticking one's nose into someone else's business was likely to have it removed, permanently. One stuck to the agreed-upon protocols—it was the easiest way to get things done. To deviate could cost too much. Any disagreements would be finalised in a closed session in front of the current ruling figure, a position held in turns by the resident tribes. The cost of such was determined by whim and what each party had to lose. Usually, both sides lost out as a result—a measure to ensure that things stayed relatively peaceful, with all parties compromising.

Shadow resumed her native dress, her appearance becoming a sure warning to others to leave her be. Few here would dare mar the path of a shaman, especially one that showed the markings of her clan. She led the way through the thickening crowds—Rad causing a stir—purchasing the items required for their desert journey. She headed to the only supplier of livestock within the walls. She was looking for camels. There were only three to be had, and none of them appeared to be in good condition. They purchased them anyway. To cross the desert, they needed to carry more water than they could carry themselves. Shadow also hired a driver to care for the beasts. Once she was done, she gathered the others around to share out the load and explain what they needed to do to survive.

'All we need now is a guide, someone who has travelled the sand many times and is willing to head in the direction we need to go. We need a sandrat.'

'That's a bit extreme, don't you think?' argued Alemrae.

'Not at all. It is whom we need, and I am hoping one may be available.'

'Alemrae, why are you against having a sandrat guide us?' asked Kai.

'They are the worst of the desert dwellers—ones who walk the sands and scavenge from the dead and dying. To have one as a guide would be to court death. They could lead us out and await our death just for the thrill of it. They can survive in conditions that would kill the rest of us, and it has been said that they can disappear into the sands themselves.'

'Nevertheless, a sandrat is what we need. I know one. I hope he may be here,' replied Shadow.

They took refuge from the midday sun in one of the few inns. Space was in short supply, so they took a room and ordered food and drinks to be sent. Shadow asked the innkeeper if any sandrats were about and if word could be passed about the possibility of a hiring. Word eventually came back to them: one sandrat was available for a hiring, depending upon where and when they were going. A meeting was agreed upon. Kai, Shadow, and Alemrae would meet with the sandrat outside the western gate at dawn, for the sandrat would never enter the town. It was a long night with little sleep to be had. The commons was noisy well into the night.

As the eastern sky lightened, Kai, Shadow, and Alemrae left for the west gate. A ball of soft light appeared above Shadow and lit their way, Rad squawking softly in Shadow's ear as he rode upon her shoulder. They meandered their way through the city, surprised at the number of people about the streets so early in the day. They moved out through the unguarded gate and walked a short distance to the south side of the gate to await their meeting. Shadow allowed her light to dissipate and leant back against the wall.

As the light grew around them, a vague outline appeared in the hazy dust of the desert. A tall humanoid figure approached. So cloaked was he that it was impossible to tell what he was. A fine covering of desert sand cloaked the clothing he wore. Shadow stood forth and offered a skin of water. The stranger reached out and accepted the skin, drinking slowly and long.

'I have a prior engagement, but if you need to go the same way, then you could join the caravan I am guiding.'

'We need to head straight west across the Plains of the Lost with minimal deviation either north or south. Time is of the essence to us. Once past the Plains of the Lost, we can head in separate directions, if need be.'

'I have to guide a party to Oesarets Reef—four to five days' travel into the Plains of the Lost, if we are lucky. Once there, my contract with the caravan ends. I can guide you the rest of the way, if you wish. It may be that Oesarets Reef is too far to the south of where you need to go.'

'We have no real choice. We will go with you. Name your price.'

'The desert will claim its own price. I am but a guide.'

'There shall be nine of us. We are already equipped. When and where do we meet to begin our journey?'

'Here. Today at dusk.'

The stranger turned and left them, heading once more into the desert sands and merging with the dust and the beginning heatwave. They returned to the inn and informed the others of their impending travel. The day passed quickly as they prepared for their desert crossing. Soon it was time to leave. Once again, they awaited the arrival of their guide by the wall of the city. Through the dust emerged a small caravan made up of six men and two boys, along with ten camels bearing loads and a small number of goats chained together in a line. Their guide stopped in front of them, said one word, and then about-faced and walked back towards the desert.

'He said, "Come",' said Shadow.

CHAPTER 49

The group began to follow their guide into the sands, the caravan bringing up the rear. They walked slowly and steadily further and further into the desert. Darkness fell. Still, they continued on.

'Drink and eat whilst you walk. We stop at dawn, not before.'

The heat from the day dispersed rapidly. The temperature dropped to a chill. The walking generated enough warmth to keep them comfortable—just. The winds shifted direction often, lifting loads of the light reddish sand and depositing it upon them in layers. In the beginning, it was not so bad; but as the night wore on, they began to feel the strain of walking on the soft sand. They became more and more tired, the pace slowing. By the time the eastern sky began to lighten, they were exhausted. The sandrat halted their progress.

'Set your camp. Sleep and rest if you can. We will start ahead again at dusk.' With that, he walked into the swirling sands and disappeared.

The sun was well up, and the heat had begun before they had finished setting up their camp and tending to the camels. Inside their domed tent, there was little talk. Everyone was too weary for discussion. Food was eaten, water drunk, and the supplies set ready for an easy start the next night. They rested easily enough until the heat of the day rained down from above. The air in the tent becoming almost unbearable.

Shadow arose and slipped outside. Circling the tent, she cast her magic, trying to limit the rise of the temperature within. Looking around, she could see nothing. Even the tents of the caravan they travelled with were hidden in the shroud of sand and shimmering heatwaves. Shadow quickly returned to the tent flaps and crawled inside. Already she could feel a difference in the temperature inside the tent. She went back to her sleeping roll and slept.

Kai woke them late in the day, and they prepared themselves for the next arduous night of walking. They packed up the tent and loaded the camels and then assisted the caravan in getting under way. As the sun neared the horizon, the sandrat once again appeared out of the swirling sands. He waited patiently for the group to be ready.

'We must push on further tonight. We have not come as far as we should have. Follow.'

Once again, he started to walk into the wind-blown sands. They followed, trying to keep up the faster pace that the sandrat set. Not long after full dark, they hit the first of the dunes. No longer would they be walking across flat sands but along the length of the ridges, occasionally crossing from one ridge to the next. As time passed, the sand dunes got higher and steeper. The effort to mount each ridge became harder to endure. Once again, the temperature plummeted. The winds picked up, throwing denser and denser clouds of sand over them.

In time, Kai called a halt. She ordered everyone, including those in the caravan, to tie themselves together with rope. Shadow was at the front of the line. As the most accustomed to the desert, she was the most able to keep track of their guide in the poor conditions. The conditions worsened. Even Shadow had a hard time of it.

Their guide came to a halt. 'Set camp. Something is wrong. The desert has been angered. Await here for my return.'

Once more, he disappeared into the wind-born sands. They slowly made camp, the task taking much longer than normal, as they kept themselves attached to the rope tying them all together. A single tent was raised, and they all huddled inside, the camels picketed near the entrance, the goats brought in under cover. They spent the rest of the night in the uncomfortable cramped conditions.

As dawn approached, the wind picked up. Kai arose and signalled to Shadow and Alemrae to follow as she stepped outside. 'We need some respite before the heat kicks in. Can you lessen the wind to allow us to erect another tent or two?'

'We can try. At least we can lessen the heat once the tents are up,' replied Alemrae.

Kai re-entered the tent to get the others. Shadow and Alemrae put their heads together to work out how to do as Kai had asked. Rad added his own chirps to the discussion. They began to work their magic. The wind began to shift direction, curling around the edge of the encampment instead of pouring straight across. The air began to clear, the sand settling back to earth. The others used the respite they had gained to set the camp to rights, putting up the other tents and arranging their supplies. By the time they had finished, the air had cleared. The winds circling the camp were a wall of sand, and the clear sky above allowed the heat of the sun's rays to scorch down upon them.

They retreated to the protection of the tents and the cooler temperatures provided by the magic of the mages. Once they were under cover, the protective wall dropped. The winds howled across the campsite, dumping loads of sand. The fury of the sandstorm increased, battering away at the tents and partially submerging them in sand.

The storm raged for the rest of the day and well into the night. Little rest was achieved until after it had blown itself out. It was almost dusk of the next day before they arose and dug themselves free.

Feeling refreshed by their extended rest, they were anxious to get under way once more. They packed up and readied themselves for the arrival of the sandrat, expecting it to show itself at dusk. The sun dropped below the horizon. Darkness fell. True night was upon them, yet the sandrat still had not shown up. What to do? Reset the camp or continue on? The sandrat had told them to await its return. A quick consultation, and an agreement was reached. They would reset the encampment and await the sandrat's return. If the sandrat had not shown up by dusk in three days' time, then they would attempt to finish the crossing alone. The camp became a hive of domestic activity. They repaired gear and clothing that had become worn or damaged on the crossing so far.

Late on the second day, Alemrae and Shadow approached Kai. 'There is something moving out there to the north. It's approaching at a very slow pace.'

'Alemrae and I will go and find it and determine if we face further trouble,' replied Kai. 'Shadow, if something happens to us, then get the rest safely away. You are the one most likely to succeed in getting them all to safety.'

Leaving the protective circle surrounding the tents was a shock. The intense heat struck them like a blow, sapping the energy out of them. 'We must hurry. We cannot stand to be out here for too long.' Alemrae led the way north, towards whatever it was that had impinged upon his magical awareness.

It did not take long to find it. It was the sandrat, barely recognisable such was its state. It had suffered many terrible injuries—it was a wonder that it was still alive, let alone able to drag its way across the sands. Alemrae used what little healing magic he had to help stabilise its life force. Once done, they carefully lifted the sandrat onto a makeshift sling made by tying their cloaks together. They took turns to slowly drag the sandrat back towards the camp. Once safely ensconced within the protective boundaries of the camp, Kai called for Shadow's assistance. The entire group rushed out to see the problem, whereupon Kai ordered everyone back under cover.

'Alemrae and Shadow will do what they can. Prepare to leave on the morrow. For we leave at dusk, however the sandrat fares.'

Once everyone else had returned to the cover of the tents, Kai said, 'Do what you can for it. Let me know how it goes.' Kai returned to her own spot in the tent to rest and meditate upon the current crisis.

Outside, Alemrae and Shadow worked what healing they could. Even with Rad's willing assistance, little seemed to do much good. 'It seems much more elemental than anything that I have come across before,' stated Alemrae. 'Perhaps raw energy may be of more use. If we tie flows of raw magic to its own healing capacity perhaps that may work better.'

'That would take too long to be of any benefit to us and tire us beyond belief,' replied Shadow. 'We would not be able to use magic again for some time, and we need to guide the party out of the desert. We don't have the food and water to last more than the time it will take to get to Oesarets Reef.'

'But if the flows were left tied to the free elements of the desert, then perhaps the desert itself could heal it as we travel,' argued Alemrae.

'That could work perhaps, but it would cause the desert to re-centre its forces upon the sandrat. We would be at the mercy of every sandstorm and crosswind that the desert produced.'

'It's worth the risk. Have Rad assist you in producing the flows of energy. I will tie them into its being. Once that is done, then together we will tie the flows into the desert itself.'

It took time for the magic to be worked. Many fine threads were woven into and through the being of the sandrat and bonded to the other strands, time and again, until a thick cord of unwieldy magic had formed. It took the abilities and concentration of all three to manipulate that final cord and tie it into the elemental matrix of the desert. They noticed its effect immediately. The slight flow of energy into the body of the sandrat was noticeable. A soft reddish glow emanated from the sandrat, and the winds of the desert picked up, becoming more violent and incessant in nature. Alemrae, Shadow, and Rad entered the tent and collapsed upon their bedding, tired out from the workings they had undertaken. They were asleep before anyone had the time to ask what they had accomplished.

CHAPTER 50

Alemrae, Shadow, and Rad awoke some fifteen hours later, only partially refreshed. They awoke only long enough to take a little food and water and to answer the few questions that Kai asked. Then they slept again. They were awoken as the others began to pack up their belongings. Once again, they took some food and water before they felt ready to move. Then they, too, started to pack. They stripped the camp. The sandrat was the last to be tied onto the back of a camel.

He awoke as they moved him. 'What have you done?'

'Tied your spirit to the energy matrix of the desert to heal you,' they replied. 'The bonds tying you together will collapse when you are healed. Until then, the desert sustains your life.'

'No! I was dead already. I can feel the one controlling me.'

'You are alive and shall stay that way. Guide us towards the one who is trying to control you. We shall deal with him as we have all the others who have been in collusion against us.'

'North. Head north.'

'Rest easy. When you are strong enough, we will let you down.'

They set off, heading north as asked, the sandstorm surrounding them intensifying as they went. The eye of the storm centred upon the sandrat—a small clear zone that slowly increased in size as the sandrat grew stronger. When they stopped for a break, the clear zone was just large enough for them all to stand in without the winds affecting them. It was a small respite, but one that was heartily welcome.

'Whoever is out there will know that we approach. They will have their own wards set against the storm and be fresh for the fight, whilst we will be at the edge of exhaustion. Be careful everyone.'

They set off again, heading in a slightly more westerly direction. The ground became stonier, less sandy, and the air became clearer as the amount of sand around them lessened. The winds, however, increased, buffeting those not able to walk within the clear eye. The wind chilled and became increasingly colder. It began to smell of water, which was very strange. Soon, they felt moisture upon the wind. Fine, misty drops at first and then becoming heavier. Where in a desert could there possibly be enough water to form a wind-blown rain?

They stopped again to consult with the sandrat. 'Ahead, not far, deep below the ground surface—a portal. Opened to let in water—trying to drown the desert. It's succeeding.'

'If we can kill off the mage controlling the portal, maybe it will close. Or maybe our own mages can close it.'

Leaving the sandrat and camels with those from the caravan, the party headed out into the storm. Staying close together, they edged forward. Suddenly, the air in front of them cleared—a definite curved edge in the storm-lashed landscape. They crossed the boundary into calmness.

'If we kill the mage, his protective boundary wards will collapse, making it difficult to close the portal as all goes wild. If we spend our energy closing the portal, you will have to deal with the mage without magical aid. I suspect he has formidable defences set,' said Shadow.

'Fair enough. You and Alemrae deal with the portal. The rest of us will find some way to destroy the mage,' replied Kai.

They spread out as they moved forward, Kai taking the centre of the line. Alemrae and Shadow followed a short distance behind.

'Once you engage the mage and his protectors, we will begin trying to disrupt the portal.'

They crept forward. Five giant scorpions were awaiting their arrival. They stood three feet tall at the join of body and leg, with a gleaming black carapace and a nine-foot-long tail tipped with a wickedly curved stinger, glistening with venom. The pincers were a creamy colour along the inner edges, stained with dull brownish-red streaks. The mage stood behind them.

'Breakfast is served, my pets. Kill them and feast.'

CHAPTER 51

The scorpions raced forward, pincers at the ready, and with their poisonous tails arched, ready to strike. Bradur walked towards the centre scorpion, trusting in his solid armour to protect him against the worst that the scorpion could do, his axe at the ready. Morannel and Frederick moved to the left. Kai and Geoffrey went to the right, giving themselves room and ensuring that they would not be attacked from behind by another of the scorpions once they had engaged their chosen foe.

In the centre, battle was already under way. Bradur had swung an overhand blow at his scorpion, which dodged backwards to escape, before lashing forward with both pincers. 'Beware. They're quick of foot!' he yelled, dodging aside.

His next blow struck, a glancing blow to the left pincer, which failed to do any damage. The scorpion's right pincer struck him hard in the side, knocking him from his feet. A hurried slash upwards connected heavily with the stinger as it plummeted down at him, causing a white fluid to flow. The scorpion backed off, its stinger hanging at an angle, no longer useable as a weapon. The respite allowed Bradur time to get to his feet.

The others set themselves to do battle. The scorpions came on, fast and furious. Defence was all anyone had time for in those first few moments. Morannel forwent his defence and allowed his battle rage to wash over him. He attacked with abandon, and this heightened his strength, allowing his sword to penetrate the thickened armour of the carapace. Despite being stung a couple of times and having one pincer grab his shield arm, doing some serious damage, he finished the beast in quick time. He then barrelled into the side of the one attacking Frederick, disabling two of its legs before it registered his presence. Frederick used the distraction to good advantage. He managed to cleave off one pincer completely and partially disable the other before the scorpion could regain the footing to attack again. The stinger whipped around towards Morannel as Frederick rammed his sword home through one of the tiny eyes and into the brain.

Kai was in trouble. She was quick enough to evade the strikes of the scorpion in front of her, but she could do no telling damage to it either. The uneven ground proved much more of a hindrance to her than her opponent, and she continually had to back up to get the room she needed to steady herself.

Geoffrey set up a methodical and superb defence. Every attack the scorpion sent his way was effectively blocked. Unfortunately, his own attacks did little more than enrage the scorpion further. His scorpion found easier prey. In her effort to evade her opponent, Kai had stumbled within range of the one next to it. It struck without warning, both pincers and the tail finding their mark in her flesh. Her own opponent struck as well, leaving her hanging between the two scorpions as their stings did their work. A large ball of flame exploded in their midst, flinging all the combatants about. The scorpions were the first to regain their footing, and they rushed to attack.

Kai lay stunned, bleeding and poisoned, unable to move. The scorpions ignored her and rushed towards the burly dwarf, who was struggling to rise. Behind them, where he had been thrown, Geoffrey climbed to his feet. Knowing he was useless to assist in that fight, he turned towards the mage who had cast the fireball and began to stalk towards him.

Frederick and Morannel surged to their feet and came to the defence of the dwarf. Battle was joined once again. Wounds were taken on both sides in the first exchange. The ferocity with which the companions attacked stood them in good stead, dealing blow after blow upon their enemies. Bradur, with one mighty strike, cleaved the skull of his scorpion in two, its death throes interfering with the mobility of its kin. Morannel and Frederick pounced, making good use of the opportunities given them, and the last two scorpions were dispatched.

Geoffrey had reached the mage and began his assault. His attacks came both swiftly and precisely, such that the mage was disrupted in his attempts to cast another spell. The end was swift. Geoffrey gutted the mage and then lopped off his head.

Magic swirled. Vast forces, which had been contained, swept inside the protective circle as it collapsed. The impact of the sandstorm was severe. Alemrae and Shadow lost control of the magic that they had summoned in their attempt to close the portal. A permanent tear in the fabric of the boundary between the planes occurred. What they had almost accomplished was now in ruins. There was no longer a way to seal the hole and stop the flow of water into the ground of the desert. A small, steady flow continued to soak the land.

The companions gathered together. Carrying Kai and supporting Morannel, who was beginning to suffer the effects of the poisoning, they turned back to where the caravan awaited. Once within the protective circle the presence of the sandrat provided, they set about making camp and seeing to their wounded.

Shadow approached the sandrat. 'I am sorry. We were unable to close the portal. At the last moment, when we had it almost closed, the death of the mage caused a flux within his protective circle. It disrupted our control over our own magic, causing the fabric between the planes to tear. There is now no way to stop the flow of water into the desert that I am aware of. It will take many years, but the desert will become swamped.'

'Then I am dead. I die with the desert. This binding you conceived to tie me with the life force of the desert has ensured my death. I shall drown as surely as the desert does. My curse shall be upon you and yours for as long as you live. The curse will only be lifted once the desert has been returned.'

With that, the sandrat departed, leaving them stranded in the desert. One small tent was all they were able to erect before the protection provided by the sandrat dispersed with his leaving. Kai and Morannel were placed on pads within the tent. The poison flowed through their veins from the scorpions' stings. Weakness and pain were what they suffered.

As Kai and Morannel writhed in pain upon their pads, the rest gathered to discuss their predicament. 'We are low on resources. Food is a major concern. Water not as much, considering what has just happened. We are at least two weeks' travel from Shadow's homeland,' stated Alemrae.

'Yes, but we are only about three days travel from Oesarets Reef. If we can make it there, then we will be able to barter for goods. If we limit our rations, we should make it, but we will not be going anywhere until Kai and Morannel are on their feet,' replied Shadow.

'Is there nothing to be done for them?' asked Frederick.

'I judge it safer to let the poison run its course. Both of them can withstand this, and they will become less susceptible to other poisons because of it. For that is in their nature,' said Shadow.

It was well into the morning of the next day before they saw any improvement in Kai and Morannel. By that time, they had managed to erect other tents and set up a proper camp, giving everyone access to cover and time to recuperate. Kai was first on her feet. She called a meeting of the party and those in the caravan. She explained the situation so that they all understood the dire straits they faced.

'Shadow is our only hope of getting out of here alive. It will be her magic that guides us to Oesarets Reef. She is also the one most used to this environment. The protective magic will have to be dropped whilst we travel, so we rope ourselves together as we did before. Shadow will lead the way. Shadow, tell us what you need of us. All that you command, we shall do.'

'We shall leave at dusk. Refill all the water bags before we go. Each person is to carry two waterbags upon their person. All the rest shall be attached to the camels. Any unessential equipment shall be left behind. Bradur, you shall have to leave your armour. All of us will have to minimise what we carry or we will not make it. Morannel will have to be tied to a camel until he is fit to walk. Start now. Once you have pared down what you will take, then rest. We have a long, hard trek ahead of us. The worst is yet to come. The past week will seem like paradise compared to what we are about to endure. Set your minds and bodies to endure and you shall survive. Give in to frustration and despair and you will die, and likely take the rest of us with you. We can do this. Now, go.'

CHAPTER 52

Dusk came, and they were ready to depart. A large pile of armour, weapons, and other goods was to be left behind. 'The sandrat was right. The desert has claimed its own cost for our travel,' remarked Bradur.

'Let us hope that the payment is enough. We do not wish to pay with our lives,' replied Alemrae.

Shadow, with Rad on her shoulder, cast out with her magic, sensing the direction that they needed to head. She set out, a slow, ground-eating walk, followed by all the rest. Occasionally, she would motion to those behind—when to eat, when to take a mouthful of water—never stopping her forward motion, always walking at the same rhythmic pace. The eastern sky had lightened through the swirling sand before Morannel was able to stand. Once on his feet, he began to walk. Still, Shadow continued. She walked for much longer into the morning than when the sandrat had led them.

It became almost unbearably hot before she stopped. 'Make camp. Once the camp has been set, Alemrae and I will set wards in place to keep the tents cool and protected from the wind. Eat, drink, and rest. We shall be under way again in a little over five hours. Take what rest you can.'

The rest they took lasted little time. It seemed that they had hardly begun to sleep before they were being woken to break camp. The heat outside the tents struck like a hammer blow. They persevered. Once again, Shadow took the lead in that slow, ground-eating walk. The others had no choice but to keep up. She pushed on into the heat of the afternoon.

The light slowly faded as the sun began to set. The cool of the night came as a slightly refreshing change but was of too little to help the party push the pace. They continued to walk throughout the night, pushing their bodies to the limits of their endurance. As dawn finally came, the first of the men in the caravan collapsed, followed swiftly by a couple of others.

Shadow called the halt and ordered camp be set. 'We have covered enough ground. We rest through this day and the following night. At dawn the next day, we make a bolt to Oesarets Reef. Drink and eat your fill. Relax and recover. At dawn tomorrow, we cover the most dangerous ground.'

Camp was slowly set by those still able to move around. The three unconscious men from the caravan were placed within their tent to recover. The little amount of magic for their healing used the last of their reserves. It would take time for Shadow, Alemrae, and Rad to regather their magical strength enough to cast even the most basic magic; so much energy had they expelled in the trek trying to keep everyone capable of continuing.

By dawn of that next day, most of the group had recovered sufficiently to continue. One of the men from the caravan had succumbed to the stresses of the forced march and had died during the night. The two boys seemed to recover much more quickly than the others in the caravan, their youth giving them a little bit more resilience to the harsh punishment. They were also the most upset over the death of their companion. He had been a distant relative and the only family they had on the trip.

Shadow had the party on the move before the true dawn of the day, leaving the deceased to be buried by the shifting sands. 'We are out of food and almost out of water. We must make Oesarets Reef before the day heats up and we cannot continue. To fail now is to die. Now, come.'

She pushed them onwards at a much faster pace than she had on the previous two days of travel. She called a halt after an hour at a place where the wind barely blew and a vast expanse of featureless sand awaited.

'This next stretch is the most dangerous section of sand to cross,' stated Shadow. 'We will not be tied together. Each of us will lead one camel. The three who don't lead a camel will each lead four of the goats. We will walk abreast of each other with a distance of about ten feet between. Those leading the goats shall be split evenly amongst the rest of us. I will take the middle. Walk when I walk; stop when I stop. If I tell you to do something, then do it immediately. Alemrae, you may need your bow—ready it. The two boys will walk to either side of me, with Alemrae and Kai beside them. Then two of you others, followed by Frederick and Morannel. We keep using the same pattern until everyone is placed. If anyone sees something, then yell out. If anyone yells, then everyone stops. Don't anyone take a step until I give the order to move out again. That large reddish-grey smudge on the horizon is our target. That is Oesarets Reef. Proceed slowly.'

They walked in their line slowly out into the waste. Oesarets Reef slowly became clearer. At irregular intervals, Shadow would call a halt and order them to watch the land in front of them. Nothing was seen, and the order to resume was given. The day began to heat up but had not yet reached those unbearable levels that had forced them to seek sanctuary in the tents. As Oesarets Reef began to loom large, they had a tendency to speed up. Again and again, Shadow had to call them back into line and slow their pace. Nearly everyone was beginning to get frustrated with Shadow's seemingly pointless efforts to slow the pace.

They were only about a mile from the reef when Nicolai, one of the boys, yelled out. Everyone stopped. 'What did you see?' the question was asked.

'It looked like a fin—the fin of a fish, but about two feet tall. But that's impossible, isn't it?'

'No, it's not. It is what I have been afraid of finding. Follow me. One at a time. Walk forward ten paces and then stop. If you see another fin, then stop immediately.'

Shadow slowly paced forward her ten steps. The others began to follow suit. By the time the third in the caravan had stepped forward, another fin, or possibly the same one, had been sighted. Shadow waited. Before long, more fins were seen. It seemed that there was a host of these things.

'These are land sharks,' called Shadow. 'They travel through the earth and sand, much like sharks do in the sea—only, you don't have any warning if one is below you. If one strikes, it always hits its target, and it is usually fatal. The only way to Oesarets Reef is over the ground through which these land sharks swim. We need to distract them. Give them other prey. Cut the goats so that they bleed and set them loose. Make them scatter ahead of us. *Do it now!* Wait for them to get well out ahead. Wait, just a bit longer . . . Now, run. Don't stop until you make it to the rocks of Oesarets Reef.'

CHAPTER 53

With that, Shadow began to sprint at top speed towards the rocky outcrop a mile ahead. She ran with the camel that she was leading. The others followed suit. The split-up party ran between the goats and the trails of blood that they left behind them. As they passed through, they saw the goats being taken, one by one, from below, by something large and black.

When a fin headed towards Alemrae, he took bead upon it and let loose. The arrow struck true. A fine spray of blood flared out over the sand. A number of other sharks bore in on the wounded one, clearing a larger passage ahead. Alemrae slowed his pace for another shot but missed as the shark dived much deeper into the sands. More and more fins began to appear in the area surrounding where the blood had been spilt.

Alemrae ran for all he was worth, trying to get to safer ground before he was cut off by the suddenly increased number of sharks. All the others had made it beyond where the sharks had gathered. None were aware of his predicament, not that they could have aided him if they were.

He ran, his feet barely making an impression in the soft sand. He staggered his run, changing direction at whim, trying to throw off any following sharks. The camel trying to follow was not so lucky. It was much heavier, and although it was able to keep pace, it could not make the same sudden changes in direction. It went down with a terrible scream as one hind hoof was torn from its leg. A sudden churning in the sands around it showed the feeding frenzy of the sharks as they feasted on the hapless beast.

It was enough of a distraction for Alemrae to catch up to the rest of the party. He called out for a slowing of their pace. The sharks had been left behind. They did not stop, however—not until the safety of the rocks had been reached. They all gathered together to rest.

'The worst of the desert is now behind us. The Plains of the Lost have been crossed. A couple of hours of travel over the rocks to the south-western edge will bring us to the small community that lives here. There, we will be able to do some trading. I think you will be astonished at just what is available. We just need to find the passage through. Come, we head due south. We will eventually come across a small gravel path. We will follow that to the west.' Shadow moved off. The others, once again, followed her lead, and Morannel, once again, was close behind her.

The journey was much easier than before. The temperature, although hot, did not get to the extremes that occurred in the Plains of the Lost. It was smoother going, with firm footing underneath, and little stumbling over uneven ground. In just under an hour, they had found the path and turned in a more westerly direction. They continued walking at a comfortable pace. The path turned into a canyon, the high walls giving some protection from the sun.

'We will slow down as we pass through. There is some rather magnificent art on the walls. Enjoy the view, for it is unlikely that you shall ever see them again. They are a representation of events. All the images have meaning, and you just have to interpret them. The meaning they have for you may be different from the meaning they have for me.'

'Shadow, who drew these images?'

'Many different people over thousands of years. A shaman will dream an image and, when they walk through this canyon, will find the right place to place it. The image is carved into the rock with magic. They will never fade, and they can't be destroyed by physical means. Some years ago, when I first learnt that I was to become a shaman, I walked this canyon. I have placed an image here, although

I did not understand it at the time. I believe I may now. It is near the far end. Come—let's continue on.'

They walked through the canyon, marvelling at the images they saw there. Some were easily interpreted—a circle of what were obviously undead—others, not so. What meaning could there be, for instance, in a small black ball resting upon a silver pillar? Kai suspected that she would dwell on every image until she had sorted them out to her own satisfaction.

They walked out of the canyon into the late afternoon light. Before them was an oasis containing a myriad of palms and grasses, small shrubs, and trees, some bearing fruit or nuts. There was a large number of circular tents scattered throughout. Many goats and a few camels wandered freely around the area. A fair number of desert tribesmen were dotted around, few paying any attention to the newcomers.

'We wait here until we are invited to enter,' said Shadow. 'This is their home, and it is not wise to intrude without invitation. There are shamans of great power here, and their view of reality is sometimes different from ours.'

'Just how many of them can use magic?' asked Alemrae.

'All of them,' replied Shadow. 'Some more than others. When I first came here, I was already more powerful than some, but there are a few here who could eliminate your existence in the blink of an eye, and with no warning given. You would just cease to exist . . . It is time to go. We have been invited in.'

'How do you know?'

'We are not dead. We have stood here long enough to be noticed, appraised, and eliminated if need be. Since we are still alive, we may enter. Keep an eye out. Someone will show us where to go if we take care to notice. Follow my lead. Leave the camels.' Shadow slowly meandered her way into the encampment.

Nicolai spoke up. 'What was that?'

'What was what?' answered Shadow.

'I don't know what it was. It was over there. I just saw a glimpse of something,' he said, pointing towards a clearing a little way away, partly hidden by some tents.

'Take us there,' said Shadow.

Nicolai led off, carefully walking on the cleared sand, not coming close to the tents, which had partially blocked the view. The oval-shaped clearing was covered with grass. A deep pool of clear water was at one end. A large tent with many smaller adjoining sections was at the other. It was made up of one large central dome surrounded by many smaller domes.

A wizened old man was awaiting them at the flaps of the tent. 'Enter, and be at peace,' he said.

He waited outside until all had entered before joining them. 'Rest and take your ease. Your trade has been accomplished. When you decide to leave, you may take anything and everything within this tent. Take or leave what you wish. Ovo-yindi, call me before you wish to go. We need to talk.' He then left.

'What of our gear, the trading, and the camels?' asked one in the caravan.

'You heard him. The trading is complete. The camels and all they carry have been accepted in trade for what has been supplied. This is how their trade has always been accomplished. You accept their terms, or you can leave with nothing. That is your choice, as it is theirs in what to offer as trade. They are usually generous in their dealings. There will be little here that we need. Most of the trade goods will be for you to accept or decline. It is time to rest. Food and water have been made available. Find the area in the tent that is most comfortable for you.'

The group split up into its various fragments, each of them finding an area suited to their needs. Kai found herself in a small, darkened tent. It contained little but a sleeping pad and a small globe of light showing the position of a reading desk with a single book upon it. A plate of food and a jug of water rested beside the book. 'Sustenance first and then sleep. Then I will read what you have left for me,' she whispered. She sat on the floor, ate the food, and drank her fill of the water before lying back on the sleeping pad. The small ball of light dimmed to almost nothing, and she slept. She dreamed that night. Many strange and peculiar things.

CHAPTER 54

When she awoke, she felt rested as never before, finally at peace with the horrors of her past. She arose and went to the desk and read the book. It told a history, but not as she knew it. Now, more than ever, things were much clearer to her. She left the tent, not seeing anyone else, and proceeded to walk back into the canyon. She studied the paintings upon the walls. The meanings behind each became clearer the longer she stayed. She walked back and forth along the canyon. Each time, she would notice another image that had somehow eluded her viewing previously. She would stop and study it. Time passed. Understanding blossomed.

Meanwhile, Shadow and Morannel found a section and made themselves comfortable. As they sat and consumed the food provided, they discussed the past events and what the future might bring. Rad snuck out whilst they paid no attention to anything but each other. He flew off to explore the oasis, the magic in use, and the surrounding lands. It would be many days before he returned.

The others also found sections to their liking—sections with armour and weapons the likes of which they had never seen. Bradur found a suit of plate armour that fit as if it had been made for him, but was so light in weight it was almost unbelievable. The others as well found items that suited their needs and natures. A bow and quiver, with two short swords for Alemrae; a helm, sword, and shield for Geoffrey.

Frederick was the only one troubled by what he found. Two things. The first was a small portrait of a woman—one he had secretly loved for years—but in this picture, she was many years older and crowned. He would carry this picture on him for the rest of his life as a talisman of sorts. The second, and by far more troubling, was a headpiece, almost a crown. He was sure that it would fit if he placed it upon his own head. He thought back through his past life—of all the decisions that he had made that had led him to this place.

He sat down and held the crown in his hands and studied it. He lost track of time as he contemplated all the ramifications of this one item. He would not wear it. But the temptation could be too much. He would take it with him as a reminder of all he had been through and just how much he had learnt about true leadership. A crown had to be earned, not taken. He buried it deep within the knapsack he carried and tried to forget about its existence. In the months to come, just occasionally, late at night when no one else was awake, he would remove it from its place and, in the light of the dying fire, study it once more.

Of those left from the caravan, they stayed but one night. They packed and left. Only one stayed. Nicolai. He had found a small nook filled with books, scrolls, and other pieces of parchment. He knew that this is why he had come on the journey—not for the adventure, nor for profit, but for the knowledge that was available anywhere other than home. He only had one problem. There was nothing here that he could read. No written language did he understand. He had never been taught. He was determined to stay until he could read it all.

Late the next day, Kai's absence was noted. The group, worried by her absence, called for the old man. 'Be at peace. There is none to harm you here. Kai will return to you when she is ready.'

Days passed. They spent the time fixing their belongings or replacing them. Discussions about the future were always stopped quickly. Without Kai, no firm decisions could be made. They relaxed and began to enjoy their respite from struggle. The bond between Shadow and Morannel deepened and intensified. Rad returned.

Shadow admonished him for his disappearance but was glad to have him back with her. Now it was just a matter of Kai's return. Once she was back, they could make their plans.

Once again, Shadow sought out the old man. 'You said we needed to speak before I left.'

'Your intentions for the tower are in error. You should leave it here instead. When you return to your people, have them journey here. If they are to survive the coming turmoil, they will require our assistance.'

'You ask for much with little I see in return. If I give you the tower, may I return and study the contents of the library within?'

'If you survive the conflicts ahead, you may return. Your place has always been within our community—you just have not seen it.'

'I know not where my place lies, excepting that wherever Morannel is, my place is by his side. He would say the same. Assist us in our travel as we leave and see to my people. Bring them here if you must.'

'Then you have chosen your path. As Kai has chosen her own. She will be with you before dusk tomorrow.'

'Then the tower is yours to do with as you see fit.'

'Then the deal is done. We shall provide the transportation that you require to hasten your journey. When you are ready to go, walk through the oasis to the west. There you will find another gravel path leading down a hillside into a canyon. Follow that path till you reach the end. Don't stop along the way or look back. Once upon the path, you only have the destination in front of you.'

'We shall do as you ask, and we shall leave as soon as Kai is ready to go.'

The old man turned and walked away. Shadow did the same. Once back in her tent, she searched her possessions for the tower. It was already gone. Shadow passed on the news of Kai's imminent return. They ate their evening meal early and retired for the night.

CHAPTER 55

The next day was spent in preparation of leaving and organising who would carry what of the goods left for them. They were so familiar with how much each could carry that it was easy to split up the load so that no one would have to carry more than they were able to cope with. They managed to arrange all the necessities so that Kai could choose which of the extra goods she wished to take without needing to carry any other burden.

It was late in the day but well before dusk when Kai returned. She stepped through the tent flaps and was immediately wrapped up in a bear hug from Shadow. The others followed suit until everyone had greeted her return. 'You all act as if I have been gone for ages. I have only been gone for a few hours,' said Kai.

'No, actually, you haven't. You have been missing for a week,' replied Frederick.

'We have all been worried about you, but they told us that you were safe and would return when you were ready,' said Morannel. 'We are ready to go as soon as you wish to leave, Kai.'

'Then we will leave in the morning. Tonight we talk about everything that happened to you whilst I was gone. In the morning, I will see what if anything I need to take from here.'

They ate and talked well into the night. Kai spent some time talking with each of the members of the group, re-establishing the connections they shared.

Kai rose early the next morning and sorted through what she thought she might need. She had left so much behind since she first began that she hardly needed to take anything. She was already down to the bare essentials. A couple of sets of desert garb was all she really wanted to take. She still had her two daggers and the briar rose pin. In her mind, that was all she needed—that and the new knowledge she had gained. The insights would be of more use than any other physical object that she could bring. Besides, she carried the burden of leadership for the rest. That was enough in and of itself. The others could manage the rest.

When she was ready, she awoke the others. They broke bread together, finished their last-minute packing, and left the tent. To their surprise, the tower was standing in all its glory near the centre of the oasis. A slight change had been made. There was now an entry at ground level—an arched doorway with a very solid-looking door sealing the way in. At the top of the tower, someone was standing at the window. It appeared that they were looking at the horizon, for they showed no sign of interest in what was happening below them.

'Come. It's time to leave,' said Kai.

'Then follow me, and don't anyone look back,' said Shadow. 'Those were the orders I was given the other day. I can guide you on to the trail we need to take, but we must continue to move forward. Don't stop or look back until we step off the end of the path.'

'Then guide us to where we need to go,' said Kai.

Shadow started off, walking at the ground-eating pace they were used to, through the oasis to its western edge. There, as she had been told, she found the gravel path leading down the hillside towards another canyon. She stepped onto the path without hesitation and continued the journey. She walked, never looking back, trusting in the others to follow and not fall behind. The walls of the canyon rose high overhead until the sky above was just a narrow white line against a dark background. She walked on, drinking when she felt the need, even eating on the move, but walk she did, one foot after the other, never stopping. She lost track of time. Time was no longer of importance. Moving forward was all that mattered.

Between one step and the next, everything changed. She no longer walked upon a gravel path between canyon walls. She was on an open rocky headland looking out towards the western ocean. A vast cliff face was before her, the ocean a long way below.

The others surrounded her. 'Where are we? How did we get here?'

'I don't know,' replied Shadow. 'I have never seen this spot before in my life.'

'I know,' stated Kai. 'This is the very spot where the ship I was on went down. I climbed that cliff with four others. I was the only one who survived the next few days. I know where we go from here. A tribe lives but two days' distance due east of here. At least, they did. We are well prepared. We can make the journey easily. Come— follow me.'

Once again, they began to walk, following Kai's guidance as they had before. The sun set in the western ocean behind them.

CHAPTER 56

'We have lost all sense of what day it is, how much time has truly passed. I feel that time is pressing in on us. If we don't get to the north soon, it may be too late,' muttered Kai.

'We shall get there when we get there. I suspect that the trip through the canyon took but a moment. We may have arrived late in the day, but I suspect we have jumped a few weeks' worth of distance in land,' mentioned Alemrae.

'Once we get to this tribe, you know, Kai, I will be able to tell you how far we have come. You know how far we must yet travel, so the timing can be worked out,' said Shadow.

'Nine to ten weeks on foot to get to where the city of Albrae stood. A couple of days after that to where the army was destroyed and Brelldan died. How much further north we then have to travel is anyone's guess. It will take more time to find the necromancers hideout. Plus we shall need to evade the undead that are out there.'

They continued to travel, stopping when necessary and trying to conserve their strength and energy. They travelled through the day or night, depending on whim. At the end of the second day, Kai admitted that they were getting close to where the tribe that they were looking for had lived. They would rest through the night and try to find them in the morning.

Dawn came. It found the group already on the march. A restless spirit had kept Kai awake throughout the night. It was earlier than she had planned when she woke the others and got them up and moving. They broke their fast whilst on the march. The sun was approaching the peak of its arc when Kai led them into the crevasse that led to the cave system she was looking for. Spirits lifted as they gained the shade and the end of their march for the day, only to plummet when they reached the cavern that housed the majority of the desert tribe.

The place stank of death. Bodies lay on the rock floor—bodies with hideous putrefying wounds and lying in pools of largely dried blood. These people had been viciously assaulted with little or no warning, probably around dusk the night before. Of their attackers, no sign was seen.

The party conducted a thorough search of the cavern. It appeared that all of the tribe had been slain, both adults and children. None had been spared the horror of the assault.

'We shall have to take the bodies outside and create a pyre with them. There is little to burn here, so we will have to use magical fire to consume the bodies.'

It took time to gather the bodies together outside of the cavern. Once they had finished, Kai spoke a few words, followed by Shadow. Shadow spoke in her native tongue, vowing retribution on those responsible, before breaking into the eulogy sung by her tribe. When she was done, with the aid of Rad, Shadow launched a ball of flame into the centre of the pyre. The blue-white flame expanded to cover all of the dead. The incineration was swift. Soon, nought but a pile of ash remained, which quickly swirled away upon the desert winds to mix with the surrounding lands.

They returned to the caverns, searching for what equipment and food remained. The destruction appeared complete. There was little of value or use that had not been desecrated beyond use. It was Shadow's knowledge of the desert tribes that led her to the stash—a small cache of emergency rations, hidden away for that desperate time when prey was scarce. They were not in need at this time for a boost to their food supplies, but there could come a time in the near future when they would be glad to have this small supplement to their supplies. The small pool of water deep within the cave system had escaped contamination. It was the reason the tribe hade made this cave their home, the sole source of fresh water for a day's travel in any direction.

'In the morning, we shall head due north. Until then, I suggest that we rest and relax as best we can. Someone should stay on guard at all times. We don't want the surprise of those who murdered the tribe coming back upon us.'

Once again, dawn saw them already on the move. It had been an uncomfortable night for all of them, and they were relieved to resume their journey. Shadow led the way, with Kai walking by her shoulder.

'That tribe was situated well north of my own. I think our magically aided travel made up all the time that passed as we stayed in Raelis. Also, we shall need to find cover well before noon, somewhere that we can hole up in until the worst of the sun is gone. Then we can walk well into the night. There should be two full moons to light our way.'

'And the farther we go, the lighter our packs will become as we consume our supplies. We have been travelling well, much faster than the last time I came this way.'

'Well, we are more accustomed to travelling on foot than you were on that first journey. We are all fit and strong. We should be able to press on and cover the distance in a few days less time than it took you all those years ago.'

'Unless we run into something that we cannot handle.'

'There is nothing much out here to have to handle. Anything of size enough to do us damage should be intelligent enough to leave our party alone.'

'And if we come across whatever wiped out that tribe?'

'Then they had best watch out, for I shall endeavour to end their existence. There appears to be a cave ahead. It is almost midmorning. Do you wish to use it to see off the worst of the heat?'

'Let's see what it offers first. If it is usable, we may as well stop.'

The cave was deemed useable, but only just. It was small and not very deep, with just barely enough room for everyone to sit up against the walls and be out of the sun. There was little in the way of conversation as they tried to conserve their energy.

As the sun lowered towards the horizon, the group set off, with Shadow leading the way once again. Darkness set in as the sun dropped below the horizon and their pace slowed. The stars lit up the night sky, with the Huntress constellation at the prime. An hour later, Sikaaris, the largest of the three moons, arose with an unusually deep red colour. 'Blood will be shed when Sikaaris rides the skies in pursuit of the huntress. So say the legends of my tribe,' whispered Shadow.

'What's that?' asked Morannel.

'My tribe has a legend about Sikaaris rising red when the Huntress rules the sky. It is an omen of bloodshed,' replied Shadow. 'Rad, lend me your sight. Fly high. Scan the land around us. I would see what is out there.' Shadow cast a simple spell as Rad took to the air.

CHAPTER 57

The party ground to a halt behind them. 'Be aware, something has Shadow spooked. She is trying to scout the land with Rad,' said Morannel.

'She should be worried. I smell smoke on the wind, and there is nothing out here to burn,' said Alemrae.

'Spread out. Ready your weapons, but stay at ease,' commanded Kai.

Rad continued to spiral up into the night sky, his silver form easily visible to those looking for it. He rose high until he was little more than a speck above. Then he swung wide and circled at speed. Three times he flew the circuit around the party, scanning the land around, each pass further out from the last. He returned, a bolt from the heavens, squawking his displeasure.

'I was right. There is something out there, hidden from view with magical energies. Let's see if I can force them to reveal themselves.'

'What do you have in mind?'

'Something unexpected.'

Shadow stepped forward and gathered her magical energies. She released them in an arc towards where she sensed her opponents to be. They spread out, settling upon the ground, softening the rock-hard surface to jelly, and then seeping down until anything of weight would have sunk down below the surface. As the energies dissipated, the rock solidified once again, temporarily trapping those hidden from view.

'Move forward. Their protections should drop anytime.'

A shimmering in the air in front of them cleared away, revealing an ugly assortment of magically created beings. What had once been either human or animal was now a mixture of both. They carried a wide variety of lethal weaponry.

'Alemrae, there must be a mage here somewhere. Find him and get rid of him. I'll flush him out. You get him,' stated Shadow.

She made a quick casting motion with her hand, and four small glowing balls flew towards the group ahead, rapidly expanding as they went. They ploughed into the front of the group and exploded, throwing bits and pieces of the enemy in all directions. The remainder rushed forward, quickly closing the gap and exposing at their rear two beings. The party surged forward, quickly providing cover for Shadow and Alemrae.

Battle was joined, vicious and deadly. Three arrows arced overhead in quick succession and found their mark in one of the two enemies behind the pack. The air around the two shimmered once again as magical energies faltered and their true nature was revealed. The human mage collapsed to the ground, dying, and the other altered shape completely. It became a towering figure of flame and smoke—triple the height of a man—with large wings darker than the night sky above. It carried a massive battle-axe wreathed in flame, with both hands wrapped around the shaft. It roared at the sky and started forward.

'Shadow, raise every magical protection you have. Surround the party. Use your circlet, or we're all doomed!' shouted Alemrae. 'Fall back. Fighting withdrawal. Converge on Shadow.'

Light flared as Shadow began to raise rings of magical energy about her. A voice suddenly sounded in her mind. *Allow me to assist.*

A strange force began to manipulate the rings of energy, changing the structure and blending them together to form a single band of energy. *Funnel as much magical energy into the ring for as long as you can. The longer you can keep it active, the stronger it will become.*

The group slowly retreated to where Shadow was laying down the protective ring. It would not stop the monstrosities, but it might be able to halt the daemon. Alemrae continued shooting arrows into the monstrous group to aid the rest of the party in their retreat. Dropping his bow, he moved next to Shadow to begin summoning magical energies to add to what Shadow could raise. Rad was already there and assisting.

The party slowly gathered, blood flowing. They had received many wounds in the short space of time they had fought. Only their much better battle skills had allowed them to fare so well against so many. There was a slight reprieve as a gap opened up between the two groups. A dome of blazing white light coalesced in the gap and encased the party. A shudder ran through the beasts in front of them, as if they were flinching from the proximity of great heat. Some began to run, away from both the party and the daemon; others began to fight amongst themselves.

Stand firm. Don't leave the dome or you will be lost. Any violent intent from within will destroy the dome and us with it. Sheath your weapons.

The last of the monstrosities fled or were cut down by the daemon for barring its way forward, the massive axe making short work of the task it was put to. The daemon approached, surprised that its victims just stood watching. It swung an overhand blow down towards the group, expecting to strike the flesh of its victims. Instead, the battle-axe struck the magical protective dome and rebounded with a flash of light. The daemon howled once more, infuriated with its failure. Dropping the axe, it punched out and, once again, collided with the dome of protection. Howling in pain and frustration, it backed off. It began to pace back and forth, circling the group and occasionally testing the dome for weakness. It found none.

'We have a problem. I know of no way to destroy that thing or return it whence it came. I don't even know if we can drive it off. All it has to do is wait for the protections to fail,' said Shadow anxiously.

'I don't think it's in its nature to be patient. It seems to be a daemon from some abyss. Fire would be its element, and perhaps water may force it to retreat.'

'If you hadn't noticed, we're in a desert. We don't have much in the way of water around us.'

'I was thinking more along the lines of a change in the weather—a storm perhaps.'

'Can you summon one? It's using all the magic I can raise just to hold this protective shield in place.'

'I can try.'

Alemrae concentrated. Using what remained of his energies, he sent a tendril of magic aloft. Like a tracer, it flew up into the highest reaches of the atmosphere, where it twisted and curled upon itself. Other strands shot out of the knot that was forming. Heading in all directions, these, too, began to curl and knot around themselves until a vast tapestry of magical light arced overhead. The sky slowly grew darker as clouds began to form and block out the light from the stars and the moons.

As time passed, the clouds got thicker, darker, and much lower. Magical light flashed from cloud to cloud, and lightning arced across the heavens. The wind picked up, carrying with it the smell of rain and the feel of moisture on the air. The daemon became more alert as it sensed the atmospheric change. The air began to feel heavy as the first drops began to fall. The daemon screamed its rage. The rain began to fall in earnest, a heavy flood of cold water pounding down from on high. Trapped within their protective dome, there was little that the party could do except await the inevitable. Within minutes, the daemon vanished—one moment there; the next, gone.

The storm continued for more than an hour before it began to subside. Soaked through to the bone, cold and weary, the group huddled together within their protective dome. They began to sort themselves out and deal with the injuries that they had sustained. The night passed slowly. It was well on towards dawn when the clouds eventually blew away, allowing the ground to begin to dry out. Sikaaris slowly drained of colour until it was back to its usual silvery blue tinge. By the time dawn arrived, the group were in their blankets, wounds bandaged, and trying to sleep.

Kai stood watch. She had been unable to sleep. Time to think was what she had needed. The night before was beyond anything she had even heard of before. She wondered for the first time if they were overmatched. Could they really manage to find and destroy the rest of the necromancers, or was this truly just a suicide mission? That they had succeeded so far was more to do with luck than anything else. They had stumbled their way through each challenge as it had presented itself to them. They had been outmatched last night, of that she was sure. The monstrosities would have been bad enough on their own. The daemon was too much. How could someone summon a daemon of that magnitude into this world and expect to control it? The mage—things had started to fall apart when Alemrae shot him. Perhaps she should go and investigate his remains and see if there was any useful information that she could gather.

Glancing around at the sleeping party, she headed off to where the man had been downed. She began to inspect the dead as she went. They carried little of value upon them. Even the weapons were not of quality. They were poorly made and had received little in the way of care—rusted and notched for the most part. Not worth the effort to scavenge. The creatures, likewise, had little going for them. Most had been carrying wounds from previous battles, wounds that had been left untreated. Only the sheer number of them had the party in trouble the night before. Now that she was seeing them in daylight, she could see that it was not as bad as she had feared.

She worked her way through the carnage to where she expected to find the mage. She found Alemrae instead. He was kneeling where the body should have been. There was no sign of the body. Instead, there was a large mark scorched into the rock—a pentagram inside a circle surrounded by a six-pointed star within another circle. All the symbols had incomprehensible glyphs written around their edges. The internal pentagram was about three feet across, the outer circle about eight.

'This is a summoning circle, a very dangerous and highly sophisticated one. It allows passage both ways by anything that happens to pass into the inner pentagram. I suspect that this one would take you to the hell from which that daemon originated.'

'What of the mage?'

'The daemon probably took him home, both to keep him alive and make him suffer. A lesson to be learnt for any would-be summoners—don't mess with those beyond your power to control. Of course, the danger is always that you don't know if you have overextended your capabilities until it is far too late.'

'Is the portal still active?'

'I have no idea, and I am not going to step into the centre to find out. It is either permanently active or it only activates with the correct opening key. Either way, we need to remove all trace of its existence. Permanently close it, if you will. Go get Shadow and Rad whilst I contemplate this some more.'

It took little time for Kai to summon Shadow and Rad. The others were already moving about and preparing to break camp. Alemrae began to discuss with Shadow the difficulties with the summoning circle. When the discussion became more esoteric, Kai left, knowing it was well beyond her own understanding.

When she reached the others, Kai gathered them together.

'They may be a while. It appears that the daemon left a way to return, so they shall attempt to seal the pathway and remove all trace of its previous existence. You can leave the camp set up. We shall not leave until tomorrow at the earliest. Rest up.'

CHAPTER 58

'**A**lemrae, there is only one way to close this portal properly, and it is extremely dangerous. We must step into the outer circle and activate it—likewise, the star and then the inner circle. Once that is done, we have to activate the pentagram. Once the entire structure is activated, we can begin to permanently close it, but we shall be at the mercy of anything that comes through whilst we try to close it. Once the pentagram is removed, we should be safe enough as the direct link should be broken.'

'How do you know all this? It is almost beyond my own training.'

'Scraethius—he studied summoning circles, remember? He had a permanent one in the top of his tower. It is from him that I am getting all this,' Shadow explained.

'How do we go about deactivating all of this once it has been activated, and how do we activate it to begin with?'

'Sheer magical power will activate each layer. Once all layers have been activated, then we need to reverse each glyph by overlaying its opposite in nature. That shall cancel their effect and nullify it. If we have done it right, the whole mess should disappear when we have finished. If we haven't done it right, I don't know what will happen. It might do enough to make it unusable or something totally different may occur. Either way, we can only have one attempt.'

'Then we had best get under way. Rad and I will channel all the power we can raise to you, then you can do what must be done.'

'Step into the ring then and start raising power.'

They proceeded to raise the power for each layer of the construct, careful to step within the boundary of that layer before raising it. By the time they had lifted the inner ring, they were both sweating from the strain.

'To stop now will just bring ruin. We must keep on. Activate the pentagram, but do so from outside its border.'

They called on even more power, quivering with the effort, until suddenly the inner pentagram erupted into flame. Each layer of the construct behind them also broke into flame. The flow of power into the construct ceased as if there was no place for it to go.

'The whole thing is now permanently active. We have to shut it down, one layer at a time. But where to begin?'

'There, at the top of the pentagram—that is the first glyph to reverse. Then proceed, following the lines of the pentagram in reverse order.'

Shadow, using knowledge passed on from Scraethius, began laying down glyphs on top of those already present. 'We have a problem. There is one glyph here that Scraethius does not know. He has never come across it before. What shall we do?'

'Make your best judgement on what should come next. Remember when we tried closing the living portal in the desert—the one that would have unleashed a flood? Use the knowledge you gained then as an insight as to what to do now.'

'I shall try.'

Shadow laid down another rune, followed by a few more. Once she had finished, a flash of light ensued, and the flames of the pentagram diminished.

'Step outside the ring, but stay within the star.'

Shadow continued placing the glyphs, this time upon those around the inner circle. She began with the glyph that was in opposition to the one at the point of the pentagram. Once again, Shadow came across the unknown glyph and used the same glyph that she had used earlier to cover it and then continued on. As before, light flashed, and the flames were diminished when she covered the last glyph.

'I need to rest a bit. Not for long. Just a few minutes—to recover. We should be safe for now.'

'Rest away. I could use the break myself. This has been far more tiring than I thought it would be.'

'We aren't finished yet. In fact, we are less than halfway through.'

After a few minutes rest, they continued on. It was taking longer and longer to raise the power to create each glyph needed to cover the next one. At last, the star flashed into subsidence, and they were able to step out of the outer ring.

'It is fully dark. Where did the time go?'

'Time evidently moves at a different pace within the construct. We must hurry before our energy loss catches up with us.'

Once again, the three of them summoned what power they could so that Shadow could begin laying down the glyphs. The outer ring was much easier to decipher and was quickly covered. When the last glyph was done, the entire construct burst into white light. As it began to fade, the light suddenly began to change colour, ranging through the whole array of the visible spectrum, and then some.

'Something has gone wrong. The portal has sealed permanently, but something else has happened.'

'What?'

'I don't know. Let's get out of here—fast!'

They staggered up the slope in the direction of the camp. The party had already begun to rush down the hillside towards them.

'Pack camp. Hurry. *Run!* We need to get out of here!' screamed Alemrae.

'What happened? You've been gone for three days,' called Bradur.

'No questions. *Move!*'

CHAPTER 59

They rushed to pack up the camp, Shadow and Alemrae struggling to match the pace of the others. 'Head north. Run. Don't stop, and keep going until you can't go any further. Alemrae and I will follow as fast as we can. We will eventually catch up to you.'

The party headed out, carrying Alemrae and Shadow's share of the equipment with them to free the two mages from having to carry anything that would weigh them down. They raced off, quickly leaving the two far behind them. They ran as a group for as long as they could.

As they began to slow, Kai yelled out, 'Keep going! We don't stop moving before dawn. There is unknown trouble behind us.'

She kept pushing them, urging them on and on, until even her own resources began to flag. As the eastern horizon began to glow, she called the halt. 'If we haven't gone far enough now, we never will. Set camp and rest.'

Alemrae and Shadow struggled after the group, going from a slow trot to a walk. Between them, they were able to track the path of the group ahead of them and follow after.

'I have sensed only vague disturbances in the magical forces around us. But something big is building back there. It appears that whatever we set in motion may take some time to come to fruition,' mentioned Alemrae as they travelled through the morning light.

'That is my assessment also,' whispered Shadow. 'Bad things tend to happen in threes, and those are two major magical mishaps we have been involved with. I wonder what the third will entail.'

'Who says they were mishaps? Perhaps we are under the guidance of an agent for change? It may be necessity that is bringing this all about. Don't forget the elvish prophecies and the Pillar of Demitrial. We are in the beginning of a new age. Perhaps we are the ones who have to alter the foundations of the last age so that the next one can start off on the right track,' said Alemrae.

'How do you come up with such thoughts, Alemrae? Isn't that just a touch aggrandising? How can you so easily pass off our mistakes as a necessary change?' demanded Shadow.

'When you have lived as long as I and lived through the horrors I have known, then perhaps you would wonder, as I do—has my life been lived as I would have wanted it, or has some higher power taken over and ensured that I face the situations that I have? I know not. Yet, I sense that had I not done as I did and not gone in search of Kai when I did, then everything would have perished long ago. So you tell me—do we do our own bidding, or do we follow another's path?'

'In my own tribe's lore, they tell of one who is a nexus—one who will bring about a calamity to this world but, upon doing so, will also heal the world. Are you that one? Are you that nexus of ruin and healing?'

'I don't believe so. I would suggest that we all, each of us, have within us a part of that nexus you speak of, and when all the parts are correctly aligned, then the change will flow. As it has already begun. But that doesn't mean that we are not being guided by a higher power. That unknown glyph—what did you use to cover it? What was the meaning behind it, and where was the source of it?'

'It is difficult to describe. It encompasses many thoughts—of love, compassion, peace, and eternity. Yet even that does not embody it all. I thought that no matter what the unknown glyph meant, surely it was in some manner in opposition to that—thus, it should be nullified. Yet I believe that it was that exact glyph that caused the malfunction. How could such a glyph, with such positive good intent, be warped to change in such a way?'

'Who said it did? Perhaps it sent the portal into a total reversal and is trying to open to all that is good for the world. That could prove to be just as catastrophic as the other. This world is meant to have both good and evil within. Too far out of balance in either direction could begin a disaster.'

'If what you say is true, then perhaps it is trying to bring everything back to a balance. A portal or portals to return what should never have been lost to begin with, both the good and the bad. Something without limits upon it, across all dimensions—even across time itself.'

'The return to balance for this world would be something great to achieve, yet as long as this undead menace is around, I don't think it has a chance of succeeding. For the undead menace, as it stands at this time, will consume all life within its reach unless it can be halted, which is why we are here to begin with. So you see, we are back to this—are we doing our own will, or are we being guided by a higher power?'

'Does it matter? We do as our nature dictates, and it is in our nature to stand up for those who cannot.'

'I wish that I had your certitude. Alas, I am far from certain that we are free to walk away should we decide to do so.'

'What? You think we would be forced to undertake this task even if we were all to walk away?'

'In the end, yes! Each of us would have to confront the challenges that lie ahead. I just happen to believe that we have a better chance of success together than alone. Thus, I bow to the will of a higher power and do what is required, to work with others for a chance of success rather than alone, where I would surely fail. Now, I do believe we have stood here for long enough, chatting. So now that we are somewhat rested, how about we try and catch up with the others?'

'Time to walk once more then.'

'I think we might be able to speed things up a bit. If I am right, they should be camped about five or six miles ahead. How about we teleport as far north as you can take us? If Rad and I raise up what magical power we can and channel it to you, then we might be able to cut down the distance we have to walk on foot substantially.'

Rad and Alemrae opened conduits for Shadow to draw upon, as they had done so before, and Shadow, using the energies from all of them combined and channelling them through her circlet, cast the teleportation magic. The view suddenly changed. They were standing at the bottom of a rocky hillside, looking up at a tented campsite. The figures moving around were familiar.

'As I said, I do believe we are being guided by a higher power, for what else could have allowed us to travel so far with unerringly good accuracy when we didn't know where we were going to come out?'

'Okay, okay, you have made a good point. How about we go up? I'm not about to race up there either—slow and steady will do.'

When they arrived, they were greeted with good cheer. Morannel went straight to Shadow and put his arms around her, hugging her fiercely and resting his head against her hair.

'I was worried about you,' he whispered.

'Nothing could keep me from your side, should that be where I wish to be,' Shadow whispered back. Rad also came looking for affection from Morannel, which was a first for him.

'You helped keep her safe for me, my fine lad. For that, I thank you.'

'Let's get everyone undercover, and you can regale us with your story,' said Kai.

CHAPTER 60

O nce they were settled and fed, Alemrae told their short tale. 'It seems we were a bit premature in our haste to leave. The resulting mishap from closing down the portal is yet to come due. It is likely to take some time for the full effects to become established.'

'Well, at least we made up a lot of ground today. We shall rest up until dusk and then move on again. Shadow, how long do you think it will take us to get to the mountains and the badlands at their end?'

'It should only take another couple of days to reach the area where we need to turn west. In order to enter the badlands, we need to get back to the coast and then head north from there. It should take us two days to reach the sea once we turn. Then it will be about a week before we clear the badlands and round the end of the mountains. Once we reach the plains, it's anyone's guess as to how long the travel will take.'

'Two weeks, then, until we reach the plains. We have travelled vast distances faster than I thought we could. I thank you all for your perseverance, but we still have much further to go. Hopefully, we shall have no more troubles until we reach the plains. Once there, I am hoping that we can come across one of the many cavalry units. I would hope that we could use them to scout the best way forward to dodge the worst of the undead horde on the plains. I know roughly where we need to head. I believe that the bolthole of this necromancer's cabal is not far from where the initial contact with the forces of Albrae occurred.'

'Kai, I believe I may be of some assistance when we get to the area you want,' said Alemrae. 'I have travelled across the north of this continent many times and have, in the past, found some cave systems that could be used, but until we get close, I could not tell you which may be the one we want.'

'We know one thing—there is one less mage to worry about. The magical ruckus we kicked up would have been sensed by anyone looking for it. Hopefully, that will draw their attention away from where we are heading, perhaps even diverge some of their resources away from where they should be,' mentioned Shadow. 'I think they know what we are up to, maybe even who we all are, but think on this—we just made one hell of a big bang for those who could hear. They know there are only two of us who can use magic, and what we just did should scare them a bit. People who are afraid tend to make mistakes. They start to perceive threats where there are none. That shall give us an edge.'

'Magic is still going to make a huge difference in our endeavours,' said Kai. From now on, I would prefer it if the two of you would hold yourselves in reserve where possible and allow the fighters in the group to deal with issues as they come to hand. I know just how formidable your fighting skills are, Alemrae, but I believe it will be your magical abilities that we will need most from hereon in, not to mention your knowledge of the lands ahead. By all means, assist if we get into trouble, but hold back if you can. Sometimes the shock of another skilled participant late in a fight can sway the balance. I have used that tactic successfully in the past. Most of where we travel now shall be fairly open terrain. I suggest we move in an arrow formation.

'Bradur, I would like you to hold the centre of the line. Morannel, move to his left side, and, Geoffrey, to the left of Morannel. Frederick will hold the right beside Bradur, with myself anchoring that end. Shadow, you and Rad can hold the middle behind Bradur and cover all of us with magical support. Alemrae, hold the rear, with bow, magic, or sword—whatever is most necessary. You are the one most able to hold alone, until one of us is free to aid you. Shadow, you will be our eyes, either with magical sight or through Rad. Keep an eye on what is around us and where we need to go. Guide Bradur as he leads us forward. We shall travel at the pace you set us from hereon in, Bradur. Rest up, people. We shall leave at dusk. I want us ready to go the moment the sun hits the horizon.'

Rest they did, although Morannel and Shadow did take some time to be alone together. Neither had liked the separation of the days before. As the sun crept low, the party dismantled the camp. They were ready to leave before the sun set. Bradur led the way as they headed north once again. They walked that night at a steady pace, stopping when necessary for meal breaks or a brief rest.

As dawn approached, the mountains began to loom ahead of them. Shadow had been right—another day of travel north, and they would need to turn west again. Bradur kept them walking well into the morning. When at last he called a halt, the others were pleased to stop.

'Not all of us have your stamina, Bradur. Let's keep it shorter tonight, shall we?'

'If we turn west from here, we will be south of where the enemy would expect us to turn. If they come looking for us, we might be able to bypass them without incident.'

'Unless they know the area. There is one valley that we must travel through to get through the badlands at the end of the mountains. They could just await us there.'

'It is unlikely that anyone would willingly wait for someone to show up in such an inhospitable place unless they were absolutely sure that we had come this way. We could just as easily turn east from here and head back to Raelis.'

'Enough. Set camp. We rest. Shadow, how long will it take to get to the coast from here?'

'It's still two days' travel west.'

'What if we push it? Travel for longer and faster?'

'It might be possible to reduce the time by a fair bit, but we would then have to rest up for far longer to recover.'

'And if we use magic to aid us, either to speed our way or hasten our recovery, what, then?'

'To travel where we go, during darkness, at speed, is likely to get us all killed. The terrain itself is too dangerous to travel through swiftly during the night. There are many sinkholes and grottoes from which there is little hope of escape. They can occasionally be difficult to spot, even in full light. To fall down one would mean one's death.'

'Then we rest for no more than two hours. We set out during daylight and travel as fast as we can, whilst we can see. Once the sun sets, we will rest again, but for four hours. Then we will travel at a safer speed until morning. Hopefully, we should be near the sea by then. We camp and rest for the rest of that day and set out again once the sun sets, but head north again. Shadow, you, Rad, and Alemrae will use your magic to aid our travel and recovery as best you can.'

The following travel was harsh. Pushed to the limits, for want of speed, their endurance began to suffer. Shadow and Alemrae laid down slow healings upon them to help their recovery, but with the continued drain of their physical resources, it did little to help them.

They made it to the coast about three hours after full light. They collapsed on the rocky ledges above the pounding waves, a cooling mist of salty spray occasionally splashing high enough to cover them. Initially refreshing, it soon became apparent that they would get little actual rest if they spent the rest of the day so close to the edge.

After regaining their wind, they backed off and found a suitably sheltered spot to set camp. Unsurprisingly, it took them longer to set up the campsite than normal, such was the state of their fatigue. Even Bradur had begun to struggle with the effort to keep going. For the first time since hitting the desert, they failed to set a sentry. There would be little need, or so they thought.

Alas, as the day wore on and the party slumbered, giant ants crept in and scavenged what was left of their supplies. When they finally awoke to the cool breezes of the evening, they found their meagre food supplies gone and no indication as to how it had happened. Magic alone could not sustain them. It could only improve upon what the body could already do, and the body needed sustenance for the magic to work.

'We are going to need to replenish our supplies. Does anyone have any idea as to how we are going to do that?'

'Kai, there are three of us here with some idea as to what plant life is edible. All we have to do is find it, with minimal energy expenditure, and Rad can go do some fishing.'

'Then each of us should take one of the others to find the plants. Bradur can stay and prepare whatever Rad can catch.'

'Before you go, allow me to scan the area. I might be able to narrow the hunt for us.' Shadow went to her pack and rummaged through it. She pulled out the globe she had taken from Ildrakol and sat down upon her bedding. She made herself comfortable and then concentrated on the globe. Clouds began to swirl within the confines of the crystal ball until they suddenly coalesced into a startlingly clear image. It showed the campsite as seen from above, and all the members of the group were easily identifiable.

As Shadow concentrated further, the image began to move, progressing in ever-increasing crescents away from the campsite. 'There—those small plants are edible. Check further in that direction.'

Shadow moved the image further south as directed. It showed a large hollow covered in small brush. 'Alemrae, take Frederick and check out that hollow. There should be many edible plants there and perhaps the odd small animal as well.'

'Shadow, keep searching. Rad, go start your fishing. Remember to bring back what you catch. We need to feed everyone. Shadow, I will go back east with Geoffrey. We passed some plants on our way here. We shall collect what we can. I suggest that you and Morannel check out the land to the north. Perhaps you will have some luck there. I want everyone back here within two hours. If we can't find what we need by then, we had best move on towards the north.'

The group split up, each pair going to search where Shadow's scouting had shown some possible vegetation. Bradur began to search the immediate area of the encampment for wood and other things in the hopes that Rad might return with a fish or two. Kai set out with Geoffrey at a slow and steady pace that would conserve their energy reserves. It would take the two of them most of the time she had allocated for travel to get to where she had seen the plants and return. The plants she was after had a large tuberous root system, which, when cooked, could be eaten.

It was almost dark by the time they reached the area and began to search. Kai found one small plant fairly quickly and showed Geoffrey how to dig it up. It had a woefully small tuber—many more would be needed to make a decent meal. It was time to go back when Geoffrey found another clump, almost hidden in the side of a small grotto. It took far longer than Kai wished to prise the rocks apart and retrieve the precious tubers—enough for a meal or two.

Feeling slightly pleased with their find, they set out in a relatively buoyant spirit. Sparks rising high into the air from Bradur's fire guided them back to the campsite. The smell of roasting fish greeted them as they returned. Rad had obviously met with success. The others had all returned before them but with little in the way of success. Shadow and Morannel had not found any edible plant life but had managed to locate a small rivulet of fresh water seeping from a cliff face. They had managed to top up all of the water containers, ensuring their water supply for the next two weeks.

Alemrae and Frederick had found the hollow they searched for, which was filled with vegetation. Alas, little of the plant life was edible. They did manage to find a single clump of purplish-yellow berries. Each berry was about the size of a thumbnail. Neither Alemrae nor Frederick had ever seen the like before. In the hopes that Shadow may know of them, they had decided to take the berries, along with the small amount of other edible vegetation that they had found. They returned before the setting of the sun to find Bradur cleaning a pair of good-sized fish.

'Rad has returned to his fishing. With any luck, we shall have a fair meal.'

'Only if Kai and Geoffrey have more luck than we did.'

As the sun sank to the horizon, Rad returned with another fish, this one larger than the previous two combined. Bradur retrieved the fish from Rad and began to clean it as well. Morannel and Shadow returned from their second trip to fill the water containers. The rest of the group had finished eating by the time Kai and Geoffrey returned. Bradur provided them with the remains of the meal and then took the plants they had brought and prepared them for cooking.

They were sitting around the fire, discussing their predicament and how to continue, when the ants returned. Their return impinged upon Kai's consciousness. 'Beware, something has surrounded us!'

They all leapt to their feet as the ants rushed in from the darkness. A wild frenzy ensued as they tried to defend themselves using whatever came to hand. They were being swamped beneath the insect horde until a sudden whoosh and flash of light erupted in their midst. Frederick had managed to get his hands on Soulburner and caused the blade to ignite. The ants closest to him fled, allowing him to assist the others.

'They fear the flame!' he yelled as he attacked.

Bradur managed to reach into the fire from under a swarm of ants and haul out a burning brand, which he began to lay about with. A whoosh of flame flared up from under another mound of ants, and Shadow emerged from beneath. The stench of burnt hair and ant drifted across the campsite.

'It has got the berries!' cried Alemrae, chasing after one of the fleeing ants.

Rad swooped in from above and breathed fire along the path that the ant was taking, frying it and a number of others to a crisp. The berries changed colour, going from the purplish-yellow colour they had been to a brightly glowing crimson. The rest of the ants fled into the night from whence they came.

CHAPTER 61

T he group slowly recovered from their unexpected assault.
'Now we know what happened to our food supplies. We were raided by the ants whilst we slept. What are those?' asked Kai, pointing at the berries they had managed to recover from the ants.

'Berries of some sort. I have never seen their like before,' said Alemrae. 'They were a hideous purple-yellow colour when we found them. We did not know if they were edible. We thought Shadow may have some idea as to what they are.'

'They are our salvation, is what they are. I have never seen them before, but members of my tribe have come across them before. They are rare, also poisonous in the extreme. You have to heat them until they glow before you can eat them. Just one berry will keep you alive for three days, even if you have nothing else. I suspect that we could force march for a day on the energy that they would give us.'

'Patch yourselves up. We rest tonight. Have a berry each for breakfast and travel north as fast as possible,' stated Kai. 'Keep an eye out for anything edible so we can forage on the way.'

They left the campsite to the ants before dawn, heading north along the rocky coastline. It was early afternoon when they stumbled upon the beach. Looking down upon it from the top of the cliff above, they saw that it was a long, wide, and sandy. Many different birds nested upon the rocky cliff, and the beach was covered with many large seals. It looked like food was not going to be a problem for a while if they could just make it safely down to the beach.

'Getting us down won't be the issue. It's getting everyone back up to the top that will be difficult,' said Shadow.

'Let us keep on for now. We can make our way down later, just before dusk. We'll set up camp at the base of the cliff and hunt in the morning. The animals may have gotten used to our presence by then.'

'Once down, how about we follow the beach until we find an easier place to come back up? We have plenty of water, and, even uncooked, the meat we get from just one of those seals will provide us with enough energy for magic to sustain us.'

'Walking on the hard sand near the water's edge will certainly be easier than scrambling over all these rocks. We may even be able to make better speed. Everyone is agreed, then? We descend just before dusk to set camp and then travel on the beach for as long as we can, or we find a suitable place to climb back up. Let's get as far along as we are able to. Lead off, Shadow.'

They continued on. Just as the western sky began to change colour, they stopped, and Shadow levitated them down to the beach, one at a time. By the time the sun had dropped below the horizon, they had set up the camp and were bunkered down for the night.

The hunt the next morning was swift, and with many hands to help—so, too, the butchering of the two animals they had slaughtered. Soon, the group was on their way once more.

They found traversing the beach much easier than the top of the rocky cliffs and made up some of the time they had lost the previous few days. As they neared the end of the beach, the cliffs dropped in height. They came down to a swampy tide-affected creek. They carefully made their way along the creek edge inland and back up towards the badlands.

Leaving the creek behind them, they crossed through a deep break in the rugged hills and emerged onto a wide, tussock-grassed plain running to the north-east. Scattered across the plain was the occasional stunted tree. Water would be scarce; an occasional rock pool near the steep-sided hills that bordered the valley would be their only source.

'Try and stay alert. There is no other option other than traversing this valley. If our enemies wish to mount another assault, it will be somewhere along this plain—probably closer to the other end, where there are numerous caves and rock outcrops to hide in,' stated Shadow.

'We should make good time here. If I remember correctly, it took me two days to walk this valley before,' said Kai.

'Let's try and do it in one, then, shall we?' said Alemrae.

He led off at a fast walk, which he knew they were capable of sustaining for some time. The others followed after. By mid-afternoon, they were nearing the end of the valley. It was becoming much narrower, and the hills to either side were steeper and more rugged. Some small caves could be seen dotted along the base of a hill.

A small pack of wild dogs trotted across the plain towards them. Obviously they were intent on investigating the strangers in their territory. The party halted where they were, spreading out and giving themselves room in case the pack decided to attack. The pack also spread out, slowly encircling the party. One by one, they moved in close to sniff members of the party and then retreated again. The demeanour of the pack suddenly changed when one got near Bradur. With its hackles raised and emitting a deep soft growl, it advanced even closer and began to circle.

'Bradur, stay still. Don't move.'

The rest of the pack moved in, passing by the other party members close enough to touch. The pack moved in on Bradur, sniffing him and trying to isolate that which was offensive. One of the dogs leapt up and began to paw and chew on Bradur's pack.

'Remove your backpack. They're after something in your pack.'

Bradur shrugged his broad shoulders and loosened the pack from his arms. He swung it around to his front and opened the flap. The pack circled faster, as he slowly removed items from the pack and dropped them at his feet. As he got to the bottom of his backpack, his hand brushed the displacer beast pelt he had collected in the tunnels beneath Ildrakol. His head jerked up, eyes widening in understanding. He pulled out the pelt and flung it high into the air where it billowed out on the wind. The dog pack went ballistic, leaping and snapping at the pelt. When they finally managed to snag it from the air, they tore it into shreds in a frenetic and vicious attack.

When they finally settled down, they calmly headed off to the south. They were perhaps forty yards away when they suddenly blinked out of sight. One moment they were right in front of them; the next, they were gone.

'Alemrae, Shadow, have you ever seen something like that before?' queried Kai.

'No,' they replied in unison.

'I have heard of these,' responded Bradur. 'Blink dogs. They can teleport and are the mortal enemies of the displacer beast. It was only when I realised what they were after that I remembered about them. They are considered to be rare but are most often seen in isolated areas of arid grasslands, usually from a distance and where the pack is heading away from the viewer. Come, let's continue on. We need to think about where we'll set up camp tonight. With that pack here, I dare say that there is nothing else of danger to us in the vicinity. If there was, we never would have seen them.'

They camped that night near one of the few waterholes at the end of the valley. In the morning, they set off once again, determined to pass around the end of the mountain range to the east as quickly as possible. It took them a week to do so. They came down off the last of the hills and began to wander through the massive grassland. The grassland stretched the width of the continent and stretched north from the base of the southern mountain range until it collided with the forests coming down from the northernmost mountains—a vast flat plain with little in the way of tree or shrub to break the monotony. Large herds of grazers and their predators were all that roamed. The occasional creek or stream bringing ice-cold water down from the mountains, which were surrounded by slightly more dense vegetation, broke up the view.

296

They travelled across the dusty grass-filled plains beyond the mountain range for three days. The wind picked up, bringing with it clouds of dust and chaff. Visibility dropped to a hundred yards or so, and with the sun beginning to set, Kai decided it was time to set camp. There would be no fire this night, despite the chill in the air. The stench of smoke on the wind could bring about some unpleasant company.

The camp was almost set when out of the swirling dust came a cavalry troupe. They bore down upon the encampment at speed. There were twenty-five riders in all—with weapons ready to spill blood, if needed—and a number of remounts. Bandaged and bloody as they were, they seemed to be in relatively good spirits, if a little bloodthirsty. They encircled the group.

'This is not a good place to camp or travel afoot. Undead have been sighted nearby, often.'

'I am surprised to see a group as large as yours out here,' said Kai. 'Orders were to keep them small, only a dozen or so at most, unless you wish to bring the undead down upon yourselves.'

'We used to be in three separate groups, but circumstances forced us to join together. Water and supplies are limited. It was deemed wiser to keep together to gather more, and swiftly. How do you know about our orders? None of the few we have come across have known.'

'Yes, well, they didn't set them, did they?'

'What, and you did?'

'Yes, I was instrumental in setting the initial orders for those skirmishers and cavalry sent beyond the northern mountains. I am Kai, princess of Raelis and the Briar Rose. Those in my company are dedicated to ending the plague of undead. We seek to find their creator and end his existence.'

'Perhaps we can help. We have enough extra horses to mount you all. We could provide an escort to wherever it is that you need to go.'

'We do not yet know exactly where we need to go. We just have a vague idea about where to begin looking—about four days' travel to the north and east of Albrae. There should be a cairn to mark the place where the first major battle against the undead took place, where the army of Albrae was wiped out.'

'We have seen it and can take you there, but there is a host of undead in and around that area. There are always undead near that cairn.'

'That is both good news and troubling. To find the hidden location of the necromancers will take time, and we can't afford to waste time trying to elude the undead. The fact that the area in question is permanently guarded tells me that the entrance should be nearby.'

'It is two to three weeks of hard riding to where you want to go. Perhaps more if the undead become more troublesome.'

'We may be able to do something to make the journey easier and take less time. Certainly we shall try. However, we can leave that until tomorrow. Camp here with us this night. There are no undead in the near vicinity. You can rest easy this night—for tomorrow, we ride into hell.'

CHAPTER 62

T he troupe set up camp beside them. A pleasant evening of camaraderie, companionship, tall tales, and true followed. New friendships were forged and an old one renewed.

Although they had a late night, the newly combined group was up with the dawn and ready to ride not long after. They rode hard, travelling fast and bypassing the few small groups of undead they came across.

Alemrae and Shadow used their magic to help sustain the horses, allowing them to run for longer than they should be able to do otherwise and stay sound. They changed direction frequently to ensure that any of the undead that followed would end up going in the wrong direction. Eight days of rapid riding, and Kai knew that they were getting close.

'We are closing in upon the cairn we raised where the army was slaughtered.'

'You are correct. Those low forested hills ahead contain many undead. Within their folds lies the cairn you speak of. I have seen it myself.'

'Alemrae, if there is a usable cave system nearby, would you know it?'

'Yes, but not close by. To the north of those hills lies a larger mountain range. On the southern spur of one of those mountains, there is such a cave system.'

'Then that is where we shall head. Let's bypass this area, circle round, and come in from the western side. Hopefully, there will be fewer undead in that direction.'

'If we cut through the western edge of these hills and head straight north for a day and then turn back to the north-east, we should come across the right mountain fairly easily.'

'Then we ride, people. We know where we are going. Let's get this thing done. I'm tired of waiting. Alemrae, lead the way.'

They rode hard and fast, pushing through the forested hills quickly, leaving the few undead they saw far behind. The land became less flat. Many small canopied hills dotted this northern landscape, with the mountains looming large behind them. The grassy plains became few and intermittent as the woods grew in density. It became harder to keep up a good pace and to find an easy pathway in the direction they wished to go. Night fell, and still they rode on. It was nearer to dawn than midnight before they stopped in a small clearing at the top of one of the hills, exhausted.

'Camp here. I shall scout out the rest of the way and return.' Alemrae disappeared into the trees on foot before anyone could stop him.

'Set camp, but be ready for trouble. Have something to eat and get some sleep. Sleep in shifts. One-third of us shall be on guard at all times. We await his return.'

It was after midday when Alemrae returned, and he returned in a rush. 'Mount up. We need to get down to the grassland below. Undead have followed. I could not shake them. They're being guided.'

The men rushed to get ready. The whole group was ready to ride in under a minute. 'This way, fast!' yelled Alemrae. He headed down slope in a rush, ignoring the path and breaking straight through the shrubbery in his haste to descend to the plain.

Something large crashed down near where they had been, taking down a couple of fair-sized trees in the process.

'What was that?'

'A boulder. They have some giants amongst them!' yelled Alemrae.

More large boulders came hurling through the air in their vicinity.

'Get to the open. We can get out of range if we can just get to the grass.'

They hit the grassland of the valley in a rush and were halfway towards the other end when they saw a horde of undead approaching from in front of them. Glancing behind, Kai saw that they were still being followed by the other undead and two giants.

'Stop! Hold here. We haven't much time. Alemrae, how close is that cave system?'

'Closer than I thought last night—just over that ridge to the north and down the other side. It's hidden by the tree line but large enough to walk in four abreast.'

'Right. We leave now. My group goes to the cave system to end the threat. You lot get to choose which group you wish to battle through to get away.'

'I will take the men and lead them away. You go do what needs to be done. My place is here,' said Morannel. 'Shadow, Kai needs you to stay by her side. I will come back for you. You have my word on that.'

'Ride! Now!' Kai led the group off towards the forest between the two approaching mobs of undead. Some of the undead from the nearer group turned off to follow.

'There are fewer undead with those two giants. Bring them all down and we should be able to get clear.'

They turned around and raced towards their possible doom. One boulder came flying towards them, but they easily evaded its trajectory. The first of the undead was ridden under; so, too, the second. Then the fight commenced in earnest as the cavalry became swamped. One of the giants pushed through the smaller undead, crushing some of them as they got in its way. It, too, was a mindless undead. The loss of its companions bothered it not at all. It swung its huge club towards the melee, crushing two of the riders, as well as a few of their attackers.

Morannel suddenly found himself in the clear. His savagery had kept him woundless, and he turned about to seek further prey. The second giant filled his sight, and he rushed in. Closing in from behind and to the side, he was able to strike a mighty blow to the leg of the giant before it realised he was there. It toppled, crushing many other undead in its fall. Its flailing as it tried to rise brought down even more of its brethren.

Morannel dismounted and ran back into the fray, hacking at whatever parts of the giant he could reach. Two of the other cavalry men joined in, and together they were able to wound it unto death. More of the cavalry broke clear as the numbers of living undead plummeted.

Finally, it was only the other undead giant that remained. The cavalry began to ride off, not realising that Morannel was unmounted. Left alone to face the wrath of the undead giant, Morannel let loose all constraints upon his battle rage. He went berserk, charging in without regard for safety.

The undead giant attacked. Slow and ponderous as it was, it would only take one blow from the club to end the struggle. The battle between them raged on, with the other undead horde slowly approaching from the east.

The cavalry commander noticed Morannel was missing and looked back. He called a halt. 'We return. Use bows to distract it. I will ride in and aid Morannel.'

They spread out as they returned and began shooting the giant with their arrows, aiming for its upper body so as to minimise the danger to Morannel. As the first few arrows struck home, the giant looked up, trying to find those causing the wounds. This gave Morannel the break he needed, and he took full advantage of it, once again slashing the lower leg muscles, bringing the giant to the ground. Sweeping its arms around in frustration as it fell, it got in a lucky strike. A backhanded sweep struck Morannel across the chest and knocked him backwards twenty feet into a spiny bush. His rage left him as he blacked out.

CHAPTER 63

Alemrae took over the lead from Kai and guided them to the cave. Some of the undead from the horde followed along slowly. 'Dismount and free the horses. If we are successful, we can regather them later. If we aren't, well, we won't be needing them. Prepare for anything. Follow as quickly as you can. Stealth is no longer an option. If we find any enemy, we'll deal with it quickly and move on. Come.'

They followed a narrow trail between the trees until they came up against the steep, rocky hillside. There, in the side of a small cliff, was a wide cave entrance.

'That goes straight back for about thirty yards and then turns to the left. After another ten yards or so, it opens up into a large cavern. On the far side, and to the right, is another exit. That is where we need to go. We could be under attack anytime from hereon in. Let's go.'

Inside the cavern, as suspected, more undead lurked—skeletons and zombies—about a dozen or so. The group piled into them, dispatching them swiftly. The horde, following them at a slow pace, entered the cavern as they ran out the passage on the far side. The passage narrowed, turned, and twisted, slowing their forward progress.

'Keep on. We can't fight such numbers.'

The tunnel widened again and then straightened. The rough natural rock turned into worked stone, and ahead, the passage stopped. Waiting in front of them was a large double door of carved wood, etched with intricate details depicting a sorcerer raising a horde of undead. A small black orb resting upon a pedestal beside him.

'This is what we have come for. We destroy that orb and we stop the undead.'

They pushed the doors open to see a large rectangular room. At the far end was a raised dais, upon which a shimmering screen of energy pulsed between two polished bronze statuettes.

'That is a portal. Pass through it, we must. On the other side, we shall find what we seek. Geoffrey, Bradur—stay here and stand guard. Seal the doors if you can and stay safe. The rest of us will pass through the portal and do what we must to end this threat of undead, once and for all.'

With that, Kai stepped up to the portal and passed elsewhere. The rest followed suit. They emerged at the end of a tunnel, lit with a low ambient light of no visible source. The air felt warm, damp, and heavy, as if being compressed by immeasurable tons of rock above. They moved forward slowly and carefully, not sure what to expect.

Frederick took the lead with his sword out and flaming, held at the ready for whatever came his way. Kai paced alongside, her hands never far from the hilts of her daggers. They came to a junction, with three possible directions to travel. Frederick paused, but Kai continued straight on.

'Hold up,' stated Alemrae. 'We should check the area down here first.' He motioned down the right-hand passage. 'If there is anyone left down here, then they will be in this direction.'

'You know this place, don't you, Alemrae?' asked Kai. 'You have been here before!'

'Yes. The path you wish to follow leads to a large cavern with no exits apart from the tunnel leading to it. The left-hand path leads to a stable of sorts, containing mounts with a difference—beasts, mostly winged. The only way out in that direction would be on the back of one of them. They would be more likely to attack than allow us to mount. That leaves this way—the war room and quarters of whoever happens to be here at this time. There could be up to eight wizards here. Necromancers and others seeking power. This area is a warren of passageways and rooms. Most interconnect in more than one place, making it easy to elude someone trying to follow, especially if they don't know the pattern.'

'Then lead us to the war room.'

'Follow me. Don't step on any blue tiles—they will teleport you to another corridor.'

They set off, keeping a careful watch upon the adjoining corridors as they passed by. Frederick brought up the rear and kept glancing behind them to ensure their retreat was clear.

They arrived at the door of the war room to the sound of voices within. They listened intently, trying to obtain whatever useful information they could before they entered.

'Our meeting is adjourned. Our guests have arrived and seek your attention. The two left guarding the entrance to our abode are already receiving their just deserts. Gargan, take those two monstrosities you created to the far north and get aid from the frost giants. They will be quite willing to take advantage of the upheaval to come. The rest of you can greet our guests in whatever manner you deem fit. They don't need to leave here alive. I shall go and raise more troops for our army.' A loud rumble of many voices began, followed by the pop of air as one teleported and then another.

Alemrae threw open the door and jumped to the right. Frederick followed but went left. Shadow sent a bolt of lightning straight down the centre of the room, which Kai followed, leaping upon the tabletop and racing down its length. The lightning bolt struck the empty throne-like chair at the head of the table and blew it into smithereens, before arcing across to the side wall and bouncing back and forth, before dissipating. A ball of fire followed its return course and slammed into the wall beside the door. It exploded into a mass of flame, engulfing Shadow and Rad, with Alemrae and Frederick barely escaping its wrath. Kai had rolled, allowing the ball of flame to pass above as she continued to the end of the table.

Frederick ran straight into the closest mage on his side of the table and knocked him from his feet. Ignoring the downed man, he continued on towards the next. Alemrae had also reached a sorcerer. This one had managed to get some of his magical defences in place and engaged Alemrae in a duel. Rad flew down the room towards the fallen mage, as Shadow picked her smoking self up off the floor, where she had been thrown by the blast. Kai tumbled from the end of the table, landing on her feet, and struck out at the mage who had unleashed the ball of fire, landing a telling blow.

The sorceress on the other side pulled a wand and unleashed a cloud of noxious gas down the room towards the door. It slowly expanded until it filled the room. It was as much of a hindrance to her own side as it was to her opposition. Frederick's rush brought him clear of the cloud before he succumbed to its effects, and he immediately engaged the mage in front of him, his sword bursting into flame as he did.

Alemrae and his opponent weren't as lucky. As the cloud engulfed them, their duel faltered. Wave upon wave of nausea and coughing brought them both to their knees.

Shadow cast a quick spell, allowing a pocket of breathable air to surround her and protect her from the effects of the cloud. A number of bolts of bright white light flew from Rad and thudded into the prone mage, ending his existence. Kai's opponent fought desperately, barely managing to keep her at bay. Frederick's opponent lashed out with his staff as Frederick swung a powerful blow, flaming sword and staff connected with a loud crack, and the staff was sheared in two. The mage had barely screamed 'no', when the resulting explosion came.

All the magical power within the staff exploded out in one gigantic blast. Frederick and the mage were thrown, in opposite directions, the length of the room. The table beside them was blown to the wall opposite, where it crushed the sorceress to death. Pieces of chair flew about the room, striking those still standing. Kai and her opponent collided with the wall behind them.

Kai slowly arose to her feet, but her opponent stayed down—the back of his head stove in by the impact with the wall. The blast also dissipated the cloud of gas. Alemrae, recovering from the effects of both gas and blast before his opponent, finished his job swiftly. Shadow once again picked herself up from the floor and went to see what aid she could give. Frederick was unconscious, which was probably a blessing, considering the fiery burns he had sustained. Shadow began to work her healing, with Rad assisting. Kai and Alemrae moved up beside them.

'That was almost too much,' stated Kai.

'More than I had bargained for,' replied Alemrae. 'There are two more to account for. One has gone beyond our reach for the present, and the other one is probably in that isolated chamber you wanted to go to first.'

Shadow's work proceeded swiftly, and Frederick was soon able to rise to his feet again. He had a number of gruesome scars as a result of his ordeal. His rapid healing was of no benefit when it came to restoring his good looks. He would no longer be the most handsome fellow at court. In truth, few outside his closest associates would tolerate his presence for long, such were his scars.

They reversed their path and proceeded back to the first junction. There, they turned down the path that Kai had originally wanted to traverse. Alemrae and Frederick took the lead, with Shadow and Kai close behind. It was a long passageway, which curved back and forth, as if whoever had made it had tunnelled through softer rock, bypassing areas too hard to cut through.

Something changed. Between one step and the next, the nature of the tunnel altered—it felt different. One moment they had been in a warm, moist tunnel with hand-carved walls, and now the tunnel was rough, more natural in its construction, and it was hot. So very hot. It had become hard to breathe. The smell of sulphides and other noxious gases assaulted their noses.

'We are much deeper underground than we were before. This feels more like a vent in the side of a volcano,' Shadow mentioned.

She led the way, ignoring everything except what was straight ahead. The temperature increased as they went on. A deep-reddish glow shone ahead. The view widened as they approached. A massive cavern lay in front of them. A deep crevasse cut across one side. It was from here that both the glow and the heat originated. Clouds of purple-, green-, and yellow-tinged gas or smoke arose from the crevasse. The haze obscured the view of the far reaches of the cavern. Near the centre of the cavern stood a silver pedestal, a small black globe resting atop it. There were hundreds of bodies lying on the ground between the cavern wall and the pedestal, and a tall robed figure walked amongst them.

Alemrae pushed past the others and walked out into the cavern towards the mage. 'Hello, Father. I told you I would return with those who could stop you.'

CHAPTER 64

Despite the distance between them, Alemrae's words carried. As did the reply.

'Returned, you have. Stop me, you will not. Will you introduce your companions? I can see you have brought two humans, a dragon, and one of mixed race.'

'They are Frederick Monfraeson; Shadow, who is host to Scraethius the Arch-Mage; Rad, a lizard of light; and Kai, princess of Raelis, and the one who will destroy you.'

'Do you truly believe that I, Delkar the Lichlord, could be impressed by such as these? Mortals all, whereas I have achieved immortality!'

'Your insanity has risen to new heights, I see. You have nothing in your favour. Become one of the undead, you have, and risen more to serve you. You may have passed beyond death in your lichdom, but this does not mean that you cannot be destroyed. Whatever protections you create, we, working together, can dismantle. You must steal other's works in order to further your own, for you cannot progress otherwise. Your thoughts are static. Always stuck in the one direction. Mother cannot be raised. She passed on to other realms centuries ago.'

'Your mother is no longer of my concern, only domination of this existence. All will be mine to destroy.'

'That is why we seek to destroy you. For you shall not succeed whilst there is still life and a will to end you, and all that is alive wishes you to end.'

Kai spoke up. 'Enough of the chatter, Alemrae. When I get to the pedestal, do as I asked all those months ago. Frederick, if you can, distract the necromancer.'

'Kai, the only thing I know of that might destroy that globe is acid. Fire will not work. Just remember, to touch it is to die. It absorbs life,' said Shadow.

Kai began to walk towards the pedestal. Frederick also moved off but towards the lichlord.

'Shadow, I need all the power that you can raise. Don't forget to use the circlet and see if Scraethius can assist you. Then hold it ready for my use. Rad, use your skills to magnify what we do and add what you can to the mix.'

Alemrae began a long and complicated incantation. Power began to build. Tensions flared. Delkar seemed to ignore their preparations. He continued his pacing amongst the dead, muttering to himself. Frederick increased his pace, closing in upon his target. The mage stopped his ambling and turned to face Frederick.

'You cannot stop nor harm me.'

'I beg to differ. I intend to see you dead.'

'I am already dead, you fool. *Akh mar skarif mahar.* Rise, my children.'

The dead began to rise. Frederick swung, connecting with the mage, but the sword seemed to just bounce off.

'I told you so. Now feel pain.'

He raised his arm and pointed straight at Frederick. A bolt of lightning flashed towards Frederick, who attempted to parry it with his sword. A high-pitched whine rang out as the electrical bolt collided with the flaming sword. Frederick was flung back, landing heavily, with arms spread wide. Somehow, he had retained his grip on the sword, its flames now flickering a blue white, a change from the orange red it used to be. Smoke rose from his clothing as he regained his feet.

He braced himself and took a two-handed grip upon his sword. His sight was blurred, and he had a ringing in his ears. The risen undead began to gather around him. He lashed out, cutting one zombie almost in half as it came within range. He sliced another on the backswing. Blue-white flames flared up turning it to ash. Another electrical bolt sheared past, missing him by a fraction. Frederick took a quick step forward and swung a heavy blow at the chest of the mage. A blinding light flared, and a concussive force erupted as the blade connected. The mage was thrown back a few feet, and the nearest undead knocked back to the ground, smoking. Frederick kept his feet but was unsteady.

Kai reached the pedestal and looked back to Alemrae. She raised her hand and dropped it.

'Now!' yelled Alemrae.

Power flooded from Shadow and Rad. He gathered it in to fuel the spell he had prepared. He cast out. The magical forces sheeted across the cavern to connect with the base of the pedestal. In the moment before it struck, Kai reached out and picked up the globe. It was much smaller than she had expected, considering the disastrous events it had caused. Pain engulfed her. She could see her hand and then her arm slowly turning grey.

She dropped to her knees and screamed out. Gathering her strength, she brought the globe up to her mouth. She swallowed the globe and then writhed upon the ground as magical forces battled within her—the globe trying to steal her life force, whilst her body tried to repair the damage the globe was doing. Slowly, her stomach acids dissolved the globe within.

They were evenly matched. Power still flowed from Alemrae, Shadow, and Rad. The ground began to shake as the forces grew. The undead, once again, crashed to the floor. Rumbling and groaning began as the rock below began to tremble. Shadow dropped to her knees. The flow of power ceased. All went quiet.

'Frederick, run!' yelled Alemrae.

Frederick turned and, upon seeing Kai writhing on the ground, started towards her.

'Frederick, leave her. If you want to live, *run!*'

A loud, sharp crack rang out. The cavern floor split in two, a large fracture running perpendicular to the crevasse. A pillar of rock shot up from the cavern floor and crashed into the roof before falling back to the floor in a shower of shattered rock. A large chunk of the floor collapsed into the crevasse as molten rock shot up.

Frederick ran as fast as he could towards the only exit from the cavern, leaping over the widening split in the floor. Alemrae was still helping Shadow to her feet when he arrived. 'Come on. Run, and don't stop for anything. Head to the portal.'

Unseen by the others, Kai rolled to her feet unsteadily. She stumbled over to where the Lichlord had regained his feet, as the ground continued to move.

'We are both dead, you and I, but I intend to end you nevertheless,' whispered Kai. She drew Brelldan's dagger.

'Do your worst. You won't stop me. Your forces are finished. With your death, the magical protections on your forces will fail and they will be sundered.'

Another bolt of lightning arced out. Kai spun, trying to dodge the strike and slice at the mage at the same time. The blade missed, but the bolt didn't. Kai was thrown backwards towards the widening crevasse. Delkar moved further away. Kai regained her feet and rushed back towards him.

'Slow, you are,' said Kai with a grin as she came in hard and fast, spinning to change the angle of her attack. The mage cast another spell, and many small arrows of white light slammed into Kai, but Brelldan's dagger had arced up from below and struck at the base of the ribcage. The dagger sliced up through the liver and lungs and hit the unbeating heart. Kai withdrew her strike, and as the mage attempted to recover from the shock of the blow, she struck again. This time, a backhanded slash sliced deeply across the throat.

She kicked out, knocking him to the ground. She took her time. She staggered around behind him, unsteady on her feet, her energies fading fast. She reached down and grabbed the hair on the back of his head. She pulled up and then sliced, completing the previous cut and beheading him. Magical energies surged around the cavern as the body in front of her turned into dust, quickly followed by the head. It was over—the menace gone.

Now she could join Brelldan in rest. She collapsed in a heap, the skin on her body aging rapidly, as if all the years that had been held in abeyance were catching up to her in an instant, and more again. As her sight failed her, the last image she saw was that of a silvery shimmer of magic engulfing everything. A sudden flash of golden light momentarily lit the cavern, and all around her shook with the mighty magic that had been unleashed. Everything went black as all signs of life faded fast.

CHAPTER 65

Alemrae, Shadow, and Frederick hit the portal at a run. Passing through, they crashed over Geoffrey, who was lying prone upon the floor. Blood welled out of the numerous gashes over his body. Bradur lay crumpled in a heap by the wall, barely breathing. Alemrae crumpled to his knees, grasping at his head as the turmoil of magical energies interfered with his grasp on reality. Piled around the room were the bodies of the undead. Behind them, the portal ceased and the bodies turned to dust. Darkness ensued. The bronze statuettes melted into irregular lumps of metal. Alemrae struggled to his feet. A soft whisper of sound, and there was light. A small pale ball rested on his palm.

It took a few moments to sort themselves out. Shadow checked on Rad to ensure his safety before turning to Geoffrey. After assessing his situation, she began casting what healing magic she had left. The bleeding slowed and then stopped.

'That's all I can do for now,' she said. 'How is Bradur?'

'He'll live,' replied Alemrae. 'But he won't want to be moving for a while. Rest. I'll go and scout the passageway out. Rad, guard them.'

Alemrae moved out slowly and quietly. He created another ball of light, which he attached to the wall before he left. He was back after a little while.

'There is no sign of the undead. If we can find Morannel and those outriders again, we should be fine.' A soft trembling of the ground reminded them of the earthquake that they had set in motion. 'We should get out of here. It's not wise to stay underground whilst an earthquake rages. Let's get Bradur and Geoffrey to their feet and get out of here whilst we still can.'

By supporting the injured, they were able to move slowly through the passageway and back out into the open. Keeping an eye out for possible trouble, they made camp and allowed Bradur and Geoffrey to rest once more. Far to the south, a dark cloud covered the horizon.

'How are you? Has Scraethius done as was agreed and left?'

'He has gone. He felt the destruction of his globe. I will be fine.'

They waited throughout the afternoon and into the night. Just as the golden light of dawn began to show in the eastern sky, a small group of riders came upon their camp. Morannel was with them, heavily bandaged. His body was almost healed from the injuries he had sustained. The horses were frisky, upset over the continued rumblings of the earth. The riders needed assistance in controlling their mounts when they dismounted. They hobbled the steeds as an extra precaution before tying them to a picket line.

After tending to the mounts and enlarging the camp, they discussed their options and traded their news. According to the riders, the undead seemed to vanish around the time the earthquakes began. The continuous rumblings were of serious concern. The magic cast the day before to open the cavern floor as a means to prevent the return of the necromancer should not have continued to cause such tremors.

Thus began 'the Great Cataclysm' that the histories would tell of.

They rested through the night, rotating the sentry duties through all those who were able. Bradur and Geoffrey were healed enough by morning to ride out with the others. As they progressed towards the east and the safest way around the mountains, they remarked upon the continued presence of the dark clouds hanging low over the mountains to the south. They tried to keep their distance from the mountains as the earth tremors appeared to be much stronger the closer they came. They continued to pick up more cavalry as they went, in ones and twos usually, although another larger band joined them on the eighth day.

After three weeks of travel, they arrived at the east coast and headed south towards Almarac. Still, they came across no undead. When they finally reached it, Almarac was in ruins. The walls and buildings had collapsed because of the continuous earth tremors. Even the docks had collapsed. The colour of the water and extremely rough conditions in the bay indicated that it was extremely shallow. No boats would ever be coming back in to this port.

As they headed up the road to Raelis, they found more debris. Avalanches and ground movement had seriously damaged the road and made for difficult progress. The land was deserted. When they finally reached the place where the first defensive wall had been built, they stopped. The wall had been destroyed. Rubble was everywhere. There were no defenders. There was also no way to get the mounts over where the wall had been. The passage was sealed. The only way through the pass was going to be by foot, if they could make it through at all. They paused to regroup and discuss their options.

In the end, all but ten decided to risk the pass. Those ten would take some of the stock and try to pass around the other end of the mountain range and traverse the badlands in an attempt to regain civilisation. The rest of the horses were released to live and breed upon the grasslands, free. The men were never heard from again.

With the band taking the lead and the other fifty skirmishers behind, they slowly made their way up the rubble. On the other side of the pile, the road was nowhere to be seen. An avalanche had scoured an entire section of the road away. A slipway down to the ocean below was all there was. It would be the first of many hazards that they would need to cross.

Loose gravel and tremors did not make for an easy passage. They tied themselves together in three groups to cross. They waited until one group was safely across before the next started. One group did not make it. A large tremor started the slide moving again, and it took the last group to their deaths, crashing into the ocean below. It swept the rock bare of loose shale but left a steep, unpassable section of rock behind them. They now had no way of return. They must pass through or perish.

After pausing for a thought for those lost, they continued on, with Bradur and Alemrae leading the way. As the most experienced in mountain hazards, it made sense to have them scout out the safest course forward. Many quakes had them hugging the sides of the pass, hoping that there would not be another avalanche.

On the fifth day, when the eastern side of the pass once again plunged towards the ocean, they glimpsed a remarkable occurrence. Two massive portals opened up—one high in the sky above their heads and another just above the sea. From the portal in the sky flew numerous large winged beasts covered in feathers. They circled once at altitude and then headed straight overhead towards the mountain peaks to the west. From the other portal near the sea, one massive creature emerged. Its body was about three times the length of the *Storm Dancer*, with its many tentacles even longer still—a couple up to four times the length of the body.

'That water is too shallow for a beast of that magnitude. I wonder where it will end up?' whispered Alemrae.

'Hopefully, far away from here,' replied Morannel.

It took them three days more to reach the far end of the pass. Low on food and water, the view as the pass opened up took their breath away. The road stopped. There was no longer a steep slope along which the road turned down to the plains below. Instead, a cliff of about fifty yards dropped down to where the road continued on.

'Now we know why there has been a cloud hovering over this entire mountain range. The quakes have started the mountains growing, and at a fast pace by the looks. I expect that there have been many eruptions as well.'

'How are we going to get everyone down?'

'I could teleport some of us down, but it would take three or four days to get everyone down to the road that way. We could levitate down. Both of us could take about six of the men. Then once they are down, you teleport the two of us back up, and we do it again. We should be able to get everyone down in one day. We leave any belongings that are not absolutely essential behind. Once the first group is down, they can start along the road to Raelis, find a place to set up camp, and await the rest of us. Then we can continue in the morning. It has been a stressful day for all of us, and it's not over yet.'

It was almost fully dark before the last of them had made it to the camp set up by the others. The shine of a welcome fire guided them to their resting place. With a meagre meal shared between close companions, it was as fine a night together as any could remember having had in the recent past. The short journey back to Raelis in the morning would be easy compared to what they had recently undergone.

CHAPTER 66

In the morning, the company led out, the rest following, thankful to be returning home at last. It was a long walk, but they took it in easy stages. The city slowly grew on the horizon. It looked different—as if something was wrong with it.

It was Morannel who finally figured it out. 'Where's the palace? I can't see the palace looming over city.'

'Maybe it has fallen because of the incessant quakes.'

'Come on. We won't find out just standing here.'

They headed off again, with a bit more urgency in their step. They had only walked for a few more minutes before a patrol of cavalry approached. Morannel flagged them down and introductions were made.

'Give us the news of Raelis. We have been gone for so long, and I need to understand the changes that have taken place.'

'My prince, the undead seem to have vanished, but the northern mountain range is erupting. Earthquakes are a daily occurrence. We lost many people during the first upheaval. To minimise casualties, we have moved the majority of the populace down to Ulmarin. A large part of Raelis is in ruins. The quakes have reduced the palace to rubble. Martial law is in effect to stop the looting. There have also been numerous deaths. The dwarven host have headed back to their citadel to see what damage needs to be attended to.'

'We shall require some mounts. Escort the rest of the men back to Raelis and see their needs attended to. Record their names so that I may reward them later for their deeds. Where will we find the command centre?'

'The Sisters of Mercy hostel is being used as the current command centre. The new head of their order is currently governing the whole community.'

'What happened to the matron mother who was in charge, as well as the Lord Chamberlain and Regent Monfrae?'

'The regent, Lord Chamberlain, and the matron mother all perished in the first earthquake, along with many others. The palace ballroom was being used as the command centre at the time. The entire dome and most of the walls collapsed. We lost almost all those giving orders in the one event—a general meeting of the leadership had been called. A couple of field lieutenants were all that was left to run the military. When the Sisters of Mercy sorted themselves out, their new head volunteered to oversee the defence. It was she who finalised the movement of the populace to Ulmarin.'

'Time to go. This is my mess to deal with,' said Morannel.

They took the offered horses and, leaving the rest in the capable hands of the patrol, headed to Raelis. They arrived at the gates to find one lying flat outside the wall and the other hanging skewed and partially blocking the entrance.

Morannel called out to the soldiers working on the downed gate. 'Forget the repair—just bring the other gate down and clear the entrance. We will be abandoning Raelis.'

He continued on, winding his way through the rubble-filled streets to the Sisters of Mercy hostel. They pushed past the guards on the gate and dismounted near the entrance, handing off the horses to those waiting nearby and issuing a command to be taken to those in charge.

When they had been escorted in, Morannel requested a private meeting of the few responsible for the current management. The new matron mother opened the meeting, introducing the other commanders.

Then Morannel stood.

'As the last member of the royal family in residence, it is my duty to oversee the management of this catastrophe. I thank you all for your work until now. You may continue to do your current duties, but keep me appraised of how things are going. We will be abandoning Raelis. The devastation suffered is too costly to repair in our current situation. The harbour is no longer useable, and it was the harbour that made Raelis into the success that it was. We shall maintain a small outpost and patrol the nearby lands in case the few undead that may have survived somehow manage to find their way here. Apart from those men, everyone shall be sent on to Ulmarin. See to it.

'Now to the news we bring back with us. We have achieved some measure of success but at great cost. My aunt Kai was lost in the final battle with the head of the necromancer cabal that was the cause of the outbreak in undead. All but one member of that cabal have been slain. That one had been sent to the far north to recruit further allies. I suspect he will follow other plans of his own devising from now on. He is no longer a current threat in any way. Perhaps sometime in the future, something may have to be done, but that will not be for many years to come. It will be someone else's problem. Of the undead, none have been seen since the earthquakes began. We believe that the sustaining force behind them was destroyed at that time.

'Also, because of other events whilst we were travelling, magic has become more unstable. Unusual events will occur. Strange beasts eradicated in the past may return, and others never seen before may show up. We have already seen some of them, thankfully from a safe vantage point. So we shall fortify Ulmarin to make it a safe and secure place to rebuild civilization in the case that the calamity is much greater and more widespread than we are currently facing. I shall endeavour to ensure that Ulmarin realises just how precarious our situation may become in the very near future.

'Geoffrey, please review the current structure of our military and oversee any changes that you deem necessary. Keep in mind the circumstances that we have been through, what we have seen, and prepare for worse to come. Alemrae, if you would, liaise with the elven nation and keep us abreast of any events that we need to be aware of. Ensure that my cousin is well cared for. You, more than any other, are aware of how important she is to our future.

'To some happier news—once things have been set in motion and are more or less under control, there shall be a wedding. In Ulmarin. I shall say my vows and take Shadow for my bride. I shall leave the story of our experiences to those more able to do it justice. Bradur, I know you will wish to journey back to your people, but please try to make it to the wedding.'

'I shall come. Just send word when it is time,' he replied.

'Frederick, you shall be my right hand. Find those whom we will need to lead my council. Also, I need you to go to Ulmarin. Talk with Zephranthe and try to start to make the changes that we need to happen. Zeph will be the key to getting Ulmarin ready for all that will come. She can work on or around our grandparents. One last thing—I want a statue of Aunt Kai erected here, in the forecourt of the palace. Or at least where the palace once stood.

'The plaque at the base shall read,

In Memory of
KAI
The Briar Rose,
Saviour,
and Daughter of the World.'

APPENDIX 1

A list of names and places.

A

Alaric, Prince – Older brother of Kai, deceased.
Albrae – the largest human nation, also the capital city thereof.
Aleen – the old nurse's granddaughter
Almarac – province and capital city, known for its' stable society and college.

B

Bay of Tranquillity – a protected and quiet bay on the edge of The Sea of Storms. Location of Raelis.
Bell - Kai's daughter.
Bocra – port and tent city on the edge of the Plains of the Lost.
Brelldan - Kai's love interest
Briar Rose – an ancient title, given to the pre-eminent fighter in Albrae, determined by competition. Due to the nature of the competition the title is rarely ever won.

C

Captain Gregorson - *see also* Gregorson, Geoffrey

Chamberlain, Lord – the second most powerful man in Raelis.
Council of Merchants – The merchant lords of Ulmarin, currently hold more political power and wealth than the monarchy.
Crimson, *see* Kai

D

Darian, King – King of Ulmarin.
Delkar the Lichlord – an undead sorcerer.
Dramas – the largest port city in the Elshgat Free States.
Druban – a swordsman, a bodyguard of the king of Albrae, deceased.

E

Elgrae Amaf - *see also* Lizards of Light
Elshgat Free States – the remains of the Elshgat Empire. A land of many city states. A violent land where banditry and slavery are well entrenched. Gladiatorial arenas are used for public entertainment.
Elspeth, Queen – Queen of Ulmarin.

F

Frederick Monfraeson - *see also* Monfraeson, Frederick.

G

Gargan – a sorcerer who specialises in creating immense monsters.
Gedry, King – father of Kai and Alaric, deceased.
Great Cataclysm – a period of magical turmoil, lasting fifteen years.
Gregorson, Geoffrey – Captain of the Northern Gate Watch in Raelis. Formerly a Knight Captain of the Kings guard. He was demoted for insubordination.
Grellor – a swordsman. A bodyguard of the king of Albrae. Deceased.

H

Hammerhand, Kralmar – a dwarven smith.
Hergath - swordsman, a bodyguard of the king of Albrae. Deceased.

I

Icarian (the Mad Seer) – an Elven seer of ancient times whose prophecies seem to contradict each other.
Ildrakol – the tower of Scraethius the ArchMage.
Iona – second largest of the three moons, golden in colour. Slow moving. Two day rotation period. Travels from ENE to WSW.
Irikani – a fierce tribe known for the number of mages and shaman they produce.
Irikani Desert – sandstone desert region.
Ironfist, Bradur – brother of King Gralden Ironfist III.

Ironfist, Gralden, III – King of the dwarves in Rockholme.

K

Kai -Princess of Raelis, the Briar Rose, also known as Crimson in the Elshgat Free States.
Kira – the old nurse's granddaughter

L

Lake of mists – A large deep lake high up in the mountains south of Albrae, perpetually covered in mist.
Laksha the Small – one of the five bodyguards of the king of Albrae.
Lasel'nar – the smallest of the three moons, red in colour. Fast moving, eleven hour rotation period. Travels from the NNE to SSW.
Lizards of Light - pocket sized dragons, highly intelligent and extremely capable practitioners of magic.

M

Maria, Sister – a healer of the Sisters of Mercy chapterhouse in Raelis.

Monfrae, Regent – currently rules Raelis, until Prince Morannel comes of age.

Monfraeson, Frederick – son of Regent Monfrae. Cousin of Prince Morannel. Current owner of the sword Soulburner.

Morannel, Prince – Prince of Raelis, first in line for the throne.

N

Nicolai – a young caravaner.

O

Oesarets Reef – a large rocky outcrop surrounding a large oasis, near the edge of The Plains of the Lost. Home to numerous wizards.

Orset – a sergeant in Raelis

Ovo-yindi, *see* Shadow (Shadow's Hand)

P

Path of Icarian – Roadway constructed in eons past under the orders of Icarian the Mad Seer.

Pillar of Demitrial – A concurrence of stars which signal the turning of an age.

Plains of the Lost – a sandy desert of extreme temperatures and inconsistent, swirling winds.

R

Rad – a Lizard of Light

Raelis – City/State, Origin of Kai, Morannel and Zephranthe. Currently the richest city due to its trading empire and central location.

Riddik the Giant – one of the five bodyguards of the king of Albrae, a half breed giant, deceased.

Rockholme - The Dwarven capital.

Roderick – a young soldier.

S

Sarah – a merchant's daughter

Scraethius the Archmage – deceased, wizard of immense power.

Seraphine, Sister - the best healer in the Sisters of Mercy chapterhouse in Raelis.

Shadow (Shadow's Hand) - a young mage/shaman of the desert tribe - Irikani.

Sikaaris -Largest of the three moons, silver in colour. Travels East to West rotation period of one day.

Sisters of Mercy -Military order of women with chapter houses across the nations.

Soulburner – a sword, capable of turning its' blade to flame. It tends to magnify the more sinister aspects of its handlers character, usually to their detriment.

Storm Dancer – a three masted ship.

T

Terino, Lakira – a hunter

Tir – the eastern continent.

Traemellin, Alemrae – A half-elven fighter and mage

U

Ulmarin – Large city, very old and rich. Corruption is rife.

Uripor (The wastes of) – Limestone desert region, also known as the badlands. It stretches from the Irikani desert up to the mountain range south of Albrae.

V

Valley of Scraethius – the land of Scraethius the Archmage where all magic gets twisted awry.

W

Z

Zephranthe, Princess - Younger sister of Morannel